One of the world's leading science fiction writers, Anne McCaffrey has won the Hugo and Nebula awards for science fiction. Brought up in the US and now living in Ireland, she is the creator and bestselling author of the unique Dragon series. Between her appearances in the States, England, Europe, Australia, New Zealand and Alaska as a lecturer in secondary schools and universities, and guest-of-honour at science fiction conventions, Ms McCaffrey lives in a house of her own design, Dragonhold-Underhill (because she had to dig out a hill on her farm to build it) in County Wicklow.

Margaret Ball lives in Austin, Texas with her husband, two children, three cats, two ferrets, a hedgehog, and a large black dog. She has a BA in mathematics and a PhD in linguistics from the University of Texas. After graduation, she taught at UCLA and then spent several years honing her science fiction and fantasy skills by designing computer software and making inflated promises about its capacities. Her most recent book publications are *Lost in Translation* and *Mathemagics*, both from Baen. When not writing, she plays the flute, makes quilts, and feeds the pets.

Anne McCaffrey's books can be read individually or as a series. However, for greatest enjoyment the following sequences are recommended:

ACORNA
The Unicorn Girl

ANNE MCCAFFREY
& MARGARET BALL

CORGI BOOKS

ACORNA

The Unicorn Girl

Preface

The space / time coordinate system they used has no relationship to Earth, our sun, the Milky Way, or any other point of reference we could use to find our way around, and in any coordinate system we use, they're so far off the edge of the chart that nobody has ever contemplated going there, even with the proton drive. So let's just say that they were somewhere between the far side of nowhere and the near side of here when their time and space ran out, and what started as a pleasure cruise ship turned into a death chamber. They are like us in many ways besides appearance. They didn't want to die if they could possibly avoid it; if they couldn't live, then at least they wanted to die with dignity and peace instead of in a Khlevii torture cell; and they would happily have thrown away life, dignity and everything else to save their youngling, who didn't even know what was about to happen to them.

And they had time to talk; what amounted to several hours by our reckoning, while the Khlevii ship closed in on the little cruiser that had run out of places to flee to.

'We could offer to surrender if they'd spare *her*,' she said, looking at the net where their youngling curled asleep. It was a mercy that she slept so well; she talked well enough that they'd have had trouble disguising their meaning from her if she were awake.

'They make no terms,' he said. 'They never have.'

'Why do they hate us so?'

'I don't know that they do hate,' he said. 'Nobody knows what they feel. They are not like us, and we can't ascribe our emotions to them. All we know is what they do.'

And they both fell silent for a while, unwilling to speak of what the Khlevii did to prisoners of other races. No one had ever survived capture by the Khlevii, but the images of what happened after capture were broadcast by the Khlevii, in full three-D reproduction, with sound and color. Was it a calculated ploy to terrorize, or simply a display of triumph, as members of a more humanoid race might display the enemy's flag or captured ships? No one knew, because the same things had happened to the diplomat-linguists who went under sign of peace to make a treaty with the Khlevii.

'Cruel . . .' she breathed after a long while watching their sleeping child.

'Their only mercy,' he said, 'is that they have already let us know to expect no mercy. It won't happen to us, because we won't be alive when they reach here.'

Since the third broadcast of Khlevii prisoner-torture, shortly after the beginning of what history might know as the Khlevii Invasion, no ship of their people had gone anywhere without certain necessary supplies. The only prisoners taken were those caught away from a ship or without time to use those supplies. The others were always far beyond the reach of pain when the Khlevii caught up with their bodies.

'But I don't like to go without striking even one blow,' he said, 'so I have made certain modifications to our engines. There are some privileges to being director of Weapons Development; this system is so recently designed that even the Fleet has not yet been fitted with it.'

His hands were not quite as flexible as ours, but the fingers worked well enough to key in the commands that would activate those modifications; commands too dangerous to be activated by the usual voice-control system.

'When anything of a mass equal to or greater than ours approaches within this radius,' he told her, pointing at the glowing sphere that now surrounded their ship in the display field, 'the dimensional space around us both will warp, change, decompose until all the matter within this sphere is compressed to a single point. They will never know what happened to us or to their own boarding craft.' His lips tightened. 'We've learned that they don't fear death; perhaps a mystery will frighten them somewhat more.'

'What happens to the space around us when

11

the compression effect is triggered?'

'No one knows. It's not something you'd want to test planetside or from a close observation point. All we know is that whatever exists within the sphere is destroyed as if it had never been.'

She said nothing, but looked at the baby. The pupils of her eyes narrowed to vertical slits.

'It won't hurt her,' he said gently, seeing and understanding her grief. 'We'll take the abaanye now, and give her some in her bottle. I'll have to wake her to feed her, but she'll go to sleep afterwards and so will we. That's all it is, you know: going to sleep.'

'I don't mind for us,' she said, which was a lie, but a loving one. 'But she is just beginning to live. Isn't there some way we could give her a chance? If we cast her out in a survival pod—'

'If we did it now, they'd see and intercept it,' he said. 'Do you want to think about what would happen then?'

'Then do it when the ship explodes!' she cried. 'Do it when we're all dying! Can't you rig those controls to eject the pod just before they reach the radius, so that they won't have a chance to change course and take her?'

'For what? So that she can spend her last hours alone and scared in a survival pod? Better to let her go to sleep here in your arms and never wake up.'

'Give her enough to make her sleep, yes,' she said. She could almost feel her wits becoming sharper in these last moments. 'Make her sleep for more hours than the pod has air. If only she were

12

old enough to . . . Well, she isn't and that's that. If the air runs out, she'll die without waking. But some of our people might find her first. They might have heard our last distress signals. They *might* be looking. Give her that chance!'

She held the baby and fed her the bitter abaanye mixed with sweetened milk to make it palatable, and rocked her in her arms, and kissed her face and hands and soft tummy and little kicking feet until the kicking slowly stopped, and the baby gurgled once and breathed deeply in and out, and then lay quite limp and barely breathing in her mother's arms.

'Do you have to put her in the pod now?' she cried when he stooped over them. 'Let me hold her a little longer – just a little longer.'

'I won't take the abaanye until I see her safely stowed,' he said. 'I've programmed the ship to launch the pod as close to the time of detonation as I dare.' Too close, he thought, really; the pod would almost certainly be within the radius when the Khlevii approached, to be destroyed with them in the explosive transformation of local space. But there was no need to tell her that. He would let her drink the abaanye and go to sleep believing that their baby had that one chance of living.

She willed her pupils to widen into an expression of calm content while he was closing the pod and arming it to eject on command.

'Is all complete?' she asked when he finished.

'Yes.'

She managed a smile, and handed him a tube of sparkling red liquid. 'I've mixed a very special

13

drink for us,' she said. 'Most of it is the same vintage as the wine we drank on our vows-day.'

He loved her more in that moment, it seemed to him, than ever he had in the days when they thought they had long years of life together before them.

'Then let us renew our vows,' he said.

One

At first Gill assumed it was just another bit of space debris, winking as it turned around its own axis and sending bright flashes of reflected light down where they were placing the cable around AS-64-B1.3. But something about it seemed wrong to him, and he raised the question when they were back inside the *Khedive*.

'It is too bright to have been in space very long,' Rafik pointed out. His slender brown fingers danced over the console before him; he read half a dozen screens at once and translated their glowing, multicolored lines into voice commands to the external sensor system.

'What d'you mean, too bright?' Gill demanded. '*Stars* are *bright*, and most of them have been around a good while.'

Rafik's black brows lifted and he nodded at Calum.

'But the sensors tell us this is metal, and too smooth,' Calum said. 'As usual, you're thinking with the Viking-ancestor part of what we

15

laughingly refer to as your brain, Declan Giloglie the Third. Would it not be pitted from minor collisions if it had been in this asteroid belt more than a matter of hours? And if it has *not* been in this part of space for more than a few hours, where did it come from?'

'Conundrums, is it? I'll leave the solving of them to you,' Gill said with good humor. 'I am but a simple metallurgic engineer, a horny-handed son of the soil.'

'More like a son of the asteroidal regolith,' Rafik suggested. 'Not that this particular asteroid offers much; we're going to have to break up the surface with the auger before there's any point in lowering the magnetic rake . . . Ah! Got a fix on it.' An oval shape, regularly indented along one edge, appeared on the central screen. 'Now what can the sensors tell us about this little mystery?'

'It looks like a pea pod,' Gill said.

'It does that,' Calum agreed. 'The question is, what sort of peas, and do we want to harvest them, or send them gently on their way? There've not been any recent diplomatic disagreements in this sector, have there?'

'None that would inspire the placing of mines,' Gill said, 'and that's not like any space mine *I* ever saw. Besides, only an idiot would send a space mine floating into an asteroid belt where there's no telling what might set it off and whose side might be worst injured.'

'High intelligence,' Rafik murmured, 'is not inevitably an attribute of those who pursue diplo-

16

macy by other means . . . Close reading,' he commanded the console. 'All bandwidths . . . Well, well. Interesting.'

'What?'

'Unless I'm mistaken . . .' Rafik paused. 'Names of the Three Prophets! I *must* be mistaken. It's not large enough . . . and there's no scheduled traffic through this sector . . . Calum, what do *you* make of these sensor readings?'

Calum leaned over the panel. His sandy lashes blinked several times, rapidly, as he absorbed and interpreted the changing colors of the display. 'You're not mistaken,' he said.

'Would you two kindly share the great insight?' Gill demanded.

Calum straightened and looked up at Gill. 'Your peas,' he said, 'are live. And given the size of the pod – too small for any recycling life-support system – the signal it's broadcasting can only be a distress call, though it's like no code I've ever heard before.'

'Can we capture it?'

'We'll have to, shan't we? Let's hope – ah, good. I don't recognize the alloy, but it's definitely ferrous. The magnetic attractors should be able to latch on – Easy, now,' Rafik admonished the machinery he was setting in action, 'we don't want to jostle it, do we? Contents fragile. Handle with care, and all that . . . Very nice,' he murmured as the pod came to rest in an empty cargo bay.

'Complimenting your own delicate hands?' Calum asked caustically.

17

'The ship, my friend, the *Khedive*. She's done a fine gentle job of harvesting our pea pod; now to bring it in and open it.'

There were no identification markings that any of them could read on the 'pea pod,' but a series of long scrolling lines might, Calum surmised, have been some sort of alien script.

'Alien, of course,' Rafik murmured. 'All the generations of the Expansion, all these stars mapped and planets settled, and we're to be the first to discover a sapient alien race . . . I *don't* think. It's decoration, or it's a script none of us happens to know, which is just barely possible, I think you'll agree?'

'Barely,' Calum agreed, with no echo of Rafik's irony in his voice. 'But it's not Cyrillic or Neo-Grek or Romaic or TriLat or anything else I can name . . . so what *is* it?'

'Perhaps,' Rafik suggested, 'the peas will tell us.' He ran delicate fingers over the incised carvings and the scalloped edges of the pod. Hermetically sealed, of a size to hold one adult human body, it might have been a coffin rather than a life-support module . . . but the ship's sensors had picked up that distress signal, and the signs of life within the pod. And the means of opening, when he found it, was as simple and elegant as the rest of the design; simply a matter of matching the first three fingers of each hand with the pair of triple oval depressions in the center of the pod.

'Hold it,' Calum said. 'Better suit up and open

it in the air lock. We've no idea what sort of atmosphere this thing breathes.'

Gill frowned. 'We could kill it by opening it. Isn't there some way to test what's in there?'

'Not without opening it,' Calum said brightly. 'Look, Gill, whatever is in there may not be alive anyway – and if it is, surely it won't last forever in a hermetically sealed environment. It'll have to take its chances.'

The men looked at each other, shrugged, and donned their working gear before moving themselves and the pod into the airlock.

'Well, Calum,' Rafik said in an oddly strangled voice, seconds after the lid swung open, 'you were half right, it seems. Not an *adult* human, at any rate.'

Calum and Gill bent over the pod to inspect the sleeping youngling revealed when it opened.

'What species is it?' Gill asked.

'Sweet little thing, isn't she?' Gill said in such a soppy tone that both Rafik and Calum gave him an odd look.

'How'd you arrive at the sex of it?' Rafik wanted to know.

'She looks feminine!'

They all admitted to that impression of the little creature which lay on her side, one hand curled into a fist and thrust against her mouth in a fairly common gesture of solace. A fluff of silvery hair curled down onto her forehead and coiled down to the shoulder blades, half obscuring the pale, delicate face.

Even as they watched, she stirred, opened her eyes and groggily tried to sit up. 'Avvvi,' she wailed. 'Avvvi!'

'We're scaring the poor little thing,' Gill said. 'Okay, obviously she's an oxygen breather like us, let's get out of the suits and take her into the ship so she can see we're not metal monsters.'

Transferring the pod and its contents back into the ship was an awkward business. The 'poor little thing' wailed piteously each time she was tilted in the pod.

'Poor bairn!' Gill exclaimed when they set her down again. The movement of the pod had dislodged the silvery curls over her forehead, showing a lump over an inch in diameter in the center of her forehead, halfway between the hairline and the silver brows. 'How did that happen? This thing's cushioned well enough, and Rafik drew it into the bay as gently as a basket of eggs and not one of them cracked.'

'I think it's congenital,' Rafik said. 'It's not the only deformity. Get a good look at her hands and feet.'

Now that he called their attention to them, the other two saw that the fingers of the hands were stiff, lacking one of the joints that gave their own hands such flexibility. And the little bare feet ended in double toes, larger and thicker than normal toes, and pointed at an odd angle.

'Avvvi, avvvi!' the youngling demanded, louder. Her eyes looked strange – almost changing shape – but she didn't cry.

'Maybe it's not a deformity at all,' Calum suggested.

'Still looking for your intelligent aliens?' Rafik teased.

'Why not? She's physically different from us, we don't recognize the writing on the pod, and can either of you tell me what an "avvvi" is?'

Gill stooped and lifted the youngling out of the life-support pod. She looked like a fragile doll between his big hands, and she shrieked in terror as he swung her up to shoulder height, then grabbed at his curly red beard and clung for dear life.

'Perfectly obvious,' he said, rubbing the child's back with one large hand. 'There, there, acushla, you're safe here, I'll not let you go . . . Whatever the language,' he said, '"avvvi" has to be her word for "Mama."' His blue eyes traveled from the pod to Rafik and Calum. 'And in the absence of "avvvi," gentlemen,' he said, 'it seems that we're elected.'

Once she had found that Gill's beard was soft and tickled her face and that his big hands were gentle, she calmed down in his arms. Figuring she might be at least thirsty from being in the pod for who knew how long, they experimented by offering her water. She had teeth. The cup would forever bear the mark of them on its rim. She made a grimace, at least that's what Gill said it was, at the first taste of the water, but she was too dehydrated not to accept it. Meat she spat out instantly and she was unenthusiastic about crackers and bread. Alarmed that what was basic to their diet

21

was not acceptable, Calum rushed down into the 'ponics section of the life-support module and gathered up a variety of leafy greens. She grabbed the lettuce and crammed it into her mouth, reaching for the chard, which she nibbled more delicately before going on to the carrot and radish. When she had had enough to eat, she wiggled out of Gill's arms and toddled off – right to the nearest interesting instrument panel and set a danger sensor blaring before Gill swooped her out of harm's way and Calum corrected her alteration.

She looked frightened, the pupils in her silvery eyes slitted to nothing and her little body rigid. She babbled something incomprehensible to them.

'No, sweetie pie, no,' Gill said, holding up a warning finger to her. 'Understand me? Don't touch.' And he reached out, almost touching the panel and pulling his hand back, miming hurt and putting his fingers into his mouth, then blowing on them.

The slits in her eyes widened and she said something with a questioning inflection.

'No!' Gill repeated, and she nodded, putting both hands behind her back.

'Ah, it's a grand intelligent little bairn, so she is,' Calum said approvingly, smiling as he stroked her feathery-soft hair.

'Should we show her the head, d'you suppose?' Rafik asked, regarding her nether regions, which were covered with a light fur.

'She doesn't have the equipment to use our

head,' Gill said, 'unless she's a he and he's hiding what he uses.' Gill began fingering his beard, which meant he was thinking. 'She eats greens like a grazing animal . . .'

'She's not an animal!' Calum was outraged by the suggestion.

'But she does eat greens. Maybe we should show her the 'ponics section. We've got that bed we use for the radishes . . .'

'And you just gave her the last of the radishes . . .' Rafik's tone was semi-accusatory.

'She's not feline or canine,' Gill went on. 'In fact, sweet-looking kid as she is there's something almost . . . equine about her.'

Rafik and Calum hotly contested that category while she became quite restless, looking all around her.

'Looks to me that she's as close to crossing her legs as a young thing can get,' Gill went on. 'We gotta try dirt.'

They did and she bent forward slightly and relieved herself, neatly shifting loose dirt over the spot with her odd feet. Then she looked around at all the green and growing things.

'Maybe we should have brought the dirt to her,' Gill said.

'Let's get her out of here then,' Rafik said. 'We've fed and drained her and maybe she'll go to sleep so we can all get back to the work we should be doing.'

Indeed, she was quite content to be led back to the open pod and crawled up into it, curling

23

herself up and closing her eyes. Her breathing slowed to a sleeping rhythm. And they tiptoed back to their workstations.

The debate about her future disposition, however, went on through an afternoon of sporadic work, intermittently adjusting the great tethering cable around the body of the asteroid and placing the augering tool in a new location. AS-64-B1.3 might be rich in platinum-group metals, but it was making them pay for its riches with a higher crushing coefficient than they'd anticipated. The afternoon was punctuated by one or another miner taking his turn to suit up for EVA in order to search out a slightly better location for the auger, to replace a drill bit, or to clear the dust that clogged even the best-sealed tool from time to time.

'Let's call this asteroid Ass,' Calum suggested after one such trip.

'Please, Calum,' Gill reproved him. 'Not in front of the infant!'

'Very well then, you name it.'

They were in the habit of giving temporary names to each asteroid they mined, something a little more personal and memorable than the numbers assigned by Survey – if any such numbers were assigned. Many of their targets were tiny chondrites only a few meters across, too insignificant to have been located and named in any flyby mission, but easy enough for the *Khedive* to ingest, crush and process. But AS-64-B1.3 was a large asteroid, almost too large for their longest tether to hold, and in such cases they liked to pick a name that used the initial letters of the Survey designation.

'Hazelnut,' Gill threw out. Their unexpected guest was awake again and he was feeding her another leaf of chard with carrots for afters.

'Wrong initial letters.'

'We'll be Cockney about it. 'Azelnut. And you can allow me a zed for an ess, can't you?'

'If there were any point to it. Why are you so set on Hazelnut?'

'Because she's a hard nut to crack!' Gill cackled and Calum smiled rather sourly. The smallest of the three men, he was the only one who could get inside the workings of the drill while wearing full EVA gear, and the dust of AS-64-B1.3 had sent him outside on this shift rather too often for him to find much amusement in it.

'I like that,' Rafik said. ''Azelnut she is. And while you're enjoying your way with words, Gill, what shall we name this little one? We can't just keep calling her "the child."'

'Not our problem,' Calum said. 'We'll be turning her over to Base soon enough, won't we?'

He looked at the suddenly stony faces of his colleagues. 'Well, we can hardly keep her here. What will we do with a kid on a mining ship?'

'Have you considered,' Rafik said gently, 'the probable cost of abandoning operations on 'Azelnut and returning to Base at high delta-V?'

'At the moment,' Calum snapped, 'I should be

only too happy to leave 'Azelnut for some other fool to crack.'

'And to bring back the *Khedive* with less than half a payload?'

Calum's pale lashes flickered as he calculated what they would make – or lose – on the trip in that event. Then he shrugged in resignation. 'All right. We're stuck with her until we make our payload. Just don't assume that because I'm smaller than you, you Viking giant, that I'm naturally suited to play nanny.'

'Ah, now,' said Gill with great good humor, 'the creature's walking and toilet trained already, and she'll soon pick up our language – children learn easily. How much trouble can one toddler be?'

'Add that to your list of famous last words, will ya?' Calum remarked at his most caustic when they found the youngling had uprooted a good half of the 'ponics vegetation, including the all-important squashes and rhubarb, whose large leaves provided much of the air purification.

Rafik ran tests to see how much damage had actually been done to air quality. She'd gone to sleep again and had awakened so quietly that none of them had been aware of her movement until she wandered back in, flourishing cabbage leaves. Calum and Gill replanted, watered, and tied up the pulled plants in an effort to save as many as possible. The infant had evidently sampled everything, pulling up those she particularly liked instead of leaving her mouth-sized bite in leaf or stalk: she had eaten all the half-ripe legume pods, staples of Rafik's preferred diet. These subsequently caused a diarrhea which upset her almost more than it upset them. They spent a good hour arguing over a dose of medicine sufficient to bind her back to normal. Body weight was the critical factor and Rafik used the mineral scales to weigh her and then the powder. She spat out the first dose. And the second, all over Gill. The third dose they got down her by covering her rather prominent nostrils so that she had to open her mouth to breathe – and thus swallow the medication. Once again, she didn't cry, but her silverish eyes reproached them far more effectively than tears could.

'We can't have her doing this again,' Calum told Gill when they had finished replanting the garden. Then Rafik came over, showing them the readout on the atmosphere gauge.

'It should be down, but it's up,' he said, scratching his head and then tapping the gauge to see if the needle moved. 'Not so much as a stink of excess CO_2 in our air and we were about due for a good backwash.'

'I remember me mum putting a cage around me,' Gill said, 'when I would get into her garden.'

They made one out of netting in a corner of the *Khedive's* dayroom, but she was out of that as soon as they turned their backs on her. So they netted the 'ponics instead.

They tried to find toys to amuse her with, but pots and pot lids to bang together and an array of boxes to nest and bright colored cups and bowls did not divert her long. She had to be attached to someone, somehow, which generally made doing their separate tasks difficult, if not impossible.

'Dependence transference,' Rafik suggested pompously.

'This is not in my job description,' Gill said in a soft voice when she had finally fallen asleep, small arms limp around his neck. Rafik and Calum helped to remove her as gently as possible.

They all held their breaths as they managed to lay her in the open pod, which remained her nocturnal cradle.

'And that's another thing,' Gill said, still whispering, 'she's growing by the hour. She's not going to fit in that much longer. What the hell species is she?'

'Born more mature than human babies are,' Rafik said. 'But I can't find out a damned thing in the Concordance or the Encyclo, not even in the alien or the vet entries.'

'Look, guys, I know we'll waste time and fuel, and we haven't got enough of a payload to resupply if we go back to Base, but do we have the right to keep her out here with us when someone might be looking for her? And Base might be able to take care of her better?'

Rafik sighed and Calum looked away from Gill, everywhere else but at the sleeping youngling.

'First,' Rafik said, since he usually did this sort of logical setting out of facts, 'if anybody's looking for her, they'd be looking in this sector of space, not at Base. Second, since we've agreed she is of an unknown alien species, what possible expertise can Base supply? There aren't any books on how to look after her, and we're the only ones with hands-on experience. And finally, we *don't* have enough of a payload to refuel. We do have what looks like a real find here, and I'm not about to let any hijackers take it away from us. We did catch that ion trail last week, and it could very well be Amalgamated spies, just checking up on us.' Gill growled and Calum sniffed his poor opinion of the competition. 'Well, we'll just have to include her in the duty roster. An hour on, two hours off. That gives us two crew working . . .'

'And one going off his nut . . .' Gill said, and then volunteered to take the first duty.

'Ahahaha,' Rafik waggled a slim finger at his crewmate, 'we all work while she sleeps.'

Somehow or other the scheme worked a lot better than any of them had any reason to expect. In the first place, she learned to talk, which kept her, and her current minder, occupied. She learned also to respect 'no' and brighten at 'yes' and, when she was bored with sitting still, would 'yes' and 'no' every object in the dayroom. She never again touched a 'no.' The third day, it was Rafik who brought out the markers and 'dead' computer printouts. He showed her how to hold the implement and, while she could not manage her digits as he did, she was very shortly drawing

29

lines and squiggles and looking for approval at each new design.

'You know,' said Calum, when called upon to admire her handiwork, 'that looks a lot like the stuff on her egg. How mature was she born, d'you think?'

That sent all three comparing her efforts with the egg inscription, but they finally decided that it was pure chance and how would a youngling know script at such an early age. So they taught her to print in Basic, using the now-standard figures. She outdid them shortly by repeating the computer printout programming language.

'Well, she prints what she sees a lot of.'

The big discovery, and the treat could take up to an hour, was bathing her.

'You gotta bathe all kids regularly. Hygiene,' Rafik said, pausing to grin at her as she splashed the water in the big galley sink. She still fit in it at that point. 'I know that much.'

'Yeah? With water on board for three and she makes four and drinks a lot, we'll be in deep kimchee on water quality soon,' Gill said sourly.

'All sink water's recycled,' Calum reminded them just as the youngling dipped her face in the bathwater and blew bubbles. And then drank the bubbles. 'No, sweetie, don't drink the bathwater. Dirty.'

'Actually it isn't,' Rafik remarked, looking at the clear liquid in which their charge sat.

'Has to be. I soaped her good.' Calum peered in and the monel bottom was clearly visible. 'That's impossible. There should be lather and she'd got her kneecaps dirty crawling on the floor and she got her fingers messed up drawing before that. They're all clean now, too.'

'Just a jiff,' Rafik said, and went off for one of his many diagnostic tools. He inserted it in the bathwater and gawked at the reading. 'This stuff is one hundred percent pure unadulterated H_2O. In fact, it's a lot purer than what I used to make coffee this morning.'

'But you saw me soap her,' Calum said in a defensive tone. 'I washed her because she *was* dirty.'

'Which neither she nor the water is now.' Rafik immersed the diagnostic tool again. 'I dunno.'

Calum got a crafty expression on his face. 'Done a reading on our air lately?'

Rafik grimaced. 'In fact I did, like I'm supposed to this time of day.'

'Well?' Gill's voice rose in a prompt when Rafik delayed an answer while scratching his head.

'Not a sign of excess carbon dioxide, and with four of us breathing air, there should be some traces of it by now. Especially as we don't have quite as many broad-leafed plants in 'ponics because she,' he pointed at *her*, 'likes them better than anything else.'

The three men regarded their small charge, who was bubbling her crystal clear bathwater, greatly enjoying this innocent occupation.

'Then there's that sort of horn thing in the middle of her forehead,' Gill remarked.

'Unicorns were supposed to purify water.'

'Water maybe,' Calum agreed as he had been brought up with some of the same fairy tales as Gill, 'but air?'

'Wa-ter?' the youngling said, dropping her jaw in what they now recognized as her smile. 'Air?' she added, though it came out in two syllables, 'a-yir.'

'That's right, baby, water and air. The two things both our species can't live without,' Rafik said, sighing at the puzzle of her.

'Let's call her Una,' Gill suggested suddenly into the silence.

'I don't like it,' Rafik said, shaking his head. 'We're in the As, you know, not the Us.'

'Acorna?' Calum said. 'Sure beats "baby" and "youngling" and "sweetums".' He glanced sideways at Gill, whom he had overheard addressing his charge with what Calum thought a nauseating euphemism.

'Acorna?' Rafik considered. 'Better than Una.' He picked up a cup, dipped it in the clear bathwater, and as he made to pour it over her head, Gill grabbed it out of his hand.

'You ain't even Christian,' he said – and, pouring the water over her head, 'I dub thee Acorna.'

'No, no, you twit,' Calum said, taking the cup from his hand and dipping it in. 'I baptize thee Acorna. I'll stand as godfather.'

'You will not. I will.'

'Where does that leave me?' Rafik demanded. Acorna stood up in the sink, and only his quick movement kept her from falling out of the improvised bath.

'Holding the baby,' Gill and Calum said in unison. Calum handed him the towel.

They had learned to dry off as much moisture as possible because, once set on her feet again, Acorna tended to shake herself and there was too much equipment about that did not need daily sprinklings.

The *Khedive* had cracked and digested 'Azelnut and was on her way to DF-4-H3.1, a small LL-chondrite that should have a high enough concentration of valuable metals to make up the payload for this trip, when the first announcements from Base reached them.

'Summary of proposed adjustments to shareholder status . . .' Gill scowled at the reader. 'Why are they sending us this garbage? We're miners, not pixel-pushers or bean-counters!'

'Let me see that.' Rafik snapped his fingers at the console. 'Hardcopy, triple!'

'Wasting paper,' Calum commented.

'Acorna needs more scratch paper to mark on,' Gill said.

'And if this is what I think it is,' Rafik added, 'you two will be wanting to read it for yourselves, not to wait for me.'

'Whatever it is,' Gill said in disgust after peering at his printout, 'it's wrapped up in enough bureaucratic double-talk that we'll have to wait for you to interpret anyway, Rafik.'

'Not all of it,' Calum said slowly. 'This paragraph –' he tapped his own hardcopy – 'says that our shares in Mercantile Mining and Exploration are now worth approximately three times what they were when we left Base.'

Gill whistled. 'For news like that, they can wrap it up any way they please!'

'And *this* paragraph,' Calum went on, 'says that they have become nonvoting shares.'

'Is that legal? Oh, well, for three times the money, who cares? We didn't have enough shares between us to make a difference anyway.'

Calum was blinking furiously as he translated the announcement into numbers without bothering to consult the voice calculator. 'The net worth of our shares has increased by a factor of three-point-two-five, actually. But if we had ever voted our shares in a block, our interest in MME would have been sufficient to influence a close-run policy decision.'

'I believe,' Rafik said in an oddly strangled voice, 'that if you two will stop jingling your pocket change and look at the last page, you will observe the important part of this announcement. It seems MME has been acquired. By Amalgamated.'

Gill flipped through his hardcopy. 'Says here it's a merger, not an acquisition.'

Rafik shrugged. 'When the tiger executes a merger with the goat, which one walks away?'

'Ah, it's nothing for us to be concerned about,' Gill said. 'We hadn't enough shares to be worth

34

the voting anyway, Calum, and besides, we were never around for their AGMs when we could vote. And it says right here that nothing is going to change in the way the company is run.'

Rafik shrugged again. 'They always say that. It's a sure sign that heads are about to roll.'

'Back on Base? Sure. But that won't affect us.'

'Not immediately, no.'

'Oh, quit spouting doom and gloom, Rafik. Since when do you know so much more about the ways of big business than the rest of us? Like I said, we're miners, not pixel-pushers.'

'My uncle Hafiz,' Rafik said demurely, 'is a merchant. He has explained some of these matters to me. The next announcement should follow within twenty-four to thirty-six hours Standard. That will be the company's change of name. The restructuring and the first revised organizational chart will occur somewhat later, but still well before we reach Base – especially if you still intend mining Daffodil before our return.'

'I'm beginning to think we should rename DF-4-H3.1 Daffy, in your honor, Rafik,' Gill said. 'You can't possibly predict all that.'

'Wait and see,' Rafik suggested. 'Or to make it more amusing, how about a small wager? I'll give you odds of – umm – three to two that you'll not recognize the old MME by the time we bring the *Khedive* in again.'

Calum grinned. 'Not very good odds, Rafik, for someone who claims to be as certain as you are of the outcome!'

Rafik's brown lashes swept down across his face as demurely as any dancing girl in his ancestors' harems could have looked. 'My uncle Hafiz,' he murmured, 'also kept racing horses. He instructed me never to bet on longer odds than I had to.'

'And even if they do reorganize,' Gill went on, 'we're independent contractors, not staff employees. It won't affect us.'

'Remembering some of your other famous last words, Gill,' Calum said unhappily, 'I rather wish you hadn't said that.'

The *Khedive* stayed out much longer than their original prospecting plan filed with MME. A case of finding Daffodil nearly as lucrative as 'Azelnut and covering a wider area. Since their water remained pure and their air remarkably clear of CO_2, they really were not at all pushed.

Acorna also supplied diversion enough to keep all three men from feeling any need to seek fresher companions. Though their arguments about her upbringing slowly verged on the 'what'll we teach her today' rather than physical concerns, the debates usually occurred while she was sleeping. She did require a good deal of sleep, growing out of nap times to at least ten hours in the hammock they devised as her sleeping accommodation. Once asleep, she was impervious to noise – except for the one time a thruster misfired and set off the hooter and she was wide awake in an instant and standing by her assigned escape pod. (Rafik had put her original pod in it, 'just in case' he'd said, and the others had concurred. As there were only three pods on the *Khedive*, and Calum was the smallest of the miners, he would share hers.) So they would discuss her lessons quite freely and sometimes at the top of their lungs.

Such EVA work as was needed was generally accomplished when she was asleep, or so involved with her 'studying' she didn't notice that one of them was gone.

'We're going to have to train her out of such dependence, you know,' Rafik said one night. 'I mean, when we get back to Base, we'll each have duties that will separate us, and she's got to learn that having just one of us around is okay, too.'

'How do we do that?' Calum wanted to know.

'Start doing short EVAs while she's awake, so she sees us going and coming back. I think once she realizes that we *do* come back, she'll settle down more,' Rafik said, shaking his head and casting a sorrowful glance to where she swayed slightly in her hammock. 'Poor tyke. Losing her family to who knows what. Small wonder she needs to see all of us all the time.'

They'd been giving her lessons in Basic, naming everything in the *Khedive* for her. At first she had reciprocated – at least they thought that was what she was doing – with sounds in her own language. But since her words sounded like nothing they'd ever heard before and their efforts to repeat them were dead failures, she soon began accepting and using their vocabulary.

'Just as well,' said Gill.

'A pity for her to lose her original language,' Calum said, 'but she's so young, I doubt she had that much command of it anyway.'

'Well, she sure knew how to say . . .' and Gill spelled the word out rather than upset Acorna by hearing it spoken.

'Avvvi?' she said aloud in response. The look of expectancy in Acorna's eyes as she looked toward the airlock of the *Khedive* nearly had the tender-hearted Gill in tears.

'She can spell?' Rafik exclaimed, grasping the important facet of that incident. 'Hey, there, Acorna baby, what does R-A-F-I-K spell?'

Diverted, she pointed her whole hand, the digits closed as was her habit, at Rafik and said his name.

'And G-I-L-L?'

'Gill.' She made the odd noise through her nostrils which the men had identified as her laugh.

'C-A-L-U-M?' demanded the last of her parent figures.

'Calum!' Now she drummed her closed hands on the table and her feet on the floor, her expression of high happiness.

A good bit of that day's segment went into a spelling lesson. That evening produced the knowledge that she had assimilated the alphabet, and with only a little help from her friends, she began to print what she spelled.

'In a ten-point type, gentlemen, if you will examine the evidence,' Calum said, holding up one of the sheets she had covered with her delicately wrought script.

38

'What's so amazing about that?' Rafik asked, turning the sheet to the other side where the printout words were also in ten point type.

'How much has she absorbed?'

'Damn,' Acorna said very clearly as the writing implement she was using ran dry.

'I'd say more than enough, mates,' Gill said, 'and he who uses foul language will pay one half credit to the box for every foul-mouthed syllable uttered from this point onward.' He picked up an empty disk box, started to write 'Foul mouth' on it when Acorna, reading it, repeated the legend. He erased it hastily and wrote 'FINE' instead.

'What is fine?' Acorna asked.

That's when they showed her how to access the *Khedive*'s reference programs. She had a bit of trouble getting her oddly shaped fingers to hit just the keys she wanted until Rafik made up a keyboard with spacings appropriate to her manual dexterity. If improving this new skill kept her occupied so that they could get on with their professional work and more beneficiated ore was sacked and stored in the drone carrier pods that festooned the exterior of the *Khedive*, she totally confounded them three days later.

'Cargo pods are nearly two-thirds full. What . . . when they are three-thirds full?'

'Say what?' Rafik asked, blinking at her.

'I think she's trying to ask what we'll do then. We take the three-thirds full pods back to Base, get paid for them, resupply the ship, and come back for more,' Calum replied, trying to speak in a nonchalant tone.

'But Daffodil is more than three-thirds cargo pods.'

'Well, you know, we send the iron and nickel back by the mag drive. The ship's own payload is merely the metals too valuable to send that way,' Calum explained, as if he really expected Acorna to understand him.

'Platinum is val-uble.'

'That's right.'

'Then palladium and rhodium and ruthenium is val-uble.'

'Are,' Calum corrected absently.

Rafik had straightened. 'Did you hear that? She knows the platinum-group metals!'

'And why not?' Gill retorted. 'Doesn't she hear us talking about them all the time?'

Acorna stamped her foot to get back their attention. 'Osmium is val-uble. Iridium is val-uble. Rhenium is not val-uble.'

'Rhenium isn't one of the platinum group,' Calum corrected her, 'but at the moment, thanks to the boom in proton accelerometers, it is very valuable indeed.'

Acorna frowned. 'Not mining rhenium.'

'We would if there was any on Daff, I assure you, honey.'

'Rhenium is. Deep.'

'No, love, Daffodil's regolith is rich in platinum-group metals, but low in iron and the minor metals, including rhenium. We could tell that from spectroscopic analysis and . . . um, other instruments,' said Gill, who left the technical task of deciding which asteroids were likely candidates to Calum whenever he could. 'That's why we're miners, hon. This is our job. And we are very lucky to have found Daffodil. 'Azelnut was good, but the Daff's been better for us.'

'Deep!' Acorna insisted. 'Use auger. Drill. Find rhenium, go back soon. Then go somewhere new?'

'To find your folks?'

Acorna's eyes narrowed and she looked down an elegant but definitely equine nose at her closed hands.

'Honey, one of the reasons we've stayed out so long is to make enough money to do a real good galactic search for your folks. Your Avvvi. Was Avvvi the only one in your ship?'

'No. Lalli there, too.'

'Your mother and father?' Gill asked, hoping that now her comprehension of Basic was so good, she might be able to make the leap to translating her mother tongue.

'No, Avvvi and Lalli.'

'Nice try, Gill,' Rafik said, laying a sympathetic hand on his arm.

'By the way, hon, three-thirds full is all full. Three-thirds make one,' Calum said, seeking to distract her from her sad contemplation of her hands. 'Thirds are fractions.'

'Fractions?' Her head came up.

'Parts of a whole. There're all kinds of fractions, halves and quarters and fifths and sixths and lots

41

and lots, and when you have two halves, you have a whole. When you have four quarters, you have a whole.'

'And five fives is a whole, too?' Her eyes were wide again as she grasped the concept. 'What is the smallest? One and one?'

'We also got us a mathematical genius,' Rafik said, throwing up his slim fingered hands in humorous awe.

One mathematical concept led to another, and it wasn't long before Acorna was accessing algebraic equations. Calum, muttering something about leaving no regolithic grain unturned, bullied the others into using the tether and auger to go beneath the fine, friable rubble of Daffodil's outer layers.

'Why not teach her something useful? Like how to watch the catalytic converter gauges and switch over at the right temps?' Rafik asked. 'Then I'd get to go out with you guys on EVAs and she'd have less of this dependency thing.'

'I think,' Calum said in awed tones, 'she was born knowing more useful things than we can imagine.' He was inspecting the latest drilling samples by remote control. 'Look at this analysis, will you?'

'Rhenium and hafnium,' Rafik said slowly, bending over the screens. 'High concentrations, too. If the drill keeps bringing up this quality of ore, we can make our payload and be back at Base sooner than if we keep working the surface regolith for platinum. And the load will be richer by—'

'Forty-two point six five percent,' Calum said,

blinking absently. 'She *said* there was rhenium down deep, you know.'

'Daffodil shows as an undifferentiated asteroid. There've been no atmospheric processes to move deposits. Logically, the deep rock should be the same metals, in the same concentration, as the surface regolith . . . just harder to get at.'

'Logically,' Gill retorted, 'looking at this analysis, it isn't. There just may be a few things the cosmologists don't know yet. But I'd give a pretty penny to know how you knew, Acorna acushla. I think we'd better teach her the rest of the metals, gentlemen, so she knows what to tell us about from now on. And as for dependency . . .' Gill snorted. 'Once you made her her own keyboard, she undepended herself, or hadn't you two noticed?'

'Some are born to be hackers, and some ain't,' Rafik said.

'Well, it won't hurt to try, now will it?' was Gill's retort, but he was as proud of Acorna as they all were. 'We're not doing so bad as parents, are we?'

'How mature was she born?' Calum asked, almost plaintively. 'She's only been aboard for . . .' He had to access the log for the date she'd been recovered. 'Hey, twelve months and fifteen days!'

'A year?' Rafik repeated astonished.

'A year!' Gill cried. 'Hell, we forgot her birthday!'

The other two, tight-lipped with anger, pointed to the FINE jar, which hadn't actually been fed for some time.

Two

'Purely superficial changes,' Gill said as the *Khedive* arrived within visual range of the old MME Base. 'You'll not claim your winnings on the basis of a few cosmetic details, will you now, Rafik?'

'I should be delighted,' Rafik said, 'not to claim them at all.'

No announcement of any reorganization had reached them, but the MME logo that had once decorated both sides of each docking gate had been replaced by a much larger sign reading, AMALGAMATED MANUFACTURING. Instead of Johnny Greene's cheerful greeting, they had been read into position by something with a dry mechanical voice that refused to give its name and complained about their failure to introduce themselves with 'the Amalgamated protocol,' whatever that might be.

The docking bay itself was much the same, but immediately within the double airlock doors leading to the interior of Base they were met by the owner of the dry voice, still complaining about their failure to use the Amalgamated protocol.

'Look, mate,' Gill said, 'like the pilot here told you –' he nodded toward Calum '– we're the *Khedive*, on contract to MME, and we didn't get word of any new approach and docking protocol. If you chaps wanted us to use something new, why didn't you send us the rules?'

'Violation of regulations to send classified company protocols via unsecured space transmissions.'

'The ancient Americans had a phrase for it,' Rafik said, smiling slightly. 'Something about a twenty-two catch, I believe.'

'And where's Johnny Greene?'

'Redundant.'

'And just what is *that* supposed to mean?'

Gill's voice had grown loud enough to echo down the corridors. A young woman in a pale blue coverall, her fair hair drawn back into a bun, hurried forward with one hand raised.

'Eva Glatt,' she introduced herself, holding out one small hand, 'TT&A – that's Testing, Therapy, and Adjustment Department. The consolidation of MME with Amalgamated has resulted in a number of organizational changes for efficiency, Mr – Giloglie, is it? I've come to take charge of the child.'

'She is in *our* charge,' Gill said.

'Oh, but surely you won't want to be bothered with her while you're filling out the docking protocol forms and reregistering the *Khedive* as an

Amalgamated ship. I've prepared everything, though your message did not give us much time to make ready.'

Rafik and Calum had convinced Gill that it would be tactful to tell Base something about the enigma they were bringing back from this latest expedition, but they had all waited until they were on the way back from Daffodil, just in case Base had any ideas about issuing an immediate recall.

'And Dr Forelle himself wishes to inspect the pod in which she was found and your tapes of the initial contact,' Eva went on. 'I'll just have that material brought off the ship and taken to him while you're registering yourselves, shall I? And you can come with me, you poor baby.' She knelt and held out her hand to Acorna, who put both hands behind her own back and stepped back a pace, narrowing her pupils to vertical slits.

'*Not*,' she said with emphasis.

'Complete sentences, Acorna acushla,' Gill said with a sigh.

'Now, dear,' Eva Glatt said brightly, 'you'll be very bored staying here with your nice uncles while they do all that tedious paperwork. Wouldn't you like to come along to the crèche and play some nice games?'

Acorna glanced at Rafik. He gave a small nod and she relaxed her guarded pose slightly. 'Will go,' she said. '*Short!*'

'There, you see,' Eva Glatt said, straightening, 'it's just a matter of elementary psychology. I'm sure she'll be quite docile and trainable.'

'That woman,' said Gill as Eva led Acorna off, 'is an idiot.'

'She said something about a crèche,' said Rafik. 'Acorna might enjoy being with some other children for a change. And I do have a presentiment that the next hour or so will be boring in the extreme.'

While Gill, Rafik and Calum worked their way through questionnaires demanding everything from grandmother's middle name to preferences in basic food groups, Dr Alton Forelle skimmed through the ship's log of Acorna's first utterances half a dozen times.

'Again!' he snapped, and his assistant, Judit Kendoro, obediently replayed the first segments of that haunting cry.

'Idiots,' Forelle said cheerfully. 'Why couldn't they have recorded everything she said? Why did they have to interfere by an attempt to overlay Basic Universal speech patterns? There's not nearly enough data here to analyze.'

'There's enough to tell that she was just a lost baby crying for somebody she knew,' said Judit softly. She thought she might be reduced to tears herself if she had to listen to that wail of 'Avvvi, avvvi!' any longer.

Forelle shut off the player. 'You're anthropomorphizing, Judit,' he said. 'How can we presume to interpret an alien speech merely from inflection and situation? We shall have to make a thorough syntactic and semantic analysis before any conclusions at all are valid.'

'And just how are we going to do that,' Judit said, 'when she's been with these people for over a year, exposed to Basic Universal and forgetting her own speech patterns?'

'We'll regress her to the time when she was found, of course,' Forelle replied, as if that should have been assumed. 'The technique is simple enough, and with the right drugs, no one resists a regression. From the number and sequence of sounds she was making when they found her, she must have had some mastery of her native language at that time. The information is still there, simply overlaid by recent experiences. We have only to strip off the overlay.'

Judit made a small, involuntary gesture. Even adults who had volunteered for the process found a full regression terrifying. What would it be like for this child? 'You'll halt the process, of course, if she appears traumatized?'

'Of course,' Forelle assured her. 'But you mustn't be so tender. We must have as much evidence as possible to back up this discovery. If she is a sapient alien, speaking a language totally unrelated to any human tongue, whatever we can learn of that language will be of inestimable scientific value. We can't let individual concerns stand in the way of Science.'

'And publication,' Judit said dryly.

'Oh, don't worry about that,' Forelle said. 'If you help me with the child, I shall certainly list you as one of the coauthors. And you must bear the other possibility in mind, too. If she's just a deformed mutant gabbling some known tongue in a way we didn't recognize from the log, what fools we should look, announcing the discovery of the first true alien language! We can't risk that, can we?' He smiled into space and went on, more to himself than to Judit, 'It's high time linguistics came into its own as a scientific discipline. We've been ridiculously hobbled all these years by a squeamish reluctance to experiment on human beings. Why, the entire critical-period theory of language learning could have been settled generations ago if someone had just had the fortitude to isolate a few dozen babies from human speech for ten or twenty years. It would be a beautifully controlled experiment, you see – take a child out every six months and expose it to language, and when they stop responding, you know the critical period has passed. Of course, one wouldn't want to contaminate the test subjects by returning the exposed children, and one has to allow for sickness, and the need to duplicate results, so rather a large initial test group would be required. I'm sure that's why my request for funding was turned down. Governments are so short-sighted about pure research. But this time I won't need to wait for a grant. I've got the subject right here, at least I *shall* have as soon as that Glatt female is through with her puerile tests, and Amalgamated's psycho-socialization lab is perfectly equipped for the examination.'

Judit Kendoro bit her lip and reminded herself

that she had been lucky to get out of the factories of Kezdet, lucky to win one of the very few technical school scholarships set aside for indigent students, even luckier to have a good job with Amalgamated that had paid off her sister Mercy's bond and would, given just a few more months, see her little brother Pal through school and into a job of his own. Even forgetting the other considerations that kept her at Amalgamated, no one could possibly expect her to throw away all those years of hard work just because some foundling child might be scared by reliving a traumatic incident of her past. Besides, what could she do?

'I'll just see how they're getting on with the child at TT&A,' she said.

Dr Forelle smiled. 'Good idea. They've had her quite long enough. And you might bring the test results with you . . . not that I expect much from the clumsy, outmoded instruments that Glatt woman uses.'

'We've completed the forms,' Gill said, leaning over Eva Glatt's desk, 'and we've come for Acorna. If you could just show us the way to the crèche?'

Eva looked surprised. 'Oh, you can't take her now!'

'Why not? She may be enjoying the chance to play with the other children, but I'm sure she will be wanting to see us by now.'

'Playing? Other children? I'm afraid you have misunderstood. We've just begun testing her

50

mental and psychological capacity. She'll be in tests most of this day. Most of the week, probably. You wouldn't be spending any more time with her in any case.'

'We would not?' repeated Rafik. 'I am sorry, that is not acceptable.'

'She is used to us,' Calum said hastily, trying to smooth things over, 'and . . . we're kinda used to her, too. We figured, unless you located her people, she could just stay on with us. She's already lost her parents. She doesn't need to lose us, too.'

Eva Glatt laughed merrily. 'How sweet! But you really couldn't expect to retain care of her, could you? Three mining engineers, isolated for years at a time . . . I'm sure you've done your best, but you hardly have the training and expertise to solve her special problems.'

'Acorna doesn't *have* any special problems,' Calum said angrily. 'She's a perfectly delightful little girl, and we *like* taking care of her. Oh, I'm not saying we might not have handed her over to a Company crèche if we'd been able to at the beginning. But she's been with us nearly two years now. We're her family. Of course we expect to continue taking care of her.'

Eva laughed again. 'Don't be ridiculous. Even if the situation were not obviously unsuitable, your PPPs would invalidate any application for formal guardianship.'

'PPPs?' Rafik repeated.

'Personal Psychological Profiles,' Eva deigned

to elucidate. 'I pulled up the Amalgamated psych files on you. All three of you are classified as maladaptive personalities who are drawn to a lonely, high-risk profession such as asteroid prospecting by a combination of self-destructive traits and romantic thrill-seeking—'

'Excuse me,' Rafik interrupted, 'I do not, myself, recall that this company has administered any psychological tests to me. Calum? Gill?'

The other two men shook their heads.

'You just filled out the personnel forms,' Eva said patiently. 'The computer analysis was routed to my mailbox immediately, since your personality problems may have a bearing on the child's psychological problems. The results are much as I expected.'

'Psychology! When we contracted with MME,' Gill said, 'we reported to the Director of Mining Engineering, who was more interested in whether we knew how to handle an ultra-low-temp vacuum blasting unit than in what we saw in the inkblots.'

'An outmoded attitude,' Eva said. 'Amalgamated considers it of vital importance to see that only socially well-adapted personnel are retained in the trying conditions of space.'

'And exactly how,' Rafik inquired sweetly, 'did you come to this . . . conclusion . . . about our personalities?'

'It's self-evident,' Eva said. 'Why else would you expose yourselves to the risks and loneliness of such a career, when you all score high enough in SGIQ – Stabilized Generalized Intelligence Quotient – and have more than enough education to obtain much better-paid administrative positions right here at company headquarters?'

'More money,' Calum agreed gravely, 'and the benefits of psychologically designed decor. Why indeed?'

Eva looked at him uncertainly. 'I . . . I'm glad you agree with me. You understand, then. The child is severely deformed and probably retarded as well—'

A hissing noise distracted her for a moment, until Rafik took Gill by the elbow. 'Do not interrupt, my friend,' he said. 'We are all most interested in the lady doctor's evaluation of Acorna, are we not?'

'By height and weight charts, she is a reasonably well-nourished six-year-old,' Eva said, 'but on the SLI – Standardized Language Interaction – she scored as a low two.'

'By my own experience,' countered Gill, 'she was an infant when we found her, and that was less than two years ago. She can't be more than three or four years old.'

'And her understanding of language is excellent,' Calum added. 'If she's lagging in expressive speech, it is probably because her brain is not wired for human language; she's having to learn it analytically, not naturally as a human infant would.'

'I'm glad to see you admit she has brain problems,' Eva said quickly.

'Differences,' Calum said, 'not problems.'

Eva fussed with her desk console for a moment. 'Given the degree of language retardation, we next administered the Colquhoun Color-Matching Test, which is of course designed for much younger children. She displayed notable clumsiness in operating the cursor—'

'Her fingers are lacking a joint,' Rafik pointed out. 'Of course she has trouble with equipment designed for human hands. What are you testing for, intelligence or manual dexterity?'

'The two have long been shown to be linked,' Eva retorted. 'Every fool knows that a child is not ready for reading or computation until he can hop a straight line on one foot; it's one of the standard crèche-readiness tests.'

'Aye, I'm sure that is one of the things every *fool* knows,' Gill agreed with a heavy irony that escaped Eva. '*Did* you test her intelligence at all?'

'Did you ask her to write a simple program for carbonyl reduction?'

'Or to calculate the concentration of platinum-group metals in the regolith of an E-type chondrite?'

'Don't be ridiculous!' Eva snapped. 'Even if the child could perform such tasks, she must have learned them by rote. Doing such extremely age-inappropriate things is another sign of the social maladjustment we will cure after her deformities have been corrected. If she is to develop into an adaptively competent personality, her upbringing must be entrusted to experts who will understand how to help her compensate for her disabilities without requiring excessive achievement from her.'

'And exactly what did you have in mind?' Rafik inquired politely.

'Well, I – she must be tested more thoroughly first, of course – but I see no reason why she should not be trainable to hold a minimum-responsibility position in a sheltered workspace.'

'Stacking trays in the company cafeteria,' Gill said.

'Or folding linen,' Calum suggested.

Eva flushed. 'I'm not a miracle worker,' she snapped. 'You've brought me a deformed, retarded child who has already suffered the effects of nearly two years in a socially maladaptive environment.'

'I would not, myself, be so quick to be assuming the child is retarded,' said Calum. 'Once you take your eyes away from the psychological tests long enough to observe that she is *not human* – which any competent biologist could verify for you – perhaps you will begin to understand that differences are not the same as defects. And yes, she has some problems with language and with manipulating equipment designed for humans. So? In any other field, Dr Glatt, the expert is the one who knows how to solve problems, not the one who wails that they're unsolvable.'

A gleam of triumph appeared in Eva Glatt's eyes. 'As a matter of fact,' she said sweetly, 'I am already preparing to solve some of the child's problems. There's no known surgical correction for the hand problem, but that disfiguring excrescence in the middle of her forehead can easily be removed.'

'That— You mean you want to cut off her horn?' Gill exploded. 'Woman, have you lost your wits? That's not a deformity; it's an integral part of her.'

'Amalgamated's on-site med team is quite capable of administering a local anesthetic and tying off any blood vessels that have infiltrated the deformity,' Eva said primly.

'I think you do not understand.' Rafik leaned over Eva's desk, his dark eyes flashing with intensity. 'Acorna is . . . not . . . human. Differences are not deformities. And her race *uses* that horn. We've already learned that she can use it to purify air and water, and we suspect it's integral to her metal-sensing abilities.'

Eva sighed. 'I think you three have been isolated too long. You're beginning to hallucinate. What you suggest is not scientifically possible.'

'We speak from our own experience,' Calum said.

Eva tapped at her desk console. 'In my capacity as head of TT&A, I shall recommend extended leave and a course of psychological adjustment for all of you before you are allowed to take out company property such as the *Khedive* again. My evaluation shows that you are not only socially maladaptive but seriously delusional.'

Gill began to hiss through his clenched teeth again, but Rafik stopped him.

'Never mind the minor insults, Gill. The first priority is to stop this nonsense of surgery on Acorna. The horn is an integral part of her. Without it she would be crippled . . . or worse. We will absolutely not, under any circumstances, give permission for an operation.'

'I think *you* don't understand. Acorna is no longer your problem. After surgery and remedial training, she is to be transferred to an orphanage pending identification of the parents who abandoned her.'

'The devil she is!' Gill roared. 'We're taking her back. Now. Are you going to send for her, or do we go and get her?'

'She was scheduled to go into surgery at 1330 hours,' Eva Glatt said. She glanced at her wrist unit. 'It's too late for you to make a fuss now.'

'*Relax*, Gill,' Calum said after checking his own unit. 'It's only 1345 now. They'll still be fiddling around with the anesthesia.' He perched on the corner of Eva Glatt's desk, one arm casually draped over her console. 'But I do think you had better tell us how to get to Surgery. Now!'

A young woman with a wrist-thick braid of dark hair hanging over one shoulder stepped into the office. 'I believe I can help you gentlemen with that,' she said. Her chest rose and fell as though she had just been running, but her manner was calm enough. 'I'm going that way myself, as it happens.'

'That,' said Gill, 'would be very helpful. We're in rather a hurry, though . . .' He steered the girl out into the hall, blocking her view of Eva Glatt's desk, while Calum slipped behind the desk and stopped Eva from reaching for one of the recessed buttons in the desk console. 'Rafik, go on ahead. I'll bring this one – keep her under my eye so that she doesn't get any ideas about calling Security.' He hauled Eva Glatt to her feet and clamped his free hand over her mouth.

'Calum,' Rafik interjected, 'we do not have time to drag a captive with us. And we do not wish to alarm our guard.' Eva Glatt's eyes rolled up in her head as he approached and she sagged limply against Calum's arm.

'Well, that's solved,' said Calum with relief. 'She's fainted.'

'No,' Rafik said, 'just weak with fear. I apologize for this,' he told Eva, who was now feebly struggling again, 'but we do not have access to your more scientific methods of quieting people.' His fist tapped her forehead, so quickly she could hardly have seen the blow coming, and this time she fell back in the complete relaxation of true unconsciousness.

Gill and the girl who'd offered to guide them were some distance ahead when they came out of the office, walking at a pace just short of a jog through the long curving corridor to the left. Rafik and Calum ran and caught up with them at an intersection where they had paused for a moment.

'Running,' the girl said severely, 'is likely to draw attention. Just walk as quickly as you can manage. I gather you three are the men who brought the alien foundling in, is that right?'

'At least somebody around here understands she's not of our kind,' Rafik said as they race-walked down the hall. 'Yes. Acorna is ours. Or we are hers. Depending on how you look at it. And she must not be put through this surgery.'

'Yes. My boss – Dr Forelle – wants it stopped, too. He was to have called ahead, to make sure they delay until I get there with the orders to release her to our department.'

'Just a minute!' Gill grabbed the girl by the upper arm. 'She's to be released to *us*, not to another department of this blasted company.'

'You,' said the girl without slackening pace, 'can't get Eva Glatt's orders for immediate surgery rescinded. I can.'

'And who might you be?' Rafik asked.

'Judit Kendoro, Psycholinguistics. I work for Dr Alton Forelle.'

'Saints defend us,' Gill exclaimed, 'is there nobody works for Amalgamated but head-shrinkers?'

'Amalgamated decided to use the old MME base as headquarters for the research and personnel departments,' Judit explained. 'They're phasing out the independent mining operations; yours is one of the last contract groups to come in. Deliveries will be handled by drone and routed to other stations from now on.' Despite the speed they were making, she wasn't even breathing hard.

'Forelle,' Rafik said. 'The man who wanted our logs of the first interaction?'

'Yes. *He* believes – or hopes – she is a sapient alien.'

'Then he's on our side?'

'I wouldn't say that exactly.' Judit skidded to a halt just before a three-way intersection with corridors painted in different patterns of yellow and green stripes. 'He doesn't want her put through surgery before he has a chance to study her. What do *you* want with her?'

'To take care of her,' Gill said.

Judit looked him up and down for a long moment, then turned to Rafik. 'I believe you mean that.'

'Believe it,' said Rafik.

'Then—' She glanced back the way they had come. Calum followed. Judit dropped her voice. 'Don't let Dr Forelle get her. He'll mine her brain for memories of language without caring what he does to the rest of her. It could be worse than the surgery.'

'Then what can we do?'

'Is your ship ready to take off?'

'We've just docked, we'd fuel and air to spare, no repairs scheduled . . .'

'Then this,' Judit said, 'is what we do next.' She outlined her idea.

'You trust us easily,' Rafik commented when she had finished.

'One must trust *somebody*,' Judit said, 'and . . . I had been listening for a few minutes outside the door before I interrupted you in Dr Glatt's office. Incidentally, dare I hope that you gagged her?'

'No time,' Calum said, catching up with them. 'Knocked her out.'

'Good.'

'If you were listening, then you know some-thing of us. But what do we know of you? Why should you take this risk for us?' Gill demanded.

Judit threw him a scornful glance. 'Have you ever heard of Kezdet?'

Gill shook his head.

'My Uncle Hafiz,' Rafik said, 'recommended it as a place to be avoided.'

'Your uncle was right. I got myself and my sister out of Kezdet,' Judit said, 'and pretty soon I'm going to get my kid brother out. Besides . . . but that doesn't concern you. Let's just say I have seen enough children suffering. If I can save this one, maybe . . . maybe it'll make up for what I ignored in order to get myself out.'

A few minutes later, Judit Kendoro walked through the swinging doors of Surgery and pre-sented her Amalgamated badge to the desk clerk. 'Here to collect Child, Anonymous, recent arrival on the *Khedive*,' she said in a bored monotone. 'Dr Forelle will have transmitted the orders.'

The clerk nodded and pressed a button. The doors behind her slid open and a tall woman in sterile scrubs came out.

'I *wish* you people would make up your minds,' she said. 'We had to give her a global anesthetic, the local didn't work. I could go ahead and get all the restorative work done right now if Forelle would just wait a day.'

Judit shrugged. 'It doesn't matter to me, I'm just the courier. You want her back when we're done?'

'If the order for surgery hasn't been cancelled by some other department,' the woman snapped. 'For now, take her with my compliments. I have enough *real* patients without getting caught in some power struggle between the psych departments.'

She nodded toward the room she had come from and a green-gowned aide wheeled out a gurney on which Acorna lay limp and unconscious. The tangle of silvery curls had already been shaved in a wide naked semicircle around her horn.

'I'll take her on the gurney,' Judit said in a bored tone, 'no need for your people to waste time with the transfer.'

As soon as Judit had control of the gurney, Rafik sprang forward and grabbed her from behind. A plasknife slid out of his sleeve and gleamed across Judit's throat.

'Thanks for showing us the way, dummy,' he growled in his best threatening tones. 'We'll take the kid back now.'

'You can't do this! You tricked me!' Judit was a terrible actress; the words came out as woodenly as someone reading a basic literacy test.

'Raise the alarm,' Rafik threatened the desk clerk and surgeon, 'and the girl gets it. Keep quiet, and we'll let her go when we're safely away. Understand?'

Gill reached down to the gurney and swept

Acorna up in one arm, and Calum held the doors while he and Rafik and Judit made their exit.

'Is she all right?' As soon as the doors swung shut behind them, Rafik dropped the pretense of holding Judit at knife point. Now he was at Gill's side, feeling for a pulse in Acorna's wrist.

'Breathing,' Gill said. 'We'll see about the rest when the anesthetic wears off. Judit, is there anything we should know about that?'

She shook her head. 'Standard anesthesia. She'll be out an hour, maybe two, depending on how long ago it was administered. Just as well, really. Gives you time to get her back on shipboard without a fuss . . . I'd better go with you, though. Keep the knife out, Rafik, and hold my arm. You may need a hostage again.'

'Which way from here to the docking bay?' Gill asked.

'We can take the service tunnels. Less chance of running into people.' Judit pressed a panel in the wall and a narrow inner tunnel opened before them, barely wide enough to admit Gill with the burden of a sleeping Acorna.

They reached the docking bay without incident. The bored, mechanical clerk who'd replaced Johnny Greene hardly lifted his head when they came to his desk.

'Warn personnel out of the bay and prepare the outer doors for opening,' Calum said. '*Khedive* departing immediately.'

'Not cleared,' the clerk mumbled without looking up from his console.

'Please,' Judit said in a shaky voice, 'do what they say. He – he's got a knife.'

This got the clerk's attention. His head snapped up, he gave a startled look at the plasknife in Calum's hand, and he dived under his desk. 'Do what you want, just leave me out of it!'

'Well, well,' said Gill softly, 'and here I thought the wee man might make trouble by trying to be a hero. Calum, d'you know the docking system well enough to clear us for departure?'

'If Amalgamated hasn't changed it too much,' Calum said. 'Here, hold this.' He handed the plasknife to Judit, who quickly handed it on to Gill. 'I'm a *hostage*, you idiots,' she hissed.

Gill laughed quietly and accepted the task of holding Judit 'hostage.' Calum, having swiveled the desk console to face him, was oblivious to the byplay. He brought up a series of screens in quick succession, nodding in satisfaction. 'Hmm,' he said at the sight of the fifth screen. 'Hmm . . . Uh-huh. Okay, next, okay, uh-huh.' He zipped through the rest of the status screens and tapped in a command. 'Okay, that clears us. But there are a couple of little problems.'

'Anything that would keep us on the base?'

'No, but . . .'

'Right. We'll discuss them later. Come on! And Judit, act normal. The bay may be cleared, but unless Amalgamated's remodeled, the loading staff can watch us from the top gallery. We don't want any of the staff to notice you're being a hostage.'

'So I'm not-a-hostage trying to act like a hostage trying to act not-a-hostage,' Judit muttered as they passed through the series of doors that protected the interior of Base when the docking bay was open to space. 'It's as bad as singing Cherubino, having to be a girl pretending to be a boy pretending to dress up as a girl.'

'You like ancient opera?' Gill asked in surprise.

Judit shrugged. 'I was in a couple of amateur productions at school. My voice isn't good enough to go professional. But one year we got Kirilatova to coach us in *Figaro*. She did Susanna, of course.'

'Kirilatova? But she's got to be about a hundred and ten by now!'

'Not quite. She was seventy then,' Judit said, 'and when she sang Susanna, if you had your eyes closed, she was a girl of twenty about to be married to her beloved. It was an incredible performance. I wish I'd been born early enough to hear her at her peak.'

'I have cubes,' Gill said. 'Early performances, originally preserved on DCVCD, then transferred to tri-D when the new format came out.'

'Are you going to invite the girl up to listen to your opera cubes, Gill? How about lifting Acorna up first?' There was an edge of sarcasm in Calum's voice. They had crossed the open bay without incident while Gill and Judit talked about dead singers.

'I might at that,' Gill said thoughtfully. He took Judit's hand. 'You could come with us. You don't belong with the psych-toads at Amalgamated, you know. As the customer said to the Vassar girl in the brothel, what's a nice girl like you doing in a place like this?'

Judit shook her head. 'As the Vassar girl said to the customer, "Just lucky, I guess." I know nothing of mining; I'd be useless cargo to you.'

Calum, who'd been on the verge of making that point, opened his mouth and shut it again with an audible snap.

'You'd better knock me out, too, before you go. The hostage act may not have been totally convincing.'

'After all the help you've been? I couldn't bear to, acushla.'

'It will lend verisimilitude to an otherwise bald and unconvincing narrative,' Judit said. 'Look, I need this job. I can earn enough here to see Pal through technical school. Anyway, I . . . I have my reasons for staying with Amalgamated. Now will you get on with it?'

'Can't,' Rafik said. 'You've no protection. If you're in this docking bay when we open the doors, and not on the ship, you're dead. You will have to walk back through the inner doors. As soon as you're safe, we'll take off. They won't have time to cancel the clearing sequence.'

Unexpectedly, Judit laughed. 'That fat little toad of a receiving clerk is probably still under his desk, and nobody else knows anything's wrong . . . yet. But I look too unharmed to have been the hostage of you brutal roughnecks. Give me the knife, Gill.' With rapid efficiency she sliced through her outer coverall at the point where Gill had been pretending to hold the knife point against her side, then pulled half the hair out of her braid and let it fall in a dark cloud over the side of her face. 'Do I look enough of a mess yet?'

'You look most beautiful,' Gill said, 'and I shall carry your memory with me through the cold of space.'

'Get on with it, you two!' Calum snapped. 'We've got Acorna webbed in. The longer you spend chatting the girl up, the more chance of somebody noticing something's wrong.'

'That's a brave girl,' Gill said as he climbed on board the *Khedive* and strapped himself in for takeoff. He watched Judit's halting progress across the floor of the docking bay. 'I hope that limp is part of the acting . . .'

'She was moving just fine on the way to Surgery,' Calum pointed out. 'Rafik! Systems ready? I want us in action the minute she's through the first doors.'

'Second doors,' Gill said firmly. 'She's too valuable to risk.'

'And Acorna? Not to mention us? And the *Khedive*?'

'We'll make it,' Gill said with confidence.

And they did.

'*Now* what?' Calum said when they were well away from Base.

Gill shrugged. 'Long term or short term? Long term, we've still got our skills and our ship, and there are other companies to contract with – or we can go independent. Short term . . . You said something about problems when you were humming over the console back there. What's our status?'

'Refueling only partially complete, but that's no problem; we've enough to make it back into the asteroid belt, and once there, we can mine a carbonaceous chondrite to supply hydrogen for the fuel converter.'

'A C-type chondrite will replenish our water and oxygen, too, if necessary,' Rafik pointed out. 'So what's the problem?'

'Food's low. We're about to be temporary vegetarians.'

'At least one of us won't mind that,' Gill said with a tender look at the net where Acorna lay, moving just enough in her drugged sleep to reassure them all that she would wake soon enough.

'And we didn't get the replacement auger bits,' Calum said. ''Azelnut cracked most of them and Daffy just about finished the rest of the box off. Our tether cables are worn, too. We were due for a good deal of refitting at Base.'

There were more immediate complications than shortage of spare parts, as they learned when they activated the com units.

'Just receiving,' Rafik advised them. 'Transmitting would give away our position.'

'Ah, they're not going to follow us out of sector for one little girl nobody had claimed anyway.'

'"Why step on me?" the ant asked the elephant. "Because I can, and because you have annoyed

68

me,"' Rafik answered obliquely. 'It is not wise to annoy the elephant.'

'I've got the Base frequency,' Calum announced. 'You two might want to listen in.'

They listened in tight-lipped anger to the repeated announcement being broadcast to all Amalgamated bases and ships.

'They're claiming the *Khedive* is stolen property!' Gill exploded. 'They can't do that! She's our ship, free and clear!'

'That ghastly female said something about the *Khedive* being theirs,' Calum said thoughtfully. 'Rafik, is there some legal mumbo-jumbo in the reorganization that could possibly make it look like we had been leasing the ship from them?'

'They can *claim* whatever they want to,' Rafik pointed out. 'And if they catch up with us, and we have to argue it out in the courts, who'll be taking care of Acorna?' He smiled benignly at his colleagues. 'We might be well advised to take on a new identity.'

'We can call ourselves whatever we want,' Gill grumbled, 'but the ship's registered and known . . .'

Rafik's smile was seraphic. 'I might know someone who can take care of that little matter for us. For a fee, of course.'

'What have we got to pay your someone with? I have a strong suspicion Amalgamated's accountants are not going to credit us for all the iron and nickel we've been sending back by drone,' Calum said dourly. 'And the platinum and titanium are sitting in the Amalgamated shipping bay – wrapped up in our only container nets!'

'We have,' Rafik said gently, 'a large block of extremely valuable, if nonvoting, shares of Amalgamated stock. I think Uncle Hafiz will be willing to convert it into local currency for us.'

There was a moment's pause, then Gill laughed and slapped his knee. 'So Amalgamated pays for the refit, after all! Good enough.'

'We'll be broke afterward,' Calum grumbled.

'We'll have our ship, our tools, and our skills,' Gill said in high good humor. 'And Acorna! Never worry, man. There are asteroids out there richer than anything we ever mined on contract. I can feel it in my bones.'

'So, onward to Uncle Hafiz?' Rafik asked, settling himself at the navigational board and posing his fingers over the keys.

'Yeah. Where is your famous Uncle Hafiz?'

'The planet is called Laboue; the location is a family secret I'm not allowed to divulge,' Rafik said, already plotting in a course. He had completed it and cleared the screen before either Gill or Calum could see what he had entered. 'Naughty, naughty!'

'Nauuughtie?' a feeble little voice queried.

'Acorna, sweetie,' and Gill, being nearest, strode to her hammock. 'Sorry, hon, sorry. We had no idea at all what those idiots were going to do to our little Acorna.'

Her pupils widened and the fear drained from her features, her hands and feet opening in relief at finding herself back on board the *Khedive* and with them.

'That stupid woman! Glad I decked her,' Calum said.

'Very stupid woman,' Acorna agreed, nodding her head vigorously and then moaning. 'Oh, my head!'

'It'll wear off, acushla,' he said, and then added to Gill, 'Get webbed. We're about to go into the wild black yonder!'

Three

Acorna was very nervous for the next few days, so they all made a big effort to divert her and promise, on their honors, that she'd never be left alone with stupid strangers again. One of the few unessential tasks that Calum had had time to do, before they went to collect Acorna, was to pick up some seed from the chandler. He was offered flowers, too.

'There are quite a few decorative broad-leafed types, flowering, too, which do give you some diversity in your 'ponics. Also some botanical oddities that do quite well on nutrient solutions,' he'd been told. 'Quick growing.'

While he had been more interested in vegetables and edible legumes and some of the new bean types, he also picked up alfalfa, timothy, and lucernes seeds, remarking that he would be making a planetfall and was doing a favor for a friend.

Setting out the seeds and using the *Galactic Botanical* from the ship's library program to figure out how to speed up their growth helped pass the time and increase the variety of their meals. Acorna had read just as much as Calum and Gill had of the *GB* and she very shortly told them she had the matter well in hand and they were to please do something else.

'You don't suppose she remembers stuff . . . racial memory?' Calum asked.

Gill shrugged. 'Who's to know? I did manage to check that blood sample we took when she scraped her knee. She's not of a known genotype. Shit!' And he obediently put a half-credit in the FINE box. It joined its fellows with a clink.

'Hey, man, how much have we got in there?' Calum asked and Gill opened the container, spilling out a good fifty half-credits.

'Won't buy much, but it's a start.'

'Uncle Hafiz will set us up, lads,' Rafik assured them from the pilot's seat. Then he leaned forward. 'Gill, d'you remember that dead ship we found rammed halfway through an asteroid?'

'What about it?'

'Wasn't it the same class as this one?'

'Year or two older.'

'But same class. Are you getting at what I think you're getting at?' Gill asked, brightening.

'Indeed I am, dear lad,' Rafik said, grinning from ear to ear. 'And that asteroid belt is also on our present heading . . . well, with a slight detour.'

'We change identities with it?' Calum asked. 'Can we *do* that?'

'With a little extra help from Uncle Hafiz, that

73

should be no problemo,' Rafik said. 'Shall we?'

Gill and Calum made eye contact.

'Well, it's worth the effort, I think, especially if Uncle Hafiz can fiddle some updates about where that ship has been while she was missing.'

'He's a whiz at that sort of thing,' Rafik said and began to whistle off-key.

'Sure get Amalgamated off our tail if they should bother to come looking for us,' Calum said, looking anxiously in the direction of the 'ponics, where Acorna was working.

'It would at that,' Gill said, after finger-combing his beard. He held up a portion of the belt-long hirsute appendage.

'Well, I wanted to have a good trim, but I'll bet Amalgamated axed the barber shop, too.'

'I'll give you a trim,' Calum suggested suavely.

'No way, mate,' Gill said, wrapping his beard up and stuffing it down the front of his tunic.

'Uncle Hafiz has an excellent barber,' Rafik said soothingly.

'I can't wait to meet this Uncle Hafiz,' Gill said.

'He will amaze you,' Rafik said with smug pride. He then added, in a much less confident tone, 'Only one thing. He isn't to know about Acorna.'

'Why not?' Gill and Calum asked in unison.

'He's a collector.'

'Of what?'

'Of whatever's going, and I'm bloody sure he's never seen anything like Acorna.'

'Won't that complicate matters a trifle?'

Rafik cocked his head to one side, then the other,

and shrugged. 'I am not my uncle's nephew for nothing. We will contrive. We can *not* lose Acorna.'

The physical exchange of their beacon with that of the wreck took, in the end, three days of sweaty labor. The first problem was that mining tools were ill adapted to the task of cutting and welding ship parts, and their mechanical repair tools were not designed to function in the vacuum, dust, and temperature extremes of the asteroid surface.

'Without Acorna to purify the air,' Calum commented at the end of their first shift, 'this cabin would be stinking like the locker rooms at the TriCentennial Games by now.'

'Water, too,' Gill agreed. With constant re-cycling, ship's air and water usually developed a stale tang that nothing could get rid of. 'Acorna, you're good fortune to us.'

Acorna shook her head, sadness filling her dark eyes as the centers narrowed to slits.

'You are that,' Calum insisted. 'What's the matter?'

'You run away. We hide. I . . .' Acorna visibly struggled to put the words together. 'If I go back, you do not have to hide. My fault!'

The men's eyes met over her head. 'We've been talking too freely,' Rafik said softly.

'She speaks so little,' Calum agreed, 'I forget how much she understands.'

'Never mind that now,' Gill said more loudly. 'The important thing is to explain that she's got it all wrong, don't you think?' He picked Acorna up and hugged her. 'Not your fault, sweetie-pie. Remember the stupid woman Uncle Calum decked? Not your fault she was such a twit, was it now?'

Acorna put the fingers of one hand into her mouth. Her eyes were dark disbelieving pools.

'Listen, Acorna,' Rafik said. 'We did not like those people at Base. We did not want to work for them. If we had never . . . met . . . you, we would still not work for Amalgamated. Would we, fellows?'

Calum's and Gill's emphatic 'No!' seemed to halfway convince Acorna; at least, the silvery pupils of her eyes slowly returned to normal and she consented to munch thoughtfully on the spinach stalks Rafik offered her. By the end of the shift, she was sufficiently recovered to pester them about why they stayed on an asteroid that she could tell held no interesting concentration of metals.

'This is a carbonaceous chondrite, Acorna,' Calum explained.

'Simplify it, will you? The kid doesn't know those big words!'

'Just because basic astronomical chemistry is beyond you, Gill,' Calum retorted, 'don't assume Acorna is as thick as you are. She knows the words we teach her, and we might as well teach her the right ones for the job.' He went on explaining that the hydrogen and oxygen they could extract from this asteroid would provide them with extra air and water, as well as with the fuel they would need to reach their next stop.

'*I* clean air,' Acorna said, stamping a hooflike foot.

'So you do,' Calum agreed easily, 'but we don't know your tolerances yet, see, and we don't want to have you doing more than you can handle at this body weight. Besides, we need fuel . . .' Every few sentences he had to stop and draw diagrams of molecular structures and conversion routines. Acorna was fascinated, and Calum drew the teaching session out until she fell asleep in his arms.

'Whew!' Calum fastened the sleeping child in her net and stood up, stretching his back. 'Okay, fellows, a few ground rules. We'd better discuss certain things only when Acorna is asleep. She's too clever by half; if she knows everything, she'll carry a load of guilt she doesn't need. That goes for the beacon switch, too. If she doesn't know about it, she won't ask inconvenient questions about it later. As far as she's concerned, we're just here to refuel, right?'

'Just as well we never got around to picking a suit small enough for her out of Stores,' Gill commented.

Rafik nodded. 'Soon she must be allowed to go outside with us. She can be inestimably useful in locating and assessing mineral deposits, and irrespective of the benefit to us, Acorna needs to feel useful. But for now, yes, it is as well to keep her in ignorance of our real reason for stopping here.'

After that it took even longer to exchange the beacons, because they had to do the work only when Acorna was asleep, officially confining their activities when she was awake to the extraction of hydrogen and oxygen. Once the onerous task was completed, Rafik reprogrammed the navigation computer for the destination he still refused to reveal, and all three men slept as much as possible on the way to planetfall.

'Are we to stay on the ship the whole time we're here?' Gill demanded.

'Rafik's probably afraid you'll be able to identify this planet's star if we set foot outside the port area,' Calum said. 'You can stop worrying, Rafik. There was really no point in those little games you played with the navigational computer. I know exactly where we are.'

'How?' Rafik demanded.

'Fuel consumption,' Calum said smugly. 'Triangulation on known stars. Time. Course corrections. I plotted the course in my head and checked the numbers on my wrist unit. We're on the fourth planet from—'

'*Don't* say it,' Rafik interrupted. 'At least let me swear to Uncle Hafiz that the name and location of his hideaway have never been spoken on board this ship.'

'Why?' Calum asked. 'What's the big deal? Anybody could compute—'

'No, Calum, they couldn't!' Rafik rolled his eyes heavenward. 'I could write a *book* on the hazards

78

of shipping with a mathematical genius who hasn't an ounce of street sense to balance the other side of his head. There are all sorts and conditions of people here, Calum, and the one thing they all have in common is a strong desire for anonymity. A desire,' he added pointedly, 'which we share with them, or have you forgotten already? Now, let's keep this simple. *You* stay right here. *I* visit Uncle Hafiz and see what sort of a cut he'll want from the profit on our shares in return for converting them to galactic credits and fixing the registration of the new beacon.'

'He's not going to do it from family feeling, huh?' Gill asked.

Rafik rolled his eyes again and sighed heavily. 'Just . . . stay . . . here. I'll be back as soon as I can, okay?'

'If you people are that big on secrecy, why couldn't we do it all by tight-beam transmission from low orbit? Why make a personal visit?'

Rafik looked shocked. 'All this time working together, and you two have yet to learn decent manners. You infidels can cut deals electronically if you wish, but Children of the Three Prophets meet face to face. It's the honorable way to settle an agreement. Besides,' he added more prosaically, 'no transmission is so tight that it can't be intercepted.'

He was back sooner than they expected, tight-lipped and burdened down with a quantity of squashy parcels wrapped in opaque clingfilm.

'You do not look entirely happy. What's the

79

matter, does Uncle Hafiz want an extortionate cut of the shares?' Calum asked.

'And how come you stopped off to go shopping?' Gill added.

'Uncle Hafiz,' Rafik said, still tight-lipped, 'is more traditionally-minded than I am. He wishes to meet the other parties to the agreement face to face before we begin serious discussions.'

'Not Acorna!'

'Port authorities reported four crew members. He wants to see all four. It'll be all right,' Rafik soothed Gill, 'he won't actually *see* Acorna. I've thought of a way around it. It's a *good* idea, too; one we might want to use from now on.'

'And it involves yards and yards of white poly-silk,' said Calum, investigating the contents of one of the packages. 'Umm, Rafik, don't take offense, but I've had previous experience with some of your "good ideas." If this is going to be like the time we tried to slip into Kezdet space to collect that titanium that was just sitting there begging to be mined and refined . . .'

'That was a good idea, too!' Rafik said indignantly. 'How was I to know that the Kezdet Guardians of the Peace had just hired a new hand who would recognize our beacon from old days at MME?'

'All I'm wondering,' Calum murmured, 'is what crucial factor don't you know this time?'

'It's nothing like that,' Rafik said. 'Just a minor costume change. Look, we don't want anybody noticing Acorna, right? So we're going to be more traditional even than Uncle Hafiz. I told him I'd been studying the Three Books – that made him happy. Then I explained that I had been inspired by the First Book to study further, and that I had been accepted into the Neo-Hadithians.'

'All of which means precisely what?' Gill asked.

'The theological ramifications are probably beyond you,' Rafik said. 'The important point is that my wives wear *hijab*, which will be the perfect disguise for Acorna.' He took a length of white polysilk from Calum and held it up with both hands so that they could see the shape of the garment: a many-layered hood atop a billowing gown of even more layers, each individual layer light and seemingly transparent, but collectively a cloud of iridescent reflective white. 'As an enlightened Child of the Three Prophets, naturally I know better than to adhere to the ancient superstitions about the veiling of women. There is actually nothing in the First Book – what you unbelievers call the Koran – that requires women to be veiled and secluded. And the Second Prophet absolutely repudiated that and other barbaric practices, such as the prohibition against fermented liquors. But the Neo-Hadithians claim that the Hadith, the traditional tales of the life of the First Prophet, are as sacred as the words of the Books. They want to go back to the worst of the bad old ways. Including the veil. Uncle Hafiz is disgusted with me, but he says he will respect my religious prejudices while waiting for me to outgrow them. He will not actually look upon the faces of my wives, but they must be present during the agreement.'

'Wives?' Calum repeated.

Rafik's eyes sparkled. 'That is the *really* brilliant part of the idea. I told Uncle Hafiz that I was accompanied by my partner, an unbeliever, and by my two wives. You see, that neatly accounts for the four people reported on this ship. And anybody looking for three miners and a little girl will probably *not* think to investigate a neo-Hadithian, his two wives, and his partner.'

'Sounds risky to me,' said Calum. 'You mean one of us stays on the ship and you pick up some local girl to play your second wife? How can you be sure she won't talk?'

'That – er – was not *quite* what I had in mind,' Rafik said. He shook out the second length of white polysilk and held it up against Calum. 'Yes. I estimated your height quite well. Now, do remember to take small steps and keep your eyes down like a proper Neo-Hadithian wife, will you?'

'I don't believe it,' Dr Anton Forelle said explosively when he read the reports on the *Khedive*. 'I – don't – believe – it.'

'I didn't want to believe it either,' said Judit, 'but the reports are quite clear.' She had been crying. 'It's so sad. Those nice men, and the little girl . . .'

'If it were true,' Forelle said, 'it would be a tragedy. The end of my chance for the research coup of the decade – of the century! But it's *not* true. Amalgamated hires fools; I should know, I'm in charge of inventing the language of the lies they feed their fools, making up nice-sounding words for inhumane policy directives.' He shot a shrewd glance at Judit. 'You don't like the sound of that, do you, girl? Don't like me to say straight out what our department's about. But you're not as stupid as the rest of them. You must have noticed. Well, I had my reasons for taking the job – deplorable, the lack of support for pure research these days, and no matter what my ex-colleagues at the university say, I *could* have completed a respectable thesis if I'd been able to get funding for my research. And I suppose you have your reasons for putting up with Amalgamated, too.'

'They pay well,' Judit said. 'I've a younger brother on Kezdet. He's not quite through school yet.'

'And when he is,' Forelle said, 'no doubt you'll find some other excuse to make to yourself for taking their money. They buy a few good minds and corrupt us, and use us to buy as many fools as they want. Including the idiots who think the *Khedive* crashed on an asteroid!'

'The beacon signal—' Judit began uncertainly.

'Faked. I don't know how, I'm no engineer, but it was faked.'

'Too hard. There'd be registration numbers on the ship body and engines.'

'Ha! Nobody went out and actually looked, did they? They just trusted the computer records.'

Judit was silent. Forelle's idea was insane . . . but

it was true, nobody had physically checked the crash site.

'I'll wager you that ship is not the *Khedive*. Yes, that's it. The beacon signal is faked, and they're in some different sector of space by now, laughing at us all. And Amalgamated will let the matter drop, because they know that no matter what legal juggling they indulged in, no sensible court would uphold their claim to the ship – so rather than pursue it, they'd just as soon write off the ship as a wreck and the dissidents as dead. But I'm not going to let it drop!' Forelle glared at Judit as if she'd dared to think of contradicting him. 'That – that unicorn girl is too conspicuous to disappear without a trace. Amalgamated has plants and bases galaxy-wide. I shall put out a standing order for any mention of a child with those particular deformities to be routed to my console with top priority. Sooner or later, they'll slip up. I'll find her, and we'll get our paper, Judit. And then I'll be able to leave these fools and take up the university position I deserve. They'll probably endow a chair for me. Well, get on with it. Compose the order, and I'll edit it so that they know it's urgent and won't question why, and won't forget it either. Finally applied psycholinguistics will be good for something besides keeping Amalgamated's work-force happy.'

Judit thought he was deluding himself, but it was a delusion she would have liked to share. However, if the child had by some miracle lived, she had no desire to see Forelle get hold of her for his experiments. So she put her best psycho-linguistic training into composing a memo that would look urgent enough to satisfy Dr Forelle, while actually encouraging anybody who skimmed it to mentally dismiss the whole matter as 'just another one of Anton's crazy ideas.'

The skimmer that Rafik rented to take them from the port area to Uncle Hafiz's residence passed over a trackless expanse of tropical vegetation, brilliant green sprinkled with blazes of red and yellow flowers. To the east, an indigo-blue sea gave off glints of silver in the sunlight; to the west, they could just see the long blue line of an escarpment that must have discouraged any building of roads into the interior of the continent.

'The Mali Bazaar,' Rafik said as they passed over a collection of buildings with flat roofs inlaid in jewel-toned mosaics.

Gill pressed his nose to the window of the skimmer to get a better view of the pictures delineated by thousands of glazed ceramic tiles. 'Anywhere else,' he said reverently, 'that would be a major tourist attraction. Why do they put it on the roof where nobody can see it?'

'Most travel here is by skimmer,' Rafik said, 'and it's a kind of advertisement for their services. Everybody knows where the Mali Bazaar is. That's where I bought your *hijab*, by the way.'

'Isn't it a nuisance not having roads to the port?' Gill asked. 'How do you transport heavy goods and machinery?'

'By sea, of course,' Rafik said. 'There are, if you think about it, many advantages in dispensing with a road network. Most of the residents of Laboue have a strong preference for personal privacy; traveling by skimmer reduces the chances of meeting other travelers who might be curious about one's errands. It certainly works in our favor, wouldn't you agree? Then, too, roads require a degree of cooperation which is difficult for the strong individualists who make their homes here. There's no central government, no taxation, no centrally supported infrastructure.'

'Expensive,' Gill murmured. 'Inefficient.'

Rafik gave him a bright-eyed glance of amusement. 'Can any system really compete with the massive inefficiencies of a well-entrenched bureaucracy? As for expense . . . one entrepreneur did attempt a network of toll roads, but he couldn't afford the cost of guarding them.'

'You have problems with bandits?'

'Let's say there are residents who find it difficult to put aside their traditional ways of life,' Rafik said, banking the skimmer into a smooth turn that brought them down in a paved square surrounded by high bougainvillea-covered walls. He handed Acorna and Calum out of the skimmer with the care a Neo-Hadithian would be expected to take of his delicate and precious wives. 'Remember,' he whispered to Calum, *don't talk*! As long as you're wearing that veil, convention dictates that you are not really here.'

The long, multilayered Neo-Hadithian robes of

white polysilk concealed Calum and Acorna marvelously; in the brilliant sunlight they looked like two moving clouds of white iridescence, shapeless and indistinguishable save that one was somewhat taller than the other.

As Gill made his exit from the skimmer, a section of bougainvillea-covered wall swung away from the rest, revealing a dark man of medium height in whom Rafik's elegant features were sharpened to a look of dangerous wariness.

'You and your family and guests are welcome to this humble abode,' he said to Rafik, with a quick gesture of his right hand from forehead to lips to chest.

Rafik repeated the gesture before embracing him. 'Uncle Hafiz! You are gracious indeed to receive us. You are well?' he asked as though they had not been conversing only a few hours before.

'I am, thanks be to the Three Prophets. And you, my nephew? You are well?'

'Blessed be the Hadith and the revelations of Moulay Suheil,' Rafik said, 'I am, and my wives also.'

A faint shadow of distaste crossed Uncle Hafiz's features at the mention of the Hadith, but he controlled himself and gave properly courteous answers as Rafik went on to inquire about the health of innumerable cousins, nephews, and distant connections. Finally, the initial greetings finished, Uncle Hafiz stepped back and invited them, with a wave of his hand, to precede him into the garden revealed beyond the walls around the skimmer landing area.

A path of deep blue stepping stones wound among flowering shrubs. As Gill stepped on the first stone, a clear pure middle C sounded in the air. The next two steps produced an E and a G; the sounds lingered on the air and blended in a perfect chord.

'You like my walkway?' Hafiz asked with a satisfied smile. 'Perhaps you have not before encountered the singing stones of Skarrness.'

'But I thought they were—' Gill choked down the rest of the sentence. The once-famous singing stones of Skarrness were virtually gone now, having fallen prey to unscrupulous collectors, who removed so many of the stones that the remaining ones could not maintain their population. But Rafik had said Hafiz was a collector of rarities and had implied that he was not overburdened with scruples. It would probably not be tactful to complete his thought.

'Quite rare, yes,' Hafiz said. 'It was my great good fortune to obtain a perfectly tuned set in C major, and an even rarer set in the Lydian mode. Very few complete sets, alas, are available now.'

Thanks to jerks like you, Gill thought, but he managed to keep his thought to himself and his face composed.

The walkway led them musically to a high wall of dark stone which Hafiz identified casually as Farinese marble. A double gate of lacy, hand-wrought metal work opened into a second garden, this one surrounded on three sides by a roofed gallery with columns of the same Farinese marble. Through the columns Gill could glimpse openings into a shadowy interior of polished floors, carved wooden screens, and silk hangings.

Hafiz clapped his hands and several robed servants appeared, two carrying cushions of jewel-coloured silk, another with a tall crystal pitcher, and a fourth behind him with a crystal bowl and a stack of towels so richly embroidered in gold thread that only a small silken square was visible in the center of each.

'We have, of course, completely modern facilities within,' Hafiz said apologetically, 'but it delights me to keep to the old customs of offering guests water with my own hands, and food and drink in my own garden, as soon as they have arrived.' He took the pitcher and poured a thin stream of cold water over Rafik's outstretched hands. Gill copied Rafik's motions and took one of the embroidered towels to dry his hands. Hafiz handed the pitcher to Rafik with a bow. 'Perhaps you would prefer to offer water to your wives yourself. I should not like to insult your new beliefs.'

Rafik bowed acknowledgment and held out the pitcher for Calum and Acorna to wash their hands, casually moving as he did so that his body blocked any view Hafiz might have had of Acorna's oddly shaped digits and Calum's masculine fingers.

Hafiz indicated that they should all seat themselves on the silken cushions, mentioned casually that the pitcher and bowl had each been carved from a single piece of Merastikama crystal, and told the servants to take back the washing implements and bring refreshment for his guests. The placement of brass trays on three-legged wooden stands, the handing round of minute glasses full of fiery liquor and delicate bowls of fruit-flavored sorbet, took what seemed to Gill an inordinately long time while Hafiz and Rafik chatted of trivialities. Rafik made a show of refusing the liquor, in keeping with his pretense of conversion to the strict Neo-Hadithian sect, which had revived all the prohibitions of the First Prophet and then some. Gill at first felt glad to be an official unbeliever and free to enjoy the drinks; then, after one burning swallow, he began considering the possibility of announcing an instant conversion to Rafik's tenets. He was relieved to see that Acorna managed to take a dish of sorbet under her veil; he'd been afraid that eating and drinking would tax her disguise too much. But it seemed the Neo-Hadithians had designed their women's costumes so that the veils need not be removed for anything. Gill wondered sourly whether they removed them in bed.

Finally, as a casual afterthought to a lengthy discussion of the problems of interstellar trade, Rafik mentioned that he and his partner had encountered a small technical difficulty with which Uncle Hafiz might be able to help them out – for a consideration, of course.

'Ah, these minor technicalities.' Hafiz sighed

sympathetically. 'How they plague us, these petty bureaucrats with their accounting details! What seems to be the difficulty, son of my best beloved sister?'

Rafik gave Hafiz a severely edited account of their difficulties with Amalgamated, leaving out any mention of Acorna and stressing the basic illegality of Amalgamated's claim to own the *Khedive*.

'If their claim is entirely without foundation,' Hafiz asked, as though motivated by idle curiosity, 'why do you not take your case to the courts of the Federation?'

'It is written in the Book of the Second Prophet,' said Rafik, 'Trust kin before countrymen, countrymen before outlanders, and all before unbelievers.'

'And yet your partner is an unbeliever,' Hafiz pointed out.

'Our partnership is of long standing,' Rafik said. 'Besides, there is a minor complication in the matter of money advanced by MME – the company with which we had previously contracted – for mining equipment and supplies. The dogs of unbelievers at Amalgamated claim our ship as security against the advance, though if they had credited us with the metals sent back by drone over the last three years, the debt would have been paid three times over. However, we left the Amalgamated base in some haste and the matter was not resolved.'

'It is also written,' said Hafiz, '"Be not in such haste to collect the silver that ye let the gold fall by the wayside."'

'A most excellent precept, O Revered Uncle,' said Rafik politely, 'but one which I found myself unable to honor under the circumstances.' He lowered his voice as if to make sure that the veiled figures on the other side of the brass tray should not hear. 'It was a matter of a woman – you understand?'

Hafiz smiled broadly. 'I begin to see why you have joined the Neo-Hadithians, my son! It is their revival of polygamy which appeals to you. So, two wives were not enough. You had to get yourself in trouble with some unbeliever on the Amalgamated base?'

'In confidence,' Rafik said, 'the taller of my two wives is so ugly one might imagine her a man, and I have no use for her as a woman; while the smaller one is too young yet to be taken to my bed. Both marriages were made to strengthen my claims to kinship within the Neo-Hadithians and not for carnal desire.'

Calum choked under his veil. Gill reached under the table and pinched some part of his anatomy through the billowing white layers of polysilk, hard enough to distract Calum from whatever he might have been tempted to say.

Hafiz laughed merrily at Rafik's account of his marital troubles, and seemed more disposed to help them out if he could get the satisfaction of teasing his nephew for the bad bargain he had made in joining the Neo-Hadithian sect. Transferring registration of their new beacon into their name, he warned, was a complicated task and would require facilitation payments to a number of individuals, not all of them so liberal in their thinking as he was. He would, however, be happy to arrange the entire matter, if Rafik could see his way to putting sufficient credit at his disposal.

'That brings up another minor point,' said Rafik, and showed Hafiz the share certificates from Amalgamated.

'These can, of course, be converted into Federation credits,' Hafiz said, thumbing rapidly through the certificates, 'although at a substantial discount.'

'The discount on shares from such a galactically recognized company, all but certain to rise in value, should be only nominal,' Rafik protested.

Hafiz smiled. 'Is it not written in the Book of the Third Prophet, "Count not the light from a distant star among your assets, for that star may have been long dead by the time its light reaches thine eyes"?' He glanced at Acorna, who had begun wriggling under her veils in a way that was causing Calum and Gill grave anxiety. 'But your younger wife is restless. Perhaps your wives would care to retire to the rooms which have been made ready for them while we settle the minor matter of the discount on these shares and the payments necessary to facilitate reregistration of the new beacon? Or would they like to stroll in the outer garden? I can call one of my women to attend them.'

'That will not be necessary,' said Gill, rising to his feet. 'I should be honored to escort the ladies.'

Rafik smiled seraphically. 'I repose complete trust in my partner,' he assured Hafiz. 'As he trusts me to complete the negotiations, so can I trust him with my honor and that of my women.'

'Particularly,' Hafiz needled him as the others left, 'since one is, by your own account, too ugly to bed and the other too young.'

'Just so,' said Rafik cheerfully. 'Now, about this discount . . .'

As soon as they were concealed among the flowering shrubs of the outer garden, Calum shoved back his multilayered veil and took a deep breath. 'I am going to *kill* Rafik,' he said.

Gill snickered. 'Remember to take tiny little ladylike steps,' he teased. 'And better keep the veil down. Even with Rafik's warning that you're as ugly as a man, Hafiz might get suspicious if he saw that you need a shave.'

'I just hope they finish dickering so we can get back to the ship,' Calum said sourly, but he flipped the veiling back over his face. 'I'm tired of fancy dress.'

Acorna tugged at Gill's sleeve and pointed at the grass that grew around each of the blue singing stones. 'What? Oh, sure, sweetie, go ahead and nibble if you like. You've been a good girl. Just remember to cover your head if we hear anybody coming. The singing stones ought to give us plenty of warning,' Gill said rather defensively to Calum.

'You didn't let *me* unveil.'

'Modesty, modesty.' Gill chuckled. 'You don't need a snack. Acorna's metabolism needs more than the occasional dish of sorbet, you know. And if Hafiz expects us to stay for a meal, it'll probably be mostly meat dishes and she can't eat those.'

Acorna, ignoring the argument, had quietly knelt down within her billowing veils and pushed the face veils back so that she could see to pluck the tender tops of the sweet grasses. 'Good girl, good,' Gill encouraged her. 'Don't make any divots, now.'

'Is rude to make holes in grass,' Acorna said. 'Is a no.'

'A very big no, in somebody else's garden,' Gill agreed. 'But the stuff has to be mowed, I assume, so it'll do no harm if you take an inch or two off the top.'

Five notes in a wailing pentatonic scale sounded in quick succession. Acorna tried to jump up, but the swathes of filmy fabric impeded her movements and she would have fallen if Gill hadn't grabbed her hand and pulled her upright by main force. She was still fumbling for her veil when Hafiz and Rafik came into view.

Hafiz' eyebrows shot up and he came forward rapidly. 'By the earlocks of the Third Prophet!' he exclaimed. 'A rarity indeed! Rafik, beloved nephew, I do believe we can come to a mutually agreeable arrangement at a considerably less discount than I had anticipated.'

'Uncle,' Rafik said in reproving tones, 'I beg of

you, do not insult the modesty of my wives and the honor of my family.' But he was too late; Hafiz was already stroking the short horn that protruded from Acorna's forehead. She stood quite still, only the narrowing of her pupils showing her distress and confusion.

'You were complaining that this one was too young to be of any use,' Hafiz said without looking away from Acorna. 'How fortunate that your new religious friends hold to the old traditions in the matter of divorce as well as of polygamy and *hijab*. Nothing could be easier than a quiet family divorce, at once freeing you of an undesired entanglement and allowing me the acquisition of a new rarity.'

'Unthinkable,' Rafik protested. 'Her family have entrusted her to me; she is my sacred responsibility.'

'Then they will no doubt be delighted to hear that she will henceforth grace the home of such a distinguished and benevolent collector as myself,' Hafiz said happily. 'I am willing to undertake to respect all the religious prohibitions of your sect. She can have the rooms which I had set aside for you and your wives tonight; I will establish them as secluded women's quarters for her and her servants alone, so that the Neo-Hadithian scruples need not be outraged. You will be able to tell her family that she is kept in every possible luxury.'

'I am sorry,' Rafik said firmly. 'I do not sell my women. Uncle Hafiz, this touches on my honor!'

Hafiz waved the objections away with an airy

hand. 'Ah, you young people are so impetuous! I would not be doing my duty as your uncle, my boy, if I permitted you to refuse in haste what will upon reflection appear to you as a most advantageous solution to all your difficulties. No, family feeling dictates that I make sure you have time to reflect upon the situation at leisure. You will remain as my guests until you have had sufficient time to perceive the wisdom of this course.'

'We cannot impose upon you,' Rafik said. 'We will return to our ship tonight and there discuss the matter among ourselves.'

'No, no, dear boy, I could not hear of it! My household would be dishonored forever should I fail to offer you appropriate hospitality. You will be my guests tonight. I simply insist,' Hafiz said, raising his voice slightly.

There was a rustle among the bushes, and suddenly two robed and silent servants stood behind each one of them.

'The singing stones, although a great curiosity, are sometimes inconvenient,' Hafiz said cheerfully. 'There are other ways through the garden for those who serve me.'

Rafik caught Gill's eye and gave a slight despairing shrug. 'We shall be delighted to accept your hospitality tonight, Uncle. You are too generous.'

Hafiz' generosity extended to the provision of separate quarters for them, one set of rooms for Rafik and his 'wives,' and another room, on the far side of the sprawling mansion, for Gill. 'You would naturally wish your women to be housed in seclusion and far from any man's sleeping place,' he explained smoothly.

'And that makes it even harder to get away,' Calum growled as soon as Hafiz had left them on their own. 'How are we going to find Gill and get to our skimmer?'

'Peace,' said Rafik absently.

'You're not thinking of giving in to him!'

'I played in this house as a boy,' Rafik said. 'I know every inch of the grounds, perhaps better than my uncle; it has been some years since he had the figure to wriggle along the low paths under the shrubbery, or to swing from cornice to pipe along the upper stories. But we *will* temporize for a day or two, Calum.'

'Why?'

'We do,' said Rafik sweetly, 'want to give Uncle Hafiz time to fix the registration of our new ship's beacon, don't we? Let him think we're cooperating until that is done; then it will be time enough to get away.'

'And how do you think you're going to get him to switch the registration and launder our shares without handing over Acorna?'

'Don't worry about a thing,' Rafik said. 'I'm a master negotiator. I learned from an expert.'

'I know,' said Calum. 'We're negotiating with the expert in question, remember?'

Four

Acorna woke to the dawn-chirping of birds in the sweet-scented flowering vines outside the window. The night had been still and hot and she had pushed all the covers off her bed; now it was cool, almost chilly. She wrapped the clinging layers of white polysilk around herself. The robes were enough to keep her warm, but she was unable to recreate the drapery of hood and robe and face veils that Rafik had arranged about her the previous day. She looked doubtfully at the sleeping Rafik and Calum. Would it be a big 'no' to leave the room like this, without the veils over her head? She hated the veils anyway; they clung to her mouth and nose and chafed her forehead where the growing horn was still tender. It would probably be an even bigger 'no' to wake Calum and Rafik and ask them to dress her, wouldn't it?

The pressure in her bladder settled the question. Tiptoeing so as not to wake the miners, Acorna quietly slid the carved wooden door open just enough to let her squeeze out. She remembered the washing-place they had been shown last night, a wonderland of blue tiles and jets of hot and cold water and minty steam rising up through wooden slats. But this morning there was no one to make the hot water come out for her, and after relieving herself she abandoned the washing-place and tiptoed down two flights of stairs to where she could see the garden through an open archway.

The blue stones sang when she stepped on them, just as they had last night. Entranced by the sweet pure tones, Acorna dropped her clinging draperies and danced back and forth, improvising a tune by leaping from one stone to another and accompanying the music of the stones with her own singing. She did not realize how loud she was getting until a discordant note interrupted her melody. She whirled and saw Uncle Hafiz standing at the beginning of the blue stone path.

Acorna's song broke off and the sudden stillness of the garden shocked her into realizing how boisterous she had been.

'Too loud?' she asked, penitent. 'If I make too much noise, that is a big no?'

'Not in the least, my dear child,' Uncle Hafiz said. 'Your singing was a delightful interruption to a boring task. No, no—' he forestalled her as she belatedly tried to wind the robes around herself again, 'there's no need to trouble yourself with those things, not among family.'

'I must be covered. Rafik said.'

'On the streets, perhaps,' Uncle Hafiz agreed, 'but among your own relatives it is different.'

Acorna thought this over. 'You are rel-tive?'

'And I hope soon to be a very close relation indeed.'

'You are rel-tive to me?'

'Yes.'

'And I am rel-tive to Rafik and Gill and Calum. So you are rel-tive to Gill?'

Uncle Hafiz was so dismayed at the thought of claiming kinship with the red-bearded unbeliever that he didn't even think of asking who Calum might be. 'Ah – it doesn't work quite like that,' he said hastily.

'How many percent rel-tive to Gill are you?'

'*Zero* percent,' Hafiz said, then blinked. 'Aren't you a little young to be learning fractions and percentages?'

'I know fraction, percent, decimal, octal, hexa-decimal, and modulo,' Acorna said cheerfully. 'I *like* numbers. You like numbers?'

'Only,' said Hafiz, 'when the odds are in my favor.'

Acorna frowned. 'Odd is not-even. Even is not-odd. Odds is not-evens?'

'No, no, sweetheart,' Hafiz said. 'The boys have neglected an important part of your education. Come along inside. I can't explain without drawing pictures.'

When Rafik came pounding down the stairs an hour later, sure that Acorna had been kidnapped while he and Calum slept, the first thing he heard from Hafiz's study was a familiar piping voice asking a question.

'That's right!' Uncle Hafiz sounded more relaxed than Rafik had ever heard him, almost jovial. 'Now, suppose you're making book on a race where the favorite is running at three to two, so you offer slightly better odds – like, say, six to five—'

'Six to five is *much* better,' Rafik heard Acorna object. 'Should not give more than seven to four.'

'Look, it's just an example, okay? Suppose you offer seven to four, then. What happens?'

'Many people place bets with you.'

'And what do you do to make sure you don't lose your money?'

'Lay off the bets with another bookmaker?'

'Or,' Uncle Hafiz said cheerfully, 'make very, very sure the favorite doesn't win.'

That was the point at which Rafik interrupted them and brought Acorna back to their rooms for the excellent breakfast Hafiz had ordered sent up to them. He and Calum wrangled over the sliced mangoes and pointed skewers full of grilled lamb like weapons at one another while Acorna quietly worked her way through the bowl of leafy greens Hafiz had ordered especially for her.

'How could you be so careless and irresponsible?' Calum demanded.

'You were sleeping in this room, too,' Rafik pointed out acidly. 'I happen to know that you slept very well last night. You snore!'

'You should have told her not to go out without one of us!'

'Look,' Rafik said, 'no harm's been done, okay? He didn't hurt her.'

'From your own account,' Calum retorted, 'he was teaching her to gamble! That's not the sort of education I want for my ward.'

'She's mine, too,' Rafik said, 'and there is nothing inherently criminal about the profession of being a turf accountant.'

Acorna chose that moment, having finished all the sweet greens and the sliced carrots, to speak up. 'Nobble the favorite,' she said clearly, and smiled with pleasure at her new word.

'I rest my case,' said Calum, arms folded. 'And what's more, you are not getting me back into those ridiculous garments. If Acorna can run around unveiled, so can I.'

'You will *not*,' Rafik said with quiet intensity, 'do anything to destroy my cover as a Neo-Hadithian. And that includes raising your voice. We're just lucky that Uncle Hafiz respects my religious beliefs enough to order the servants to keep away from these rooms, or we'd be blown already.'

'I think we are blown,' Calum said. 'Blown clear out of the water. Now that he's seen Acorna, what's the point of wrapping ourselves up like white tents?'

'My conversion to Neo-Hadithian tenets,' Rafik said, 'is an essential part of my negotiating strategy. And it's not such a bad thing that Acorna has charmed Uncle Hafiz, either. He'll be all the more inclined to complete the transaction and speed us on our way.'

Calum stared. 'You sound as if you actually mean to give him Acorna!'

Acorna's eyes narrowed until the silver pupils were all but obliterated. She leaned across the table to grab Calum by one hand and Rafik by the other.

'It's okay, sweetie,' Calum soothed her, 'we're not going anywhere without you. *Are we, Rafik*?'

'Want Gill,' Acorna said firmly. 'All together.'

'We will be together, darling, in just a little while,' Rafik promised.

'Want Gill here *now*!' Acorna's voice rose.

Calum's and Rafik's eyes met over her head. 'I thought you said she was over the dependency,' Rafik mouthed.

'Being auctioned off as a curiosity makes a girl insecure,' Calum whispered back.

'*Gill*!' Acorna wailed on an even higher note.

'Just so you understand,' Calum said some time later, 'I'm only doing this for Acorna.'

'Darling, I would *never* ask you to put on *hijab* for my sake,' Rafik said sweetly. 'White isn't your color.'

They were strolling in the garden, Calum and Acorna decently veiled so that Gill could join them without outraging Rafik's supposed Neo-Hadithian sense of propriety.

'Explain to me again,' Calum said while Acorna skipped ahead, holding Gill's hand, 'exactly how wrapping me up in a bolt of polysilk is an integral part of your negotiating strategy. *And don't giggle*!' he added sharply, almost tripping over some of the lower layers of robes.

'Don't hike your skirt up, it's not decent,' Rafik

said. 'If you'd take small steps, like a lady, you wouldn't trip all the time. Ah, Uncle Hafiz! The benevolence of your smile lights the garden more brightly than the summer sun.'

'What joy can be sweeter than the company of beloved relatives,' Hafiz replied, 'beloved relatives and, er, um . . .' He looked at Gill's flaming red beard and freckled skin. '. . . relatives and *friends*,' he finished with an audible gulp. 'I trust you have had time and privacy sufficient to confer with your family and your partner, dear nephew?'

'We accept your offer,' Rafik said. 'Transfer the registration of the ship's beacon and sell the shares for us, and . . .' He nodded at Acorna, who was happily chattering to Gill about the new kinds of fractions she had learned, such as three-to-two and six-to-four.

'Excellent!' Now Uncle Hafiz was truly beaming. 'I knew you'd be reasonable, dear boy. We're two of a kind, you and I. If only your cousin Tapha could do as well!'

Rafik looked slightly queasy at being compared to his cousin, his uncle's heir. 'Where is Tapha, by the way?'

Hafiz's smile vanished. 'I sent him to take over the southern half of the continent. Yukata Batsu has been running it long enough.'

'And?'

'I don't know where the rest of him is,' Hafiz said. 'All Yukata Batsu sent back were his ears.' He sighed. 'Tapha never had what it takes. I should have known when I abducted his mother that she didn't have the brains to give me a worthy successor. Yammer, yammer, yammer, all the time complaining at me that she could have had a career dancing topless at the Orbital Grill and Rendezvous Parlor. Her and her perky breasts. Yasmin, I told her, all the girls have perky breasts in zero-G, you were nothing special, you're lucky a good man took you away from all that. But would that woman listen?' Hafiz sighed and brightened up. 'However, I'm not too old to try again. Now that I've found a woman with intelligence to match my own . . .' His eyes strayed to Acorna. 'Don't you mind her holding hands with that dog of an unbeliever?'

'She's only a little girl,' Rafik said stiffly.

'Not for much longer,' Hafiz said. 'They grow up faster than you think.'

A sputtering sound escaped from behind Calum's layers of white veiling. Hafiz looked startled. 'Your senior wife? She is unwell?'

'She suffers from nervous fits,' Rafik said, grasping Calum's wrist and hauling him away from Hafiz.

'A sad affliction,' Hafiz said. 'Meet me within the house when you have calmed your women, Rafik, and we will pledge faith to our agreement over the Three Books.' He turned away, muttering, 'Ugly, prone to fits, big feet, and what a hairy wrist! No wonder he is reluctant to give up the other one . . . but with his ship and his credits, he can easily buy another wife.'

'And just what were you snickering about?'

106

Rafik demanded in a whisper when Hafiz had passed back into the house.

'"They grow up faster than you think,"' Calum quoted. 'If he only knew *how* fast! Would he believe Acorna was a toddler when we found her less than two years ago?'

'Let's not tell him,' Rafik suggested. 'This whole deal depends on mutual trust, and he'd be sure I was a thumping liar if I tried to tell him how fast Acorna grows. Besides, she's not going to be here long enough for him to find out.'

'But it's the truth!' Calum said.

'Truth,' Rafik said, 'has very little to do with verisimilitude.'

Gill kept Acorna amused in the garden while Rafik and Calum went into the study to meet Hafiz. He was seated behind a gleaming, crescent-shaped desk with the usual consoles and controls, plus a few that Calum did not recognize, inlaid flush with the surface so as not to spoil the smooth lines of the desk. Incongruously stacked atop the modern equipment were two antique books, the kind with hard covers enclosing a stack of paper sheets, and an old-fashioned databox with only six sides.

'You admire my desk?' Uncle Hafiz said pleasantly to Calum. 'Carved from a single piece of purpleheart . . . one of the last of the great stand of purpleheart trees on Tanque III.'

'My wife prefers not to talk to other men,' Rafik said sharply.

He's rumbled us, Calum thought in despair. *He knows I'm not a woman. Rafik and his damn silly games!*

'Dear boy,' Hafiz said, 'surely within a family as close as ours, and soon to be united even more closely by the exchange of wives, even you Neo-Hadithians can drop some of these ridiculous . . . oh, all right, all right, I didn't mean to insult your . . . religion.' He pronounced the last word with the faint distaste of someone directing the servants to remove whatever it was the cat had dragged in and failed to finish eating.

Rafik bridled, scowled, and gave what Calum thought an excellent imitation of a man on the verge of taking mortal insult.

'Your ship,' Uncle Hafiz said, 'is now registered as the *Uhuru*, originally of Kezdet.'

'Why Kezdet?'

'That was the original registration of the beacon you appropriated. It would have been extremely expensive to delete all traces of the beacon's history. I think it suffices that we can now show an electronic trail of three transfers of ownership. Appropriate insignia have been applied to the body of the ship, along with some . . . ah . . . cosmetic changes.'

Calum choked.

'Every rascal in the galaxy registers under Kezdet,' Rafik protested. 'They're a known cover for all sorts of thieves, desperadoes, con men, and cheats.'

Uncle Hafiz' brows rose. 'Dear boy! My own modest personal fleet has Kezdet registration.'

'Exactly,' muttered Calum, too low for Hafiz to hear him. He jabbed Rafik in the side with one veiled elbow, hoping to remind him of the other problem with using Kezdet as their port of registration.

'And,' Rafik said, 'as it happens, I have had an . . . unfortunate encounter with Kezdet patrols. One of those pesky matters of trespassing that can occur with the best of will on both sides, but I am afraid they took it in a poor spirit.' There was no way of knowing for sure, but it seemed a safe bet that the Guardians of the Peace were still unhappy about the patrol cruiser he, Calum, and Gill had crippled and marooned before taking off with that load of titanium.

'Then,' Uncle Hafiz said smoothly, 'you will have an excellent excuse for not returning to your port of registration, will you not? Now, your shares have been converted to . . .' He named a sum in Federation credits that made Calum gasp through his veils.

Rafik actually managed to look disappointed. 'Ah, well,' he said sadly, 'that would be after your discount, of course?'

'By no means,' said Uncle Hafiz, 'but I propose to take no more than twenty percent of the gross, which I assure you will barely cover my expenses in arranging . . . facilitation payments . . . to all the bureaucracies concerned.'

'It was seventeen percent yesterday.'

'Delay,' said Uncle Hafiz, 'increases the expense. How fortunate that you have come to a wise decision! It only remains to complete the transaction. If you will swear on the Three Books to honor our agreement, then call Acorna in and divorce her, I

109

shall marry her immediately and you will be free to depart.'

Rafik looked mournful. 'If only it were that easy!' he said. 'But I must warn you that the Hadith require a waiting period of at least one sunset and dawn between a woman's divorce and remarriage.'

'That is not in my understanding of the Hadith,' Uncle Hafiz said sharply.

'It is a new revelation of Moulay Suheil,' Rafik countered. 'He had a dream in which the First Prophet, blessed be His Name, appeared and expressed his concern lest women, being weak in understanding and easily led, might be drawn into error by too much haste in the matter of divorces and remarrying. A divorced woman must spend one night in prayer, seeking the will of the First Prophet, before she may enter into any new alliance.'

'Hmmph,' muttered Uncle Hafiz. 'I would scarcely describe the young rarity out there as being weak in understanding. I've never seen anyone catch on so fast to the idea of keeping a double set of accounts, one for the Federation and one for private purposes.'

Calum choked and Rafik trod on his foot. This was no time to resume the argument about whether Hafiz was teaching Acorna suitable things!

'However,' Rafik said, 'to allay your anxieties, I will do better than swearing on the Three Books. I will swear on this copy of the Holy Hadith them- selves, authenticated by Moulay Suheil, and most

110

sacred to me and to all true believers.' He drew a datahedron from his pocket and kissed it reverently before extending it in his cupped hands. Uncle Hafiz recoiled as if from a snake.

'You swear on your Hadith,' he said, 'and I will make my oath on the Books of the Three Prophets. Thus each of us will be bound by that which one holds most sacred.'

'An excellent idea,' said Rafik.

Calum's attention wavered during the lengthy oath-taking which followed, most of which was not performed in Basic Interlingua but in the language of Hafiz and Rafik's culture of origin. It sounded to him like a group of birds choking on something unpleasant, but it seemed to make sense. At one point they called for Acorna to be brought into the room; she stood quite still under her veils while more of the unfamiliar language spouted over her head. At the end Hafiz kissed the topmost of his Three Books, and Rafik pressed his lips to the datahedron again, and both men smiled as if in the satisfaction of a bargain concluded.

'With your permission, Uncle, I will now escort my former wife to the place set apart for her, that she may begin her vigil of prayer. I know you will not wish to delay the final ceremony,' Rafik said.

'Since I myself am not a Neo-Hadithian,' Hafiz said, 'I see no need at all for this delay.'

'I must report to her family that all has been handled decently and in good order,' said Rafik. 'It is a matter touching my honor, Uncle.'

Hafiz muttered and grumbled but finally let

them go, after receiving Rafik's assurances that Acorna's prescribed time of prayer need not interfere with her attending the wedding feast that night. 'Only family,' he promised. 'Only ourselves and your partner.'

Rafik looked surprised. 'You will break bread with an unbeliever?'

'You consider him as family and entrust him with your honor in the persons of your wives,' said Hafiz, looking as though he had just swallowed something very unpleasant. 'In loving respect to you, my dear nephew, I can do no less.'

'What,' Calum demanded as soon as they were safely in the secluded rooms upstairs, 'was all that about?'

'Well, you didn't *want* me to hand Acorna over to him then and there, did you? I had to come up with some reason to delay. Now that the credits and registration are in order and he's told me the passwords to access them, we can sneak out tonight. Have to wait until after this blasted feast, though.' Rafik frowned. 'I wish I knew why he insists on having Gill there. He obviously didn't like the idea above half.'

'Makes it convenient for us,' Calum pointed out.

'That,' said Rafik, 'is what worries me.'

Out of consideration for Rafik's supposedly strict religious views on the seclusion of women, Hafiz arranged that no servants should be present at the celebration feast that night.

'You see, dear boy,' he said, gesturing at the

spacious dining hall with its carved lattice-work screens and colorful silk-covered divans, 'all is prepared. The table is, after all, adequately furnished with heating and chilling chambers to keep food at the proper temperature. What could be pleasanter than a simple dinner *en famille*? The employment of dozens of servants to carry trays and pour drinks is merely an outmoded tradition of conspicuous consumption, something which the Third Prophet enjoined us to abjure at all times. Do you not agree?'

Gill was glad that he, as an unbeliever, and Calum, as Rafik's senior wife, were not expected to reply to this statement. All he had to do was keep a straight face as Rafik praised the modesty and simplicity of Hafiz' arrangements . . . and try to keep his eyes from wandering over the incredibly lavish display before them.

A long, low table stretched between two rows of divans covered in emerald and crimson silk. Dishes covered the table from one end to the other: bowls of pilau, silver trays of sizzling-hot pastries, sliced fruits arranged as an elaborate still life on a specially inset chilling tray, skewers of grilled lamb, dishes of yoghurt with chopped mint, Kilumbemba shellfish fried in batter, crystallized rose petals and sugared golden-hearts . . . Between the dishes stood tall tumblers frosted with ice, and a pitcher of some sparkling fruit drink rested in another cooling tray beside Hafiz' divan at the head of the table. The far wall of the dining hall appeared to be a cliff of moss-covered rock with a

113

veil of water running down its surface and splashing into a recirculating stream at the bottom of the miniature cliff. From behind the carved lattices, a recording of Kitheran harp music provided a softly tinkling counterpoint to the sound of the falling water.

'We shall even pour our own drinks,' Hafiz said, gesturing toward the pitcher. 'I have seen that as a good Neo-Hadithian you follow the First Prophet's words and abjure wine, rather than accepting the dispensations of the Second and Third Prophets. I myself usually enjoy a Kilumbemba beer with my dinner, but for tonight I will share the iced madigadi juice prepared for my guests.'

Rafik nodded, rather sadly. Actually, as both Calum and Gill well knew, he would have liked a mug of cold Kilumbemba beer, the other specialty of that planet, to wash down the fried shellfish.

'Don't even think about it,' Calum muttered in his ear. 'If I can wrap myself up like a white balloon to substantiate your conversion, you can drink fruit juice for one evening and like it.'

'Your senior wife is disturbed?' Hafiz inquired. 'Not another fit, I trust?'

Rafik tried to step on Calum's foot, but only succeeded in trampling the hem of his robe. 'She is in excellent health, thank you, Uncle,' he replied, 'only inclined to chatter about trifles after the manner of women.'

'Women who are not kept veiled and secluded,' Hafiz pointed out rather acidly, 'have more of a chance to develop interesting topics of conversation – oh, all right, all right! I won't say another word against the revelations of Moulay Suheil.'

'We are returning to the pure traditions of our original faith,' Rafik said stiffly.

'Then let us enjoy another tradition tonight,' Hafiz said, 'and drink from the same pitcher in token of perfect trust within the family.' He made a show of pouring the iced madigadi juice into each of their cups, finishing with his own and taking a deep draught from it as proof of the drink's harmlessness. Rafik raised his own cup, but a sudden commotion outside the room surprised him into setting it down again. There was a babble of excited voices, then the high-pitched wail of a woman: an old, quavering voice.

'Aminah!' Hafiz sighed and stood up. 'Tapha's old nurse. She treats each bit of news from the south as another installment in a vid-drama. I had best calm her. Forgive the interruption. Please, go on with your meal; I may be some time.' He strode out of the room quickly, a frown between his brows.

Gill took a handful of the batter-fried shellfish and crunched them with enjoyment.

'Well, he did say to go on,' he said when Rafik raised an eyebrow, 'and even if the table does keep these things hot, it can't keep them crisp indefinitely.' He took a deep breath and reached for his own cup. 'Must say, I've never had them served quite so hot and spicy before.'

'Any decent food tastes overspiced to you barbarians,' Rafik said. 'Acorna, what are you doing?' She kept pushing and pawing at her veils

115

until they were a tangled mess around her face.

'Here, honey, let me fix that for you,' Gill said. 'Any reason why she shouldn't put her veils back for dinner, Rafik? It's not as if Hafiz is gonna see anything he hasn't seen before.'

'Only that he may wonder why I do not permit my other wife to unveil,' Rafik said with resignation. 'I suppose I shall have to explain that she is so ugly, I fear the sight would put him off his food.'

Calum kicked him under the table.

'That's odd,' Gill said, feeling Acorna's forehead. 'Do you think she has a fever?'

'Her skin is cool enough. But look at her horn!'

Great drops of clear liquid were forming on the fluted sides of Acorna's horn. She mopped at them ineffectually with the end of her veil.

'Have a cool drink, sweetie, it'll make you feel better,' Gill suggested, holding her cup for her.

Acorna stared at it blankly for a moment, then took the cup from Gill and, instead of putting it to her mouth, dipped her horn into it.

'What the deuce?'

'She does that with the dirty bathwater too. Acorna, sweetie-pie, do you think the juice is dirty? It's okay, that stuff floating in it is just madigadi pulp.'

'Is not dirty,' Acorna said firmly.

'Well, that's good—'

'Is *bad*.' She dipped her head again, this time plunging her horn into Gill's cup. 'Now is one hundred percent good,' she informed him.

The three men looked at one another. 'He made

a great show of pouring all our drinks out of the same pitcher,' Gill said.

'Why would he want to poison us? He thinks – I mean,' Calum said, choosing his words carefully in case of unseen listeners, 'we have agreed to all his wishes.'

'Oh, it's just a foolish fancy of the kid's,' Rafik said easily, but he rose to his feet as he did so and offered Acorna his cup and Calum's. 'Nothing to worry about. Let's go on with the meal!' At the same time a subtle head shake warned both the other men not to take his words literally.

Acorna's horn broke out in drops of sweat again as she brought her face close to Rafik's cup. She dipped her horn into the juice for a moment, then smiled in satisfaction.

'Ah – just a minute,' Rafik said as she moved to repeat the treatment on Calum's cup. He put that one back on the table and offered Acorna the cup Hafiz had been drinking out of. Her horn showed no reaction.

'How did he do it?' Gill mouthed soundlessly.

'The drug must have been in the cups, not in the pitcher,' Rafik replied in the merest thread of a whisper. Quickly he exchanged Calum's cup with Hafiz', then sat and served himself a plate of rice and pilau. 'Come on, wives,' he said loudly and heartily, 'let us feast and rejoice!' He piled Acorna's plate high with fruit and greens just as Hafiz rejoined them.

'I trust the news from the south is not bad, Uncle?' Rafik inquired.

Hafiz' thin lips twisted in an unpleasant grimace. 'It could be worse,' he said. 'It could be better. Yukata Batsu has sent back the rest of Tapha. Alive,' he added, almost as an afterthought. 'Aminah cannot decide whether to bewail the loss of his ears or celebrate the return of her nursling.'

'Felicitations on your son's safe return,' said Gill. 'And – er – I'm sorry about his ears.'

Hafiz shrugged. 'My surgeon can replace the ears. No great loss; the original ones stuck out too far anyway. As for Tapha himself . . .' Hafiz sighed. 'No surgeon can fix what should have been *between* the ears. He, too, expected me to congratulate him on his return, as if he did not realize that Batsu freed him as a gesture of contempt, to show how little he fears Tapha's attempts against him. He is as foolish as his mother was.' He twirled a ball of sticky rice on two fingers, dipped it into the pilau, and downed the combination in a single gulp. 'Eat, eat, my friends. I apologize for allowing this minor contretemps to interrupt our pleasant family dinner. Do try the madigadi juice before it loses its chill; as it warms, the subtleties of the flavor are lost to the air.' He took another lengthy pull from the cup beside him.

'Indeed,' said Rafik, following his uncle's example, 'this particular juice has some subtle, lingering aftertaste that is unfamiliar to me.'

'Almost bitter,' Gill commented. 'Good, though,' he added, quickly taking a deep drink before Hafiz could become too alarmed.

118

Since none of them had any idea what drug Hafiz had put in the cups or how quickly it was supposed to act, they watched him for cues. Within fifteen minutes Hafiz had all but stopped eating, as if he had forgotten the food on his plate. His speech wandered and he began forgetting what he had said and repeating himself.

'Ever hear th' one about th' two racehorses, the Sufi dervish and the jinn?' He launched into a long complicated story which Gill suspected would have been extremely obscene if Hafiz had not kept losing the thread of his own narrative.

Rafik and Gill ignored their own food, leaned forward over the table and laughed as loudly as Hafiz did. Calum leaned back against the wall, an anonymous white bundle of veiling, and produced a rattling snore. Acorna's eyes went from one man to the next, the pupils narrowing to slits until Gill surreptitiously squeezed her hand.

'Don't worry, sweets,' he whispered under cover of Hafiz' raucous laughter, 'it's just a game.'

Finally Hafiz abandoned the Sufi dervish in midsentence and slumped forward into his rice. The other three waited tensely until his snores convinced them that he had lost consciousness.

'Okay, let's get out of here,' Gill whispered, standing and swinging Acorna to his shoulder. Calum followed suit, but Rafik bent over his uncle's form for a moment, fumbling in his stained silk robes.

'Come *on*, Rafik!'

Finally Rafik, too, stood, showing them a

119

holographic card that flashed a complex three-dimensional image of interlaced knots.

'Uncle's skimmer key and port pass,' he said happily. 'Or were you planning to *walk* to the port?'

Five

'Hey, Smirnoff?' Ed Minkus called to his office mate in the Kezdet Security Office.

'What?' Des Smirnoff replied without real interest, for he was scrolling through some routine ID checks as fast as he could and had to keep his eye on the screen, just in case something interesting turned up in the latest haul of dockside indigents.

'Gotta match on an ooooold friend.'

'Who?' Smirnoff was still not dividing his attention.

'Sauvignon,' and he immediately had Smirnoff's complete attention.

'I told you then,' and Smirnoff savagely stabbed the hold key, 'that perp wasn't dead. He may have had to lie low a while . . . Send the item over here.' He drummed his fingers for the few seconds it took for Ed to transfer the file to his screen. 'Registered as the *Uhuru* now? Couldn't change the origin, could he? So the ship's still Kezdetian.'

'I can't imagine a clever perp like Sauvignon ever returning . . .'

'Voluntarily, at least,' Ed interjected with a sly grin.

'. . . into our own dear jurisdiction. But you . . .'

'Never know, do you?' Ed had a habit of finishing Smirnoff's sentences for him.

'I can,' and Smirnoff's thick fingers stabbed each key as he typed in a command, 'make sure that we, and our dearest nearest neighbors in space, are aware that the *Uhuru* is of great interest to us here in Kezdet.'

He gave the final number of the code sequence such an extra pound that Ed flinched. Keyboards suffered frequent malfunctions at Smirnoff's station, to the point where both Supply and Accounting now required explanations. They always got the same one: 'Get a new supplier, these boards are made of inferior materials or they'd stand up under normal usage.'

Since most of such equipment was made in the sweat-levels (and quite possibly out of inferior grade plastics), the ones who suffered were the unfortunates who eked out a bare living anyhow. Who cared how many got fired and replaced? There were always enough eager youngsters with nimble fingers to take over.

Having instituted a program that would apprise the office of Lieutenant Des Smirnoff the instant the beacon was scanned in any of the nearby systems which cooperated, however unwillingly, with Kezdet Guardians of the Peace (a piece of this and a piece of that was what the neighbors said), the proximity of the *Uhuru* would now send off bells, whistles, and sirens.

'So the report of Sauvignon's death is greatly exaggerated,' Des said, grinning with evil anticipation of future revenge. 'How delightful.'

'Sauvignon may be dead,' Ed suggested. 'The new reg lists three names, and none of them are Sauvignon's.'

'Whose are they?'

'Rafik Nadezda, Declan Gilogley and Calum Baird,' Ed replied.

'*What*?' Smirnoff erupted from his chair like a cork from a bottle of fizzy. 'Say again?'

Ed obeyed, and suddenly the names rang the same bell in his head. 'Them?'

Smirnoff punched one big fist into the palm of his other hand, jumping about the office in what had to be some sort of a victory gig, waving his arms and hollering in pure, undiluted, spiteful joy.

'Is everything all right?' said their junior assistant, a female they had to employ to keep the Sexist Faction satisfied, though Mercy Kendoro's role in their table of organization began and ended with taking their messages and supplying them with quik-sober. On seeing Smirnoff's unusual antics she had hoped that one, he'd been poisoned, or two, was having a fatal heart attack or convulsion. Sometimes, not even getting out of the barrios of Kezdet made up for the humiliation she suffered at their hands.

'I got 'em. I got *all* of 'em,' Smirnoff was chanting as he bounced from one large boot to the other. '*Close the door*!' he roared when he saw Mercy's head peering in at them. Her reflexes were excellent and he missed her when his big boot slammed the door shut.

'Weren't Nadezda, Gilogley, and Baird those miners who marooned three of us on an asteroid before they made off with a fortune in titanium?'

'They were, they are, and they will be ours,' Des Smirnoff said, rubbing his hands together. The expression of great gleeful anticipation intensified on his face. His thick upper lip curled: a sight that made many timorous souls tremble in fear. He was not a man to cross and he had sworn vengeance on these three by all that he held sacred. Instead of prayers, Smirnoff had a nightly litany of those who had crossed his path and on whom he was sworn to take revenge. This not only kept the names alive, but topped up his capacity for vengeance, certain in his own little mind that he would one day cross paths with every one of those in his bad books. This mining crew would pay dearly for the indignity and suffering he had endured at their hands. He was still paying off his share of the repairs to the patrol cruiser. Kezdet Guardians of the Peace were not a forgiving authority and you ponied up out of your own credits for any damage above normal wear and tear. And for rescue and salvage.

In point of fact, *he* hadn't actually paid out of his

own private account, but out of the public one into which he had dribbled the credits required for the monthly payments from his little side business of protection monies. But he had other plans for that credit and meant to take it out of the miners' hides if he ever had the chance.

'So Sauvignon's off the hook?'

'Nonsense.' Des Smirnoff swiped the racks of data cubes off their rack. 'They've got the ship, they've got the fines accrued against it.' The thought had him settling at his keyboard again while he accessed those fines and chuckled at the amount of interest that had accrued since Sauvignon's disappearance.

'You'll own the ship, too, at that rate,' Ed said, sniffing enviously. He tried not to show it, but he did really, honestly, deeply, sincerely feel that Des kept more than his fair share of the covert rewards of their partnership. He was waiting for the day when he found some little inconsistency in Smirnoff's duties that he could use as a handle to bargain for a larger percentage.

'What'd I do with a crappy old tub like Sauvignon cruised? It was all but falling apart as it was. Amazing he survived. I was sure we'd penetrated the life-support system with that last bolt we fired at him.'

'Yeah,' and Ed scratched his head, 'sure looked like a direct hit, if I remember correctly.'

'You better remember my aim is always accurate.'

'Odd though that the ship survived, isn't it?'

Des Smirnoff held up one hand, his big, bloodshot brown eyes widening.

'Wait a nano . . .'

'It didn't survive,' Ed said. 'Those miners have switched beacons.'

'Do we have their IDs?' But he didn't wait for an answer, his big fingers slamming down the keys as he completed his own search. Then he flipped the offending keyboard up, pulling it out of the desk socket and spinning it across the room, where it crashed and split against the far wall. 'We don't. We should. They were MME, weren't they?'

'MME's been absorbed by Amalgamated, I heard,' Ed replied, disguising his sigh as he opened the com unit to Mercy Kendoro. 'Bring in a replacement keyboard. Now.'

When Mercy entered, she handed the keyboard to Ed rather than approach Smirnoff, who had his hands tucked up under his arms and was clearly seething over whatever had caused him to break the latest keyboard.

'Rack up those cubes, too, while you're in here. This office must be kept neat and up to standard at all times,' Des said and smiled anew as he saw the trembling assistant bend to her task.

Later that day, Mercy Kendoro took her midday meal break at a workers' canteen near the docks, where the balding owner teased her affectionately about moving into the tech classes and forgetting her origins.

'That's right, Ghopal,' Mercy replied as always,

'if I'd remembered how terrible your stew is, there's no way I'd be eating here! What did you put in it this morning, dead rats? At least three of them, I'd guess; I've never seen this much meat in it before.'

Ghopal took the teasing in good part and personally cleared away Mercy's bowl when she had finished eating. Later, when the midday rush had petered out, he put in a call to Aaaxterminators, Inc. 'We've found three dead rats in various spots too near the kitchens for my liking. If you'll send out a man I'll give him a list of the specific locations so he can find where the vermin are hiding and clear them out. And – as usual, no need to trouble the Public Health office with the matter. Eh? After all, I'm dealing with it promptly, like a good citizen.'

Ed Minkus came across that transcript when reviewing the day's tapes of private calls from citizens in whom Security took an interest.

'Hey, Des,' he called, 'time to pay a little semi-official visit to Ghopal. He's having problems with vermin again, and he'd probably be grateful not to have the matter called to the attention of Public Health. About fifteen percent grateful, I estimate.'

'Small-time,' Des grunted. 'If I catch those miners – and I will – we won't need to bother shaking down dockside bistros any more.'

But by then the representative of Aaaxterminators, Inc. had called at the back door of Ghopal's kitchen and had gone away with the note Ghopal handed him, promising to take care of the rat problem.

On his way back to the office, the Aaaxterminators man stopped at a kiosk and bought a cluster of happy-sticks, paying in real paper credits from an impressive wad he kept in his inner coverall pocket. He flirted outrageously with the girl who sold him the happy-sticks, which might have explained why she seemed a bit flustered and took longer than usual to give him his change.

That evening, as always, Delszaki Li's personal assistant went out to the same kiosk to buy a flimsy of the racing form sheets for the next day. He and the kiosk girl laughed over the old man's refusal to subscribe to the racing news via personal data terminal and agreed, as they always did, that if a nice old man was embarrassed by his fascination with this form of gambling and thought that buying flimsies with hard credits would preserve his anonymity, there was no need to disturb his illusions. The folded flimsy sheet Pal Kendoro took back to the Li mansion was thicker than usual. After he had unfolded it and read the contents of the inner page, he dissolved that page in water, poured the water down the drain, and requested an immediate interview with his employer.

'Sauvignon's ship has been reported in transit, sir,' he said, standing as straight as a military attaché before the old man in the specially equipped hover-chair. A wasting neuromuscular

128

disease had rendered Delszaki Li's legs and right arm all but useless, but the intelligence in those piercing black eyes was as keen as ever, and with one hand and voice commands he had remained in charge of the Li financial empire for fifteen years after enemies had predicted his speedy demise. Pal Kendoro was proud to serve as Li's arms, legs, and eyes outside the mansion.

'And Sauvignon?'

'I don't know. There is still a party of three aboard the ship, but the names are not those of our people. It is now registered to Baird, Gilogley, and Nadezda,' Pal recited from memory.

'Would have been most unwise for Sauvignon and party to retain same names,' Li pointed out. 'Do you think they attempt to make contact with us again?'

'Unlikely. This information came from a Guardians' office.'

Delszaki Li's black eyes snapped fire. 'Then is most urgent to find them before Guardians do. Must be you who goes, Pal. Wish I could keep you here, but who else would be believed as doing errand for me and at same time reestablish contact with Sauvignon?'

Pal nodded agreement. Most of the members of the league were from the underclass, with no visible means of going off-planet, no obvious reason to go, and no off-planet passes. The few, such as Pal, who had risen through the tech schools, were the only ones who could travel freely without inconvenient questions being asked. But he didn't like leaving Delszaki Li with only his regular servants, at least half of whom were secretly in the pay of Kezdet Guardians of the Peace – and secure in the belief that their second source of income was a secret.

'If I might make a suggestion, sir, you will need a personal assistant while I'm gone. My sister might be able to oblige.'

'Mercy?'

'No! She's too useful where she is. My older sister, Judit; I don't think you've ever met her. She's brilliant. Finished Kezdet tech schools at sixteen and scored highly enough on the final exams to win a scholarship to study off-planet. She's working in the psych section at Amalgamated's space base.'

'Would be willing to leave this fine job?'

'Like a shot, sir. She hates the place, was only working there for the money to put Mercy and me through school so we, too, could escape the barrios. It should be safe enough for her to return to Kezdet. Due to leaving so early, she's never been . . . active,' Pal said delicately.

'And therefore is unknown to the Guardians' offices, except as sister to girl who works as their assistant.' Li nodded his satisfaction. 'Could hardly have a better guarantor.' Li chuckled quietly. 'Is good, Kendoro. Send word to sister, but do not wait for her arrival. I shall manage well enough for few days, and Sauvignon may need help.'

'If it is Sauvignon,' Pal said under his breath, but the old man heard.

'And if is not Sauvignon, then maybe ship in hands of those who kill our friends. In which case . . .'

'Terrorism is against the principles of the league, sir. Despite what they say about us in the newscasts.'

'Is extermination of rats,' Li snapped, 'is not terrorism.'

So the chain of information from the Guardians' office to the Li mansion ended as it had begun, with a discussion of dead rats.

'I want that boy,' Hafiz told his trusted lieutenant, Samaddin.

'With respect, patron, I thought it was a girl.'

'What? Oh – the curiosity. Yes, well, of course I want her, too. But I want young Rafik more. The son of a camel and a whore outsmarted me!'

'With all respect, patron!' Samaddin bowed even lower. 'Forgive me, but the patron would not wish, later, to recall that he had spoken of his sister in such terms.'

'Family!' Hafiz said in disgust. 'When they double-cross you, you can't even curse them properly. Get me that sheep-buggering boy, Samaddin.'

'Consider it done,' Samaddin promised. 'Er – you want him with his balls or without them?'

'You idiot! You misbegotten son of a jinn's meeting with a jackass, may the grave of your maternal grandmother be defiled by the dung of ten thousand syphilitic she-camels!' Hafiz indulged the bad temper resulting from a major drug hangover and the loss of his prized unicorn by abusing Samaddin for several minutes, while his lieutenant's expressionless face grew steadily closer to purple than its normal creamy tan. Finally Hafiz calmed down enough to explain that he wanted Rafik back alive and unharmed, and especially with his generative capacities intact.

'He'll pay for what he did to me, never fear. But after he works off his debt, I've got plans for the boy. Do you know how long it's been since anybody double-crossed *me*, rather than the other way round, Samaddin? He's got the brains and the guts to take over after me, and I want him to have the balls to sire more sons, too. I'm going to adopt him and name him my heir. Well? What are you staring at? Perfectly normal practice – good families, no son to carry on, bring in a young relative.'

'The patron has a son,' Samaddin murmured.

'Not,' said Hafiz grimly, 'for long. Not after the way he screwed up the southern operation. Soon as his new ears are fixed, I'm sending him back to do the job right this time.'

'Patron! This time Yukata Batsu will kill him!'

'Sink or swim,' Hafiz said with a benign smile, 'sink or swim.' He considered for a moment. 'Better not send him until you've got Rafik safely back here, though. The family is short of young males at the moment. Tapha is, I suppose, better than nothing.'

'Waste not, want not,' Samaddin said helpfully.

*　　*　　*

132

In the curtained room where Tapha lay with his head wrapped in bandages, old Aminah whispered with the servant girl she'd sent to dust the latticework outside Hafiz' office. She raised her hands and eyes to heaven in horror when she heard Hafiz' plans for his own son.

'What shall we do?' she wailed. 'If he goes back to the south, that fiend Yukata Batsu will surely kill him. And if he stays here, that other fiend, his father, will kill him. We must smuggle him away as soon as he has healed from surgery. There must be some place where he can hide.'

Aminah's wailing awakened Tapha, and he struggled to sit up in his bed. 'No, Aminah. I will not hide.'

'Tapha, nursling! You heard me?' Aminah fluttered to his side.

'Yukata Batsu took my outer ears, not the brain which hears and understands,' Tapha said sourly, 'and a deaf beggar would have been awakened by thy wailing, old woman. Now tell me all that you know.'

When Aminah had poured out her story, Tapha lay back on his pillows and considered. His face was somewhat paler than it had been, but that might have been from the exhaustion of sitting up.

'I will not hide,' he declared again. 'It is unbefitting a man of my lineage. Besides, there is no place where my beloved father, may dogs defile his name and grave, could not find me if he wished. There is only one thing to do.' He smiled sweetly at Aminah. 'You will tell my beloved father that I am not recovering from the restorative surgery, that it is feared I will lose my life to an infectious fever brought back from the southern marshes.'

'But, my little love, you grow stronger with every hour! You have no fever; I, who have always nursed you, should know.'

'Try not to be more stupid than you were made, Aminah,' Tapha said. 'Since when is it necessary to declare to my father the exact truth of what passes in these rooms? Or will you no longer protect me as you did when I was your nursling in truth, and you lied to deflect the wrath of my father over minor escapades?'

Aminah sighed. She had lied for Tapha too many times to stop now.

'But the deception must soon be discovered, my darling,' she pointed out. 'You cannot pretend to lie abed with the marsh fever forever.'

'No. But while my father is staying well away from these rooms for fear of the infection, I can get off-planet. I do not think he will kill you when he discovers the deception,' Tapha added after a moment's thought. 'He may not even beat you very badly, for you are old and weak, and it is shame to harm one's servants.'

'Dear Tapha,' Aminah said, 'don't worry about me. My life is as nothing compared to a single hair of your head.'

Tapha had no quarrel with this assessment.

'And so you will hide after all?'

'By no means.' Tapha smiled. 'By no means.

134

Running away and hiding offers only a temporary safety. There is only one way to make sure that my position as my father's heir remains unchallenged, and that he treasures my life as a loving father ought. I shall simply have to find my cousin Rafik,' he said, 'before Samaddin does.'

The *Uhuru* was unloading a collection of miscellaneous minerals on Theloi when Calum was approached by a courteous stranger.

'I could not help overhearing your discussions with Kyrie Pasantonopolous,' he said. 'Allow me to introduce myself – Ioannis Georghios, local representative for . . . a number of businesses. I had the impression that your dealings with the Pasantonopolous family had been less than satisfactory? Perhaps you would allow me to inspect your cargo. I might be able to make you a better offer.'

'I doubt it,' Calum said sourly. 'It's the mineral resources around Theloi that were unsatisfactory. We had to go all the way out to the fourth asteroid belt to find anything worth mining, and then all we recovered from the ferrous regolith was gold and platinum. Hardly worth the cost of the journey—'

He stopped abruptly as Rafik stepped on his foot and interrupted him. 'But, of course, the value of anything depends on how much the buyer desires it and how little the seller cares for it,' he continued smoothly. 'Perhaps one of the businesses you represent, Kyrie Georghios, would find some slight use for our trivial and insignificant cargo. *Don't* run down our payload in front of a purchaser,' he added to Calum out of the corner of his mouth as Georghios followed Gill to inspect the samples they had shown the Pasantonopolous concern.

'And just what were *you* doing?' Calum demanded indignantly.

'Being polite,' Rafik said. 'It's a different thing altogether. I think your bargaining instincts have been dulled by too many safe years under contract to MME. You'd better let me do the talking from now on.'

'He wants to take samples for his own office to test, and we're invited to dine with him tonight to discuss an asteroid he wants us to explore,' Gill said, joining them. 'He hinted it might be a good source of rhenium. I suppose you think my bargaining instincts are atrophied too, Rafik?'

'My dear Gill,' Rafik said amiably, 'you never had any talent for bargaining in the first place. We would do better to hand over the dealing to Acorna, who, at least, has a flair for numbers.'

'Better if she's not seen too much,' Calum said. 'She'll have to stay on board the *Uhuru* tonight.'

The other two agreed. Acorna had grown so fast that she could now pass for a short man, and in miners' coveralls and with a bulky cap concealing her silver hair and nascent horn, she could just get away with passing through the bazaars of Theloi without attracting too much attention. But they doubted her ability to pass for human through a prolonged evening of bargaining and formal dining.

'Better,' Rafik said, 'if all three of you stay on board. Then you can't put your foot in your mouth again, Calum.'

'Calum stays with Acorna, I go with you,' Gill decided after a moment's consideration. 'We don't know this Georghios, and I don't think any of us should be going off alone with strangers at present. We've annoyed too many people recently.'

'He may not be willing to tell a loudmouth like you about the rhenium asteroid,' Rafik warned.

'No,' said Gill cheerfully, 'but he won't bop me over the head in a dark alley, either.'

'You're paranoid,' said Rafik, but in the end it was he who recognized the trap Georghios had laid for them.

'He wants all four of us to dine with him,' he reported after a telecom conversation with Georghios. 'Says he prefers to know that all partners are in agreement before committing to a possibly hazardous venture like this . . . it seems the rhenium asteroid is closer to Theloi's sun than we usually work, and we'll need extra radiation shielding as well as protection from solar flares.'

'Partners? Well, that lets Acorna out, anyway.'

'He specifically requested all of us,' Rafik said, frowning. 'Hinted that if we didn't all show up, there'd be no deal. Now who does that remind you of?'

'Sounds like Hafiz,' Gill said, nodding. 'In

which case we'd better take Acorna along to check for poison.'

'No,' Rafik said slowly, 'in which case we'd better leave *now*. I'll accept his invitation – that will give us the afternoon to unload our payload, get what we can out of the Pasantonopolous family, and take off for Kezdet.'

'We don't dare go to Kezdet,' Calum pointed out.

Rafik smiled. 'All your survival instincts have atrophied. I knew it. Kezdet makes as good an official flight plan as any, don't you think? We haven't decided where to go next, and I wouldn't want to accidentally file a plan for someplace near where we're actually going.'

What they were able to get from the Pasanto-nopolous concern for their gold and platinum barely paid their expenses. They had to stop at the first system with any mineral resources at all. That was Greifen, where the planetary government was building a series of orbiting space stations for zero-G manufacturing and could use all the pure iron the *Uhuru* could refine and send back into low planetary orbit by drone. The profit per load was not much, since Greifen was only willing to buy space-mined iron as long as the cost was less than that of lifting their own planetary iron into orbit. But it was steady work, and while the mag drive shipped buckets of iron back, they slowly accu-mulated a payload of more valuable metals. They were almost ready to look for a buyer on Greifen when Calum, who had been amusing himself during long refining processes by breaking the security codes on bureaucratic messages from Greifen, raised the alarm.

'I don't think we'd better try to sell this stuff on Greifen,' he told Rafik when the other two miners checked the status of the latest processes. 'In fact, I think we'd better leave – *now* – and sell it someplace far, far away.'

'Why? Getting bored? Another hundred tons of iron and we should have accumulated enough rhodium and titanium to make the trip seriously profitable.'

'Listen to this.' Calum flicked a switch and the com unit replayed the results of his last few hours' eavesdropping on official Greifen business. 'Somebody has landed with a claim against the *Uhuru* for debts and damages incurred on Theloi.'

'We didn't *do* any damage on Theloi,' Gill said indignantly. 'We didn't have time!'

'Would you like to explain that to a court that's been thoroughly bribed by Rafik's Uncle Hafiz?' Calum asked. 'He must be really mad at us. I didn't think he'd follow us out of Theloi.'

'He didn't,' said Rafik, examining the flimsy of the transmissions Calum had decoded. 'At least . . . this does not have the flavor of my uncle's work. He prefers to avoid the courts. And look at the name of the supposed creditor. That's not a Theloian name.'

'Farkas Hamisen,' Gill read over Rafik's shoulder.

'Farkas,' Rafik said, 'means "wolf" in the Kezdet dialect . . . I think maybe it was not such a bright idea after all, to file a flight plan for Kezdet. That must be how they caught on to us.'

'They'd have no reason to go after this ship,' Gill protested. 'Officially we're not the *Khedive* anymore. We're the *Uhuru*. We've even got the beacon to prove it.'

Rafik shrugged. 'Do you really want to stick around and find out what they've got against us?'

'No way,' Calum and Gill said in unison.

They agreed to forget about their credits from Greifen for the last drone loads of iron. As for the payload, as Rafik pointed out, any number of systems would be happy to get supplies of titanium. Nered, for instance, was a high-tech and highly militarized planet suffering from a severe shortage of mineral resources . . .

'The trouble with selling to Nered,' Gill pointed out gloomily after they had reached that planet and concluded their transaction, 'is that there's nothing in this system for us to mine. We've got an empty ship . . .'

'And a great many Federation credits,' Rafik said. 'They really wanted that titanium.'

'Yeah, but these people are military mad. I bet there's nothing to buy here except paramilitary gear and espionage gadgets.'

'We'll spend it elsewhere,' Rafik said. 'Most of it. Tonight, let's celebrate solvency by taking

Acorna out to dinner in the best restaurant on Nered.'

'Oh, boy,' Calum said, 'I can hardly wait to check out Nered haute cuisine. What's the main course, bandoleers in hot pepper sauce? With gingered grenades for afters?'

'She can't go dressed like that,' Gill announced, gesturing in her direction.

Over the course of the past year, Acorna had shot up in height until even Gill's coveralls were short on her. Inside the ship she preferred to relax without the binding, too-small clothing. Calum and Rafik turned and stared now at Acorna, where she rested in a net, happily perusing a vid on carbonyl reduction techniques for nonferrous metals. Her silvery curls had grown into a long mane that tumbled fetchingly over her forehead and tapered down her spine. Her lower parts were covered in fine white fur. She was taller than Gill and as flat-chested as a child, with nothing of an incipient mammary development visible.

'I wonder how old she is?' Calum speculated in a low voice, so as not to attract Acorna's attention.

'Chronologically,' Rafik said, 'probably about three. It's been two years since we found her. Physiologically, I'd guess around sixteen. Evidently her species matures quickly, but I don't think she's come to her full growth yet; look at the size of her wrist and ankle bones relative to her height.'

'Six feet six and counting,' Calum muttered.

And that would shortly pose a serious problem.

141

The *Khedive* had been designed for three small-to-average-size miners. Gill's broad shoulders and excess height had put a strain on the system; sharing the quarters with a fourth passenger had necessitated some fancy reshuffling of the interior arrangements; fitting a seven-foot-tall unicorn into the small confines of the mining ship was virtually impossible.

Acorna looked up from her vid. 'Calum,' she said, 'could you explain, please, how this sodium hydroxide reduction process forms liquid $TiCl_2$?'

'Umm, that's a late stage,' Calum said. He bent to draw a quick diagram on the vid screen next to the explanatory text and pictures. 'See, you have to pump dilute HC1 into the electrolysis cell . . .'

'They should have said so explicitly,' Acorna complained. Her language use had asymptotically approached standard Basic in the last year; only a slight formality in her speech, and a faintly nasal inflection, gave any suggestion that she was not a native speaker of the galactic interlingua.

'And developmentally,' Rafik murmured, watching Calum and Acorna threshing out the details of electrolytic metals separation, 'she's four going on twenty-four.'

'Yeah,' Gill agreed. 'She knows almost as much as we do about mining, metallurgy, and navigation of small spacecraft, but she doesn't know anything about, well, you know . . .'

'No, I don't know,' Rafik said, watching Gill's face turn as red as his beard.

'*You* know. *Girl* stuff.'

'You think it's time for one of us to sit her down and have a little talk about the human repro-ductive system? Frankly, I don't see the point,' said Rafik, fighting his own embarrassment at the idea. 'For all we know, her race may reproduce by – by pollinating flowers with their horns.'

'That fur doesn't cover everything,' Gill said, 'and anyway, I bathed her as often as you did last year. Anatomically, she's feminine.' He looked doubtfully at Acorna's long, slender body. 'A flat-chested female, but female,' he amended. 'And she can't go on lounging around in nothing but her long hair and white fur.'

'Why not? Maybe her race doesn't have a nudity taboo.'

'Well, mine does,' Gill shouted, 'and I'm not having a half-naked teenage girl parading around this ship!'

Acorna looked up. 'Where?'

She never found out why all three men exploded in laughter.

They still had the yards of white polysilk that Rafik had bought at the Mali Bazaar to clothe his 'wives' in approved Neo-Hadithian style. Gill hacked off a length of fabric, Calum came up with some clip fasteners, and together they wrapped the material around Acorna's waist and threw a fold of it over her shoulders. A second length of fabric provided a loosely wrapped turban which disguised her horn . . . well, sort of.

'This is not comfortable,' she complained.

'Honey, we're not dressmakers. You can't go

143

out to a nice restaurant in my old coveralls. You'd better buy her some clothes while we're here,' Gill said to Rafik.

'You buy the clothes, you're the one who cares,' Rafik retorted, 'and you'll be lucky to find anything but army fatigues on this planet.'

Rafik had maligned the shopping resources of Nered unfairly. Both men and women at the Evening Star restaurant were dressed like peacocks: the men elegant in formal gray-and-silver evening wear, the women a colorful garden of fashions and styles from across the galaxy, all interpreted in brilliant jewel-toned silks and stiff rustling retro-satins. In such a gaudy gathering the miners hoped that they would escape notice. Their own formal wear was respectable, but not comparable to the silver-flashed suits currently in vogue on Nered, and Acorna, with neither jewels nor colorful silks to adorn her, should have looked quite dowdy next to the fashionable upper class of Nered. Instead her appearance had quite the opposite effect. Her height and slenderness, the tumble of silvery curls falling down from her improvised turban, and the simplicity of her white polysilk sari made her stand out in the crowd like a lily in a bed of peonies. Heads turned as they were shown to their table, and Rafik could tell from the swift calculation in the maître d'hôtel's eyes that they were being given a far more prominent table than the one originally intended for four working miners from off-planet. Bad luck, that, but there was no sense in making a fuss over it now; that would only draw more attention their way. They would simply have to make it through dinner as best they could, and he would watch like a hawk to make sure Acorna's turban didn't fall off. He also looked around to see if any one else was wearing a turban, or was as slender as Acorna. You never knew in an interstellar area what sort of oddities you'd encounter. Returning Acorna to her own people would solve a great many problems!

He was so intent on shielding Acorna from notice that the real danger, when it did come, took him completely by surprise. A tense young man in dark brown military fatigues thrust his way into the restaurant, knocked down a waiter carrying a tray of soup bowls, and took advantage of the confusion to level three bursts of laser fire at Rafik before making his escape.

Gill knocked over his own chair in his haste to get to Rafik, but Acorna was faster, kneeling over an ominously still figure. The shock of the attack sent isolated nightmare images flitting through Gill's brain. Rafik wasn't moving; he should have been screaming in pain – half his face was burned. Acorna fumbled at her turban. Shouldn't let her do that. She had to stay covered. Doctor! They needed a doctor! Some idiot was babbling about catching the assassin. Who cared about that? Rafik was all that mattered.

Acorna bent over Rafik, her horn exposed now, her eyes dark pools with the pupils narrowed to virtually invisible silver slits. She – nuzzled – at him with her horn. It was heartbreaking to watch; a child mourning a parent. Gill thought numbly that he should take her away. Let her grieve in private. Hide her before too many people noticed the horn. But moving to Rafik's side felt like swimming through heavy water, as though time itself had slowed around them, and when he reached Acorna and Rafik, Calum gripped his shoulder and held him back.

'*Wait*,' he said. 'She can purify water and air, and detect poison. Maybe she can heal laser wounds.'

Even as they watched, the charred flesh on Rafik's face was replaced by smooth new skin wherever Acorna's horn brushed it. She lingered for a moment with her horn just over his heart, as though urging his shocked system to continue breathing and circulating. Then he stirred and opened his eyes and said irritably:

'What in the name of ten thousand syphilitic she-devils happened?'

Calum and Gill tried to tell him at once. Then those at the tables nearest them came over, now that it seemed safe to approach, to add their impression of the assassination attack. Those further away, of course, were demanding to know what had happened. When they saw no visible damage but overturned chairs and food spilled on the floor, they turned back to their own tables to resume their interrupted meal. Calum managed to put the turban on the back of Acorna's head, and

Rafik pulled it over her horn. Then both he and Gill had to explain to those nearest that no, Rafik had not been hit. No, the laser hadn't even touched him.

Eventually all agreed that an assassin had fired at Rafik and that the young lady had fortunately reacted quickly enough to save him by knocking him out of his chair, so that he was not even singed by a near miss. A small vociferous group wanted to discuss their idea that the would-be assassin had looked remarkably like Rafik. Gill and Calum let the story of the miraculous near miss stand and discouraged plans to hunt down Rafik's attacker who had eluded his pursuer; all they wanted was to get back to the *Uhuru* at once. They had attracted far too much attention this evening!

Six

Delszaki Li and Judit Kendoro were finishing their evening meal when the dining room com unit beeped in the rising arpeggio that meant a scrambled message had been received.

'That will be Pal,' Li said. He depressed a button on the left arm of his float-chair and the sequence of jagged, screeching noises that constituted the scrambled message became audible. After a moment of silence, the com unit's decoding module whirred busily and the original message was heard, Pal's voice somewhat distorted and metallic due to the limitations of the coding process.

'There are four crew, not three, presently using the *Uhuru*. None of them is Sauvignon. They have enemies; one of the crew was the target of an assassination attempt this evening in a fashionable restaurant. The consensus of opinion is that the assassin missed his target, but I was sitting close by in an attempt to listen in on their conversation and I believe what actually happened was quite different – and very interesting. The miner Rafik was actually struck by three bolts of laser fire; I saw the burns myself. I also saw them healed with astonishing speed by the fourth crew member. This person appears to be a very tall young woman with slightly deformed fingers and a small . . .' Pal's voice paused for a moment and only the faint background noise introduced by scrambling and decoding was audible. 'Sir, you're not going to believe this, but she seems to have a small *horn* in the middle of her forehead. And when she nuzzled the man Rafik with this horn, his burns healed and he was conscious within seconds. Sir, I saw this with my own eyes; I'm not making it up or repeating gossip.' There was another pause. 'These people have no discernible connection with our friends. But they are very interesting. I have decided to maintain contact with them until you send further instructions.'

'A *ki-lin*!' Delszaki exclaimed as the message ended. He turned exultantly to Judit, who had been sitting as still as stone ever since Pal had mentioned the horn. 'My dear, we have been granted a portent of inestimable value. This strange girl may be solution to Kezdet's tragedy . . . or she may only portend coming of solution. We must bring her here!'

'Acorna,' Judit said. 'They called her Acorna . . . I thought they had all died; their ship's beacon was found transmitting from a crash site. I cried for them then, those three nice men and the little girl. Acorna.' There were tears standing in her eyes now.

'You knew of a *ki-lin* and did not tell me?'

'Mr Li, I don't even know what a *ki-lin* is! And I thought she was dead. And it was my fault, because I helped them get away . . . They wanted to cut off her horn, you see . . .'

'You must tell me all this story,' Delszaki Li said. 'But first, you must understand the importance of the *ki-lin* and why I need her here.'

'*Ki-lin* . . . is that Chinese for "unicorn"?'

Li nodded. 'But our beliefs are somewhat different from your Western tales about the unicorn. Your people have stories of trapping and killing unicorns. No Chinese would ever kill a *ki-lin*, or even hunt one. The *ki-lin* belongs to Buddha; she eats no animal flesh and will not even tread upon an insect. We would not dream of trapping the *ki-lin* as a gift to a ruler; rather, the wise and beneficent ruler hopes that his rule may be blessed by the arrival of a *ki-lin*, who, if she comes to his court, is received as one sovereign visiting another. The appearance of a *ki-lin* among humans is an omen of a great change for the better or of the birth of a great ruler.'

'And you yourself believe this?'

Delszaki Li cackled at the expression on Judit's face. 'Let us say I do not *disbelieve it*. How could I? I am scientist first, man of business only from necessity. No *ki-lin* has ever appeared in recorded history, so there is no evidence to prove or disprove the legends. But I am also man, not only scientist, and so I hope. I hope that this *ki-lin* will presage the change which Kezdet – and Kezdet's children – so desperately need. And so I shall instruct Pal to make these miners an offer they cannot refuse. They will, in fact, be quite useful for one of my other projects. And while we wait for their arrival, you shall tell me what you know of this Acorna and her friends, and we shall search the Net for more information about them. Never go into a bargaining session unprepared, Judit – even if you are bargaining with a *ki-lin*!'

It was Acorna who suggested they measure her to know how long the legs of pants and sleeves of shirts should be, though why she needed to cover herself, when her fur kept her quite comfortable, she couldn't understand.

'Didn't you like what the women were wearing in the restaurant last night?' Rafik asked. 'I saw you looking around like your eyes would pop.'

'Her eyes don't pop,' Gill said loyally, and then added, 'but your pupils were out to the edges of your eyeballs.'

A sort of dreamy expression crossed Acorna's face briefly and she gave a resigned sigh. 'None of those things would last a minute crawling down a conduit or in an EVA suit.'

'That's another thing we have to get for you,' Calum said, for he had worried about that lack. She could do with some hands-on mining experience to round out her education in asteroid extraction techniques.

'You would need to measure me for that,' she said.

From somewhere they unearthed a flexible tape in an old mechanic's kit. They made most measurements using the instrumentation on board because most of what they needed to measure was out in space and their EVA suits were equipped with gauges. So they dutifully took down what they felt they needed to buy appropriate sizes.

Then they argued over who was to go: Gill would definitely be useless in a dress shop, or even a straight women's-apparel outfitter. Calum's taste, according to Rafik, reposed only in his mouth. Rafik would have to go.

'Not when there's an assassin out there somewhere waiting to snuff you out and this time we can't take Acorna with us for emergency first aid.'

'You all go,' Acorna said reasonably and before the decision-making turned into one of the interminable arguments the men all seemed to enjoy so much. 'I am safe in here and will not answer any summonses.'

That was debated, too, but it was finally decided that with Gill bulking along behind Rafik and Calum at his side, he would be less of a target and he would at least not be able to complain when either of the others came back with what he felt to be unsuitable raiment.

They got the EVA suit first, since those could be custom-made and produced within an hour. They'd collect it on their way back.

Despite Gill's snide comments about the militaristic bias of Nered, it was still a wealthy planet with the usual supply of flea markets, bazaars, and good used-apparel shops. With proper measurements, they could also find the right sizes of work clothing for their growing charge. Rafik even found attractive upper-body wraps, made of an elasticized material that was guaranteed 'to fit any female form comfortably.'

'She'll like that,' Rafik announced, and got three plain colored ones in blue, green, and a deep purple that he felt would look well with her silvery hair, and two figured ones: one with flowers that might never have bloomed on any planet in the galaxy, and another with daisies. At least that's what he told the other two they were.

After looking in several used-apparel shops, he also found some skirts with elasticized waistbands, also guaranteed to fit any form comfortably.

'It doesn't say "female",' Gill said, about to discard a splendidly patterned one.

'Mostly females wear skirts,' Rafik said, and took the skirt from his hand. He found another that was filmy but opaque, in a misty blue that he thought Acorna would like for the flow of it – a saleslady modeled the item – the texture of the material, and the color.

It was the saleslady, having discerned that the three attractive miners were buying for a female they all knew, decided to inveigle them to buy accessories, such as 'lingerie.'

'You men are all alike. Concentrate on the outer wear,' she said teasingly because the big, bearded redhead blushed to the color of his hair at the first mention of underclothes, 'and forget there has to be something underneath.'

Rafik beamed at her. 'My niece has just reached puberty, and I don't know what girls do wear underneath . . .' and he wiggled his fingers in helpless innocence. 'Her parents were killed in an accident and I'm her only living relative, so we've sort of inherited her.'

'Very good to do so, too, if I may say so, Captain,' Salitana said with more than usual fervor, losing her suave salesperson persona. 'When you think of the traffic in orphaned children in this curve of the Milky Way, it's nice to know some will take on responsibility for blood relations instead of selling them out of hand to who-knows-what miserable existence.'

'Like Kezdet?' Gill asked, having glanced around first to be sure they were not overheard.

'Out-system visitors call us paranoid,' Salitana said, 'but if your planet were this close to Kezdet, you'd have a major defense budget, too.'

The two locked eyes, but Salitana immediately smiled her salesperson smile and turned to her keyboard, accessing the stock for the sizes the niece needed: she had the measurements before her. Rather than embarrass the men any further, she ordered up what she felt would appeal to a young girl – what would have appealed to her had she had any options in what she could wear in puberty. While those were on their way to her station, she frowned down at the chest measurement. Poor child was absolutely flat-chested. Well, maybe a training or an exercise bra would suffice. She ordered several of those and the merchandise arrived, already wrapped.

'You'll find these suitable, I assure you,' she said, handing them over.

The redhead looked most grateful as the covered items slipped into the carisak he held open.

'You have been shopping. What about shoes, now? I can show you—'

'No, that's fine. We got footwear in the bazaar,' Rafik said, and hastily proffered the plastic card used on Nered for purchases. He didn't like using a card because it could lead back to the *Uhuru* more quickly than credits would, but credits caused delays, since the shop had to check that these credits were legal and backed by a respectable credit authority.

'We should get her some shoes somewhere,' Gill said when they were out on the mall walkway again.

'The skirts measured long enough to cover her feet, and you know how she hates constriction,' Rafik said. He was tired – probably a remnant of having been dead yesterday for a few minutes – and he was eager to show her what they'd managed to find for her pleasure and adornment. 'Let's get a hovercraft back to the dock.'

'I thought you looked tired,' Gill said solicitously, and waved his long arm to attract a hire vehicle from the rank at the end of the mall.

One zoomed in to the head of the rank and blinked its 'hired' sign to show it would take them, but they had to wait until it could get in the traffic pattern above the busy area. It was just turning at the far end when the saleswoman rushed out to them.

'Don't take that one,' she cried, and frantically pulled them back into the store. 'You've been followed. Your charges were monitored. Come with me.'

The urgency with which she spoke and Rafik's so recent problem with an assassin impelled them to obey without question. Within the store again, she led them through the crowd of shoppers in a circuitous route to the rear, down two flights of steps, which had Rafik panting from exertion, and into a clearly marked 'Store Personnel Only' room, which she had keyed to open.

'I'm sorry to act so presumptuously,' she said, her face pale and eyes dark with worry, 'but for the sake of your niece, I had to intervene. Anything to save her if she has been orphaned in this quadrant of space. I don't know who's tracing you, but I do know it isn't Neredian-generated, so it has to be illegal and you are in danger.' She held up both hands defensively. 'Don't tell me anything, but if you'll trust me just a little longer, I contacted a friend—'

'From Kezdet?' Gill asked gently.

'How did you know?' she said in a soundless gasp, one hand to her throat, her eyes wider than Acorna's last night.

'Let's just say, we know a bit about what happens on Kezdet from . . . other friends . . .' Rafik said, 'and we appreciate your help very much. Someone is after me and I do not know why. Is there another way out of here?'

'There will be shortly,' she said, glancing at the chrono on the wall. 'I cannot linger, or my absence will be noted. The . . . party . . . will tap like this.' She demonstrated with a long index finger nail on the door. 'The . . . party . . . knows the access code,' and she gave a helpless little shrug. 'You need it to get in or out. But the party is absolutely trustworthy.'

'A child labor graduate?' Calum asked.

She nodded. 'I must go. Your niece is so lucky to have you! She has the right to have you in good health and one piece.'

She was out the door again so fast they hadn't time to see what digits she had pressed.

'So, who's after us? Or you, in particular?' Calum asked Rafik, leaning back against a table.

'She was a nice woman,' Gill remarked, regarding the closed door with a bemused expression on his face. 'Not as nice as Judit . . .'

'Judit?' Rafik and Calum said in unison, staring at him.

'She came from Kezdet.'

'And has a brother still stuck there . . . but one begins to wonder about the main occupation of those lucky enough to leave it,' Rafik said, then shook his head. 'Nah, it's more likely to be Hafiz who's after me . . . but Uncle's style would be more

157

along the lines of kidnapping me to take the place of that idiot son who lost his ears.'

'So long as the idiot son didn't lose what's between them,' and Calum inadvertently paraphrased the subject of his sentence, 'maybe it's him who found out and is going to put an end to Uncle's future plans for you.'

'Or it could be our erstwhile friends from Amalgamated. They're still after us for our ship,' Gill said.

'Or maybe it's that spurious claim of the Theloi?' Rafik said, rubbing his chin thoughtfully.

'So who's this Farkas Hamisen who hates your guts and registered the claim?' Gill asked.

'Possibly my earless cousin,' Rafik said, nodding his head, as that fit the parameters of such a relative.

'Or it could be the Greifen, after the ore . . .' Calum suggested.

'Well, the ore's gone.' Rafik dismissed that option. 'Could it have anything to do with our new beacon? And here Uncle Hafiz was so certain he was doing us a real favor . . . I wonder . . .'

'What?' Calum and Gill said in chorus.

'Who died in the wreck?'

Gill's eyes popped and his mouth dropped.

'You mean,' and Calum recovered more quickly, 'we got people we haven't even annoyed after us, too?'

The tap startled them in the silence that followed this observation.

The door opened and a slender youth, with dark

eyes that were wiser than his countenance, gestured imperiously for them to follow him. Though they did, Rafik hissed a bombardment of questions at the man's back as they had to jog to keep up with him.

'Shush,' he said, holding up one hand, which Gill then noticed pointed at a spy-eye in the corner of the corridor.

They shushed and he hunched over the pad of a heavily plated metal door at the end of the corridor. It opened slowly, because it was ten centimeters thick at least, Rafik estimated as he slipped through when the space was wide enough. They had to wait a few seconds longer for Gill to squeeze through. Their guide had judged it finely enough – he'd already tapped in the close sequence, hauling Gill's leg out of the way. The door closed a lot faster than it opened. The youth then gestured to a goods van, thumbed open its back doors, and pushed the three inside.

They could feel it rising on its vertical pads and then it moved forward. Very shortly they were all aware that they were in a traffic pattern of some kind, for the van was not soundproof. What it had originally carried was moot since there was nothing in it but three sweating miners. Rafik slid down one wall and onto his rump, and mopped his forehead.

'Dying takes more out of you than I ever realized,' he said. 'I'm bushed.'

'Are we *am*-bushed, I want to know?' Calum asked, hunkering down on his heels. Gill sat, too, as his head was brushing the ceiling of the van.

'No, you would have been,' a new tenor voice said softly. 'Salitana said you have taken a niece from Kezdet . . .'

'No, that's not correct,' Rafik said. 'She has been our charge for nearly four years. She needs new clothes.'

'Ah! But you know of Kezdet?'

'Yes,' Gill answered, 'we met someone who got out of there. Still trying to get her brother off that damned planet, too.'

'Really?' Surprise more than a prompting to continue colored that one word. 'Now, we are out of the mall. Where do I take you that you may safely descend?'

'The docks,' Rafik said.

'We should pick up Acorna's EVA suit first,' Gill said, and cowered at the dirty looks the other two gave him for mentioning her name.

'At which chandler's?' the youth asked in such a natural tone of voice that some of their fury at his indiscretion was dispelled.

'The one on Pier 48B,' Rafik answered, still glaring at Gill.

'Can do.' And they all felt the van make a left-hand turn.

That was right, Rafik thought and sneezed. Gill and Calum did, too. In fact they all were in such a paroxysm of sneezing that they inhaled a more than sufficient quantity of the sleep gas that circulated through the rear of the van.

*   *   *

Some very astringent substance was being held under his nose and Rafik roused to avoid it. To his utter surprise, a slim hand was held out to him.

'I am Pal Kendoro and it is my sister Judit who was working at Amalgamated who had paid for an education that would lift me out of the barrios of Kezdet. Are my bona fides sufficient to restore me to your good graces?'

Rafik glanced over at the still unconscious forms of his two friends.

'All of you would overpower me. One I can handle,' Pal Kendoro said, tilting his head – evidently a family trait; Rafik saw the resemblance to his sister in that pose. 'I apologize for . . .' and he waved his hand toward the front of the cab, '. . . the necessity, but I was seeking another whom I thought might be you.'

Rafik straightened up. He'd a crick in his neck from lying in an uncomfortable position, but the back door of the van was open and, while the air it let in smelt of fish and oil and other unpleasant odors, the last of the gas was dissipating.

'And who might that be?' Rafik asked in a droll tone. 'There's a waiting list.'

Pal grinned. 'So I have discovered.'

'How long were we out?' and Rafik rubbed at his neck. 'Oh migod . . .'

'She will not worry,' Pal said, reaching out a hand to steady Rafik when he tried to leap to his feet. 'I sent a message to your ship . . . She believes you have stopped to eat.'

'How the devil did you access our security

codes . . . ? Oh.' He groaned. 'I think I know. You're looking for the legal owners of the beacon we borrowed. Believe me, the ship was split like a nut when we found it wedged in an asteroid. Nothing could have lived.'

'Would you at least remember where you found the derelict?' Pal asked, his dark eyes intent.

'Sure can, but I don't know what good that'll do.'

'We . . . I . . . would be obliged.'

'We . . . I . . . owe you one,' and Rafik left off rubbing his neck.

Pal Kendoro got off his haunches now and went to wave his restorative under Calum's nose before he handed the bottle to Rafik to tend to Gill. Rafik chuckled at Kendoro's innate caution. Gill did indeed come out of his inadvertent nap ready to do mischief to whoever did that to him. A few brief explanations and harmony was restored, thanks for their escape offered and dismissed.

'Can we get back to—'

'Our ship,' Rafik hurriedly interjected.

'Yes, and with one stop at the chandlers on Pier 48B,' Pal said, exiting the van and adding as he closed the sides, 'this time I let you see where I am driving you.'

He was as good as his word, for the opaque panel between the goods section and the driver's turned transparent.

'I have had fresh words with Salitana,' he told them as he eased the van out of the side road and

162

into a busy traffic pattern, 'and there was considerable interest in you which she was unable, of course, to answer, since you were strangers buying clothing for female friends and she, naturally, wanted no part of the offers you made her.'

'She wouldn't have imparted to you a description of the interested parties, would she?' Rafik asked with a weary smile.

Pal Kendoro slid three quik-prints through a small slot in the panel.

'She is efficient.'

'Hey, that looks like . . .' and Gill closed his mouth on 'the assassin.'

'No, but there's a resemblance to the uncle,' Calum said, 'and if I'm not mistaken this shot shows quite new ears on him.'

Rafik had also noticed that.

'He is registered at the port as Farkas Hamisen,' Pal Kendoro said over his shoulder.

'She's not the only efficient one,' Calum murmured.

'Okay, why have you involved yourself with the cause of utter strangers, and don't tell me because we have succored a minor female?' Rafik said. He was getting very tired of being chased and helped and then chased again.

'I have also had a word with my sister, Judit, who is currently assisting my employer during my absence on the mission to discover who caused the death of our friends who owned the ship whose beacon you have appropriated for use in yours.'

Rafik was not the only listener who blinked at the long and involved and grammatically correct sentence.

'And . . .' Rafik prompted when Pal seemed to take a long time to make up his next sentence.

'Would your niece be a young female of unknown origin with a curious protuberance on her forehead?'

Rafik exchanged glances with his mates. Gill nodded solemn approval, but Calum looked wary.

'I think this lad is in an . . . efficient . . . position to help us on a number of vexing matters,' Rafik murmured. 'Yes, that is our niece, and Judit has already helped us save her. She isn't still with Amalgamated, is she?'

'No, and one of the reasons is your ward.'

Rafik raised his eyebrow over that term, but it was more accurate than 'niece' had ever been, technically speaking.

'Here's the EVA shop,' Gill said, pointing to the right.

'So it is,' Rafik said and started to move.

'Oh, no you don't,' Calum said, pushing him back down. 'I'll get it. No one's been killing me.'

'You are both wrong,' Pal said, twisting around. 'You will undoubtedly have a chit that indicates the merchandise has been paid for.' He paused to don a cap that said clearly 'Nered Messengers GmBH, Inc & Ltd' on the peak. He held his hand at the slot and Rafik slid the receipt through.

Pal got out whistling and entered the shop

while the three miners watched . . . and watched all corners for anyone watching Pal's activities. But by then he was out of the shop, still whistling, the EVA suit in its protective covering thrown over his shoulder in a careless fashion. He threw it through a barely adequate opening at the back of the van, winking as he did so, and slammed the door shut before resuming his position as driver. His forward motion could scarcely be called either furtive or fast. Clearly he was a messenger determined to increase the time of his errand for a larger fee.

Clearly he was also very adept at inconspicuous trips because, although the three miners observed the twists and turns he made, they almost did not recognize the *Uhuru* when the van stopped at its closed hatch.

Then a lot of things happened all at once: Pal Kendoro grabbed the EVA suit, jerked them out of the van when they didn't appear to move quickly enough to suit him, and said that whoever had the command to open the *Uhuru's* hatch had better activate it *right now* because 'they' were here and waiting for them.

Rafik activated it and the hatch had opened just enough for them all to get inside, even Pal, though he had to be pulled through with the suit encumbering him.

Acorna was at the pilot's controls. 'We have cleared for take-off, just as you asked, Uncle Rafik,' she said as he slid into the second seat.

'I did?'

'You did!' At the sound of his own voice so cleverly imitated, Rafik turned around to see Pal behind him. 'And I advise the most speedy departure this ship can make and an even quicker jump to these coordinates.' He laid a flimsy beside Acorna.

'Well, go ahead, Acorna,' Rafik said, waving his hand in submission.

'Where?'

'To a place of absolute safety,' Pal said, trying very hard not to stare at the slender figure with the mane of silver hair who was in control of the ship.

'I trust him,' Rafik said, uttering what would soon be added to the list Calum kept of his Famous Last Words, 'he's Judit Kendoro's brother.'

Acorna had no more than finished keying in the course than Rafik began to sneeze again. So did Calum, Gill – who tried to reach out to Pal, who held a mask over his face – and Acorna.

Seven

In the end, it was Judit who conveyed Delszaki Li's invitation to the *Uhuru* when the ship reached Kezdet. 'Pal can negotiate with the miners,' she'd pointed out, 'but if you want Acorna to come and stay with you—'

'She must,' Li insisted. 'I may not know how or why yet, but this I do believe: the *ki-lin* is vital to our goals!'

'I have met these men,' Judit said. 'They have been betrayed before; they will not entrust Acorna to strangers again. To me, perhaps, but not – forgive me – to an unknown businessman on a planet that has not treated them well.'

'Name of Li is scarcely unknown in world of business and finance,' her employer remarked dryly.

'They would probably trust your financial expertise,' Judit agreed, 'but will they trust you to care for a young girl?'

She was not entirely sure, herself, that she trusted Delszaki Li to recognize that Acorna was a little girl as well as a *ki-lin*. Pal had described her as a young woman . . . but that was ridiculous; after all, Judit had seen the child herself, only a year ago.

And, with the image of that drugged child in her mind, she was taken aback at first by the tall, slender young woman in a sophisticated deep purple body wrap and misty blue flowing skirt who greeted her when at last she received permission to board the *Uhuru*. For a moment she wondered wildly if there could be two Acornas, if this could be the mother or older sister of the child she remembered.

On her part, Acorna stared at Judit as soon as she spoke, and her silvery pupils narrowed to vertical slits.

'I think . . . I know you,' she said in confusion. 'But how?'

'She saved you from surgery at Amalgamated's space base,' Gill said. His big hand briefly enveloped Judit's; she felt a wave of warmth and security emanating from his touch. 'But you were unconscious at the time, drugged for the operation. You can't remember.'

'I remember the voice,' Acorna said. She looked thoughtfully at Judit. 'You were very much afraid . . . and very sad. You are not so sad now, I think.'

'Then it *is* you!' Judit exclaimed. 'But you were so tiny . . .'

'It seems my people mature more rapidly than do yours,' Acorna said. 'Not, of course, that we know anything about my people . . .' Her pupils

168

narrowed to slits again, then widened as she turned her silvery gaze on Judit and dismissed that subject. 'So you are Judit. Gill and Rafik and Calum have told me often of your heroism.'

'Then they have exaggerated wildly,' Judit said. 'I didn't do anything, really.'

'You will allow us to differ about that,' Gill put in, still holding Judit's hand clasped inside his.

'And you were not harmed afterwards?'

Judit smiled. 'Oh, no. They bought the hostage story . . . I think Dr Forelle had some doubts, but nobody else could quite believe that a barrio girl, even one who'd made it through university, would have the brains or independence to go against so many rules. And to keep them from thinking it, I made sure to act *very* stupid for some time thereafter. I think they were glad to get rid of me when Mr Li offered me a position as his assistant.'

'Ah, yes,' Rafik said. 'Your famous Mr Li. Pal has been telling us all about him, and his fortune, and his great plans—'

Judit felt the blood draining from her face.

'Pal, how could you?'

How *could* Pal have trusted these men with such dangerous secrets! Oh, Gill, she would trust, but these other two . . . no doubt they were good men, but Pal didn't have the right to risk the lives of children on his intuitive judgment of them.

'– plans to establish lunar mining bases on Kezdet's moons,' Rafik went on, and Judith breathed again. 'He seems very eager to give us a contract to oversee the establishment and development of the work . . . a remarkably lucrative contract to offer three independent asteroid miners.'

'As I've explained to you,' Pal cut in, 'Kezdet is a technologically underdeveloped planet. We have planetside mines, of course, but they are of the crudest sort, dependent on manual labor for nearly everything. And there is no local expertise in low-G mining. Kezdet's moons are far richer in valuable metals than the planet itself, but up to now we have lacked the capital and the technology to exploit the mines. Mr Li proposes to provide the capital, but he needs men like you to consult on all the problems of mining in space – protection from solar flares, high-friction coefficients, lack of the usual reagents for extraction, and so forth.'

'You seem tolerably well informed on the problems, anyway,' Calum remarked.

Pal flushed. 'I've studied a few vid-cubes. That doesn't make me a space mining expert. That's where you come in.'

'I should perhaps point out,' Rafik said softly, 'that hijacking our ship and taking us, unconscious, to a planet we have every reason to avoid is not the most persuasive of bargaining maneuvers.'

'Pal,' Judit said sorrowfully, 'you *could* have tried explaining to them!'

Pal's flush deepened and he rounded on his sister, palms out. 'A minute ago you thought I *had* explained to them, and I was in deep kimchee for that, too. Can't I do anything right?'

'Not with a big sister, kid.' Gill chuckled. 'Rafik, Pal, both of you calm down. Whatever the rights and wrongs of it, we're here now, and it won't hurt us to listen to Mr Li's offer . . . and personally, I'm dying to hear the explanations.'

'I think Mr Li would prefer to present his case to you personally,' Pal said, 'and he very seldom leaves his mansion. Will you trust me so far as to accompany me there, where we can discuss the matter in greater comfort?'

Gill glanced at the others, smiled wryly and shrugged. 'What the heck . . . we're already on Kezdet, how much worse can it get? Just lay off the sleep gas this time.'

'Kezdet,' Pal said somberly, 'can get much, much worse than any of you can imagine.'

Just before dawn there was a subtle change in the quality of the darkness of the sleep shed. Unrelieved blackness faded slightly, revealing the slumped outlines of what looked like piles of rags on the earthen floor. After three years working Below, Jana could sleep through the twenty-four-hour rumble and thump of the slagger, but the faint light in the shed woke her, most mornings, before the call. That was the good thing about being on day shift. Night shift, you didn't have that bit of warning. It worked today; she was on her feet, rubbing the sleep out of her eyes, when Siri Teku came through the shed with his bucket of icy water, splashing it on the heaps of rags until the children underneath stirred. He grinned at Jana and aimed the last of the bucketful at her, but she dodged so that he only got her bare feet.

'Thanks,' she said. 'I was meanin' to wash my feet today anyway.'

She dived into the corner and caught little Chiura by the arm, hauling her upright and clapping one hand across her mouth before the kid could wail and earn a slash from the long, flexible rod Siri Teku held in his other hand. The other kids knew better than to cry about a little thing like cold water, or to take too long scrambling to their feet, but Chiura was new, the only new one their gang had got from last week's intake. The others had grumbled when Siri Teku shoved her into their shed.

'How we gone keep up our allotment with babies on the soojin' gang?' Khetala demanded.

Khetala, two years older than Jana, broad-shouldered and black-browed, was the unofficial leader of their gang. She kept the rest of the kids in line with pinches, slaps, and threats to tell Siri Teku on them. But she also kept their ore carts full and the draggers moving so that they weighed in with a full allotment most shifts. That meant supper. Gangs that didn't earn supper didn't last long; the kids got tired too easily, then they couldn't keep up their allotment, they started getting sick, pretty soon the sick ones disappeared and the ones that were just puny got sold off to other gangs. Or worse, Kheti said darkly, but Jana

172

wasn't sure what could be worse than being a dragger on a gang.

'She's too little to go Below,' Jana said. Chiura's bare legs were dimpled with baby fat; her round, full face was tilted upward to Jana and Khetala as if she expected them to pick her up or something. She'd learn soon enough that there wasn't any time at Anyag for playing with babies.

'No backtalk!' Siri Teku's rod whistled against the backs of Jana's legs. She didn't jump, so he lashed her a couple more times until tears stood in her eyes. 'She's not going Below. Not yet, anyway. She can help Ganga and Laxmi sort.'

Jana and Khetala looked at each other. They needed another sorter. Siri Teku had taken Najeem away right after wake-up a couple of days ago, when he noticed Najeem's morning cough. But how were they going to teach a baby who couldn't be more than four, maybe only three, to sort ore?

'She wants to eat, she'll learn,' Siri Teku said. 'You'll teach her.' He left the shed to fetch their scanty morning meal.

Now Jana knelt beside Chiura, dipped a corner of her own kameez in the water bucket and wiped the kid's face clean. She'd been crying again in the night, there were dried tears and snot caked around her upper lip. A bruise was starting to show on her cheek.

'Who hit you, Chiura?'

Chiura didn't answer, but she glanced toward Laxmi and back, a quick, darting, furtive glance that she'd learned in this first week at Anyag. Jana glowered at Laxmi.

'The brat kept me awake with her snuffling,' Laxmi said.

'We all cried at first,' Jana said. 'You hit her again, Laxmi, and I'll break your arm. See how long Siri Teku keeps you on the gang when you can't work!' She wiped Chiura's face as gently as she could and ran her fingers through the curly dark hair, trying to work a few tangles out of the matted ringlets.

'You're wasting your time,' Laxmi said. 'She'll hafta get clipped like the rest of us, or she'll get lice. I donno why Siri Teku hasn't done it yet.'

'You mean there's something you don't know?' Jana jeered. 'An' here I thought you was the Divine Fountain of Wisdom come down to Anyag to instruct and save us all.'

Siri Teku kicked the door open and set down a round platter of bean paste just inside the shed. Beside it he dropped a stack of patts, letting them fall on the dirt so the bottom ones would be all gritty. He said it trained the kids to grab their food fast and not waste time, but Jana figured it was just meanness. She'd never seen anybody who wasn't hungry enough to bolt their patts and bean paste so fast they hardly chewed.

The first day, Chiura had wrinkled up her face and spat out the gritty patt and bean paste Jana rolled for her. She was hungrier now; she would've dived right under the trampling feet of the older kids if Jana hadn't held her back.

'It's okay,' she told Chiura. 'Kheti sees to it, there's fair shares for everyone.'

'More,' Chiura wailed when the rush had slowed and they got their patts and beans, one apiece.

'Fair shares,' Jana said firmly, but she tore her rolled patt in half and slipped it to Chiura when nobody was looking. And while the rest of the gang shuffled off to the shaft, she lingered to ask Laxmi how the baby was doing.

'Plays too much, less'n I clout her,' Laxmi said. 'Doesn't know good rock from bad. She's bringin' down our count.'

'Don't hit her,' Jana said. 'She won't learn if she's scared. Let her watch what you're doing. She'll learn.' She knelt by Chiura and hugged her. 'You'll watch Laxmi, won't you, sweetcake? Watch and learn how to tell good ore from rocks. Watch for Mama Jana.'

'Sweetcake?' Chiura repeated. 'Mama?'

'Aah, she's too dumb to know what you're saying,' Laxmi whined. 'Only way to teach her . . .' She doubled over in a silent cough. Her thin face turned dark with the effort to hush the convulsions that shook her body.

'You don't hit her,' Jana said, 'and I don't tell Siri Teku you got Najeem's cough. Deal?'

Laxmi nodded in between convulsions, and Siri Teku's rod came down across the backs of Jana's legs. This time Jana yelled good and loud, to give Laxmi a chance to let some of the coughing out. And Siri Teku was so busy telling her off for lingering behind the rest of the gang, he didn't even notice the way Laxmi wheezed for breath. She hoped.

Going Below was the part Jana hated worst, the sickening drop in the cage full of scared kids. It was usually all right, if the minder was awake and paying attention to his engine. If he let it run a few seconds too long, the cage would slam into the pit floor like a dropped basket of eggs. Coming back up was just as dangerous; an inattentive minder could drag the cage and all into the engine to be chewed up like a lump of ore in the slagger, but you didn't think about that so much – by the end of shift, all you could think of was getting Above again. Above belonged to light and flowers and Sita Ram, whom Jana imagined like a mother who smiled and hugged you close and wanted to keep you forever. Below belonged to Old Black and the Piper, and if you prayed to Sita Ram or even thought about Her, they'd maybe get angry and send one of Their messengers for you: a rock falling from the tunnel roof, a flood of water when the hewers broke through into old workings, or the stinking air that made your chest forget how to breathe.

The cage rattled to a stop, thudding on the pit floor but not falling, and the gang moved off to their places under Siri Teku's direction.

'Buddhe, Faiz, you boys are dragging for Face Three today. Watch how Gulab Rao handles the compressor, Buddhe. You're getting too big for a dragger and I just might put you to work on the face pretty soon if you show me you can get a load of ore without spraying the gallery with rock splinters. Israr, you trap for Face Three. You girls go to Five. Khetala and Jana drag, Lata trap.'

Buddhe and Faiz set off at a run down the opening that slanted down to the tunnel to Three, but Kheti called them back and made them strap on their knee and arm pads.

'Girl stuff,' Buddhe said scornfully, flexing his skinny ten-year-old arm while Kheti tried to tie on the pads she'd made out of old rags. 'When I'm a hewer, I won't fool with stupid girl stuff like padding myself.'

'Wear the pads, maybe you don't get so many cuts, maybe you live long enough to make hewer,' Khetala snapped.

Jana didn't argue about putting her own pads on. They were another of Kheti's good ideas. Other gangs, when they got new kameezes, sold the ragged bits of their old ones to a picker for a cornet of curried peas or some other luxury. Kheti made them save the old cloths to make these pads that protected their knees and elbows from the sharp rock floors of the tunnels. While the pads lasted, their gang didn't come down with half as many scrapes and cuts and infections as the other gangs. The only trouble was, they never could get enough cloth. Kheti said she was going to talk to Siri Teku some day when he wasn't drunk or angry and point out how much the pads saved them, try and talk him into giving them some extra cloth. But it could be a long time waiting until Siri

Teku was in a mood to be approached.

The hewers had been working at Five since well before first light; they went on shift and off shift earlier than the draggers, so that the kids could find full corves of ore waiting when they started work and could finish off the hewers' last production of the day before they went off shift. This morning there were three full corves waiting for them. You couldn't hear anything over the whine of the compressors, but one of the hewers – Ram Dal, it was – wasn't wearing his face mask, and Jana could guess from his scowl what he was saying to them. If the draggers got behind, then he wouldn't have an empty corf to pile his ore into, his production would go down and the gang wouldn't meet their allotment. It wasn't her and Khetala's fault that Face Five had turned into an easy vein that the hewers could strip faster than Siri Teku had expected, but they'd be the ones to get the stick if Ram Dal told Siri Teku that they were holding up the line. Jana buckled the belt about her waist, straddled the chain attached to the first corf, and set off back up the long slope of the tunnel without a word or a nod to Khetala. Halfway up the tunnel, Lata pulled the ventilation fan back so that they could drag the corves through.

'Come back soon,' she begged. 'It's dark here. I'm scared the Piper will get me.'

'Don't worry about the Piper,' Jana said as she passed. 'I left an offering for Him at the face. And we'll be back in a minute.'

It was always dark in the tunnel, and they always came back as fast as they could. Lata really was simple; you could see it in her face, the funny tilted eyes and the moon-round cheeks. She could never remember anything from one trip to the next. But being so simple, she didn't get bored and fall asleep, either. Jana liked having Lata as trapper and didn't mind saying, every trip, that she would come back in a minute.

'Liar,' Kheti whispered when they were past Lata and the hum of the fan blocked out their words. 'You never. Piper's gonna get you.'

'Huh. Piper won't want me. I'm too skinny. Piper's gonna take *you*, Kheti – your chest getting big now.'

The first trip wasn't so bad, except for being in a hurry because the hewers were getting ahead this morning. Jana figured about the third trip was the worst; by that time everything was bugging you. Your thighs ached from the pull of the loaded corf, you had scrapes on the places your pads didn't protect, the chain between your legs chafed and sweat dropped down into the chafed places and made them sting worse than ever. In some ways Jana reckoned it was better later on in the shift, when you were too tired to care, almost too tired to remember that there'd ever been anything but pulling loaded corves, tipping them into the cage basket, and drawing the empty boxes back. Finally the hewers quit for the day, and then they knew end of shift was almost there and all they had to do was clear the last loaded corves.

Then there was the creaking cage again, this time taking up draggers and trappers instead of baskets of ore, and cool clean air and the first stars of evening, and shivering because your kameez was soaked with sweat and you weren't used to the coolness. Jana helped Khetala to herd the other kids of their gang over to the pump that spewed out water from the lowest mine workings, nagged them all to pull off their kameezes and wash. The littlest ones, Lata and Israr, were so tired they were about to fall asleep, even though they had been sitting still all day instead of hauling corves. They gasped and crowed indignantly at the shock of the tepid water. That helped; Buddhe and Faiz wanted to show they were tougher than the little kids, so they splashed rowdily under the pipe. Jana and Khetala took the last wash. Faiz tried to pinch Khetala's chest and she splashed water into his eyes and everybody had a good laugh.

'I wish we had spare kameezes, and spare pads, too,' Kheti said as they trudged back to the shed. 'Then we could wash our clothes and pads and leave them to dry next day.'

'Yeah? Long as you're wishing, why don't you wish for the moon to hang in our shed and a cloud to fly through the tunnels on?'

'The better we keep clean,' Kheti said firmly, 'the less we fall sick.'

Jana didn't see the connection herself. Everybody knew that sickness was caused by annoying Old Black and the Piper so that they laid a cough in your chest. She'd been at the mines five years now, since she was only a little bigger than Chiura. Kheti was all the time setting herself up as some kind of know-it-all because she'd only come to the mines two years ago, when she was eleven already, and she claimed to know all sorts of things about the world away from the mines. But she did know a lot of good stories to tell at night, and it was true that since she'd joined them they had only lost two kids from the gang to illness. Besides, if you argued, she hit and slapped, and Jana had taken enough blows that day from Siri Teku and Ram Dal – she didn't need a fight with Kheti to finish the day off.

The sorters had come in when it got dark. They were supposed to light a fire and heat water to cook the evening beans and meal porridge, but half the time the sleep shed was dark and cold when the rest of the gang got there. This evening was one of those times. Laxmi and Ganga were bickering about whose turn it was to fetch sticks for kindling. Khetala waded in and sorted the argument with a couple of brisk slaps, sending Laxmi for kindling and Ganga to fill the bucket.

'What about *her*?' Laxmi jerked her head at the pallet where Chiura lay, chubby arms and legs flung out in exhausted sleep. 'She don't sort her share, she don't help fix the fire . . .'

'She's little,' Jana said. 'She'll learn. Give her a chance.'

'I say, if she doesn't work, she doesn't eat!'

'That's dumb,' Jana said. 'If she doesn't eat,

181

she'll just get sick. I'll help you get the dinner ready if you'll give her a share.'

Her legs ached all over from hauling corves of ore all day, but walking and carrying kindling was a different kind of work anyway. It probably did her some good to stand upright for a while. Some of the older hewers hobbled around half bent, unable to straighten up after years of lying on their sides in wet tunnels to hack out the last ore in a narrow vein.

When they got the fire going and the water began to bubble, Khetala made Laxmi stir, even though Buddhe and Faiz complained that she would cough all over their food.

'Never mind them,' Kheti told Laxmi. 'Steam's good for the breath-sickness. You stir every night for a while, and lean over the bucket while you stir, hear? Breathe in that steam.'

'Why?' Laxmi whined.

'Easy,' Jana said before Khetala could lose her temper and slap Laxmi, which was how she usually settled disagreements. 'Steam goes up, right? Sita Ram is Above, Old Black and the Piper are Below. Chest cough comes from Old Black and the Piper. Steam carries it up to Sita Ram.'

Khetala rolled her eyes but didn't argue. 'Just do it, Laxmi. Breathe the steam, and hope Siri Teku keeps you on sorting for a while and doesn't make you drag a corf.'

'Right,' Jana agreed. 'She goes Below, it'll just give Old Black and the Piper another chance to lay a curse on her.'

Jana took Chiura to sleep beside her that night. She wouldn't mind if Chiura cried, and she wouldn't hit the kid the way Laxmi did. Anyway Chiura didn't cry much; she snuggled in between Jana's arm and body and burrowed her head into Jana's armpit like a kitten butting its mother for milk. There'd been a litter of kittens once, all soft and fuzzy . . . but that was before the mines . . . Jana blinked away tears. It didn't do no good to think about before. That was the first lesson anybody learned. You were bonded to your gangmaster, Siri Teku or whoever, and he took the cost of food and clothes out of your wages and kept the rest to pay off the advance your family had gotten for bonding you, and when you were paid off, you could go home or you could stay at work and send the money back to your family. It took a long time to get paid off, though. But it must happen for some kids. Sometimes kids just disappeared, and they weren't sickly or anything, and you never saw them around the mine again, not working the other shift or working in another gang or whatever. Like Surya. She'd been a year older than Khetala, but she wasn't on the gang anymore. So she must have earned out her bond and been sent home. Jana wasn't sure what she would do when she earned out. She didn't know how to find her family. She'd been too little when they bonded her – she only knew it was a long way off. They maybe wouldn't want her back anyway; there were too many kids and not enough to eat. Maybe she'd go to the city and find some easier work.

183

Anything had to be easier than dragging corves ...
She fell into an uneasy dream of dragging bigger
and bigger corves up a worse slope than any in the
mine, with the Piper behind her dark and faceless
and threatening, and her legs jerked and twitched
all night as the overstrained muscles tried to
remember how to rest. But whenever she woke up
there was Chiura's little body warm against her,
and that was some comfort; almost as good as
having a kitten of her very own.

The miners were tense as they followed Pal into
the Li mansion, unsure what to expect. The house
was darkened against the heat of the Kezdet sun,
with cool, scented currents of air fanning though
high-ceilinged rooms. They were still blinking
with the sudden change from brilliance to
shadows when the soft whir of a float-chair
heralded Delszaki Li's arrival.

While Pal and Judit made introductions, Calum
hung back, studying the man whose power and
influence had brought them here. A wasted body
was largely concealed under stiff, brocaded robes;
all that he could see was the man's wrinkled face,
with sharp, intelligent eyes. Those eyes lit up
when Acorna was introduced, and Calum tensed.

She *is what he wants*, he thought. *The rest is just
an excuse*.

But his suspicions were lulled by the long,
intense discussion that followed the introductions
and ritual offering of food and drink. Li had
evidently studied and anticipated all their tastes;

there was Kilumbemba beer for Gill, chilled fruit juice for Acorna, and a variety of cold and refreshing drinks for Calum and Rafik. But the man was obviously eager to be done with social niceties and get on with his business; the clawlike fingers of one hand trembled over the float-chair buttons while they made polite conversation. He seemed relieved when Gill downed his beer and said bluntly, 'Now, Mr Li, we have been promised some explanations. Exactly what made you so eager to bring us here, and why are you so sure we will accept your offer?'

'Require your assistance,' Li said, 'to destroy illegal but well defended system of child slavery on this planet.'

'There are unpleasant rumors about the fate of unprotected children on Kezdet,' Rafik agreed.

'The reality,' Judit said, 'is worse than the rumors.'

Gill put one arm around her shoulders.

'And exactly how will the establishment of lunar mining bases help to eradicate the current system?' Calum demanded. 'And why *us*?'

'Second question is more easily answered than first,' Li replied. 'I have chosen you because of personal reports from Judit Kendoro, also substantiated by reading of classified files of Amalgamated. Men who will break contract and incur wrath of intergalactic company to defend one child might be willing to take some further risks to save many children.'

Calum had the feeling that Li was not revealing

all his thoughts, but then, the head of a multi-billion-credit financial and industrial empire seldom did reveal everything he was thinking.

'For answer to first question,' Li went on, 'small introduction to current system is necessary.' He paused for a moment, his bright black eyes darting around the table until he was sure that he had everyone's attention. 'Kezdet, like Saturn, eats its children. Small population of highly paid technical workers, bureaucrats, and merchants rests at top of a pyramid of underpaid and exploited human labor. And at bottom of pyramid are children – those of Kezdet, and the unwanted children of many other planets. Kezdet labor contractors visit an overpopulated, impoverished world where planetary government is already struggling to provide basic social services. They make promises of employment and education for homeless children, training in basic job skills, and the chance for a better life. Reality is sadly different. Training? Yes – employers claim child is "in training" for long years during which no wages at all are paid. Employment? Yes – as much as twenty hours a day in some cases. And education?' Li smiled sadly. 'All most of these children learn is that if they do not work, they will not eat. And they learn that lesson very well. Illiterate, half-starved, separated from their families if they ever had any, they are utterly dependent on their employer's good will. Enslaved children are backbone of Kezdet economy.'

'Child labor and slavery are both violations of

Federation law,' Rafik said. 'Surely the law applies on Kezdet as elsewhere?'

Li's smile was infinitely sad. 'Inspections are always announced in advance, to give factory owners time to hide children or pretend they are only working in allowed roles such as carrying water and snacks to adult workers. Kezdet Guardians of the Peace are paid, what you say, under the console?'

'Under the table,' Rafik supplied.

'Sometimes Child Labor League makes public some company's violation of law. But judges are also paid off. Small fine, company continues business as usual.'

'It doesn't make sense,' Calum protested. 'Adult workers are stronger and do more. I'm sure conditions are terrible for the few children who have to work, but you make it sound as though they are the entire workforce.'

'Kezdet has specialized in industries where children are especially useful,' said Li. 'In primitive mines, their small size is convenient. In glass factories, they can run faster than adults and calculate a path more intelligently than 'bots, bringing molten glass to blowers. Small nimble fingers are useful in match factories, where the sulfur poisons them, and in carpet factories where they are crippled from hours of sitting in a cramped position and half-blinded from working in the dark. Adults,' Li said dryly, 'might protest such conditions. Children provide cheap, uncomplaining labor. And Kezdet as a whole is too

187

tight-fisted and short-sighted for kind of capital investment it would take to modernize industries and improve appalling conditions. Children do here what machines do in more civilized places – and it is *always* cheaper to buy another batch of children from a labor contractor than it would be to automate a factory. System perpetuates itself. And children themselves are kept in perpetual slavery by system of financial juggling. Most bonded child laborers incapable of calculating "debt" they owe for transportation to Kezdet and fee of contractor who brought them here. As legal fiction,' he explained, 'debt is owed by adult head of child's family, if such exists. Everyone knows debt is to be paid only by child – but cannot prosecute on basis of what "everyone knows," especially on Kezdet, where entire legal and peace-keeping system is corruptly in pay of factory owners. Meanwhile, employers cheat children in every possible way, charging their food and clothing at ridiculous sums against their wages, docking them for breakages, keeping high rate of interest on original debt. While all of them think that someday they will work off their bond, very few ever achieve that.'

'I was lucky,' said Pal. 'I had a sister who won her freedom with a scholarship, then spent years working hardship posts on space stations and sending back every penny of her salary until Mercy and I were bought free as well.'

'Success of Judit required brilliance, tenacity, and luck,' Delszaki Li said. 'First element of luck was that she was not sent to Kezdet until she was fourteen, when she and Pal and Mercy were orphaned by a war that left their home planet burdened with thousands of displaced children. She fell into barrios of Kezdet later than most, with good health, a basic scientific education, and – most important of all – knowledge that a better way of life was possible. But none of that would have saved her if she had not been an exceptionally brave and intelligent young woman.'

'You don't need to tell *me* that,' Gill rumbled. 'Remind me to tell you sometime about the first time I met this girl.'

'But for every Judit who escapes the Kezdet system are hundreds of children who do not escape. Too poor, too weak, too ignorant to fight . . .'

'But what happens when they grow up?' Rafik demanded.

'Mostly,' Pal said, 'we don't. Grow up. What do you expect, with poor food, hellish conditions, no medical care? The healthiest and best-looking children are regularly bought from the labor contractors for city brothels, and even they don't last long there. The rest work until they get sick, and then they die. And the few who survive to adulthood are too weak to do much besides breed more children whom they can sell to the labor contractors for a pittance.'

Calum looked about him at the luxurious furnishings of the room where they sat: windows of high-tech Kyllian solar glass, walls draped in

189

sound-absorbing Theloi silk, an entire wall covered with shelves of expensive antique flat-books. Delszaki Li intercepted and interpreted his glance.

'No, this is not paid for by labor of children,' he said, 'although you would be hard put to find another such house in all of Kezdet.' He sighed. 'I was young and idealistic when I inherited my family's holdings on Kezdet. I swore never to employ child labor or any bonded laborers; I have devoted a lifetime to demonstrating that it is possible for business to flourish – even on Kezdet – without exploiting children. Experiment has gained me many enemies, but it has had no other effect. In recent years I have turned to more direct action. Child Labor League achieved some successes at first, but now has been made illegal by order of Kezdet government, which has accused members of terrorist action.' Li smiled. 'This means, among other things, that my contri-butions to the league are not tax deductible.'

'It also means that his house is watched, his assistants questioned, and his projects ruined wherever the corrupt Guardians of the Peace can find out what he is doing,' Pal put in.

'If this room is bugged,' Rafik pointed out, 'this entire conversation is extremely indiscreet.'

'Is indiscreet anyway,' Li said calmly, 'but I have made decision to trust you. As for other listeners, I believe my off-planet technology is still better than their off-planet technology. Guardians of the Peace are just as cheap as any other group on Kezdet; they buy second-rate espionage equipment and have it copied in barrio factories where workers do not know what they are supposed to be doing and hence make many mistakes . . . Actually, it is remarkable how many mistakes they make on contracts for Guardians of the Peace; suspicious man might think someone were alerting them and suggesting subtle ways to sabotage equipment.'

'I like the way this man thinks,' Rafik announced.

'You would,' Calum said, 'he's almost as twisty as your Uncle Hafiz.' He glanced at Li. 'No offense intended, sir.'

'If you are referring to Hafiz Harakamian,' Li said, 'no offense taken. He is brilliant man with admirably subtle mind. Your people sometimes find subtlety morally suspicious; mine do not.'

'About the mines?' Gill prompted.

'Peaceful demonstration has failed,' Li said. 'Education efforts on Kezdet have been hampered by Guardians of the Peace, who destroy com systems belonging to Child Labor League and break up schools established to teach bonded children how to read and calculate, so that they may know how much their employers are cheating them. Now I try third approach: direct action. Remove children from Kezdet. Only two problems: how to find children who have been well trained to hide from strangers, and what to do with them when found.'

'Just two little problems, huh?' Rafik drawled.

191

'You will solve second problem. Li consortium owns mineral rights to all three of Kezdet's moons, sold to me personally by stupid government officials who thought moons too expensive to mine. Not willing to make capital investment, train modern workers. Li consortium has plenty of capital. You three men have expertise. You will establish first lunar base city on primary satellite, Maganos. You three will train freed children to operate equipment. Judit will be head of school system and medical services. Children will work, but will also learn.'

Gill blinked at the scale of the project presented in these few clipped words. 'Mr Li, I think you don't realize how many trained personnel it takes to run an efficient lunar mining base. We're contract miners, independents. We know how to strip an asteroid and ship the separated metals where we'll get the most money for them. What you're proposing is a much bigger operation.'

'I know that,' Li replied. '*You* do not realize how many children are enslaved on Kezdet. I will supply personnel. You will train them.'

'It's going to be extremely expensive,' Calum warned. 'Setting up shielded living quarters, importing equipment from other systems . . . It could be years before you see any return on your investment.'

Li waved his one working hand disdainfully. 'Li consortium has capital. Initial return on investment will be lives saved. In fifty, maybe hundred years, will be fully working concern. Li descendants will be rich and happy. I will be dead, but will be one happy ancestor.'

Rafik asked Li for the chance to sleep on the proposition and Li smiled, murmuring something erudite about prudent men. Pal was designated as guide for the men while Judit took charge of Acorna.

As the three miners watched their ward make her graceful way up the anachronistic flight of stairs to the second level of this amazing house, they each experienced a sense of moment.

'She's grown up . . . all of a sudden,' Calum said plaintively.

'She belongs in a place like this,' Rafik remarked, beaming with pride at the look of her, courteously inclining her body to the shorter Judit and smiling at something said.

'She's grown out of us, that's for sure,' Gill said with a sad sigh, and then focused his attention on Judit.

She'd cried when she thought we were all dead and gone. Who'd've thought it? They'd met so very briefly. He hoped Rafik and Calum would be willing to go along with Li's scheme. He'd have a lot more chance to be with Judit and he found he wanted that, suddenly, at his time of life. Well, he wasn't *that* old, after all was said and done. Time he gave a thought to settling down. Mining was a grand life when you were young, but it was isolating and he'd had enough of the females available for short-term liaisons. Would Judit mind that he'd played around a lot? He'd been careful: always insisted on seeing an up-to-date cert before he did *anything*.

'You're right on that count,' Rafik said with a wistful expression on his face. Ah, well, they were due for a change.

Calum had entirely different thoughts, though they were centered on Acorna. They had managed to bring her to her species' maturity, or close to it. But they hadn't done what they ought to have done a long time ago: found who and where her people were. Caring for her was one thing. He couldn't fault any of them on that, but they really should now, especially with the resources available to them if they picked up on what Li was suggesting, be able to employ the experts they needed – discreetly, of course – to find her home system. They owed her family that. They owed *her* that. She was female and shouldn't be deprived of a mate because a proper member of her own species wasn't immediately available.

Pal showed them into a suite of rooms, three bedchambers off a spacious, beautifully furnished lounge, and each bedroom had its own bath facility.

'Boy! Have we come up in the world!' Calum said, pivoting on one heel with his arms wide open, taking in the luxurious appointments.

Pal smiled at such an ingenuous remark. 'You are very welcome guests. I do hope that you can find it in your hearts and minds to forgive my actions, but perhaps you see why such cautions had to be taken.'

'If Li's up against an entire planet, I suppose he's got to be doubly, triply careful,' Rafik said as he settled himself into a wide chair that immediately conformed itself to him. 'Hey, I can get to like this!'

Pal stepped to the nearest wall, pressed an ornate button, and a panel slid back to reveal not only a well-stocked bar but other supplies.

'In case you require sustenance or refreshment before the morning. In the meantime, I will wish you a comfortable night's rest. And if you have any requirements, speak into this grill and the house of Li will supply whatever you lack.'

'I believe it could,' Rafik said with a grin.

Pal left and closed the door quietly behind him.

'I think we ought to . . .'

'This is the chance of a lifetime . . .'

'Be our own bosses . . .'

They had spoken all at once and broke off, laughing. Gill and Calum found chairs, which they pulled closer to Rafik's semithrone so they could have a good natter about their amazing new prospects.

'First,' Rafik said, taking charge and ticking off the points he wanted to make, 'I think we'd be stupid not to take Li up on the offer because we're not getting any younger and mining asteroids for huge corporations like Amalgamated is no longer the wide-open, friendly game it used to be.' The others nodded. 'Exploiting the riches of a moon . . .

and nonexploiting our employees at the same time
. . . much less not having to worry about what'll
happen at our next port of call . . . I wonder . . .'
Rafik paused, '. . . if Li can find out who else is after
us and why.'

'Whaddaya wanna bet that's already being
handled?' Calum said. 'But, look, fellas—'

'Look, there must be hundreds of technies and
experienced men who're as cheesed off with
Amalgamated as we are. We take our pick of *good*
men to start this project up: builders, engineers,
environmentalists, medics . . .' Gill's eyes gleamed
with such rosy prospects. 'We could hold out for
the best there is.'

'Not to mention the fair Judit.' Rafik shot a sideways look at Gill, who blushed to the beard and
beneath.

'Now . . .'

'Ease off, Gill,' Calum said, holding up his
hands between them. 'Before we get our heads all
warped with plans, there's one other thing we *have*
to do.'

'What?' They both turned on him in surprise.

'Find out where Acorna comes from. We ought
to have done something about that a long time
ago.'

'Yeah, when we've had so much free time,'
Rafik began, and then stopped. 'That kind of
search could take a lifetime.'

'Not if Li will let us hire a metallurgic specialist
and get us the spectroanalyses of primaries.'

'*All* of them?' Even Rafik goggled at that.

'Naw, we can narrow it down,' Calum said. 'She hadn't been in that pod very long – the oxygen supply wasn't down by as much as half—'

'But she could have kept it clean,' Gill put in.

'It took a few weeks to do ours, remember,' Calum said. 'Any way, we go back to the old 'Azelnut group and use the evaluation of primaries in that area, widening the search. She can't have been from that far away. Besides which, I'll bet anything that some of her people visited Earth, or that sort of a legend wouldn't have grown.'

Gill frowned at him and waved his hand in dismissal of the idea.

'Now, wait a minute, Gill,' Rafik said, holding up one finger. 'A lot of those old legends did have bases in fact when modern science took a look at them. There's no reason Acorna's people didn't start that one. Just remember how beautifully that escape pod ... a mere escape pod ... was designed. They've been in space a lot longer than we have.'

Gill stroked his beard. 'Yeah, I guess it's possible.'

'That would be a real coup,' Rafik said. 'Furthermore,' and he settled back into his chair, locking his hands behind his head as he stretched out, 'I think Li would really go for the research.'

'At least he's respectful of Acorna,' Gill said. 'Not like others I could name,' and he shot a glance at Rafik.

'Or that awful surgeon who was going to remove the "disfigurement"?' said Calum who had never forgotten his outrage over that and by what a slim margin they had saved her. If they'd been just a fraction of a moment later . . . he shook himself.

'So we broach that tomorrow, too?' Rafik asked.

'Look, let's get an idea of what we're going to *need*,' Gill said, 'draw up a plan of attack—'

'A visit to the moon?' Rafik put in, grinning.

'Among other things.' Gill was opening cupboards to find out where the computer terminal was hidden.

Rafik removed one hand from behind his head and laid it on the edge of the table beside him. It lifted and exposed a state-of-the-art system that made him sit up and whistle. He rolled the chair around the corner of the table, toggled it on, and raised his hands over the keypads.

'Okay, what's first?'

When they had revised their order of the priorities half a dozen times and finally reached one they could all agree (mostly) on, which did include a visit to the moons, which headhunter to contact for the most essential personnel, and what Calum would require for his search, they did 'sleep' on it.

Eight

'Wake up, Jana!' Somebody was shaking her, dragging Jana out of the lovely second sleep she'd fallen into after she woke at dawn and Siri Teku didn't come. The sleep shed door was locked and nobody brought them food, so Jana went back to sleep so she wouldn't think about how hungry she was.

Kheti's face was gray with fear. Jana'd never seen her like that, not even that real bad time when Siri Teku got so drunk he was seeing demons here Above and started whipping all the kids, screaming that he would drive Old Black and the Piper out of them. Kheti'd kept her head then, helping the little kids to scramble into hiding places, making Buddhe and Faiz throw rocks to distract Siri Teku until they all got out of reach, keeping them safe until the gangmaster threw up and fell down on the ground to sleep it off. She'd taken a lash across the face that would mark her for life, but she hadn't been frozen by fear the way she was now.

'I got to get out of sight,' she whispered. 'I'm too big now, she'll take me for sure.' She tugged her ragged kameez up, trying to bunch it up over her chest where she was bumpy now but there wasn't enough fabric to cover her top and bottom, too. Buddhe snickered and pinched her on the butt, and Faiz yelled that he could see some hair that wasn't on her head.

'Who'll take you?' Jana demanded.

'Didn't you hear the whispers? Didi Badini's coming.'

Didi meant big sister. 'Your *family*?' But why wouldn't Khetala want to go with her sister? Nobody's family ever came for a kid. Only the real little ones, like Chiura, even thought it would happen.

Khetala tried to laugh. It came out like a grinding fall of rocks.

'Oh, Didi Badini's everybody's big sister, didn't you know? Piper sends her at night to take the pretty little kids, boys and girls both, and the girls that're getting too big to be draggers, like Surya . . . didn't you ever wonder what happened to Surya?'

'She worked out her bond,' Jana said slowly. 'She went home. Didn't she?'

Khetala laughed again. 'Don't you know *anything*? Nobody ever works out their bond. Does Siri Taku ever show you how much you owe, how much you're earning, how much he takes out for your keep?'

Jana hung her head. 'I don't know my numbers so good.'

200

'Well, I do,' Khetala said, 'and the first time I asked to see my records, he knocked me across the shed.' The color was coming back to her face now, her eyes sparkling; she loved to instruct people. 'The second time, he said I'd have to come to his room, he kept the datacubes there. Huh! He didn't even have a reader. Had somethin' else he wanted to show me, though. So I know all about what Didi Badini's coming for.'

'You said she comes at night. It's not night.'

'I can't help that. Dunno why she's coming in the daytime this time, but I heard the whispers. Besides, why else would Siri Teku keep us locked in here? Missing a half day's shift work, we are.'

Khetala's fear was infecting Jana, but she didn't want to show it. She yawned and turned over on her side.

'So what? Me, I get a chance to sleep, I'll take it . . . Besides, whatever Didi Badini wants kids for, can't be worse than this place.'

'*Can't it?* She works for the Piper, dummy.'

'Piper's a story to scare kids down Below.' Or maybe not. But they were Above now, even if they had been locked in the sleep shed since before dawn. They were in Sita Ram's realm of sky and sun. Piper couldn't have power here.

'Piper's real, and he takes kids to the bonk-shops in the city. You catch worse things than chest-cough that way, too. You get the burnies, and the scale, and if they don't kill you by doing it to you too much, then your nose falls off and your

201

crotch rots and they throw you out on the street to beg.'

'How do you know all that?'

'I know what Siri Teku did to me in his room,' Khetala said, 'and I got away from Ram Dal a couple of times when he wanted to do the same. And I been in the city, too, before my mum died and her boyfriend sold me here. You can see the beggars all over the place . . . and pictures of kids outside the bonk-shops. Why do you think she takes the prettiest kids? And Siri Teku and the other gangmasters, when a girl gets too tall to drag, they practic'ly give her to Didi Badini . . . and I'm going to be tall. You'll be okay for a while, Jana, you've been living on patts and bean pasta since you were a baby, you'll always be a little shrimp. Me, I had eleven years of good food and standing up straight before I came here. I've got big bones. I won't be able to drag much longer. You know that.'

Jana nodded slowly. Sometimes Kheti got stuck in the narrowest tunnels, the ones leading to Face Three. That was one reason she usually worked Five now. And if she grew much more, she wouldn't be able to get through the low pitch on the tunnel from Five.

'You're not pretty, though,' she said slowly. 'Not since . . .'

Kheti rubbed the pink weal that crossed her right cheek.

'I know. But I'm big. That's bad enough. If I thought gettin' my face messed up would keep

Didi Badini from takin' me, I'd go stand by the compressor and let the flying chips cut me to pieces. But that won't make me small again.'

A new fear struck Jana. 'Chiura!' Her face was burning up, but her hands felt icy cold. 'She wouldn't take . . .'

'I reckon that's why Siri Teku didn't clip her curls,' Khetala said. 'He never figured to train her for a sorter. She's a little sweetcake of a kid, specially the way you been keeping her washed and her hair combed so good. He figured it was worth feeding her for a few weeks, then sell her to Didi Badini. He'll make lots of creds off that one. He won't get much for me though. Maybe if I can keep out of sight . . .'

Jana didn't hear the rest. She darted to where Chiura was playing with a pile of cast-off rocks and snatched her up, ignoring the baby's wails of protest.

'Come on, sweetcake. We got to get you fixed up good for the visitors. Faiz, give me your knife.'

Faiz rolled his eyes. 'Who me? Got no knife, got nothing.'

'I seen you stroppin' that bit of steel,' Jana said. 'Give it here. You can have it back when I'm through.'

'You going crazy,' Faiz said. 'Old Black eating your brain.'

But he fumbled in his pallet and came up with a thin band of metal, gleaming sharp along one edge and rusty dull on the other.

Chiura cried when Jana pulled her hair to hack

203

off the curls, and she'd only got one side of the kid's head when they heard steps outside.

'Sita Ram, help me!'

Jana rubbed her hands in the dirt and smeared it over Chiura's face. The tears and snot mixed with the dirt until Chiura's round little face looked truly revolting. Jana rubbed some more dirt into the long ringlets she hadn't had time to cut, spat on the dusty hair and patted it into muddy strings that hung down over the side of Chiura's face. That was good – she looked almost ugly now, probably worse than if Jana'd had time to finish cutting her hair. She tossed the knife back toward Faiz and pushed Chiura into a corner.

'You sit there and *don't make a noise*!' she hissed at Chiura.

The little girl pulled her knees up and sat rocking back and forth, eyes wide. She was probably scared to death that 'Mama Jana' had been so rough with her. All the better, if it would keep her quiet.

'I'll give you a honey sweet when they're gone,' Jana whispered, though she had no idea where she'd get one. 'Just keep quiet now, Chiura, sweetcake, you don't want them to notice you.' She squatted in front of Chiura, shielding her with her body.

There was a clanking noise – that would be Siri Teku unlocking the door. Then light flooded in. It was full day. Jana felt a cold sweat of fear over her body. She didn't want to believe in Kheti's panic, but Siri Teku had to have some good reason for 'wasting all this work time. Time was credits, he always said, and here he'd lost a lot of time keeping them in the shed – how much she hadn't realized until the door opened and she saw all that light. The golden rectangle of the open doorway hurt her eyes; she had been working day shift so long she couldn't remember when she'd last seen so much sunlight. It had to be something big to make it worth his losing all those hours at work. Just for a moment she believed all Kheti's horror tales about Didi Badini, and more, too.

The man and woman who followed Siri Teku into the shed didn't look evil, though. The man was a pinch-faced little gray fellow, no fangs or nothing, so Jana reckoned he couldn't be the Piper. And she didn't have much attention to spare for him after she caught sight of the woman. She was the most beautiful thing Jana had seen since she'd been brought to Anyag as a bondchild. To begin with she was clean, with no dust dulling the sheen of her smooth brown skin. And instead of being skinny and bony, she was plump and solid. And her *clothes*! The kameez was all pink and gold, and it was made of something so light and gauzy that it seemed to float over her body and caress her full curves like a cloud of butterflies; below the gold-embroidered hem of the kameez Jana could see the cuffs of deep pink shalwar, half hidden under gold anklets. Without meaning to, Jana made a small sound of longing and reached out, then snatched her hand back. She wanted to feel the fine stuff of the kameez, but she'd get it dirty. She was just a dirty little girl of the mines and Siri Teku would beat her if she messed up this fine lady. *Maybe she'll take* me, Jana thought, *and I'll wear silk shalwar under my kameez and eat every day and . . .*

Didi Badini's eyes met Jana's for a moment. The eyes were not beautiful like the rest of her; they were cold and dark and hard, as if Old Black had sneaked up Above to look through the beautiful lady's face. And when she saw the eyes, Jana remembered seeing Didi Badini before. Only she'd thought it was a dream. She'd come at night last time, inspecting the children by lamplight. Jana had rolled over and buried her head in her pallet, too tired to care about the dream-people talking and moving the lamp; in the morning Surya had been gone.

'Too skinny, too plain,' Didi Badini said now to Siri Teku. 'If that's your best, you're wasting my time.'

'I've a big girl here, getting too big to drag the tunnels. Where's Khetala?' Siri Teku demanded of the children.

Jana hadn't noticed where Khetala had gone, she'd been too busy with Chiura. But Israr's eyes flicked toward the corner farthest from the door, where several pallets of rags seemed to have been heaped up together, and simple Lata said, 'She's playing hidey, but I saw her.'

Siri Teku kicked the pallets with all his force. Something gasped. He reached into the heap of rags, fumbled for a moment, and pulled out Khetala by one arm.

'She won't want me,' Khetala sobbed. 'I'm too ugly. Look!' She stood in the sun and turned her face up so that the pink weal crossing one cheek showed.

'Mmm,' said Didi Badini. 'Stand still, girl.' She ran one hand over Khetala's chest, felt her buttocks, and reached in between her legs. 'Marked *and* used,' she said. 'And no more use here, as you said yourself. I'll take her as a favor.'

'She still owes on her bond,' Siri Teku said.

Didi Badini looked amused. 'Don't they all?'

She and Siri Teku haggled for a moment and agreed on a sum in credits that left Jana gasping.

'No! I won't go!'

Siri Teku had let go of Khetala to wave both his hands during the bargaining; now she ducked between the adults and made for the door. Didi Badini's fat brown arm flashed out, quick as a snake, and caught the fat braid of dark hair that hung down Kheti's back. Kheti hit the floor on her knees, only the hand on her braid holding her upright.

'Please,' she sobbed. 'I'm ugly, see, you don't want me.'

Didi Badini's smile was full of Old Black. 'Some of my clients like them that way,' she told Kheti. 'You'll have more marks soon enough.' She nodded at Siri Teku. 'Put the fight out of her. I'm not wrestling a screaming cat all the way back to Celtalan.'

Siri Teku casually punched Kheti on the side of the head. Her head bobbed limply from the braid that Didi Badini still held. He hit her again and her whole body hung limp. Didi Badini let go the braid and Kheti fell onto the mud floor. Siri Teku slung her over his shoulder and carried her out the door.

'That is not what I came here to see,' the gray man said in a voice like dry leaves blowing in the winter wind.

'Your mister told me there was something worth coming here for,' Didi Badini said to the rest of the children. 'Where is it? A pretty child, he said, something really special, and too young to be worth training for work.'

Jana looked at the floor. Maybe if she didn't look up, if she didn't see Old Black peeping out of Didi Badini's eyes, maybe the woman wouldn't see her and wouldn't question the way she was crouched awkwardly in front of the corner where Chiura sat.

'Was it you he meant?' Didi Badini tipped up Faiz's head with one finger under his chin. 'Sweet brown eyes, but the teeth are hopeless and you look old enough to be a good worker. Not you.' She moved on to Lata, who looked up with a vacant smile and tried to focus her one good eye on Didi Badini. 'If he meant this one, he's wasting my time.' Her chubby brown feet moved on with a tinkling of the little gold bells that were attached to her golden sandal straps, until she stood in front of Jana. 'Look at me, child!'

The sweet cloud of perfume that wafted from the folds of Didi Badini's kameez almost choked Jana, it was too much, too sweet.

'Nice,' said a little voice behind her. 'Pretty.'

'Ahhh,' Didi Badini breathed on a long satisfied sigh. She bent and took Jana by the nape of the neck. Her fingers were surprisingly hard and strong; she threw Jana onto her side without even breathing hard. 'So this is the prize.'

'Pretty lady,' Chiura said, looking up. She grasped Didi Badini's kameez with muddy fingers.

'A lovely child, indeed, if she were clean.'

'No,' Jana gasped, coming up to her knees and pushing Chiura back. 'No, lady, you don't want her, she's simple, and sick already, she's got a bad sickness, she'll make you sick, too.' If only Kheti were there, Kheti who knew so many words and knew all about the city! She'd be able to think of a good story. But Kheti was gone, head lolling against Siri Teku's back, sold to the pretty lady with Old Black in her eyes and her smile.

'Don't talk nonsense, girl.' Didi Badini slapped Jana aside with a backhanded blow. Her hands were covered with rings; the ornate settings cut Jana's cheek. 'I suppose you're the one who tried to make her ugly? A right mess you've made of her, too, half cutting her hair and all that mud. But I can still tell she'll clean up fine. You come with Didi Badini, little one,' she crooned to Chiura. 'Come and live in the city, sleep on silk and have sorbet to drink every day.'

Chiura lifted her muddy arms to Didi Badini, then looked over her shoulder. 'Mama Jana?'

'Your mister will take care of Mama Jana,' Didi Badini said. 'She's not coming with us. Not this time.' The cold black eyes flicked a scornful glance over Jana, sitting on the mud with blood running down her grimy face. 'Maybe the mister will give her away when she gets too big for a dragger.'

'No. Don't take her. *Please*,' Jana begged. Siri Teku had come back in; she clasped his knees. 'I'm teaching her to sort, she'll be a good worker, I'll take care of her, she won't be any trouble.'

Siri Teku kicked Jana away. His boot landed in her stomach and knocked the air out of her. She lay on the floor and listened to her own breath whistling like something far away and unimportant, while Chiura babbled in Didi Badini's arms and somebody counted out credits. Then Didi Badini and the silent gray man were gone with Chiura. And Siri Teku had raised his cane.

'I'll teach you to try and hide my stock,' he said before the first blow landed, burning across Jana's chest.

There was something about waking up on a planet that always excited Acorna. Maybe it was the flavor of the air: not dead-pure as on the ship, but mixed with an infinite variety of scents and the tantalizing hint of exotic goodies to eat – tender new leaves, sweet crunchy roots, hectares of grass blowing in the wind instead of the carefully tended blades grown for her in the ship's 'ponics system. This morning she woke with her head filled with vague dream-images of a sunny garden

210

full of flowering shrubs and the music of trickling streams . . . and another music, too, from little animals that danced in the tree-tops and sang in sweet harmony. Was that a real place, or something she had concocted in her dream? The images were so strong, she could almost imagine they were a true memory of something she had seen when she was a child. A long, long time ago, because she'd been quite small in the dream/memory . . . before Nered, before Greifen, before Theloi, even before Laboue . . . hadn't there been a garden where the grass was soft and blue-green, and a pair of arms that held her up to see the singing-fuzzies? But when she tried to chase down the elusive memory, it vanished like a bubble on the water, leaving her with only the feeling that nice things happened on planets if you went for a walk in the early morning.

There was some vague discomfort and guilt associated with the clearer memory of the gardens on Laboue with their singing stones, though. Hadn't Rafik and Calum and Gill been angry with her for going out? Oh yes – she had forgotten to wear those robes that were supposed to cover up her horn. Well, she'd been a silly baby then. She was grown up now. They'd said so last night. And she certainly knew better than to make *that* mistake again!

Feeling quite proud of her forethought, Acorna donned not only the clinging body wrap and long skirt Gill now insisted she wear, but also a scarf of filmy green to match the skirt which could be draped casually across her head so that instead of a horn, she seemed only to have a bouffant hair style from which a few silver curls escaped. Thus fully prepared, she slipped out of the mansion where they'd been brought by skimmer and prepared to explore Kezdet's capital city of Celtalan in her own way, by walking.

The restricted life of a mining ship left Acorna with few chances to stretch her long legs. She worked out daily in the ship's exercise room – exercise *closet* was more like it, she thought, admiring the broad open spaces before her – but it wasn't the same as having a good run on nice hard-packed dirt.

Not that the immediate prospect from Delszaki Li's house offered any good opportunities for a run. Already, early though it was, the open space between rows of town houses was filled with people in skimmers darting back and forth on urgent errands. They flew low, obviously not expecting to have to dodge pedestrians, and Acorna prudently kept to the narrow stone-covered strip alongside the houses. She congratulated herself on her intelligence and forethought in keeping away from the skimmers. Gill and the others were all wrong when they said she didn't know how to take care of herself dirtside. True, she'd never been alone on a planet before. She'd gone out only on those carefully chaperoned shopping trips where they stopped to sell their payloads. But how dangerous could it be? This wasn't like EVA from the *Uhuru*, where a slight mistake could leave you without air to breathe or send you spinning dizzily away from the ship into space. Planets were *easy*; they had gravity and atmosphere. What more did she need?

But this part of this planet was boring – row after row of faceless walled houses with metallic grills across their windows, and the only people awake were locked away in their skimmers and darted past her with no chance for interesting conversations. Acorna raised her head, looking to the horizon for something more amusing, and her sensitive nostrils caught a whiff of something green and growing not too far away. She followed the scent along stone pedestrian strips, her feet clacking on the smooth-worked stone, until she reached its source.

Though Acorna did not know it, the Riverwalk was Celtalan's glory of city planning – at its western end – and its shame at the eastern end, where the river that gave the park its name had long been allowed to degenerate into a polluted, half-choked stream. She entered by the arches cut through hedgerows on the western side of Celtalan, where everything was neatly manicured and controlled to a fare-thee-well. The view through the first arch gave the illusion of spacious countryside with rolling hills; it was only after Acorna had walked through the entranceway that she realized how clever landscaping and tricks of perspective had made this park surrounded by city buildings seem so much larger than it really was. Little streams (carefully purified before they were guided into their preformed channels) trickled over miniature waterfalls of moss-covered boulders; half-size gazebos and follies, perched atop grassy mounds, gave the illusion that one was looking down vistas of limitless space laid out by a landscape architect of infinite means. Acorna beguiled half an hour in a flowering maze before the sweet smell of the fresh green buds next to the flowers became unbearably tempting. Rafik and Gill had impressed upon her strongly that it was considered a social faux pas to eat other people's gardens. If she went back to the big house, that nice Mr Li would probably find her something she could eat. But she wasn't tired yet, and at the far side of the maze she could see that the careful landscaping of the Riverwalk began to degenerate into something wilder and less carefully manicured. Instead of the gravel path that hurt her feet, there was a path of hard-packed earth, a perfect surface for running on . . . Acorna glanced around, saw no other early risers who might be surprised or offended by her actions, and carefully kilted up her long flowing skirts to above her knees. After all, she assuaged her conscience, she had only promised Gill that she would *wear* the skirt; she was still doing that, wasn't she?

Two Kezdet Guardians of the Peace, observing the park from overhead scanners, saw the tall girl take off at a galloping run down the dirt path that led to the river on the eastern edge of the Riverwalk Park. They shrugged and continued sipping their morning kava. Most members of the wealthy techoclass who inhabited the west-side mansions knew better than to go anywhere east of the river without an armored skimmer and armed bodyguards. Doubtless this girl would turn back before she reached the river bridge. And if she didn't – well, there might be a reward in it for them if they got her out of trouble and saw her safely home. Before she got into trouble, there was no reason to bestir themselves.

Pounding down the dirt path, her horn-covered feet landing solidly on the earth, Acorna felt more alive than she could ever remember. Some atavistic instinct deep inside her told her that *this* was what she was born for – not the sterile confines of a ship, but long glorious runs up grassy slopes and down the other side, effortless leaps over the ragged brambles that impeded her way after she left the path, the morning breeze blowing through her tangled curls. The blood throbbed in her veins and she increased her speed until she felt as though she were flying over the grass and bushes, flying down a long weed-infested downhill slope . . .

The same instincts that had urged her into a run saved her from a fall into the stinking river at the bottom of the slope. Without consciously thinking about the obstacle, she shortened stride, collected her balance, and launched herself from the bank in a long, glorious arc that carried her safely over the ten-foot expanse of stinking, gray-green water.

On the far bank the park ended abruptly and the expanses of pavement resumed, but with a difference. Instead of long regular rows of tall, faceless houses there were clusters of humbler dwellings, with dirt paths winding off between the buildings. Instead of businessmen in skimmers, the main road was full of people: stalls and carts selling bangles and snacks and fruit and vegetables, a knife grinder squatting in the corner made by two mud walls, a huddle of street urchins playing some game that involved mad rushes in pursuit of something Acorna couldn't quite see. She grinned happily. This was *interesting*. She would explore a little, get an apple or some other snack from one of these stalls, and be back at the house before anybody else woke up.

Overhead, in the scanner tower, one of the Guardians of the Peace nudged the other one. 'D'you see that?'

'See what?'

'That girl. She jumped the river!'

'You've been burning too many happy-sticks,' grunted his partner. 'River may be down to a miserable trickle, but it's still too wide to jump. Besides, why would anybody take the risk of falling in there when there's a perfectly good bridge upstream!'

'Maybe she didn't want to detour. Maybe she didn't want to explain her business to the bridge guards. This could be interesting. Let's take out a skimmer and follow her.'

The fried meat pies being hawked from the first rolling stall didn't appeal to Acorna, but the second wagon held a tempting display of fruits and vegetables . . . rather more tempting from a distance, she realized with regret, than on closer inspection. The apples were soft and wrinkled, the madi-fruits covered with brownish spots.

'Do you not have anything fresh?' she demanded of the owner.

'All fresh, gracious lady, picked just this morning from my cousin's farm.'

'Huh!' the meat pie seller grunted, just audibly, 'just fell off the back of your cousin's skimmer, more likely.'

Acorna did not wish to get embroiled in the men's bickering. She pointed at random to a cluster of ruta roots. They looked slightly limp, but ruta aged well, and they'd be something to nibble on while she walked back through the park. She tasted one while the stall-keeper wrapped the others in a scrap of plastifilm for her; the insides, at least, were still sweet and crunchy.

'That'll be five credits,' the stall-keeper said, holding out the package.

From the way his neighbor's eyebrows shot up, Acorna guessed that she was being charged at least double the going rate for a bundle of slightly overage rutas. But that wasn't important. What *was* important was that this blasted skirt had no pockets, and she hadn't been thinking of money when she left the house that morning.

'Charge it to the account of my guardian, Delszaki Li,' she said.

The stall-keeper's face turned ugly. 'Look,

techie, we don't run charge accounts this side of the river. Credits in hand is my rule.'

'Then keep the rutas,' Acorna said, 'they weren't that fresh anyway.'

'You'll pay me for the one you've eaten! I been robbed already once this morning by one of them thieving street brats, I'm not having some techie come along and make a free meal off my stall on pretense of sampling the goods!'

'Hey, Punja, we got the little thief for you!' called one of the street urchins whose game Acorna had noticed just before she inspected the stall.

Now, with a sinking heart, she realized that the quarry in their 'game' was not a youngling from their group, but a much smaller child, bruised and bleeding from a cut lip, who struggled madly as the larger boys hauled her bodily toward the stall.

'And a lot of help that is,' Punja snarled, 'you can tell by looking that she hasn't a clipped credit to pay me back.'

'What did the child take?' Acorna interrupted.

'Three of me best madi-fruits. Gobbled them down on the run, she did. I suppose you'll be wanting that placed to the account of your guardian, too, will you?' the man asked Acorna with heavy sarcasm.

'You could give us a reward for catchin' her,' one of the boys holding the child grumbled.

'What good's it to me that you caught the brat? You can give her a good beatin' if you like, teach her not to steal from respectable merchants,' Punja

218

suggested. 'That should be enough reward for you. Have a little fun before you turn her loose.'

The boy's heavy-browed face lit up with an expression of sickening glee, and he slammed a fist into the child's stomach before Punja had finished speaking.

'That's just for starters,' he told the gasping, white-faced child. 'Now you can come along wif me and me mates and see if you haven't got something to pay us back for our effort.'

'Scrawnier'n a bondworker,' one of his pals demurred.

'But free,' the first boy pointed out, 'or did you suddenly get rich enough to patronize a bonkshop, huh? Now me, I'm . . .'

He never got a chance to finish articulating his philosophy of life. All that had delayed Acorna's intervention was the need to tuck her flowing skirt farther out of the way. Now she executed another leap from her perfectly balanced standing position, came down with one foot on the first boy's stomach and swung the other to crunch into his mate's nose. Rather pleased with the results of her self-defense classes with Calum, she recovered her balance and pulled the starving child up by one wrist while the rest of the gang of boys, seeing what had happened to their biggest and strongest members, melted away into the network of dirt paths behind the main thoroughfare.

'You,' she told the child, 'had much better come with me. No one shall beat you again.'

The child struggled feebly and tried to pull away from Acorna's hand.

A skimmer settled in the dusty roadway, and two uniformed Guardians emerged.

'What's all this?' the first one out demanded.

A chorus of voices informed him, variously, that the girl was a techie out to make trouble on the wrong side of the river; that the child was a thief and ought to be bonded to honest labor; that the girl was a foreigner who had viciously attacked two innocent boys who just happened to be standing by the stall.

'And who's to pay for the damage to my stock?' wailed the stall-keeper, virtuously holding up a handful of bruised fruit which he reckoned he could blame on Acorna's part in the brief fracas.

'My guardian, Delszaki Li, will cover all charges,' Acorna said.

'Aye, she keeps naming Li, as if she thought the sound of his name would carry all before!' said the stall-keeper virtuously. 'Y'ask me, she ought to be confronted with Li himself. If, as is no more than I suspect, she's lying, he'll know how to deal with impostors. Why don't you make her go there now?'

'I should like nothing better,' declared Acorna, 'but this little girl comes with me!'

'You'd best be telling the truth,' one of the Guardians warned her, 'Kezdet doesn't treat impostors and thieves lightly. Maybe you'd rather step off with me and we'll ... ahh ... see if we can't work something out, hmm?' He eyed the long shapely legs, which were by now almost fully exposed by the way Acorna had tucked up her skirts for battle. Strange kind of furry stockings the girl wore under the skirts . . . some new techie fashion, no doubt. Never mind, he'd soon have those off her.

'Not without me, you don't go nowhere!' the stall-keeper interrupted. 'I got a right to me damages.'

Acorna's prompt willingness to call on Delszaki Li had given him second thoughts. If the girl *was* telling the truth, he should be able to get more 'damages' out of Li than his entire stall was worth; Li was far beyond the need to count credits when appeasing a poor man.

Nine

No one had yet missed Acorna when the two Guardians of the Peace brought her back to the Li mansion, one holding Acorna's left elbow firmly in his right hand, while she supported the waif against her with her right arm, Punja dancing behind this quartet. None of the street children had been able to keep up with the skimmer as it set about on its lawful errand, but they followed as far as they could: right up to the rancid water.

'Jeesh, how'd she get across this?' the leader of the group wanted to know. 'She dint come by the bridge, like.'

One of Delszaki's many discreet servants peered through the spy hole before exclaiming and calling for the nearest girl to summon the master. Trouble was on the doorstep. Then he flung the door open, kowtowing before Acorna until his nose nearly touched his knees.

'Missy, missy, why are you here? You have not arisen from your bed as yet,' he said, bobbing in his consternation.

'Will you please inform Mr Li that I am here and not in my bed and need him. If he is in his bed, I am truly sorry to disturb him . . .'

Pal and Judit came down the massive stairway as if it had turned into a slide.

'Acorna!' cried Judit, and then exclaimed more loudly when she saw the bedraggled girl Acorna was protecting.

'Mr Li is on his way this very moment, Guardians,' Pal said, gesturing for them to enter. 'If you will be so good as to step inside . . .' and, with a very deft push of his rear against the front door, Pal closed it right in the stallkeeper's face.

Oblivious to the howls outside and imprecations which could be heard, if muted, through the thick panels of the door, Pal courteously guided the Guardians of the Peace, who were exchanging bemused and gratified glances, while Acorna was trying to get the child's arms from around her neck so that Judit could take charge. The child was moaning and weeping in the desperate way of her age: all the more effective since such 'lost' noises demonstrated that she had been bereft of comfort for long enough not to expect any to come her way.

'You know this . . . this . . . person,' the first Guardian said, for by now the kerchief on Acorna's head had been pulled off and the distinctive horn was visible.

'Of course we know her,' Pal said so stoutly that both raised hands in defense of their query. 'She is the Lady Acorna, beloved ward of Mr Delszaki Li, who is surely known to the Bureau of Guardians . . .'

'Indeed he is, and very generous he is to our retirement and the vacation funds,' the second man said, bobbing not unlike the doorman but not as deeply, as much because he couldn't have folded his paunch as because Guardians are not supposed to show respect to any but their superiors.

'Are you all right, Acorna?' Pal asked, taking her by the arm and leading her to the nearest chair. She looked very shaky indeed to him. 'Where did you go? Why have they brought you back?' he whispered.

'I wanted to run on the grass,' she said in a very tiny voice.

Just then Rafik, Calum, and Gill entered the room, having obviously thrown on the nearest clothes to hand.

'Now, Guardians, just what is the problem?'

'Well, the . . . the . . . female there . . . said she was Mr Li's ward and she got into a bit of a spot, so we thought we'd better check it out.'

'You mean, you did not believe the word of a gently bred girl who is obviously well dressed and clearly not the sort of person who gets into spots?' Rafik said, but the look he shot Acorna indicated to her, at least, that he was going to have a few choice words with her.

She got very interested in brushing the dirt off her hands and then her arms. She could do little about the stains on her lovely skirt right now, but she did straighten her head covering. Not that it mattered.

Delszaki Li appeared in his float-chair, and so the reception room became quite cramped.

'Now, Acorna, my dear, why did you go out without someone to escort you wherever you wished to go?' He turned to the Guardians. 'Cordonmaster Flik and Constable Grez, what seems to be the trouble?'

In the background, someone was kicking the door steadily. To the rhythm of the blows, Cordonmaster Flik, who was extremely gratified to realize that Mr Li knew both his name and that of his partner, explained the circumstances. Since the cameras on the exterior of the house had taken pics of the two Guardians and their identities had been verified by Central Guard Headquarters, the knowledge surprised only the two Guardians.

The matter was shortly resolved and Punja paid exactly what his merchandise was worth – and the look given him by Pal as he handed over the half credits made Punja very certain that this was not the person to haggle with – and sent his way. A junior servant very quickly appeared to remove the scuff marks of Punja's plastic shoes on the fine wood of the door so that when the Guardians, invited to have some refreshment, left, there was no mark remaining of the morning's fuss. They also left with sufficient credits, yet not too many, to ensure that the incident would be 'suitably' reported in their log as a 'lost child returned to her home.'

'Whatever possessed you, Acorna?' Rafik demanded when the Guardians had been sent on their way, well, but not overly, paid for their rescue work.

'I wanted to run on the beautiful grass,' she said, gulping back a sob.

'Now, now.' Judit was back and slid into the seat beside her. 'It's all right, dear. No one is mad at you. Just terribly upset that you had such a fright.'

'I wasn't exactly frightened,' Acorna said, raising her delicate chin, her eyes slits of remorse, 'I was furious to see a little child beaten like that for taking damaged fruit.' She had clenched her fists and brought them down so hard on her knees that Calum winced. 'Where is she? She was so terribly frightened and hurt and hungry.'

'She's fine, dear,' Judit said. 'She's being fed, carefully, because she hasn't had any food in quite a few days and to eat too much would be unwise. Then we shall bathe her and make sure she sleeps. Although,' and Judit's delightful laugh eased the tension in the room, 'I have a suspicion that once her tummy is full, she will fall asleep before we can clean her up.'

'So why did you go out? Why so early? Didn't you know how dangerous it is out there?' Calum demanded. He turned to the rest of them. 'She's not *stupid*; I've never seen anybody pick up the basic concept of Fourier transforms so fast. I can't understand why she would do such a stupid thing.'

'How would she know Kezdet could be dangerous?' Gill leapt to her defense. 'She's never been
planetside for more than a day or two, and always
with one of us.'

'The park was beautiful,' Acorna said. 'It was
like the one in my dreams . . .' She realized that was
a lame excuse. But maybe no one would realize
that the park was so far from the house that she
couldn't have known about it when she ventured
out.

'Your dreams?' asked Mr Li in a coaxing voice
and waved Rafik and the others away. 'You men,
stop harassing the child. You will make her more
afraid of you than of Kezdet!' While Calum and
the other men took the seats he indicated at a good
distance from Acorna, he turned his attention back
to her. 'Tell me about these dreams . . . while Judit
fixes you a refreshing drink. I think you may need
one.'

Judit handed her the glass and she was grateful
because her throat was dry.

Acorna sipped something cool and green and
tangy and then told him about the dream,
and how the park had seemed so like it.

'At least the first part of the park where it was
truly lovely,' she said, ending lamely.

'No, we will not try regression, Mr Li,' Judit
said suddenly. 'The method produces enough
problems with cortices we are beginning to understand.'

'It was but a thought.'

'I think her . . . adventure, though, has proven a

227

thing or two to the others,' Judit said, smiling at her employer.

'Has it? Well, that is advantage then,' and he leaned over to pat Acorna's arm, below the mud. 'No action without some profit, if the eye can see it. You rest now, later we talk again.'

Acorna stood. 'I am very sorry for any trouble I caused.'

'Must make errors in order to learn,' Mr Li said understandingly and pulled his float aside so she could leave the room.

'Do you need any assistance, Acorna?' Judit asked gently.

She shook her head. Distress still narrowed her pupils to vertical slits. 'I must think. It is sad . . . I have never seen such terribly poor people.'

The two watched her make her way in slow repentant steps up the stairs and to her quarters.

'Reality has touched Acorna,' Delszaki said with a heavy sigh of regret.

'*Ki-lins* must know of reality, sir,' Judit said as gently as she had spoken to Acorna.

'A rude awakening,' and he sighed again.

'She had healed the child,' Judit added. 'I hope that the Guardians of the Peace did not notice.'

'They have been taken care of,' Delszaki said. 'Their interest has been redirected into useful paths.'

'So what is next to be done?'

'Meet with the miners and discuss the Moon Project and this dream world of Acorna's.'

*   *   *

228

It was Delszaki who noticed that Rafik and Gill did most of the talking, while Calum seemed more intent on covering the notepad in front of him with light-pen doodles: most of which were primaries with satellites whirling around them in impossible astronomical patterns.

'What is it that you see in those patterns, Calum Baird?' Delszaki asked, pausing the conversation on double domes versus linked units.

Calum sat straight up and pretended he had been listening to every word said. Rafik glared at him, but Gill looked surprised at his inattention. Last night he'd been full of good suggestions.

'I think we have got to find Acorna's home world first,' he said, letting the sentence out in a rush, then he colored as redly as Gill could.

'How can we possibly find what the child only remembers as a dream?' Delszaki asked.

'But she does remember something. I was just thinking . . .' and he ran dots on the primaries, 'that every star has its own spectroanalysis. And every star throws out satellites, if they do generate planets, that are made up of their constituents. Maybe a bit more metal on that one, maybe just gases on another, but if you knew what metals a primary had to disperse, you could find the right one,' he waved a hand heavenward, 'and find Acorna's.'

Rafik shook his head. 'There's not enough difference in constituents. Stars are all basically made of the same stuff – at least, all the ones that generate Earth-type planets are going to look pretty much alike to spectroanalysis. Certainly they'll all have the conventional metals.'

'The pod Acorna came in,' Calum said stubbornly, 'is *not* composed of conventional metals. Not entirely, anyway. We never did figure out exactly what-all was in the alloy, but it's not like anything we – humans – use for space and industrial construction. Lighter. Stronger.' He waved his hands. 'I'm a mathematician, not a physicist. It's worth studying, don't you think?'

'You have original spacegoing container?' The fingers of Li's left hand tensed over the com pad on his chair. 'And you have not mentioned the artifact before?'

'Well, it scarcely came up in conversation, after all,' Calum said apologetically. 'We always *meant* to study it one day.'

'Ah, well, it takes but a little arrangement . . .' and, even as Delszaki turned to Pal, the young man was tapping out an access code, '. . . to make appointment to discover what we may from it.'

Actually, it took considerably longer because Rafik, Gill, Calum, and Pal had to bring a collapsible crate to the *Uhuru* so that anyone watching would not see what they were unloading. Of course the vehicle Mr Li could put at their disposal for the transfer was state of the art and undoubtedly left a number of watchers gawking at its speed and maneuverability so that the precious pod was at its destination before they had managed to achieve altitude in the traffic pattern.

Delivered to the impressive cube of one of Mr Li's business acquaintances, it was taken by grav-lift down to the bowels of the cube, through several alert and noncurious security checks and into the appropriate room for its closer examination.

'You can call me Zip,' said the white-coated older man who greeted them there. He had an oriental cast to his features and olive skin, but he spoke in an accent that suggested he had learned many other languages before the Basic he now used. He was also minus the first joint of both small fingers and the tip of one ring finger. 'Mr Li says you have a puzzle for me, Pal. I love puzzles.'

The three miners decided they liked his style and, with Pal, quickly uncrated the pod for him.

'Ah!' he exclaimed, raising both hands in awe, and his eyebrows and letting his mouth hang open. Then, he prowled around it, kneeling down to see the underside of the ovoid and standing on tiptoe to look over it. 'Ah!' he said again, seeing the inscriptions and delicately tracing them with an index finger as lovingly as a mother would trace the features of a child. 'And you've done nothing to discover if this language is known?'

Rafik looked at Gill and Cal and they all shrugged. 'We're miners, not linguists.'

'What about the occupant? Well, there was one, wasn't there?' Zip said testily. 'Or so I was given to understand. I do have Mr Li's complete confidence, you know. But I need some clues.'

'I thought . . . well . . . maybe,' Calum stuttered, no longer so sure of his promise.

'That if we had some idea of what metals comprise this alloy, we might use the spectro-analysis of stars to find out which ones are more likely to have produced satellites with similar material,' Pal said with a polite nod to the tongue-tied Calum.

'Not very likely,' Zip said briskly. He repeated Rafik's argument.

'Then there's nothing we can do?' Calum looked cast down.

'How come you believe him and not me?' Rafik muttered.

'I did not say there was nothing to be done.' Zip looked at them severely. 'You must listen more carefully if you wish to be true scientists. The avenue of approach you suggested is not likely to succeed . . . but there are some other things we can play with. Cosmology has advanced slightly since the days of planetbound observatories,' he said with a slight sneer. 'Have you ever heard of upsilon-V testing? Planetary emissions separ-ation? Mass diffusion imaging? Do not tell *me* how to do my job.' He tapped the pod and ran his hands across the top, around the sides. 'Come, come, gentlemen, it is enough of a puzzle by itself without me having to waste time discovering the opening mechanism.'

'We wouldn't,' Calum said sweetly, 'want to interfere with the expert.'

'But we *would* want to cooperate. Wouldn't we,

Calum?' Rafik reached over and showed how the pieces slipped into each other, then the lid slowly opened upward.

'Ah!' Once again Zip threw up both hands in delight at the furnishings within. He was feeling over every inch of it while the four watched and, bored by his diligence, began to shift their weight from one foot to another. Rafik finally gave a little cough which interrupted the tactile examination. 'Ah, yes. This is not something that can be solved in a trice. Or even a nonce. Go,' and he flicked one hand at them in dismissal while, with his other, he reverently felt the lining in which the baby Acorna had once lain. 'I will report when I have discovered anything of interest. My respectful greetings to Mr Li,' he said to Pal, and turned back.

They were passed through the various checkpoints and back to the roof where their vehicle awaited them.

'Say, I thought the ID was 87-99-20-DS?' Calum said, pointing to the craft. 'And I'd've sworn blind it was blue.'

'I smell fresh lacquer,' Gill said as they closed the gap to the machine.

'It's the same type,' Rafik said, because he hadn't noticed the ID or the color.

'A little precaution that might, or might not, be necessary,' Pal said as he opened the door. 'The color is dry.'

Calum entered, perplexed. Gill was frowning, but Rafik began to like Delszaki even more. A cautious as well as a prudent man.

233

*   *   *

As Judit had predicted, the child Acorna had
rescued fell asleep before she had finished eating,
clutching a piece of bread so tightly that it could
not be removed from her chubby fist without
reducing it to crumbs.

'Maybe we can just sponge her off while she
snoozes,' Judit suggested, but Acorna resisted the
suggestion fiercely. 'Let her sleep! She must be
exhausted, poor little thing. I'll bathe her when she
wakes up.'

Acorna sat over the sleeping child for the rest of
the morning, watching the gentle rise and fall of
her chest under the light blanket Judit had thrown
over her. She *was* filthy, but that could be rem-
edied; too thin, too, but regular good food would
take care of that. The bruises and scratches she had
borne after the scuffle in the street were slowly
fading, encouraged by an occasional gentle nuzzle
from Acorna's horn to heal into clean new flesh.

'She's only a baby!' Acorna thought indignantly. 'Why isn't somebody taking care of her?'

She did not realize she had spoken her thought
aloud until Pal Kendoro answered her.

'Someone is, now,' he said. 'You are.'

He had been silently watching for some time,
entranced by Acorna's rapt attention to the
sleeping child and the tender look on her face as
she nuzzled the baby's scratches with her horn.
Some people, he realized, might have found the
scene outlandish or alien. To him it was simply the
most perfect expression of motherly love he had

ever seen. It didn't matter that Acorna was of a different species, that she might never have children if they couldn't locate her home, or that those children would be physically very different from the starving beggar she had snatched up out of the streets of East Celtalan. The bond of love was there.

'But how could she have been simply abandoned to starve?' Acorna smoothed the ragged curls away from the right side of the child's face. On the left side of her head the hair had been crudely hacked short. 'She must belong to *somebody*.'

'I don't think she was abandoned,' Pal said. 'She's a beautiful child. The way her hair was hacked off, it looks as if somebody was trying to make her look ugly. Probably the same person helped her to run away.'

'What is wrong with beauty? And what would she be running away from?' Pal sighed and prepared to recapitulate Delszaki Li's lecture on Kezdet's system of child labor, bondage, 'recruiting,' and outright kidnapping. What Li had told Acorna and the miners had probably been too much for Acorna to take in all at one time. Calum went into rhapsodies about the speed with which Acorna absorbed mathematical and astronautical theories, but learning emotional facts was something else again.

'There are many children on Kezdet with no one to look after them,' he said. 'Some are orphans, some are unwanted children from other planets who have been brought here to work in mines and factories, some are bought from their parents to do the same work. If they don't work, their only alternative is to starve in the street.' He frowned. 'She does look young to have run away, though. Mostly it's the older children who have the gumption to escape and the wit to make some sort of plan. Perhaps when she wakes we can find out more about her, at least get some idea what workplace she was bonded to.'

'Not to send her back!' Acorna said, flinging a protective arm over the little girl.

'No. We won't send her back. And if . . .' Pal had been about to say that if the child's bond-owners traced her, Delszaki Li would surely buy her freedom. But he decided not even to mention that possibility in the face of Acorna's fierce protective instincts.

'If what?'

'If we can find out her name,' Pal improvised, 'she might have parents who are looking for her.' Personally he doubted it; most children who ended up in Kezdet's labor system did so precisely because they had parents so desperately poor they had no option but to sell their children. But he found himself wanting to put the best possible face on the child's situation for Acorna's sake.

Acorna's eyes narrowed to slits, then she took a deep breath and deliberately widened them again.

'Yes,' she said sadly, 'all lost children like to think that their parents are searching for them. If this one has not travelled too far, perhaps her people may be found.'

Pal could have kicked himself for his clumsy words. How could he have forgotten, even for an instant, that Acorna too had been a foundling, and one who did not know even where her race was to be found, let alone her own parents? No wonder she identified so instantly and protectively with this little waif. He stammered, trying to find some words of apology that would not deepen Acorna's pain, and was saved by the abrupt awakening of the waif.

'Mama!' she wailed, and pushed Acorna away when she would have cradled her in her arms. 'Mama Jana. Chiura wants Mama Jana.'

'There, you see,' said Pal, deftly catching up the flailing child and carrying her toward the bathroom before Acorna could realize how thoroughly she had been rejected, 'she knows her own name and that of her mother. We're making progress already.'

Most of the progress they made in the next half-hour consisted of transferring large quantities of warm water from the tub and onto the carpets, draperies, and themselves. Finally Chiura calmed down, exhausted by her hysterical sobbing, and sat quietly patting the remaining few inches of water in her tub and watching the soap bubbles that formed and popped under her hands. Pal took advantage of the peaceful moment to question Chiura gently. Did she know how she came to the city? In a skimmer? Who piloted the skimmer? How did she come to be alone? Where was she before she came to the city?

Chiura babbled and wandered from topic to topic while Pal tried to make sense of her words and kept her going with questions, always sheering away when Chiura's eyes crinkled up and she started to look upset again. Acorna wrapped Chiura in a towel, took her on her lap, and tried to comb out the long ringlets that had been caked in mud before the bath and the first three rinses. Chiura babbled that 'a bad man' had piloted the skimmer and they had come from 'the bad place' . . . and Acorna was pulling her hair, and she wanted Mama Jana *now*!

'It's no use,' Acorna said despairingly.

'Oh, I wouldn't say that,' Pal said. 'You don't know enough about Kezdet to work out the clues, but I'm getting a pretty fair idea where she was before she was brought to the city . . . and why she was wandering the streets alone.' It was as he had suspected when Acorna cleaned her up and he saw how lovely the child was.

'Kheti *said*,' Chiura piped up. 'Said when she made Didi Badini busy, run, run away, hide. There was a little fire.' She thought it over. 'Maybe big fire. Didi Badini was mad, but Chiura hid quiet-quiet under the stinky sacks.' Her eyes crinkled and a tear plopped down her cheek. 'Didi Badini hit Kheti, but Kheti didn't tell. Then Kheti jumped on Didi Badini and they roll around and get all muddy and Chiura ran, long way, got lost. Chiura bad?'

'*No*, darling,' Acorna said, hugging her and kissing her tangled curls. 'Whoever this Didi

238

Badini was, she does not sound like a nice person at all and I am sure Kheti would not have wanted you to go back to her.'

'You see,' said Pal, 'we're getting somewhere. It's not as hopeless as it seems. And I'd like to meet this Kheti,' he added. 'Anybody who'd set a bonk-shop on fire to give a kid a chance to get away . . .'

'Hopeless? Oh – I meant her hair,' Acorna explained, ruefully lifting a rat's nest of tangles in one hand. 'It will all have to be cut.'

'Would have had to be anyway,' Pal pointed out, 'to match the other side. Or did you want her to go around looking lopsided?'

Acorna managed a smile at that. Chiura bounced up and down on Acorna's knee and cried, 'Lop-side! Lop-side!' until both adults were laughing helplessly. And Pal managed to put off explaining what he had deduced of Chiura's fate until after she had demolished a bowl of sweet patts and beans and had fallen asleep again.

'The name of Didi Badini is a dead give-away,' he explained then. '"Didi" literally means "older sister" in the original language, but in Kezdet children's slang it means a woman who procures young girls for . . . um . . .' He blushed under the unblinking gaze of Acorna's wide silver eyes. 'For immoral purposes,' he finished in a rush.

'You mean, so that men can have sexual inter-course with them?' Acorna translated calmly. Then, at Pal's look of surprise, 'Calum and Rafik and Gill have an extensive library of vid-cubes on the ship, and I have watched many of them – and

239

not only the interactive training cubes on mining techniques! I do not think I was supposed to know about the others, but sometimes it was *very* boring when they were all working outside and there was not yet any crushed ore for me to run through the refining processes. Those vid-cubes that Calum kept behind his bunk were boring, too,' she added reflectively. 'I do not understand why anybody would want to do such uncomfortable and undignified things – and over and over, too! Except that I gather from the *Encyclo* that it is necessary to make babies. Still, some of the actors in the vid-cubes seemed excessively enthusiastic about their work.'

'The enthusiasm is something that . . . um . . . develops as one matures,' said Pal, making a mental note to tell the miners that their charge had a rather more extensive education than they realized. Then he had to explain to Acorna that, yes, some men were so enthusiastic they paid females to partner them in this undignified activity – and some were so perverted that they preferred the use of very young females.

'But Chiura is only a baby,' Acorna protested. 'It would hurt her!'

'The men who buy the use of children,' Pal said grimly, 'don't care if it hurts them. Mercy—' He stopped. Mercy had made him promise never to tell Judit what had happened to her after Judit won the scholarship to get off-planet. Neither Pal nor Mercy wished to burden her with unnecessary guilt about things she couldn't have stopped anyway. 'Well, this little one seems to have been lucky. Apparently this Kheti went to a lot of trouble to give her a chance to run away. It probably wasn't as easy as Chiura makes it sound, either.'

'Lucky? To beg and starve on the street!'

'Better,' Pal said. 'Believe me . . . better.'

'Then we have to find this other girl, this Kheti, and get her free, too.'

'And what,' Pal inquired, 'do you plan to do about the hundreds of others in like situations?'

'Saving one is better than saving *none*,' Acorna said firmly.

Pal could hardly disagree with this statement, but neither could he believe that Acorna would accomplish much by starting a crusade against the Didis of East Celtalan and that mysterious powerful figure, the Piper, who was said to support the brothel industry and to be supported in wealth by its proceeds.

Delszaki Li had been trying for years to identify the Piper, and when Pal joined him he had brought the Child Labor League's network of gossip and spies to bear on the problem. But not one of their covert sympathizers had turned up a whisper of the man's identity. Even Mercy, ideally situated as she was in a Guardians of the Peace office, had been unable to give them a clue; even the Guardians, it seemed, did not know who the Piper really was. All they knew was that he was wealthy, powerful, and absolutely ruthless in crushing any opposition.

There were rumors that he reserved some of the children bought by the Didis for his personal use, and that these children were the ones found strangled and floating in the river from time to time . . . unable to bear witness against him. Pal imagined Acorna's long silvery body mangled and tossed into the polluted water, and felt physically sick.

All things considered, it was almost a relief when Chiura woke up crying for 'Mama Jana' again and Acorna was distracted into trying to identify Chiura's mother. To take her mind off the plight of the children in the brothels, Pal enthusiastically tackled the task of decoding the clues they could extract from Chiura's baby recollections . . . a little too enthusiastically, he realized, as they neared success.

'This Jana can't be her real mother,' he said after another lengthy questioning session, interspersed with games of stacking vid-cubes, rolling a wheel that had fallen off a household trolley, and other improvised amusements. 'Look at what she played with the vid-cubes.' Chiura had built a completely enclosed space, then went around the room putting all the small objects she could find inside the space and naming each one. 'Lata. Faiz. Buddhe. Laxmi. Jana. Chiura. Khetala.'

'She was telling us that all these people were on the same level, all trapped.'

Chiura had reacted vigorously when Acorna tried to lift the little bronze box representing Jana out of the enclosure.

'No, no, no!' she shrieked. 'NO run away! Siri Teku beat!'

Then, in an abrupt change of mood, she had swiped at the stacked vid-cubes, scattering the 'walls' she'd built all across the room, and moved every one of the figures out onto the open floor.

'She was confined with a group of other children, probably all bonded laborers,' Pal interpreted. 'Jana must have been one of the older ones, like Khetala, who tried to take care of her.'

He tried to get some idea of where Chiura had been kept, but she had only the vaguest notions of place. There had been a big hill with no trees, only rocks. The sun went down behind the hill. Chiura had not been sent to work with the other children and had no idea what they did, only that they came back dirty and tired. What had Chiura herself done?

'Stupid Chiura,' she said, her face puckering up. 'Laxmi hit Chiura.'

That night Pal consulted Delszaki Li's extensive atlas of Kezdet.

'I think it must be someplace relatively close to Celtalan,' he explained his reasoning to Acorna, 'because Chiura says they were not very long in the skimmer – and anything over an hour's flight would be "long" to a child that young.'

He drew a line out from the depiction of Celtalan on the screen, representing the distance a skimmer could fly in an hour, and requested detailed overlays of the region. Then he narrowed the search by looking for treeless mountains with factories situated on the eastern side of the mountain. There was only one. 'It has to be the Tondubh Glassworks,' he concluded. 'Unless . . . No. That's the only mountain that fits her description.'

'Then we will go there tomorrow,' Acorna said, 'and find Jana.'

'I don't think that's such a great idea,' Pal demurred. 'Mr Li is working on his own plans for freeing the bonded children. We could mess things up for him by going out and making a fuss at the glassworks.'

Acorna gave him a disgusted look. 'Naturally we will tell Mr Li. But he will not stop us. That child has already lost her home, her parents, and her trust in the rest of humanity. Now you want to deprive her of the only person who cared for her and completely destroy her? I *know* what it feels like to be separated from the people who take care of you,' she said, remembering the terror of the barren, chemical-scented corridors of Amalgamated space base and the mean lady who would not take her back to Gill and Calum and Rafik. But they had come for her. Who would come for Chiura? They *had* to find this Jana.

After the beating Siri Teku gave her for trying to hide Chiura, Jana lost her position as dragger on Face Five. Her partner Khetala was gone, and anyway she couldn't drag. That last kick Siri Teku gave her had crunched something in her right knee; she could no longer put any weight on that leg at all, and she certainly couldn't crawl up the narrow shafts dragging a full corf of ore behind her. Buddhe and Faiz took over the lucrative Face Five work. By way of apology for taking her place, Faiz appropriated a slat from the roof which he whittled into the shape of a rough crutch, so that at least Jana could drag herself outside to the sorting slopes and the latrine trench. She supposed it was kind of him, but she didn't much care any longer. She hurt all the time since Siri Teku's beating, and the weals were hot and swollen and not healing properly. Kheti would have fussed about bad food and dirt, would have made her wash the wounds and choke down nauseating stews of the weeds growing on Anyag's mountainous slag heap to supplement the unvarying diet of patts and bean paste. Without Khetala to nag her into it, though, Jana just couldn't bring herself to take the trouble. She was tired and achy and there didn't seem to be much point in making herself even more miserable with cold water and weed stew.

Siri Teku had cursed when he saw that she was temporarily crippled, but her unfeigned wince when he drew back his foot to kick her bad knee again restored his good humor.

'Knew I'd break that cheeky spirit of hers someday,' he exulted, not even troubling to address her directly. 'She can take Chiura's place sorting ore until she can walk again.'

Laxmi grumbled that Jana wasn't much more use sorting ore than 'that baby' had been, and it was true. She wasted long hours just sitting on the ore heap, watching clouds drift across the sky, watching the evening shadows lengthening in front of the slag heap that blocked off half the sky, desultorily turning over bits of broken rock in her fingers from time to time. Laxmi made a point of separating her work from Jana's so that Siri Teku would be in no doubt about who had done what at the end of the day.

'You can be lazy and starve if you want to,' she warned Jana, 'I'm not working double for both of us. Hafta move fast if you want to earn your dinner.'

'Who cares?' said Jana.

Choking down the gritty patts was just another pointless thing that seemed more trouble than it was worth. She had to concentrate harder than she liked to make the connection between missed dinners and the constant, gnawing knot of pain in her middle. It wasn't the worst pain anyway, nothing near as bad as the throbbing of the infected whip marks on her skin, or the sharp pain whenever she dragged her bad knee somewhere. She knew, somewhere in the back of her fever-ridden mind, that if she didn't eat she would get even weaker and die soon, but that didn't seem to matter anymore, either. Without Kheti to bully them all into taking care of themselves, the whole gang wouldn't last long; already Faiz had a festering sore on one hand, and Laxmi's cough was worse than ever. Anyway, what was the point of working so hard just to keep alive? Nobody cared whether Jana lived or died, and since they

246

took Chiura away there was no little soft warm kitten-girl to cuddle and love. If Jana had been given to putting her thoughts into words, she might have told Laxmi that without someone to love, there was no reason to live. But talking was too much trouble. She listlessly pitched another ore-bearing rock into her sorting box, to shut Laxmi up, and went back to her dreamy contemplation of the clouds.

Pal had half hoped that Delszaki Li would flatly refuse Acorna's request to visit the Tondubh Glassworks in search of Chiura's 'Mama Jana,' or at least would insist that she go surrounded by a small army of House Li servants and bodyguards. Acorna had in mind to go unannounced and unescorted, except by Pal, and pointed out that bringing a large group would almost certainly cause the supervisor of the glassworks to treat their visit like an official inspection, hiding all the children.

'I think he will do so anyway,' Delszaki Li said, his eyes twinkling at Acorna, 'but if you wish, shall go with only Pal and one other.' He tapped one of the buttons on the com pad of his float-chair.

'*One*?' Pal began in outrage. 'But that's totally inadequate to protect—' He stopped and took a deep breath at the sight of the woman who had answered Li's button.

'I think you will find Nadhari adequate to any emergency,' Li said dryly.

Pal nodded, dumbstruck. Nadhari Kando was an all but legendary figure in the Li household. Rumors said that before coming to work for House Li, she had been one of the infamous Red Bracelets of Kilumbemba, or possibly a commander of one of Nered's elite shock troops, or maybe she had personally created and led the Army of Liberation that freed Anrath from its despotic rulers. Logic said a woman who looked no more than thirty could not possibly have done *all* those things, but when Pal looked at Nadhari, he could never decide which stories to discount; she appeared capable of having done all three before breakfast. Whatever she had once been, though, it had ended in an episode whose truth was unknown to anybody in House Li. She had been dismissed in disgrace for a savage combat action, or she had been sent to assassinate Delszaki Li and instead had fallen under the spell of his uniquely personal charm, or Li had saved her from summary execution at the hands of the Kezdet Guardians. Again, all three stories seemed perfectly possible.

Five feet six inches tall in her bare feet, lean and as tough as a length of braided leather, Nadhari Kando was expert in three forms of knife fighting and six forms of unarmed combat – none of which she had many chances now to use in the line of duty, since she went everywhere armed with an arsenal of miniaturized state-of-the-art weapons that could appear in seconds from her tight black braids, her gleaming skin-tight red boots, or ... Pal gulped and tried not to think about the other places where she probably concealed weapons. Rumor also said that Nadhari could read minds and that was why she always appeared somewhere where her opponent was not expecting her, just outside of his blows or behind his laser fire. But of course, nobody could read minds. That was just a superstitious story.

He hoped.

'I shall be honored to accept Nadhari Kando's escort,' Pal said through lips suddenly gone dry. 'If . . . that is . . . if you are sure you can spare her?' Nadhari's primary duty was to accompany Delszaki Li on all public appearances.

Li waved his good hand. 'Nadhari is bored. Do not go out often enough or encounter enough assassins to amuse her.'

The silent, black-braided woman in the doorway nodded once in confirmation of this statement.

'Mission?' she queried tersely.

'Ah . . . the Tondubh Glassworks,' Pal said. 'Acorna will tell you all about it as we are going along.'

Acorna's sunny mood gradually dimmed as they moved into the gray, dry industrial district east of Celtalan proper, and by the time they reached Knobkerrie Mountain she was hardly talking at all. The desolate landscape, spoiled by decades of dumping industrial waste and punctuated by walled compounds enclosing factories and housing, seemed uglier and more barren to her than any airless asteroid.

'Does it *have* to be like this?' she whispered as the skimmer banked and hovered over the compound bearing the Tondubh Glassworks logo.

'Kezdet,' said Pal, 'is ruled by the bottom line and the quarterly balance sheet. In any given quarter there is more profit in spoiling the land than in preserving it, just as there is more profit in buying new bond laborers than in keeping those you already have happy and healthy. If you don't care whether your workers live or die, and if they are too ignorant and frightened to complain, then why bother to give them decent lodgings or attractive surroundings?'

The skimmer settled gently into the space set aside for official visitors to the Tondubh facility, and Pal jumped out, ready with the story he had prepared to cover their interest in the facility. He spun the security guards a story about an off-planet vid-artist who wanted to feature Tondubh as one of Kezdet's success stories, a concern that had contributed to giving this resource-poor planet one of the higher gross planetary products in the sector.

'No vid equipment allowed in the plant,' the guard said.

Pal gave in on this point after minimal arguing, since he had no idea what he would have done if they hadn't insisted on this restriction; there hadn't been time to procure the kind of recording equipment an intergalactically known vid-artist would expect to use. The guard reciprocated by unbending slightly and allowing as how they could arrange a brief guided tour for the lady, if she and her companions would just wait an hour or so.

'No time,' Pal said, 'her time on Kezdet is measured in hours. Of course, if it's not convenient for us to see this facility, I'm sure the Gheredi Glassworks would do just as well. If you'd just give me a note of your name and number, so that I can explain to InterVid exactly why Tondubh proved unsuitable . . .'

The mention of Tondubh's biggest competitor on Kezdet plus Pal's veiled threat that he would see the guard took blame for letting this publicity opportunity go to the competition, got them inside the glassworks without more ado. As they passed the second security wall, Pal caught sight of a pair of slender, scarred bare legs winking out of sight around the corner.

'Damn kids,' the guard said genially, 'they're all over the place, bringing messages to the workers, begging a bite of the hot meals Tondubh provides to the hands, generally getting in the way.' The roar of the furnaces within the main manufacturing facility almost drowned out his words. They picked their way over a floor covered with shards of broken glass. The heat from the open furnaces was like a blow in the face; all the signs pointed to a factory in full production, yet the immense room was curiously empty. Only a handful of emaciated adults squatted in front of the furnaces.

'Do you not employ children, then?' Acorna asked.

The guard looked shocked. ''Deed, no. Why, that would be in violation of the Federation Child Welfare Statutes! Mind you, I'm not saying an occasional one as is underage may not sneak onto the payroll; these people breed like flies and don't keep no records. But Tondubh has always done its best to abide by Federation standards, madam. Get out of the way, there,' he roared at a boy who trotted into view with an iron rod taller than himself, the end covered with a blob of molten glass.

'P—please, sir, I was just bringing the glass to my gang leader,' the boy stammered, the end of his sentence all but drowned out by another outraged roar from the guard. 'Don't you know you kids aren't allowed to do anything but carry water? Now put that glass down! You could get hurt, messing with hot glass!'

The little boy dropped his rod with a clang. Molten glass spattered into the air; Pal and Acorna had to jump back to save themselves.

'Sorry about that, madam. You see why it would be better for you to wait and take a proper tour,' the guard said. 'It's hard enough to enforce proper safety regulations here at the best of times, and with these brats infesting the place for what they can pick up, well, it's no place for a lady like yourself and that's a fact. I'll just escort you back to the skimmer now.'

Nadhari glanced at Pal and raised one brow

252

inquiringly while she shifted her weight in a manner he found ominous.

'No,' Pal said under his breath. 'We will go as requested.'

Looking disappointed, Nadhari relaxed slightly.

The guard watched while Pal took off and cleared the factory airspace.

'That,' Pal said grimly, 'is just one of the problems we have to solve. Not employ children, indeed! That factory is ninety percent child-operated, and everybody knows it. But they have guards and gates and delaying tactics, and the children are trained to hide when any strangers come. I had hoped that a party of three would not be enough to alarm them. I was wrong.'

'*I* could have alarmed them,' Nadhari said in her gravelly voice, with a smile that sent a cold breeze along the back of Pal's neck.

'I am sure you could take on the entire security force of Tondubh Glassworks,' said Pal tactfully.

'Piece of cake,' Nadhari confirmed. 'Soft slugs. Poor defensive position.'

'But I think Mr Li might be annoyed if we started a private war.'

Nadhari nodded sadly.

'I do not understand why the children hide,' Acorna said. 'Don't they want to come out and ask for help?'

'They do not have much experience with strangers who make their lives better,' Pal said. 'Usually it's the other way.'

'That poor little boy. The guard was lying about his not working there. Did you see his feet? They were covered with burns and scars. If he hadn't run away, I could have healed them.' Acorna sighed. 'I suppose, if they do not admit to hiring children at all, it is useless to ask if they have a bonded child laborer named Jana?'

Pal agreed. He could have predicted this outcome to the trip, but it had appeared the only way to convince Acorna of the enormity of the task was to let her see for herself the kind of obstacles they faced. Now, however, he felt her disappointment as keenly as if it were his own.

'There is one other place we might try,' he said. 'I've been thinking . . . It's true that Knobkerrie is the only treeless mountain this near Celtalan that has a factory beside it. But to a little girl like Chiura, who's to say what counts as a mountain?'

'There isn't much else that *could* be considered a mountain,' Acorna said, looking down at the featureless landscape below the skimmer.

'Some of the pit mines have pretty high slag heaps near the sorting bins,' Pal said, banking the skimmer slightly. 'And one of the oldest mines – with one of the biggest slag heaps – is not too far from here. It wouldn't hurt to pay a visit to Anyag. This time, though, we're going to think up a better story.'

'We are?' Acorna had been tremendously impressed by the speed and fluency with which Pal had spun his tale at the Tondubh Glassworks.

'We'll have to,' Pal said. 'The children at

Tondubh had plenty of time to hide while I was convincing the guard that they couldn't afford to alienate a galactic vid-artist. This time we're going to use a story that will make them want to keep the children for us to inspect.' He glanced at Acorna. 'Good thing you dressed up this morning. But you need to be a little gaudier.' He guided the skimmer down toward a walled compound of courtyards and gardens, brilliant in the surrounding near-desert as an emerald in the sand. 'Wait in the skimmer,' he said over his shoulder as they landed.

A slim, pretty girl with long black hair ran out of the nearest arcaded passageway, calling excited greetings to Pal. He met her too far from the skimmer for Acorna to hear what they said, but there was no need; his exuberant kiss of greeting and the way he picked the girl up and spun her around in his arms told her all she needed to know about their relationship. They disappeared together into the maze of buildings and Acorna slumped in her seat, feeling remarkably foolish. Of course Pal had a girlfriend. She'd seen enough story-cubes to understand that this was the normal arrangement of human society. They spent twenty years or so growing, and then they were ready to mate. Gill was showing every sign of preparing to mate with Judit, and that didn't bother her; why should she feel so depressed at seeing that Pal was in the same situation? Probably because there was nobody for *her* to mate with. Not that she had the least interest in the kind of sexual acrobatics displayed in Calum's secret vid-cube collection, but it would have been nice to have somebody to share secrets and jokes with, somebody who came running out with a joyful face when you came to their house, somebody who would hug you and spin you around like that.

Ridiculous to feel sorry for herself, just because she was the only one of her kind, when so many people had worse problems. Acorna glanced at Nadhari, who was sitting upright and watchful in the backseat. Nadhari was alone, too, and it didn't seem to bother her. She didn't even need to talk to people except about her work.

Acorna shivered. She didn't want to be quite *that* self-sufficient. How lucky she had been to be found by Gill and Rafik and Calum, instead of by somebody who would have sold her to a labor factory on Kezdet! Acorna sat up very straight and concentrated on remembering how lucky she was and what a good life she had. She managed to such good effect that when Pal reappeared and climbed into the skimmer, the first thing he said was, 'What's the matter?'

'Not a thing,' Acorna said. 'Not a thing. I don't need to know what your plans are. I just do what I'm told.'

Pal tightened his lips to conceal a smile. So Acorna could take a huff, just like any other young girl, when she felt left out and ignored! She might look different, but she was completely and gloriously female. And that thought pleased him inordinately. He couldn't quite figure out why he should be so pleased to see her displaying signs of jealousy, but . . . well, it was nice to know that at least emotionally she was very human, indeed.

'Irodalmi Javak's family is very wealthy,' he said, 'and her father would not approve if he knew that she was a secret sympathizer with the Child Labor League. He doesn't approve of me either, but pretending to be a penniless and unacceptable suitor for her gives us an excellent cover for an occasional secret meeting – even if anybody found out, they'd just think I was sneaking into the compound to steal a few kisses.'

'Oh.' Acorna digested this. 'Then it's just . . . pretense? You two certainly looked happy enough to meet!'

'I am very fond of Irodalmi,' Pal said truthfully. 'She is a good, brave girl and she risks a lot for the movement. But she has no use for boyfriends; she wants to get off-planet and study to become a starship navigator.'

'That must be very sad for you.'

'Nothing to do with *me*,' Pal said so cheerfully that Acorna began to feel much happier. 'She's got her life planned out, and I am developing plans of my own. Our "courtship" is a convenient cover, that's all. I didn't want her to see you because the less she knows, the safer for all of us. But she lent me enough of her jewelry to deck you out in the necessary style.' Both his hands were fully occupied now with lifting the skimmer and piloting it back toward Anyag. He nodded at the dark green

257

case he had brought out of Irodalmi's house. 'Open that, will you, and put the stuff on.'

Acorna was dazzled by the sight that met her eyes when she lifted the lid of the case. A profusion of rings, bracelets, chains, and stick pins glittered in the sunlight that filtered through the skimmer windows. Most of the jewelry was in a heavy, ornate style of gold work that would suit neither the slender Irodalmi nor Acorna with her silvery coloring, but there was one ring of blue starstones set in platinum, and a matching chain with a very large starstone pendant. She put these on and longed for a mirror in which to check the effect.

'How do I look?' she demanded of Pal.

He glanced sideways and grunted. 'I said, put it on. *All* of it.'

'I do not know much of fashionable dress,' Acorna said, 'but I think that to wear all this gold at once would constitute a vulgar display of wealth, as well as being *most* unattractive.'

'Yep,' Pal agreed, 'that's Javak Senior's style, all right. Irodalmi doesn't care for the stuff herself. Says that if she wore her father's gifts, she'd look like the senior Didi in a high-class bonking shop. Which is what made me think of her. That's precisely the effect we're after. Now put the jewelry on. Please.'

Acorna did her best to follow his instructions, but most of the rings designed for human fingers would not fit on her less-supple digits, and she ran out of room for bangles on her arms.

'The larger bangles are for your ankles,' Pal instructed without taking his eyes from the skimmer's instrument panel, 'and can't you thread some of the rings through that turban kind of thing you wear on your head?'

'Try not to crash this thing in a lake,' Acorna said after following his instructions. 'I'd sink like a stone. I'm not even sure I'll be able to *walk* with this much jewelry hanging off my body.'

'Excellent,' Pal said. 'We want you to look extremely rich and extremely vulgar. Too bad you don't wear scent. A heavy dose of musk and jasmine essence would finish off the picture nicely.'

'*What* picture?' Acorna demanded.

'Just came to me,' Pal said, 'in a sudden flash of inspiration. We geniuses often work that way. If Didi Badini is welcome at Anyag to inspect the children, why not Didi Acorna? Explains Nadhari, too,' he added. 'Any Didi as rich as you're pretending to be would naturally travel with a bodyguard.'

'You want me to pretend to be a Didi!' Acorna exclaimed. 'That's a truly revolting idea.'

'It's a truly brilliant one,' Pal said. 'Just leave the talking to me, and nothing can go wrong this time.'

Acorna regarded him with some suspicion.

'Sometimes,' she said, 'you remind me very much of Rafik.'

'Act arrogant,' Pal warned her just before they reached Anyag, 'and leave the talking to me.'

Acorna had no trouble following either of these instructions. Shock at the sheer unrelieved ugliness of Anyag, the gigantic slag heap and the piles of separated ore and the endless roar of crushers, kept her silent. The stench of the latrine trench behind the sleeping sheds kept her nose up in the air, and the unaccustomed weight of jewelry on her body forced her to move slowly. The effect was all Pal could have wished: she appeared to be an incredibly wealthy young woman with vulgar taste, slow dignified movements, and too much pride to speak a civil word to the mine superintendent. It was easy for him to believe that she was a new and unprecedentedly successful Didi looking for fresh young stock to build up her expanding network of houses. He all but fell over himself apologizing for the poor condition of most of the children in the mine and issued no orders at all to hide them.

Pal demanded curtly to be shown to where Siri Teku's gang slept, and the superintendent showed some relief. He had heard that Siri Teku had scored a coup from a labor contractor just last month, picking up a curly-headed, fair-skinned girl child who looked like just the sort of fresh young thing a Didi would buy off him at twice or three times what he'd paid for her. He started to apologize that Siri Teku's crew was on day shift and would be unavailable right now, then stumbled to a halt as he decided that Siri Teku wouldn't have been fool enough to send a pretty piece like that baby girl Below. He'd have her working

Above on some easy task like sorting ore or sweeping tailings to not spoil her looks . . .

Pal interrupted him. 'Just point out the sleep shed. We won't need your company.'

The superintendent was disappointed; he'd expected a cut of the profits from any sale made on his shift. A discreet transfer of credits salved his disappointment and bought Pal and Acorna privacy while they picked their way through the debris of the mine to the area where Siri Teku's gang sorted the ore they had dragged to the surface.

There were only two children on the sorting bench. One of them was working so fast her fingers seemed to fly as she picked through the broken rocks and assessed them with an expert eye. The other stared through them with blank, empty eyes that made Acorna's own eyes narrow in anguished sympathy.

'Jana?' she asked, expecting the active child to answer.

'I'm Laxmi,' said the girl who was working so hard. 'She's Jana.' She jerked her chin toward the other child. 'She don't talk much, not since . . .' A rattling cough interrupted her words.

'Get her some water, Pal!' Acorna said.

''S okay. 'S nothing,' Laxmi croaked, wiping her chin. 'Don't tell 'm . . . I'm not sick!' There was desperation in her cry. '*Not!*'

'Of course you are not sick,' Acorna agreed soothingly. 'You are a fine, strong worker.'

Laxmi edged suspiciously away from her as

Acorna came closer, until she was on the far side of the bench with a pile of broken rocks between her and the visitors. Acorna sat down beside Jana and put an arm around her. Jana winced away with a gasp of pain.

'Best not touch 'er,' Laxmi warned from a safe distance. 'She ain't healed from that beatin' Siri Teku give 'er.'

Jana's ragged gray kameez was stuck to her back and sides in several places. When Pal came back with a bucket of scummy water, Acorna looked at it in despair, then deftly stripped off the scarves that swathed her head. Laxmi gasped and fell into another coughing fit at sight of the small white horn in the middle of Acorna's forehead.

Acorna dipped her horn into the water for a moment, then used her silk scarf to dab the now-clean water onto the worst of Jana's marks. When she was finally able to lift the kameez without pulling at the broken skin underneath, she laid her forehead against each swollen, infected weal. Laxmi edged closer and closer, eyes round as she saw clean new skin replacing the raw stripes on Jana's back and sides.

'Please, lady,' she whispered, 'I dunno what you're doing . . . but could you do her knee, too? That's what hurts her the worst. Can't walk without a stick . . .'

Acorna bent her head to the swollen knee for a long moment. Jana sat unmoving and unresponsive, but the swelling visibly went down.

'Come to me,' she said, and Laxmi, a look of

262

surprise on her face, slowly moved toward Acorna.

'If you c'n fix me, too,' she said hoarsely, 'reckon I'll go with you. Kheti allus said goin' with a Didi was worst thing as could happen to a girl . . . but Kheti dint see *you*.'

Acorna laid her face against Laxmi's throat and slowly moved the horn down along her chest. Laxmi drew in a deep breath and hardly coughed at all; she took another breath and another, and color crept into her face.

'What you think you're doing, bint?'

The angry roar came from the mouth of the shaft behind them. A moment later a tall, lean man in brown robe and turban leapt out of the cage-lift, brandishing a long, flexible rod in one hand.

Quickly swathing her horn, Acorna lifted her head.

'I have a use for these children,' she said. 'You will be compensated for them.'

Siri Teku's eyes narrowed in crafty speculation. It must be Laxmi the Didi wanted; Jana wasn't much use to anybody now. She was trying to confuse him by pretending an interest in both children.

'I might consider letting you have that one,' he said, nodding at Jana. ''T'other's too valuable to me. Last trained sorter I got, see.'

'I need them both,' Acorna replied firmly.

Siri Teku mentally evaluated the worth of this new Didi's gold jewelry and decided to take a gamble. It was true that he needed Laxmi's services. He wouldn't have pretended not to notice her cough for so long if he'd had anybody else half so good at sorting ore. But a month would give him time to buy some new children and have Laxmi train them. And if this Didi was really so interested in Laxmi, Old Black knew why, she'd come back at the end of that month . . . by which time he should be able to trade, steal, and buy enough really handsome children to make her a constant customer of his.

Besides, he thought he recognized the silent bodyguard who stood behind the Didi. Was House Li getting into the bonk-shop business? And if so, did old Li himself know, or was the old man so senile that his employees were able to take off on their own? He needed time to check the rumors so that he could figure out how to turn the maximum profit from this situation.

'This un's not for sale yet,' he repeated, grabbing Laxmi's arm and jerking her away from Acorna and Pal. 'Come back next month, after I've had time to train some new sorters. And for the other, it'll be fifty credits.'

'Who're you kidding?' Pal demanded, using a rough accent Acorna had not heard from him before. 'We'd be doing you a favor to take her off your hands. Ten credits, no more.'

'You wish to rob an honest working man of his livelihood? Besides, I will have to give a percentage to the mine superintendent. Thirty-five.'

'Fifteen,' Acorna said.

Siri Teku hesitated, and Acorna turned on her heel.

'Come,' she snapped to Pal. 'My time is too valuable to spend haggling over one child.'

'Seventeen and a half!' Siri Teku cried.

'Very well,' Acorna said, 'seventeen it is.' She dropped a bundle of credits in the dirt and turned toward the skimmer.

'And a half?'

Acorna laughed and kept walking.

'Remember,' Siri Teku called after them as Pal carried Jana toward the skimmer, 'come back next month! I'll make it worth your while!'

Laxmi's eyes followed the skimmer as it rose over the mountainous slag heap of Anyag and banked west, into the afternoon sun, toward Celtalan.

Pal tarried long enough at Irodalmi's house to return the jewelry, which Acorna was only too happy to remove, despite the surprise that it caused Jana.

'I am no Didi, little one,' Acorna told Jana, stroking her no longer sore back. 'I am taking you to Chiura, who has been crying for her Mama Jana.'

'Chiura?' Jana exclaimed. Miracle upon miracle this day had for her. Not only had her pains been soothed and she had been taken from bondage with Siri Teku, but Chiura was at her destination. Furthermore, her well-honed instincts told her that this marvelous lady with the funny horn in the middle of her forehead was good, and Jana

265

had had so little of 'good' in her life, she wondered that she could believe in any. Yet why heal her when she wasn't pretty like Chiura or useful like Khetala? That name sprang from her lips. 'Khetala? You will find and free her from Didi Badini?'

The man who drove the skimmer groaned. 'One rescue a day is all I can cope with right now, and there'll be a lot of explaining to be done for this day's work – that I can assure you.'

'But surely, Pal, we must save these children. The other one who coughed . . .'

'Laxmi?' Jana asked hopefully.

'Mr Li has a large house, but there are limits to what hospitality he can extend. That is why we must make the moon colony. *Then* we will have a safe place for all the abused and misused children in those mines. First things must come first, Acorna.' He spoke as severely as he could, and yet the melting look in Acorna's eyes over Jana's head was almost more than he could bear. What amazing powers this most unusual female had!

In December 1936, the English king, Edward VIII abdicated his throne to marry an American divorcee, Wallis Simpson. Before Christmas of that year, schoolchildren from Land's End to John o'Groats were chanting, 'Hark, the herald angels sing, Mrs Simpson's pinched our king.' No one ever figured out how the song spread so quickly; it certainly hadn't been part of a BBC broadcast.

The tale of a silver goddess with a horn in the middle of her forehead, come to Kezdet especially to heal and help children, spread with similar rapidity. As with the song about Mrs Simpson, the only certainty is that it wasn't disseminated by anyone in authority.

When the rest of Siri Teku's gang came up from their twelve-hour shift Below, Laxmi told them that Sita Ram, Lady of the Sky and Above, had visited Anyag disguised as a Didi, had healed her, and had taken Jana to live with her in the sky. The other children might have scoffed, but it was a fact that Laxmi's racking cough was gone; she breathed as easily and deeply as any of the newest arrivals. A child sold from the mines to Czerebogar took the story and the hope of that healing with him.

In the carpet works at Czerebogar, where the children squatted on hanging benches and tied knots in the famous Kezdet carpets until their fingers bled, Laxmi's Sita Ram was transmuted into Lukia of the Lights, and they whispered that the unicorn's white horn shed a magical healing light that restored the sight of squinting, half-blind carpet weavers. An itinerant teacher from the Child Labor League, entering Czerebogar in disguise, found her way made easier by this legend and suggested to her colleagues that they spread it as a way of overcoming the children's ingrained fear and distrust of all strangers.

'Should we try to overcome it?' one of the other

part-time teachers asked. 'Most of the time they're right to fear strangers.'

'Not us,' said the young woman who'd slipped in and out of Czerebogar, bringing counting games and stories and taking away the legend of Lukia. 'If they fear us, we can't help them.'

In the Tondubh glassworks, the story became part of the legend of Epona, the horse-goddess who bore tired glass-runners on her back and galloped from furnace to blower with the molten glass to spare the children's weary legs.

Everywhere on Kezdet, where there was a mine or factory keeping children at work in cramped, poisoned, miserable conditions, there was also some legend of a rescuing goddess, spun out of the older children's hazy memories of a mother's arms and given strength by the younger children's need for hope. But never before had one of the legendary goddesses taken mortal form and given solid, practical healing to a sick child. All the legends suddenly took on new life; hope flourished like an underground stream of pure water running through all the dark factories; over-seers wondered why the children had begun to sing and laugh, and worried about the change.

The repercussions from Acorna's adventure were less than Pal had feared. Judit was frankly relieved to have Jana take over the care of Chiura, who had never ceased wailing for the older child whom she evidently regarded as a mother.

Delszaki Li and the miners were somewhat

more vocal. 'You did *what*?' Rafik bellowed when Acorna proudly reported the results of her trip to him.

'I told you that I was going to look for Chiura's "Mama Jana,"' Acorna said.

'Yes,' said Calum unguardedly, 'but we didn't think you'd succeed, or we wouldn't have let you go off with just Pal and one bodyguard.'

Nadhari Kando shifted her weight slightly, from one foot to a balanced pose on the balls of both feet. The slight movement should have gone unnoticed, but instead it drew everyone's attention. She looked straight at Calum until his eyes dropped.

'That is . . .' he mumbled, 'of course you were perfectly safe with Nadhari. After all, if Mr Li entrusts his own life to her . . .'

'Quite correct,' Nadhari said. Her low, grating voice was almost without expression.

'Don't you *want* Jana?' Acorna put her arm around the bewildered child.

'Sure we do,' Gill said heartily. He dropped to one knee before Jana, who shrank back involuntarily at the approach of this red-bearded giant. 'We need you here, Jana. Chiura needs you. We all do. Plenty of room in this house for another little girl.' He glanced at Delszaki Li and received an approving nod. 'We were just . . . surprised that Acorna found you so quickly.'

'We underestimated her,' Rafik said gloomily.

'Probably not for last time,' Delszaki Li chirped. His dark eyes were bright with amusement.

269

Pal's private nightmare, that the Guardians of the Peace would somehow trace him and 'Didi Acorna' back from Anyag to the Li mansion and accuse him of procuring children for immoral purposes, never came true. He was not sure whether that was because they had not been traced, or because the Guardians were too bright to try to shake down so powerful a figure as Delszaki Li, or because they simply accepted as a matter of course that any man who was so inclined might buy himself a few girl children for private use whenever he felt the urge. He suspected the last.

Even Acorna, after a few wistful comments about the amount of room there was in those upper stories and how many beds they could fit into the long parlor, seemed to accept Pal's strict injunction against collecting any more children before Delszaki Li had started the safe haven of the lunar colony. She didn't even promise Jana to go out and look for Khetala – thank goodness! Pal sweated when he remembered the risks he had already allowed Acorna to run in their mad escapade. The last thing he needed was to have her opening those wide silvery eyes at him and politely requesting a tour of the East Celtalan brothels. Especially since he had a terrible suspicion he would give in. The urge to give Acorna everything she wanted was only growing stronger the more time he spent in her company.

All things considered, he should have felt relieved when, after a few days spent quietly with

Chiura and Jana, her only request was to go shopping with Judit.

'I am sure you must have many more important things to do,' she apologized to Judit, 'but you see, I have promised Mr Li not to go out alone again. There are a few things I need from the stores, and somehow I do not think that Nadhari . . .'

'Of course,' Judit said. 'You're quite right. I'm pretty sure Nadhari doesn't have a black belt in shopping. And I have been quietly going mad with inactivity while I wait for Delszaki and your friends to come up with something for me to do. Really, if he's going to spend all his time locked in Dr Zip's lab or cruising the Lattice on his com unit, Delszaki hardly needs one personal assistant, let alone two!'

'I'll go with you,' Pal volunteered, and felt unreasonably annoyed when Acorna stammeringly refused his help.

'Don't be silly, Pal,' Judit said in her best bossy elder-sister tones. 'One of us must stay here in case Delszaki comes out of his brown study and wants something.' Adding, after she sent Acorna off to get a heavier wrap on the pretext that there were cold winds coming in from the north, 'I expect the child wants to buy feminine fripperies, Pal. She'd only be embarrassed to have you tagging along. Nadhari will come, and she'll be quite protection enough.'

Nadhari cleared her throat, and Pal hastily agreed that no one could want more protection than she could supply.

271

Relief though it must be to have Acorna safely occupied, Judit could not repress a slight scorn when she saw the girl counting the credits in her purse before they set out. Was all the work of the Child Labor League to be set aside for Acorna's convenience? Here was Delszaki Li off on a wild-goose chase to find Acorna's home planet, instead of completing the plans for his lunar colony; Acorna herself, it seemed, was perfectly happy to go shopping for the latest fashions. It was true that Delszaki had advanced the credits to her himself, saying that he wished his 'ward' to be dressed as befitted the house of Li rather than continually washing and wearing the same three outfits the miners had casually picked out for her. And it was true that the plans of the Child Labor League were in much more danger from hasty enterprises such as Acorna's rescue of Jana than from a few days of neglect. Still, Judit could not keep from fretting over all the problems remaining: the lunar colony yet to be designed, let alone set up; how the children were to be gathered together when every factory owner had trained them to hide whenever strangers approached; worst of all, how to neutralize the shadowy, malevolent figure known only as the Piper, whose fortune derived entirely from the worst forms of child labor and who was supposed to be behind most of the official and unofficial bedevilment the league members had suffered. The Piper would surely find some way to stop Li's latest and boldest plan if he got word of it, as he was sure to do sooner or later in Kezdet's spy-riddled society.

She was further surprised when Acorna first proposed that they should walk, then stopped not five minutes from the house and hired a skimmer, directing the pilot to take them to the Gorazde Bazaar.

'Acorna, are you sure that is where you wish to go?' Judit remonstrated as the skimmer rose and hovered over the heart of Celtalan's wealthiest district. 'The Gorazde is not at all fashionable. Respectable, yes, but it is the sort of place where Delszaki's servants buy their daywear. It is not equipped to cater to a young lady of fashion.'

'I am not a young lady of fashion,' Acorna said calmly, 'and I inquired of the house staff before making my decision. I am confident that I shall find *exactly* what I need at the Gorazde.'

'And why rent a skimmer?' Judit went on. 'We could have used one of the House Li skimmers.'

Acorna hung her head. 'I wanted to do this *myself*,' she said, 'with my own credits from the work I have done for Calum and Rafik and Gill.'

'Do what, for heaven's sake?'

'That little boy at Tondubh,' Acorna said, 'his feet were all burned and cut from running over hot and broken glass. I thought . . . he could use a pair of sandals.'

'What a nice thought!' Judit approved.

'And all the other children there,' Acorna said. 'That is why I thought of the Gorazde, you see. They say it is a good place to find cheap but durable clothes.'

273

She proceeded to occupy the few minutes required for the skimmer to cross the city by asking Judit about her brother. Judit played down the misery of the first years on Kezdet, when she and Pal and Mercy had been bond-laborers with no hope of freedom, by saying truthfully that they had all three been sent to different places and she really knew very little of Pal's life during those years. Instead she concentrated on tales of Pal's progress through technical school and the stories he had told her about his work with Delszaki Li. It was a pleasure to talk at length about her beloved little brother to such an attentive audience, and Judit was almost sorry when they reached the Gorazde. She had been meaning to ask Acorna a few things about Gill ... subtly, of course, so as not to betray how much more interested she was in him than in the other two miners who composed Acorna's foster family.

Once the skimmer pilot had set them down and had been requested to wait, Acorna changed from passive audience to taking charge of the expedition once again.

'I think *this* is exactly the place I have been looking for,' she said, walking past a handful of clothing stalls to enter Sopel's Sandalarium with its flashing lighted sign proclaiming, 'Wholesale, Discount Sale, and Going-Out-of-Business Sale Every Day.'

A clerk hurried forward to serve them, every line of his demeanor announcing that he had never hoped to see two well-dressed young ladies

274

from West Celtalan in Sopel's Sandalarium. When he offered to measure their feet, Acorna informed him that this would not be necessary, as she knew what sizes she wanted. Judit gave a small internal sigh of relief; they really did not need the kind of attention that a close inspection of Acorna's unusually shaped feet would draw. Acorna specified a range of sandal sizes that would fit anything from a toddler to a child of ten and selected a cheap and long-wearing style in re-cycled syntho-foam. When the clerk mentioned a price that Judit thought far too high, Acorna glanced at her and immediately counter-offered for little more than the wholesale cost of the sandals. She pointed out the advantages of good relations with someone who was prepared to buy in bulk, gave the impression that she might be a buyer for some large consortium who could be enticed back by a very low price on this first order, and eventually acquired the Sandalarium's entire stock in the requested sizes at less than half the price originally mentioned.

'You see,' Acorna said when a slightly dazed clerk left to order porters to carry their purchases to the waiting skimmer, 'I told you I would require some help with my parcels.'

Almost as dazed as the clerk, Judit said the first thing that came into her head. 'Where did you learn to bargain like that?'

Acorna gave her an impish smile. 'I have spent two years listening to Calum selling payloads of ore and drone buckets of iron all over this quadrant. The basic principles are not dissimilar – and I have always liked working with numbers.'

'Working with numbers is hardly an adequate description,' Judit said with feeling. 'Anybody who can juggle all those prices and quantities in her head ought to be looking at a career in gambling.'

'Seven to four,' Acorna murmured, smiling at a private memory, '"Nobble" the favorite . . . I think we had better watch the sandals being loaded, don't you? Mr Sopel is not making as much of a profit as usual on this transaction; he may try to redress the balance by making a few slight mistakes during loading.'

In fact, Acorna discovered no fewer than three 'minor discrepancies' between her receipt and the goods being loaded on the skimmer in the first few minutes. With the discovery of the third shortage, she instructed the porter to inform Mr Sopel that any more discrepancies would cause her to lose faith in his ability to conduct a business and would force her to take her credits elsewhere. Thereafter all proceeded smoothly.

When the skimmer was fully loaded, Acorna directed the pilot to take them to the Tondubh Glassworks, with a sidelong glance to see if Judit would countermand her orders.

'You promised Delszaki not to collect any more children,' Judit murmured with a warning shake of her head.

Acorna lifted her long chin slightly. 'I did not promise not to *help* them. Surely no one can object if I give a few things to make their lives easier?'

And in fact, when Acorna swept into the Tondubh compound with the imperious air she had been practicing, she met with almost no opposition from the startled overseers. Judit was rather surprised to find that the Tondubh staff suffered from the illusion that Acorna was a galactically famous vid-star come to film a complimentary documentary on Kezdet's 'economic miracle,' but she said nothing to dispel the idea.

'We do not film today,' Acorna said loftily, 'so I amuse myself by bringing a few gifts for the children I saw here the other day.'

The manager started his practiced spiel claiming that no children worked in the glass factory, but Acorna cut him off.

'Of course, I understand perfectly, they do not *work* here,' she agreed with a complicitous smile and wink at the manager.

'Exactly,' said the manager, returning the wink. 'They are only hanging about here to run errands and beg meals from the generosity of the management. As long as that is understood, there can be no objection to the lady's kind gifts.'

'They will perhaps "run errands" more swiftly if their feet are protected from the hot glass and broken shards in the factory,' Acorna said. 'Let them come to me here and select sandals to fit each one.'

The manager frowned. 'I think they will not come. They are shy of strangers, gracious lady. It would be best if you left the sandals here for me to distribute.'

Already he was calculating how much he could get from Sopal's Sandalarium if he returned the merchandise still in its original wrapping – not full price, of course, but even a percentage of the discounted cost would make a nice little addition to his salary.

But, although the child workers in the factory had scattered as usual when Acorna's skimmer arrived, they were not that far away. A few of the braver and more curious ones had lingered to learn what they could of the new arrival, and they spread the word to the others that the whispered rumors were true: the Lady Epona had come to Tondubh! Who else would care to bring sandals to protect their burned and blistered feet?

At first slowly, by ones and twos, the children crept out of concealment to receive their gifts from the Lady Epona. At the sight of the first boys' burned feet, Acorna's eyes narrowed to silver slits.

'Distract that man,' she murmured at Judit, nodding at the greedy manager.

Judit smiled sweetly at the manager, flirted shamelessly, and persuaded him to take her inside for a restorative cup of kava. The other overseers, not to be left out, crowded after her, and Acorna was left alone with the children for a few precious moments.

As soon as the adults were gone, Acorna pulled off the scarf wound about her head. At the sight of the white horn rising from the tumble of silvery curls on her forehead, the children murmured in awe. A few of them dropped to their knees, all doubt removed; the younger ones clung to her skirts and begged her to take them away.

'I cannot take you now,' Acorna said, her eye-slits narrowing until they were almost invisible. 'I have promised . . . and I have no place for you yet. But I *will* come back. And when I come, you will not hide? You will come to me?'

The children were awed into silence as Acorna knelt before the first boy to claim his sandals and touched her horn to his scarred feet. When they saw the blisters and infected cuts disappearing under the touch of the horn, they were momentarily frightened. But little Donkin jumped and shouted in happiness.

'They doesn't hurt! They doesn't hurt anymore! Come on, noodle-tops, get yours!'

'Shh, shh,' Acorna cautioned Donkin, and the children quieted immediately.

They were so pale, so quiet, so obedient! There was hardly any pushing and shoving as they lined up to receive their sandals and, an even greater gift, the healing touch of the Lady Epona's white horn.

By the time the last child had been cared for, Acorna was exhausted and shaking. She was relieved by Judit's prompt reappearance from the manager's quarters and hardly noticed Judit's disheveled, flushed look.

'Take me home,' Acorna whispered to Judit, 'I am so tired.'

'With the greatest of pleasure,' Judit said between her teeth. She gave Acorna a hand into the skimmer and leapt in after her, accidentally stepping on the manager's hand as he reached in to wish them farewell. 'West Celtalan Riverwalk,' she told the skimmer pilot. That would put them within an easy walk of the Li mansion – or a hundred other wealthy homes, so anybody questioning the skimmer pilot later would not be sure just where they had gone.

But Acorna fell into an exhausted slumber on the flight back, and with resignation Judit altered her orders and told the pilot to take them to Delszaki Li's private landing pad.

'*With* pleasure,' said the pilot, 'and won't nobody find out from me where you went, neither! I thought as it must be somebody from the CLL.'

'Delszaki Li has no connection with the Child Labor League,' Judit said.

'Righty-ho,' the pilot said with a cheerful wink, 'and I'm the president of Kezdet. Don't you worry none, little lady. Truth to tell, I was just fixin' to go in and get you, claiming some kinda emergency, when you come on out of the offices. Nice girl like you hadn't ought to be alone with the kind of scum they use to run those factories.'

'You're telling *me*,' Judit said with feeling. She straightened her tunic and twisted her hair back into its usual severe knot.

'Pulled you about some, didn't they? Like me to go back and beat 'em up?'

Judit chuckled. 'If you want to be helpful, my friend,' she said, 'let's not start by getting you thrown into a Peacetower. An anonymous skimmer could be useful from time to time.'

'Here's my call sign,' the pilot said. 'Any time you want me, just take the nearest public com unit and put out this sign. Double the last two digits and I'll know it's you, see; then I'll be there soon's I can. If it's an emergency, triple the last two digits and I'll ditch my passengers and be there sooner.'

The children were not the only ones to hear about Sita Ram, Lukia of the Lights, and Epona: Didi Badini did, too, and she was livid. She asked a few questions of various informed sources and learned, to her astonishment, that no, there was no new bonk-shop opened with a Didi named Acorna. She was even more annoyed to learn *that*! In fact, she became obsessed with this Didi Acorna personage and travelled all the way to Anyag to question Siri Teku at length. He knew only that she had come in a rented skimmer—

'To keep us from knowing her location, no doubt!' Didi Badini said, tapping her elegant foot and forgetting that the mud would get between her painted toes, done only that morning in silver: a color she intended to take off the moment she got back. Silver was definitely 'out.'

'Quite possibly, Didi Badini,' Siri Teku said, bobbing continuously in his desire not to alienate one of his better customers – although in the back of his mind was the thought that if the mysterious new young Didi could, indeed, heal his sickly children, it would be worth more to cultivate her patronage than placate this old fiend.

More aggravated than ever, Didi Badini paced her apartment, ignoring the cool drinks and tasty titbits offered to her. Only the news that a new patron awaited her inspection diverted her from her annoyance.

The customer introduced himself as Farkas Hamisen, an off-planet merchant who had, he said, been told that Didi Badini's house would show him the best Kezdet had to offer.

He was a handsome young man, if one over-looked the ears that sat rather oddly on his head and did not seem to quite match the café-au-lait tone of his face. Didi Badini was far more inter-ested in Hamisen's expensive clothes and the jeweled ring that twinkled on his hand; she had no problem at all ignoring the ears, especially when he initiated the conversation by flattering her shamelessly. He could well believe that an estab-lishment with such a lovely proprietor was the finest on Kezdet, he said, but it was hard to believe the owner did not outshine her merchandise. Perhaps she would do him the honor of an evening's conversation, just to get acquainted, before they discussed business?

Didi Badini smilingly agreed. Surely she could serve him better, she agreed, if she knew his tastes and personality.

A few more fulsome compliments gained him entrée into her private rooms, where poufs of silk-covered cushions invited visitors to relax at their ease. Hamisen praised the room as well and said that surely no establishment on Kezdet could boast such a lovely lady and such luxurious settings. He almost dared to confess the secret fantasy that had never yet been satisfied.

'On Kezdet,' Didi Badini said, smiling, 'anything is possible . . . for a price.'

Hesitantly, almost shamefacedly, she thought, Farkas Hamisen confessed to a fascination with *unusual* girls. After some beating about the bush Didi Badini established that 'unusual' meant deformed rather than very young.

'You have come to the right planet, my friend,' she said, searching her memory for the children she'd recently rejected as too odd to appeal to her customers. There was that one-eyed child at Anyag . . .

Still acting shy, Hamisen said that there was a particular deformity that had always excited him beyond measure, although he had only seen it in a dream. A Didi in the next street had attempted to satisfy him by offering a girl with an obviously false horn pasted onto her forehead, but of course he had been revolted by the trickery.

'You want *her*?' Didi Badini gasped unguardedly. 'I don't believe it!'

'You know of such a girl?' Farkas murmured. 'Truly I was well guided by those who recommended your establishment.' In fact he had been touring the bonk-shops of Kezdet in no particular order, amusing himself with a girl at each one while at the same time he pursued this inquiry for Acorna, who would lead him to Rafik. 'Do tell me about her.'

'There are rumors of such a one,' Didi Badini said, thinking quickly. If she told Hamisen that the horned freak was setting up as a Didi on her own account, he would go straight to Didi Acorna and she herself would lose the lovely profits promised by his clothes and ring . . . as well as the pleasurable caresses with which he was entertaining her while they talked. She never 'went' with clients anymore, but that didn't mean she was averse to affectionate fondling of the kind that knowledgeable men and women exchanged. Just now he was stroking her hair, which she felt was her best feature: soft, silky, curly, and without a single white hair. He knew just how to do it, too, without catching his fingers or his nails, which she had noticed he kept properly manicured.

'Only rumors?' he repeated, withdrawing the caressing hand.

Then again, Didi Badini thought, if she professed too much ignorance he might leave and pursue his interests elsewhere. That must not be allowed to happen! Not only would she lose the money and the pleasure he promised, but the half-formed plan which was floating in her mind would never come to fruition.

'Only rumors to most people,' she said, 'but I have seen her, and I . . . might be able to find her again.' The thought of delivering her impudent new rival to Farkas Hamisen, drugged into a state of compliance, gave her far more pleasure than anything Farkas Hamisen could do with those elegant, long, brown hands.

'Really? You must let me know if you learn anything else,' Hamisen said in a bored tone. The underlying message was clear: she would have to do better if she wanted to retain his interest. Didi Badini searched her memory for some scrap of information that would intrigue Hamisen and keep him close to her, without giving him enough of a clue to actually locate this girl.

'Her bodyguard used to work for the Li consortium,' she said reluctantly. 'There may be some connection there . . . but you would be well advised not to pursue it, my dear. Delszaki Li is powerful, corrupt, and utterly ruthless. It would be too dangerous for someone who does not know the ways of Kezdet to inquire into House Li affairs.'

'A man does not shelter behind a woman's skirts,' Hamisen said firmly. 'How are you going to find out about the girl?'

Didi Badini smiled and stroked his arm with one long, elegantly oval fingernail. 'I have my friends . . . here and there. Amuse yourself with some ordinary girls tonight, Farkas – on the house, of course,' she added hastily, 'and come back to me in a few days for more information.' She treated him to the sleepy smile that had beguiled the elder Tondubh into parting with more jewels than the glassworks could afford, back in the days when she still did her own work.

'You *will* come back . . . won't you?'

He answered her question with one of his own. 'You *will* find the unicorn girl for me . . . won't you?'

It was Gill who brought home news of the legends that permeated Kezdet through kava shop to bazaar and even to the sacred rooms of the Miners' Guild. He had all he could do to keep from pounding a few faces in for the smutty suggestions about horn-nuzzling that went on. What had Acorna done to generate such speculation? Well, it would have to stop right now! Mr Li's house was impregnable, but Acorna had lately been given to such bizarre . . . escapades . . . even when she was supposedly being guarded and / or chaperoned by Pal and Judit.

Then it occurred to him that maybe he had best join any more outings, to guard Judit as well as Acorna.

The high-pitched laughter of happy children greeted him as he palmed his entrance to Mr Li's mansion. He stood for a moment, listening to the enchanting mirth. Laughter was a lovely sound and suddenly he realized that he could not make Acorna suspend her lifesaving activities. But the sooner they initiated the Moon project, the better . . . the safer.

Rafik was busier than he had ever been in his life in the spacious office which Mr Li had given over to him, and the use of state-of-the-art communications devices that allowed him to speed messages to an incredible number of destinations. He was not a member of his particular family without having an innate natural instinct for trading. He often wondered why he hadn't gone into that respectable profession as his mother had wanted. Not that he felt himself at any loss in the bargaining and badgering that were part and parcel of making successful deals. In the odd moments he had, he decided that as a callow youth he had only been kicking over the traces to go a-mining. And yet, he wouldn't have had the opportunity to do this now if he hadn't done that. Kismet!

He had managed to make contact, again through Mr Li's amazing network of contacts, with a lunar engineer: an elderly man, one Martin Dehoney, now retired, who had been responsible for the ingenious structures that were almost compulsory on moon mining installations for their high safety factors and low budget requirement. He was also said to be a treasure chest of innovative ideas which conservative agencies, such as large corporations and governments, would not consider. So, when Rafik contacted him, at first the Architect Dehoney had demurred by virtue of his age and debility, but Rafik's gentle persuasion – and the explanation that the plan would ruin the system of Kezdet's child-bondage system – won him over. He allowed that he had quite a few novel ideas for moon installations which he felt might be eminently suitable, and which someone of Rafik's breadth of understanding might appreciate more than bureaucracies. To know that some of his best work would see the light of a sun would be very nice indeed before he slept. It took a moment for Rafik to realize he meant the 'long sleep' of death.

To his and Mr Li's intense gratification, a veritable harvest of plans, complete with specifications (although some of these were improvements and annexes to some of Dehoney's existing lunar facilities – fascinating in themselves) arrived by special courier three weeks later.

'It's not just the innovative design for integrating living facilities and life-support hydroponics,' Calum marveled. 'The man has an incredible instinct for mining engineering problems! Look at this bootstrap proposal. It's so elegant, it's beautiful!' He was looking at Dehoney's projected Phase II of the lunar base. In Phase I the lunar regolith would be raked for metal grains, which would then be reduced to their component elements by the gaseous carbonyl process. At the same time, a related chemical vapor deposition process would be used to fabricate large-sized, ultra-lightweight mirrors from the carbonyls of iron and nickel. In Phase II, when the regolith had been raked down to the underlying rock, these mirrors could be used to concentrate solar heat and break up the rock without the use of explosives, which would have to be imported, or mechanical drills, which as Calum knew all too well were subject to frequent dust clogging and friction wear in near-vacuum conditions.

'And he uses by-products of the regolith ben-eficiation to provide shielding from solar flares in the first habitats,' Gill pointed out, 'then, in Phase Two, we can construct extensive living quarters in the rocky areas we excavate. So there's very little added cost for habitat construction and radiation shielding.' They were poring over the double-domed, lock-connected habitat and hydroponics design when Judit interrupted them to turn on Universal News and the report of Dehoney's demise: in his sleep.

'He must have just sent the plans off to us,' Rafik said, awed and chagrined. Had his urgency contributed to a fatal fatigue?

'I wouldn't have thought you could care about such things,' Judit said, giving him an odd look.

'You malign me,' Rafik said, though he knew that she had overheard him dealing rather ruth-lessly with some suppliers. He laid one hand on his heart, allowing his hurt to show. 'I would be callous indeed to work an old man to death. Even if children are being done so daily here, until we can get this underway.'

Mr Li regarded Judit over his nose as he had a habit of doing when he wished her to do some-thing that she did not wish to do.

'My apologies, Rafik.'

'We will name the main dome Dehoney after his inestimable contribution to the project,' Rafik announced, though he looked at Mr Li for confirmation of this sudden whimsy. Then, with a deep sigh, which could be interpreted in any way she chose, he unrolled the rest of the plans and studied them.

With such detailed plans, even to the environmental shifts as the population increased, Rafik was able to send out tenders to the construction firms which Gill had been checking out for integrity and the reputation of finishing jobs on time and within budgetary parameters. They sent the tenders out with a return address of the *Uhuru*, so that Mr Li's privacy would not be invaded by the importunate. When word of the size of this job got out, they would be besieged by every penurious sub-contractor looking to make more than his work was worth. Better that the office of record be a space ship so that dock security could be tipped to see that the worst did not gain entrance.

That meant that Rafik and Gill would have to have a discreet and secure modem link to Mr Li so he could supervise affairs.

'Rafik has the energy this project has needed,' Mr Li said, smiling beneficently at Judit and patting her hand, 'while I can still supply the wisdom of experience which his young head has not yet had time to accumulate.'

Judit had just discovered the packet of disks, part of the consignment and, exclaiming with delight, loaded them into the computer. Almost instantly, the sketches became three-dimension drawings, moving as the strained voice of Marty Dehoney added explanation to his vision of a lunar mining station that could also vie for use as a holiday resort, so complete were the amenities.

'And look at this!' Gill exclaimed as Dehoney went into his expansion plans. 'To cut down the hazard of fire, he suggests we capture small carbonaceous asteroids and release their nitrogen.'

'Not to mention we can get sulfates and phosphates from the same source, if needed, to supplement the lunar minerals,' Calum pointed out. 'If you hadn't been so single-minded about collecting valuable metal payloads, you'd have thought of that yourself. We passed up plenty of carbonaceous chondrites in between E-types.'

'I didn't notice you coming up with the suggestion, either.'

'Didn't need it to support a crew of four,' Calum said smugly. 'If we'd been trying to stabilize life-support and atmospheric systems for an entire colony, naturally I would have mentioned it.'

'Oh, naturally,' Gill drawled with heavy irony.

They were still viewing the comprehensive disks when Pal came to announce that dinner was ready. On noticing their intent faces, he very quickly called down to ask the butler to hold the meal for at least half an hour.

Tapha's tongue stuck out between his pinched lips as he worked his way through the cipher program built into his personal com. His father was so stupidly old-fashioned, requiring all his operatives to use a cipher that depended on recalling large chunks of the Books of the Three Prophets from memory. He'd probably have a fit if he knew that Tapha had reprogrammed his personal com to generate enciphered messages automatically, always using the First Verse of the First Book as the key . . . and even so, there was more hands-on labor involved than Tapha cared for. When *he* took over the organization, one of the first changes he'd make would be to modernize the communications system, using an automatic encryptor instead of this cumbersome system. Hafiz was overly concerned about security, anyway. Why, Tapha had been using the same encryption key for every message he sent from Kezdet, and there was no sign that any of them had been broken.

Nor was there any sign that any of them had been received, though he knew they must have been. Hafiz was just being mean and petty, refusing to advance the credits necessary for Tapha to live in the style befitting the heir to the Hafiz Harakamian empire, forcing him to sell off one by one the jewels he'd collected when he fled. Well, all that would change now. With satisfaction Tapha completed the encrypted message telling his father that he had located his prized unicorn girl and would return her . . . for a price. He could not resist adding the cryptic comment that he had also found the way to solve another family problem here on Kezdet. Without help! Well, without very much help, anyway. Didi Badini's mention of House Li had been enough of a clue for Tapha to locate Acorna and Rafik on his own. He

wouldn't need to go back to her for information . . .
though he might go back for his own amusement.

After handing in his message at one of the
public comsuites on the main streets of Celtalan,
Tapha went on his way to arrange the solution of
that nagging family problem. How proud his
father would be when he learned that Tapha had
not only recaptured the unicorn girl but had also
revenged the trickery practiced on their house by
Cousin Rafik! More to the point, with Rafik safely
out of the way, there would be no more plots to do
Tapha out of his rightful position as his father's
heir apparent. This time Tapha did not intend to
make any stupid, impulsive moves, such as the
attack at the restaurant . . . although that *should*
have worked; he still couldn't figure out how
Rafik could have moved fast enough to avoid
taking even one blast of laser fire. No matter. This
time his disguise would allow him to get close
enough to make absolutely sure that Rafik was
quite thoroughly dead.

And once that little matter had been cleared up,
he had only to wait until his father's emissaries
arrived with enough credits to make it worth his
while to tell them where the unicorn girl was. No
need to put himself to the effort of capturing
her; that was work for subordinates. He, Tapha,
was the mastermind behind the plan, and that was
quite enough. No, he would simply relax at Didi
Badini's until Hafiz responded to this latest news.
The old bat would give him anything for a few
kisses and sweet words . . . and when he was ready

293

for something fresher, he would offer to help train this new acquisition, the scarred girl from the mines. An enjoyable way to wile away the days of waiting, and one advantage accrued to this child, since she was already marked, was that presumably the Didi wouldn't care if she acquired a few more scars during 'training.' There'd be no need to be careful as he had been ever since that unfortunate accident with the joy-toy girl on Theloi.

As was routine on Kezdet, Tapha's latest message and all other messages with off-planet tags were routed through a Guardians of the Peace office on their way to their final destination. Ed Minkus browsed through the day's mail list with a casual eye out for any interesting anomalies or potential profits, stopping at the obviously encrypted message purporting to concern differing religious interpretations of the First Verse of the First Prophet.

'Hey, Des,' he called to his partner, 'here's some more crap from that Tapha guy. You know? The one with the funny-looking ears who keeps writing home for money and uses the same encryption key every time.'

'So?' Des grunted. 'Unless he actually *gets* some money, he's no use to us.'

'This one is something different.' Ed activated the decryption program and scanned the cleartext as it appeared on the screen. 'He's found something valuable . . . might be worth a cut of the action . . . oh, and it looks as if he's planning to assassinate some guy named Nadezda.'

'Nadezda?' Des rolled out of his chair and into a standing position over Ed in one savage movement. 'Nadezda! He can't do that! That triple-timing, two-tailed miner is *mine*! Nobody kills Nadezda before I get my own back on him!'

Delszaki Li's payment of the 'fines' owed by Calum, Gill, and Rafik to Kezdet had left Des without official excuse to persecute the miners, but with none of his original lust for vengeance diminished in the slightest.

'Well, then,' Ed replied mildly, 'we'll just have to stop this Tapha before he gets there, won't we?'

The vid-screen in a corner of Didi Badini's luxuriously furnished sitting room transmitted only a jagged pattern of neon flashes that made the Didi's head hurt.

'Drop the bloody scramble, can't you? It hurts my eyes – and it's not as if I'd never seen you before.' Immediately she made that last comment, the Didi regretted it. It was not wise to remind the Piper that you were one of the few people on Kezdet who had seen his face . . . even if you had no idea where in the ranks of Kezdet's techno-aristocracy he led his 'real' life.

'I have already been careless enough,' a dry voice whispered from the speaker grill surrounding the screen, 'accompanying you to that mine. And for what? First sight of a pretty girl-child whom *you* managed to lose before she was back in your house!'

Didi Badini cringed at the anger in the whispering voice and forbore to remind the Piper that he, too, had been in the skimmer when that little beast Khetala distracted them and gave Chiura her chance to run away. Never mind. She dared not express her anger at the Piper, but she could take it out on Khetala later. The brat had been locked below long enough to take the fight out of her; now she would turn her over to Tapha to break her.

'A thousand apologies, master,' she said, swallowing her rage at this unfair criticism. 'How may I serve you now?'

'There are rumors—' the voice whispered, while neon-green and bile-yellow stripes crawled and writhed across the vid-screen, 'rumors that the goddess of some children's cult walks the soil of Kezdet. She has a thousand names but only one face, long and narrow, with a horn like a unicorn's sprouting from her forehead.'

'Didi Acorna!' Didi Badini sat upright on her pile of cushions. 'I knew she was no true Didi, for none of the sisterhood knew of her!'

'Didi, goddess, what does it matter?' the Piper interrupted her. 'The tales they are spreading of her healing powers are gross exaggeration, but that does not matter, either. What matters is that the children *believe*. The Child Labor League and that malcontent Li are stirring up enough trouble now; we do not need some goddess cult serving as the focal point for more resistance. This horned freak must disappear. And I must not be seen to be involved in it. I will not have

296

my official position compromised.'

Didi Badini's plump powdered face creased in an unpleasant smile. 'Nothing,' she assured the Piper, 'would give me more pleasure. And there need be no hint of politics about the removal, either. For impersonating a sister without paying dues to our guild, she has already earned punishment. And there are those who would pay well for that horn of hers; powdered unicorn's horn is an aphrodisiac of unparalleled power.'

'But will removal of the horn kill her?' asked the voice, like dry leaves rustling.

'I think we can be sure of that little point,' said Didi Badini, smiling as the vid-screen display abruptly went gray.

Then her face sagged with relief. She might not be able to see the Piper, but she knew he could watch and interpret every change of expression on her face. A little longer, and she might have been rash enough to let him find out exactly how she proposed to locate this Didi Acorna. She saw no need to tell him that she counted on young Tapha to lead her to the girl. The Piper might think that he could more profitably deal with Tapha directly . . . and Didi Badini had not been lying when she mentioned the resale value of a unicorn's horn. She had customers whose natural powers were failing, to be revived only by some special treat such as a very young virgin or the whipping of a recalcitrant girl; they would pay handsomely for this by-product of Acorna's death.

Ten

Tapha gave his borrowed dock workers' coveralls a last nervous hitch and strode through the workers' gate to the spaceport, giving the security guard a jaunty wave as he passed. He could scarcely conceal his jubilation. The disguise had worked! The coveralls were a gift from Didi Badini, who had bought them from a lower-class Didi whose establishment of aging ladies was patronized by the poorer dock mechanics and by transients who knew no better. It had been a simple matter for Didi Hamida to slip a trank into one of her clients' drinks, remove his uniform while he slept, and subsequently remove his unclothed body to a gutter some distance from her establishment.

Women helped him, Tapha thought as he paced down the cavernous hangar where ships in for repairs were being disassembled and worked on. He definitely had a way with women . . . and once this little job was taken care of, he looked forward to returning to Didi Badini's establishment to have his way with the new girl. Experienced women were all very well, but there was nothing quite like the young and untouched . . . and if they were frightened as well, that added spice to the encounter.

'Hey, you!' a real mechanic bawled at him. 'Get me a hydraulic splitter! Not that way, you idiot,' he went on as Tapha sauntered on his way. 'Stores are the other side of the hangar!'

Tapha waved and mouthed something intended to be totally unintelligible. The mechanic shrugged in disgust, said something to his mates about fardling idiot foreigners who didn't even speak Basic properly and what was the Guild coming to, and went to get his own hydraulic splitter – whatever that might be. Tapha neither knew nor cared, but he quickened his pace so as to reach the *Uhuru*'s docking space outside the hangar before anybody else could delay him. It would be a real pity if the fiendish cunning of his new disguise and improved weaponry were spoiled by encountering somebody who expected him to actually know about mechanicals. Tapha patted the sagging pocket of his coveralls and grinned. This time there would be no possibility of a miss.

From a borrowed office high on the hangar wall, Des Smirnoff and Ed Minkus watched Tapha's sauntering progress. 'Idiot thinks he got through the security check by dressing up like a mech,' Ed commented. 'He doesn't even guess that we had the weaponry and retinal scanners turned off and

299

told the guard not to check IDs when the little guy with the funny ears showed up. Why *did* we let him through the check, anyway? Would've been easier to've picked him up there. Or did you change your mind about letting him off Nadezda for you?'

'Hell, no,' Des replied, 'but he hasn't done anything illegal yet. He hasn't even cheated the scanners, since they were turned off. It would be exceeding our charter as Guardians of the Peace to stop a man who, for all we know, is paying an innocent family visit.'

'And very nice that'll sound if there's an inquiry,' Ed applauded. 'Now what's the real reason?'

Des gave a wolfish grin. 'It won't hurt to put a bit of a scare into Nadezda before we take this one out. Besides, if we stop a suspicious-looking character at the gate and find unlawful arms on him, we're just doing our duty. If we shoot him down just in time to prevent an assassination attempt, we're Heroes of the Republic.'

Ed sighed. 'You already got your money back. Now you want revenge on Nadezda *and* a Hero of the Republic medal? Ever hear the story of the fisherman's wife who wished to be pope?'

'Pope who?'

'Never mind. He's coming into range now; let's see if the scanners can pick up just what he's carrying in that bulging left pocket.' Ed activated the beams, focused them, and gave a long, low whistle. 'Holy Kezdet . . . we shouldn't have

300

disabled the weapons scanners at the main gate.'

'We didn't want him stopped for carrying a pocket laser or something like that,' Des reminded him.

'Pocket laser! Ha! The idiot's got a tungsten bomb in there!'

'You're kidding!'

'Wish I were. Here – take a look at the reading.'

Des glanced at the scanner screens and blanched. 'He didn't mention this was a suicide mission. If that thing goes off, he won't only get Nadezda. He'll blow up the bloody ship!'

'He'll blow up the whole bloody hangar,' Ed corrected him.

'Maybe the whole spaceport.'

'A chunk of West Celtalan.'

'Hero of the Republic,' Ed said, 'is *not* what they're going to hang around your neck for letting this one through, boyo.'

'If we don't stop him,' Des said tersely, 'I won't have a neck left for them to hang me by. And if he sees us, he might panic and set the thing off prematurely. . . . Hell, he's so dumb he might set it off by accident anyway!'

Both men were jogging down the internal security hall by the middle of this conversation, so well attuned to each others' thoughts and reactions that they didn't even need to discuss what to do next. If they could round two sides of the hangar and cut off Tapha before he reached the *Uhuru*, if one of them could get a clear shot at him, they just might be able to save themselves and a largish chunk of West Celtalan from molecular disintegration.

'Alarm?' puffed Ed as they passed a security station.

'Nope. Don't want to startle him.' Des was in no better shape than his colleague, but his adrenaline high was enough to keep him from feeling out of breath yet.

They made it to their target corner with seconds to spare, Ed leading. He drew his stunner, peered around the wall, and swore. 'Too many fardling workers in the way. I can't get a clear shot.'

'Screw the workers,' Des said. 'They'd rather be shot in passing than disintegrated by a tungsten bomb, wouldn't they?' He leaned over Ed's crouching form, utilizing every advantage of his superior height and reach, and squeezed off a series of narrow-band stunner shots without even seeming to pause to take aim.

'Got him,' he said with satisfaction, and sprinted for Tapha's fallen form to defuse the bomb, Ed close behind him. 'Let's hope it's a standard arming device,' he said, reaching into the baggy pocket they had spotted as containing the weapon. 'Be a damn shame to lose the hands that have such perfect aim to a misfired tungsten bomb.'

'This thing goes off,' Ed said sourly, 'you'll never have time to miss your hands.' He knelt over Tapha and watched, breath held, as Des twirled the combination detonator on the tungsten bomb without a trace of nervousness. Three clicks, an

302

agonizing pause, and then the bones of Ed's skull registered the cessation of the almost subliminal buzzing that had signaled an armed tungsten bomb ready to detonate on signal. Now for the first time he noticed the people around them; the crowd of mechs shouting misinformation at one another, and two of the miners pushing their way through the crowd. Rafik Nadezda was the first to reach them.

'Hey,' Rafik said, looking down, 'that's—'

'A tungsten bomb,' Des Smirnoff said, rising to his feet with the dismantled halves of the bomb held one in each hand. 'Whoever this was *really* didn't like you, Nadezda – even more than I don't like you. You owe me one. Another one,' he said with heavy meaning.

'I was about to say,' said Rafik with dignity, 'that's my cousin Tapha.'

'You got the tense wrong,' Des said with a tight-lipped smile. 'That *was* your cousin Tapha. I set my stunner on max when I got a maniac with an armed tungsten bomb wandering around the port, Nadezda, and he took half a dozen shots to the head. Fried his brains.' He thought that over. 'His hypothetical brains.'

'How did he get past security?' somebody wondered aloud.

'These terrorists are fiendishly cunning,' Des said, raising his voice to roar over the noise of the crowd.

'Terrorists?' Gill repeated. 'I thought it was a personal—'

'The Guardians of the Peace have been watching this man for some time,' Des said loudly. 'We have reason to believe he is closely associated with the Child Labor League, those notorious terrorists who are doing their best to wreck the economy of our happy, peaceful, and productive planet.'

Gill's face turned as red as his beard. Rafik stepped backward and landed heavily on his toe.

'A happy end to an unfortunate situation,' he said over Gill's rumblings of anger. 'Allow me to congratulate you on your prompt handling of the crisis, Guardian Smirnoff. And – er – that little episode on the asteroid was a mistake. We had no idea you would be marooned there for any length of time. I owe you an apology for that incident.'

Smirnoff's face darkened. 'You owe me more than an apology,' he said under his breath, 'and I still intend to collect, Nadezda. Later!'

'How about a formal report and recommendation that you be nominated as a Hero of the Republic?' Rafik suggested in equally low tones. 'You've definitely earned it today.'

Smirnoff paused, visibly undecided.

'And no inquiry as to how this . . . terrorist . . . made it through security,' Rafik added.

'You can pull that off?'

'An off-planet miner may not have that much influence,' said Rafik, 'but the heir to the Harakamian Empire has.'

'You?'

Rafik stood looking down at Tapha's body, his face expressionless. 'I am now. You'll permit me to collect his personal effects?' he added after a moment's silence. 'I should have something to send to his father.'

'Go right ahead,' Des offered. 'And—'

Rafik's lips curved slightly. 'I won't forget the report, no. Congratulations – Hero of the Republic!'

Calum missed the excitement of Tapha's second assassination attempt, as he had missed most of what was going on around him since Dr Zip produced the results of his study. Zip had concentrated on the sector of space nearest where Acorna was found and had been downcast to report that the upsilon-V studies of stars in that sector showed a very low chance of any primary producing planets rich in the precise mix of metals used in the pod, a report that was borne out by the mass diffusion imaging of the nearest M-type stars and their planets.

But Calum rather thought Zip, in his pride at being able to report the constituents of distant planets through new technology, had overlooked a few things. The one sure thing they knew about Acorna's people was that they had a sophisticated space-faring system. If he and Gill and Calum could take rhenium from the asteroid Daffodil to make solar thermal-thrust chambers on Theloi, why couldn't Acorna's people also have mined a number of systems to collect the metals for this alloy?

That concept turned the problem of locating

Acorna's home world from a straightforward task of astrophysical analysis to a complex optimization program requiring sophisticated operations research techniques.

'You see,' Calum had explained to Gill when he started working on the program, 'we are also going to assume, going from what we know of Acorna, that her people are not stupid or wasteful. They wouldn't go farther than necessary to get their metals. So first I have to use Zip's data to design a program to find all the subsets of stars within a given volume of space that would, collectively, provide the necessary substances, then, for each such subset, find the M-type planet that most nearly approaches an optimal location for all the required mining missions.'

'Hey,' Rafik said, 'if Zip can come up with planetary emissions studies for all these systems, why don't we use him to locate good mining areas for us?'

'Costs too much,' Calum said. 'You wouldn't *believe* what Li has spent on this problem already.'

He quoted figures until even Rafik reluctantly agreed that it wouldn't be cost-effective to retain Zip's services as a prospector.

'But,' he said, brightening, 'he has already produced all this data in search of Acorna, has he not? Surely there would be no objections to our using it for other purposes?'

'Probably not,' Calum agreed. He was rather annoyed at the way his friends kept missing the point. Who cared about mining? He wanted them to appreciate his elegant approach to the problem of identifying Acorna's home. 'I'm treating the entire collection of stars as overlapping subsets, each containing one or more M-types. By the Axiom of Choice, there must be—'

Rafik had left abruptly then, muttering something about mad dogs and mathematicians. Calum was a bit surprised that Rafik didn't share his joy in the beauties of applied linear programming, but then it took all sorts, didn't it? Whistling under his breath, he commandeered one of the parallel-processing units used by the banking branch of the Li consortium, raided another branch for statistical analysis software that could be perverted to serve his ends, and proceeded to put together his very own astronomical and mining optimization program. For the past weeks his conversation at mealtimes had been limited to cryptic statements such as, 'I'd have it done if I didn't have to put the data structures from all these different bloody star charts into canonical form first,' or, 'No, the fact that it's in an infinite loop doesn't mean the program doesn't work; it just entered a state with which I was previously unfamiliar.' And whenever Judit would let him get away with it, he skipped meals altogether in favor of a quick snack that he could eat one-handed while gliding through visual displays of his program in the windowless room dedicated to the project.

Now, at last, he was getting results. Inconclusive, maybe, but results. He barely heard

307

Gill's excited account of the assassination attempt and its aftermath. 'Tapha's dead? Good, that's one less person after us.'

'And I think Rafik's squared Des Smirnoff. So the Guardians of the Peace won't be bothering us, either. Calum, you should have seen Smirnoff defusing that tungsten bomb! The man may be a corrupt cop, but he can take a place on my bomb squad any day. Talk about nerves of steel!'

'Mmm. Good job he defused it,' Calum said, nodding over the latest printout. 'A bomb like that could've caused a power outage as far as here, couldn't it? I could've lost a lot of data.'

Gill suggested that Calum take his data and do something anatomically improbable with it, then stomped off to find a more appreciative audience. Calum barely registered his disappearance; he was thinking about ways to narrow down the long list of possible planets to check out. The trouble with his brainstorm was that they'd gone from zero possibles to over a hundred, none of them conveniently close. *Of course, they wouldn't be close.* He snorted at his own naïveté. *If they were nearby we'd've met Acorna's people by now.* And he might not be able to rule out any of this long list of possibles, but he could rank them for the search by running a second optimization, this time minimizing the total travel time and distance required. It would be a simple variant of the classic travelling-salesman problem.

The only trouble was, then what? Calum longed to test his results, and the only way he could see to do that was to go and look for himself. Delszaki Li would probably be willing to retrofit the *Uhuru* with superdrives that would minimize the travel time. But it would still be a five-year project just to check out the nearest group of possible planets. How could he abandon his buddies and take their ship for five years? Rafik and Gill *needed* him; neither of them was enough of a mathematician to manage subspace navigation on his own.

Calum came out of his particular haze when he realized he had *not* seen Rafik and, at breakfast, asked if Rafik was living aboard the *Uhuru*.

Acorna giggled. 'I told you that eventually he would notice,' she said to Mr Li, who was smiling benignly on her.

'Well? Is he?' He addressed this query to Gill.

'In a manner of speaking, he is,' Gill replied around a mess of kippered herrings which Mr Li had imported especially for him. Though Calum was as British in origin as himself, the mathematician did *not* like kippered herrings.

Waiting for Gill to continue, he even wrinkled his nose as the reek of the delicacy wafted in his direction.

'He's on a sorrowful mission,' Acorna said, giggling again.

Calum wished she wouldn't giggle. It wasn't like his Acorna. *She* had never been silly, but maybe it was part of the girlish things that Judit was teaching her. Although he couldn't remember Judit giggling.

'What?' and Calum addressed this inquiry to Mr Li as the only sensible member at the dining table.

'His cousin, Tapha,' Mr Li supplied.

'Can no one give me a straight answer?' Calum complained.

'Considering that all we've had out of you recently has been either statistical probabilities or astronomical variables,' Judit said, a touch peevishly, 'a straight answer is improbable, isn't it?' Then she relented as Calum did indeed look hurt and had been trying so hard to locate Acorna's home world. 'He decided he'd better take Tapha's ashes back to Uncle Hafiz and explain how he met his death.'

'Oh!' Calum digested this along with several mouthfuls of a delightful breakfast omelet before he let his fork fall from his hand. 'But he's now his uncle's heir.'

'We know,' Judit replied.

'Will he come back at all? Gill said something about Rafik finally finding his element in all the trading he's had to do for the Moon Mines.'

Gill glowered at him. 'He won't leave us until he's finished that, because *that* will prove to Hafiz that he's really sown his wild oats and is ready to settle down and represent House Harakamian.'

'Oh!' Calum said, digesting that before he picked up his fork. 'Yes, it would rather, wouldn't it? But Rafik wouldn't do that, would he? Not yet, when we haven't finished the moon base or found Acorna's planet.'

'I don't think he would,' Gill said, half his mind on getting the last flake of kippered herring onto his fork and into his mouth.

Pal entered, looking concerned. 'I just heard that Hafiz Harakamian's fastest ship docked here this morning, in fact, in the berth the *Uhuru* was using.'

'Uh-oh,' Gill said, looking at Acorna. 'That idiot son of his must have told him you're here.'

'How could he know?' Acorna was dismayed.

'How could he know?' And Gill went falsetto in mimicry. 'Because you've been doing your Lady of the Lights and the healed wounds and purified water act all over Celtalan is how he knows. How many unicorn horns are there on Kezdet?' He stood, throwing down his napkin, the bristles of his beard trembling with sincerity. 'And I'm going to stick as close to you as your shadow.'

'Oh, good, when Calum goes back to his computers, we can go out. I have just a little errand to do. I would have asked Pal, but he's doing something for Mr Li, and I have a call in to Pedir,' she spared a glance at the elegant antique carriage clock on the mantelpiece, 'and he will be here shortly. Do say you'll come?'

'You better go,' Calum said, 'because I haven't spent hours, days . . .'

'Weeks?' Judit put in, grinning from him to Gill.

'. . . trying to locate where you came from, to let Uncle Hafiz get you first.'

'So Pedir found out where she is?' Judit asked.

Acorna nodded. 'He's been so helpful.'

Judit looked as if she were about to add something, then saw the belligerent look on Gill's face. 'I can't come this morning.' She turned to Mr Li. 'We have that appointment with the head of the Public Works about proving the moon base design meets the code.'

'That sounds like an engineering problem,' Gill objected.

'It's politics,' Judit said. 'He knows the base design is safe, and he knows we know it. At this stage, Delszaki doesn't need an engineer to reiterate the facts and get red in the face. He needs a psycholinguist to maneuver the talks the right way.'

'You mean, Kezdet's objecting?' Gill asked, for he'd heard rumors which Rafik had discounted.

'Nothing that can't be discreetly settled, my boy,' Mr Li said, and moved his hover-chair back from the table. 'Come along, Judit. Gill, I'd rather you accompanied Acorna and Nadhari since Judit cannot.'

'As you wish, Mr Li,' Gill said, but he wasn't looking forward to it. Nadhari Kando wasn't his idea of a pleasant female companion for an excursion. 'You'll be safe with me.' Actually, he didn't think they needed Nadhari at all, but it was better to be safe than sorry.

He could add that to Calum's list of famous last words. Climbing into Pedir's skimmer – he'd met the man previously, since his vehicle seemed to be constantly in use by Judit and Acorna for their 'shopping trips' – he had no idea where they were going. Pedir started right in telling Acorna about some very useful items he heard were going for nothing in the market which he thought she should check out. That ought to have warned Gill, but he was thinking about Tapha and Rafik and worrying that Rafik's wily uncle might somehow hold him on Laboue, and the Li Moon Mining Company Ltd might grind to a halt. Rafik had so much in his head and not on paper that it would take Gill months to catch up if Rafik didn't return in a timely fashion.

He was roused out of his contemplation when Pedir landed the skimmer, and Gill was astonished to find themselves in the very worst possible neighborhood.

'You will wait in the skimmer,' Nadhari told Acorna. 'I will fetch the girl.'

'She won't come to you,' Acorna said.

Nadhari bared her teeth. 'She will if I tell her to.' She slipped out of the skimmer, which barely fit in the narrow courtyard where they had landed, and trod through puddles of slime to where a short flight of stairs led to a basement door in the wall. She tapped a special sequence; the door opened a crack, then swung shut again.

'Wait, wait!' Acorna cried, scrambling after Nadhari. 'They don't know you! She's afraid! You'll have to go back to the skimmer!'

'Delszaki Li ordered me to protect you.' Nadhari planted her booted heels firmly in the mud and glared at Acorna. 'You go, I go.'

'Nobody's going in,' Acorna said patiently.

Gill thought it was time he joined the discussion. 'Acorna, acushla, this is not exactly a shopping trip, is it? Want to tell me what's going on?'

Acorna looked at her feet. 'Not really.'

'Not good enough,' Gill said sternly.

Acorna drew a deep breath. 'Well . . .'

The door creaked on its hinges. 'You talk too long!' whispered a woman. She put her face to the open crack, where the daylight cruelly illuminated the shiny red burn scars that disfigured the right side of her face from cheekbone to chin. 'Someone will come! The lady must come in and pay the price. No one else.'

There was a moment of tense bargaining, as both Gill and Nadhari initially refused to allow Acorna to go into the dark rooms at all, and the person on the other side of the door wanted them to go back to the skimmer, and Nadhari clearly wanted to blast her way into the rooms and take whatever it was Acorna had come for with no more talking. Finally a compromise was reached: Nadhari and Acorna were allowed in while Gill waited outside.

'We are only women here,' the veiled figure said. 'Only women come in.'

'And if they think that makes them safe,' Gill muttered, pacing the short length of the courtyard and back again, three strides each way, 'they obviously don't recognize dear Nadhari.'

There was a cry from inside, then the door bolt snicked, the door was flung back, and Acorna's arm pushed a very young girl out of the entry. Her arm did not follow as he hoped, but was yanked back inside.

'They'll kill her,' the child squeaked, and managed to jam her foot in the door. She cried out with pain as the closing door compressed her foot, but only for a heartbeat; then Gill had his shoulder to the door, forcing it open again.

The sudden change from light to darkness startled him. He had a confused impression of figures struggling in the confined space. Was that Acorna? He was afraid to move for fear of hurting her or Nadhari.

An elbow jammed into his solar plexus and Gill backed up two steps, banging into the door. 'Be some use, can't you!' Nadhari's low rough voice excoriated him. 'Open the fardling door!'

Gill pulled the door open, and the daylight showed him that two at least of the figures he'd seen were going to give nobody any trouble. Two men lay on the floor, one with a trickle of blood coming from his open mouth, the other staring wide-eyed and blank at the ceiling. Acorna was breathing hard. Nadhari was not. In the light from the open door, her right hand flicked and sent a knife into the shoulder of the young woman who'd insisted that Acorna come inside.

'Don't hurt her!' Acorna cried.

'It was a trap,' Nadhari's toneless voice grated. 'You have paid the price. Now come, before there is more trouble.'

Gill could see that the woman's face, though

315

contorted with pain, was now smooth with new clean skin where the burns had disfigured her before. 'I didn't mean for you to be trapped,' she cried to Acorna. 'They must have followed me.'

Nadhari made a sound of disgust and took Acorna's arm, pushing her out of the door.

The child in the courtyard had been trying to get back in to help, but now she was hindering their escape by blocking the door. Gill swooped her up in one arm, pushed Acorna toward the stairs with the other, and was up the stairs, down the alley, and into the skimmer in seconds.

They were actually in and Pedir was making a hasty lift out of the courtyard when more figures erupted out of the basement. The child started shrieking, clinging to Acorna.

'They'll get me. They'll get me,' she cried.

'Who?' Then Gill did a double-take on one of the male figures who had joined in the futile attempt to catch the rising skimmer. 'By all the saints, that's Uncle Hafiz!'

'Uncle Hafiz?' Acorna swiveled round, but the courtyard and its occupants was now out of sight and Pedir had pushed the speed bar as far forward as it would go, kicking the skimmer into full power.

'So, after all, Tapha told him you were here? And there's Rafik trying to make a good impression on Uncle!' Gill gave a snort of exasperation. 'Where was that? And who's this?' He decided these were safer topics than speculating about Rafik's annoyance when he discovered that Hafiz was here and might even know that his son had been trying to kill his nephew. Or maybe that wouldn't surprise him.

'This—' Acorna smiled proudly down at the young girl who was hugging her rescuer's waist in a stranglehold, still chanting her litany, 'she'll get me/he'll get me' '—this is Khetala, who saved Jana and so many of the children and guarded them as best she could until Didi Badini took her away. And we've taken her away from Didi Badini!'

'That won't help now,' Khetala blurted. 'He's after you and the Piper always kills those he's after.'

'The Piper?' Pedir said, noticeably blanching.

'The Piper?' Acorna's tone held contempt and scorn.

'The Piper?' Gill asked, wanting to understand the diverse reactions.

'He's the one who's supposed to be behind the child bondage schemes here on Kezdet . . .' Acorna began.

'He is,' Pedir said in an awed tone, jiggling the controls to get more speed out of the skimmer as he aimed it toward the nearest congregation of vehicles exactly like his.

'But we have Khetala now and she's safe with me,' Acorna said.

'I'm not sure I am,' Gill said, and sucked his bloody knuckles.

'Did you have a chance . . . I mean . . .' Pedir floundered and craned his head around to look at Acorna.

317

'Of course, I did. That was the bargain, wasn't it?' Acorna said stoutly.

Gill decided that since Pedir seemed to care what happened to the scarred girl, it might not be tactful to mention that they had left her with a knife through her shoulder and suspected her of setting them up. Nadhari and Acorna seemed to be working through the same thought processes, for they were both silent on the trip back. For Acorna, at least, that was unusual.

They reached Delszaki Li's home to discover that the population had been augmented by one that very morning, and a three-way fight was raging in the entrance hall.

'*Now* what?' Pal demanded, taking in their disheveled condition and the girl clutching Acorna like a life-preserver. 'Oh, never mind, don't tell me. I've got enough trouble this morning already, what with Mercy running out on her job.'

'I'm *sorry*, Pal,' said the slender young woman facing him. Her delicate yet firm features and the thick braid of dark hair that hung down her back reminded Gill of Judit, though this girl wasn't half as pretty. Her dark eyes didn't flash like Judit's, and she didn't have Judit's way of tilting her chin up just before charging into battle. 'I know you – we – need the information I was getting from the Guardian's office. But there wasn't going to be much more information that way. Not through me. Even Des Smirnoff noticed eventually that there were too many people named Kendoro around him. You and Judit haven't exactly been keeping a low profile, you know. Smirnoff and Minkus started being careful what they said around me last week. Today I came in to find they'd changed the passwords on all their files . . . and then I saw one of those windowless skimmers from Interrogation on the landing pad. I had to get out. I'm not brave like you and Judit, you know that. If they took me to Interrogation, I don't know what I might have told them.'

Surrounded by unknown people, Khetala clung with bruising fingers to Acorna. She quietly led the child away to the kitchen, hoping that the probably unusual experience of having all she wanted to eat would soothe and reassure her.

'Stop apologizing!' Calum snorted. He put one arm round Mercy's shoulders, as if to hold her upright. 'I've heard about some of the methods Interrogation uses. One jab of the needle and you spill all no matter how you try to keep from talking. I doubt I could stand up against them myself. You did exactly the right thing – not just for yourself, but for all of us – by getting out before they could take you.' He glared at Pal. 'What were *you* thinking of, to let the kid stay there at all after they started suspecting her?'

'I had no reason to think she was under suspicion,' Pal said stiffly, 'and the inside information she has provided on Guardians of the Peace activities has been invaluable. She's warned three of our field agents to get out before the Guardians could break up the hedgerow schools they were running for factory children and arrest our people.'

'With that kind of record, even the Guardians would have had to figure out there was a fly on the office wall somewhere,' Calum exclaimed. 'What was your plan: save the field agents and sacrifice the local one?'

'There was no need for any suspicion to have fallen on Mercy if she had been discreet,' Pal said.

'Discreet? Didn't you *listen* to the girl? It was her name, not her actions, that got her in trouble,' Calum said, blithely reversing his previous argument. 'If you two hadn't been taking Acorna all over Kezdet to stir up trouble, maybe it wouldn't be so dangerous for her to be a Kendoro.'

'Were you followed here, Mercy?' Pal asked, ignoring Calum.

The girl shivered. 'I don't know. I don't think so . . . I used the old route, through East Celtalan, and then the tunnels under the Riverwalk Park.'

'Let's hope you haven't compromised it, then.'

Calum snorted. 'Pal, if the Guardians are watching out for people named Kendoro, you can be sure they've got a watch on this house. What *difference* does it make whether Mercy was followed? The house is already under surveillance. But they're hardly likely to break into Delszaki Li's private residence to get a girl who's committed no crimes . . . are they?'

At this point Judit returned from her appointment with the head of Public Works and entered the fray.

'Pal, leave Mercy alone!' Judit commanded. 'She's had the hardest job of any of us, and if she says it was time for her to clear out, the least you can do is to trust her judgment.'

Pal threw up his hands. 'I give up! *Two* big sisters in one household is more than any man should be expected to take.'

'Fine,' Judit retorted, 'next time *you* can go and talk to the Public Works Department. Tumim Viggers is refusing to certify our base on Maganos for colonization. He says it's an untried technology and the architect needs to come to Kezdet to explain his plans in person.'

'The architect happens to be dead!' Gill exclaimed.

'Precisely. It's a stalling maneuver.' Judit frowned. 'Usually that means they want more bribes. But Viggers didn't hear any of Delszaki's hints in that direction. Maybe he really doesn't understand the base design. It is a radical departure from standard practice in some ways . . . and Kezdet's Public Works Department doesn't even have any experience with standard space environment designs.'

Delszaki Li had steered his float-chair in behind Judit and had been watching the argument with quiet amusement.

'Perhaps would be wise for some people to go to Maganos,' he suggested. 'Report, please, on how lunar base construction progresses; demonstrate success of habitat and ecological system.'

'I'll go,' Gill said. 'Rafik may not be back for a while, and heaven forbid we should tear Calum away from his astronomical optimization programs.' He looked at Acorna. 'And . . . I didn't have a chance to tell you yet, but we spotted Hafiz this morning. Three guesses what *he's* doing here! I think Acorna had better come with me. That'll keep her out of his way.' *And out of trouble*, he added silently to himself.

'I'll go with her,' Pal said immediately. He shot a dirty look at Mercy, who didn't notice. Her attention was all on Calum, who was talking quietly with her in a corner. 'This house is entirely too full of sisters.'

'Judit,' Delszaki Li said while Pal and Gill started discussing how they would produce a convincing report for Public Works, 'I wish you will accompany them.'

'Why me? Not that I mind,' Judit said hastily, 'but you need an assistant.' She glanced at Gill. For some reason the idea of studying a half-completed lunar colony with Gill sounded as attractive as a month-long holiday on the rainbow beaches of Erev Ba.

'Also need someone with sense to keep these children out of trouble,' Li said, which made Judit feel like the aging spinster governess in a Victorian household. Or the maiden aunt. 'As for assistant, Mercy can take over in your absence. Continue tradition of a Kendoro as my personal assistant.'

He cackled under his breath. 'You and Pal need to get busy, produce next generation of Kendoros before this old man wears out all three of this generation.' His glance at Gill was full of meaning.

Judit blushed and tried to think of some way to disguise her eagerness to go.

'Seems hard on Pal,' she murmured. 'He's going to Maganos to get away from his big sisters, and now you're sending one of us along to keep tabs on him.'

Li cackled again. 'I think maybe Pal has other reason for wishing to go to Maganos.' He looked meaningfully at Pal, who was staring at Acorna with an expression his loving older sister could only categorize as goopy in the extreme. 'Just when I have an assistant who understands my mind,' he sighed with pretended disappointment, 'his gets bent in another direction. You will go to Maganos, Judit,' he said firmly, a little too soon for Judit to be sure that his previous complaint had been meant to apply only to Pal. 'Mercy will stay and take care of poor old man in his declining years.'

'If you're sure she can do it . . .' Judit began doubtfully.

'You people don't appreciate Mercy!' Calum reentered the conversation with a bang, still clasping Mercy's shoulders. 'For years she's had the hardest job of any of you, working undercover for the Guardians of the Peace. Wasting her intelligence on pretending to be a secretary and carrying trays of kava! It's criminal. Do you realize this girl has an advanced degree in linear systems optimization theory? She's coming down to the basement now with me to see the programs I've developed to search for Acorna's home world.'

Li sighed as they left, but his dark eyes were twinkling.

'At least is not etchings,' he murmured, 'but is getting harder and harder to keep good help these days!'

Eleven

Brantley Geram, the subcontractor in charge of
building the living quarters and life-support
systems for Maganos Moon Base, was only too
happy to have representatives of Delszaki Li
coming to look at the work in progress. He was
in general a happy man, working on Maganos in
almost complete autonomy, developing the last
designs of the legendary Martin Dehoney, and with
the financial backing of the Li consortium allowing
him to make sure that for once everything was done
exactly as it should be, no corners cut in construction processes and no inferior materials used.

This did not, he hastened to assure Pal and
Acorna, imply any extravagance. Quite the
reverse. Mr Dehoney's plans were far-reaching,
ambitious, futuristic, perhaps, but *not* impractical
or extravagant.

'As you see, we started with minimal living
quarters, due to the expense of lifting shielding
materials into orbit. But as soon as the beneficia-
tion and reduction processors for the regolith

were in place, we were able to expand significantly, using the dust and by-products of reduction as our radiation shield.'

Acorna looked over the one large room he was showing them.

'Is this all?' she asked.

'We will, of course, be able to expand the living quarters even more as the processing of regolith continues,' Geram said, 'but there's no need for that at present. We have ample space for the contractors and work crews here.'

'You'll need more space,' Acorna said. 'How fast can you expand the quarters? We'll need dormitories, schoolrooms—'

'Schoolrooms?'

'Children may take up less space than adults,' Acorna said, 'but they must be educated. Or did you think Delszaki Li had gone into the business of exploiting child laborers like the rest of Kezdet?'

Brantley Geram sputtered unintelligibly and finally managed to convey that nobody had told him anything about children.

'That's why Mr Li wants all the machinery designed for easy maintenance and operation by people with little upper-body strength,' Pal told him. 'But I suppose you weren't involved with the mining machinery contract.'

'No,' Brantley said, with a regretful glance down the tunnel leading to the processing section of the base.

Gill had disappeared almost immediately upon arrival to inspect the technical workings, taking

Mr Li's other assistant – strange how all of Li's assistants seemed to be named Kendoro – along with him and reducing Brantley's audience to two. The funny-looking girl didn't even seem to be interested in the technical obstacles they had overcome to get this much of the lunar base operational in such a short time. Women! Let them into a place and they were mentally hanging curtains and planting flowers before you even had a decent oxygen-nitrogen balance established.

'And don't start turning the whole space into communal living quarters,' young Kendoro added to the girl. 'Remember, we'll have adults here, too, and they'll want some privacy. Make sure there are some shielded bedrooms for staff.'

Young men, Brantley thought, were even worse than women. All *they* thought about was bedrooms. Too bad that middle-aged miner, Gill something, hadn't stayed to inspect the base living quarters. He had looked like a sensible man.

'Privacy is necessarily a low priority in this phase of the project,' he said. 'Later on, when the miners start excavating below the regolith, the tunnels should provide enough living space to satisfy everyone's needs. In fact, it will be quite luxurious. With solar power from the hyper-mirrors that we're now constructing, we will have abundant energy. And by incorporating Mr Nadezda's suggestion of capturing a cometary asteroid for its ice core, we will be able to maintain a large base of water which can be passed through a swimming pool, a series of decorative ponds, and the hydroponics facility before it is purified for reuse.'

'Excellent,' Acorna said. 'You're quite right, privacy isn't important now. We need to provide a safe habitat for as many children as possible. We can wait as long as necessary for the luxuries.'

Pal sighed. 'I'm willing to wait as long as I have to,' he said.

Acorna, of course, didn't notice his double meaning. At the moment, she was so entranced with the vision of refuge for Kezdet's children that he wasn't sure she had even noticed his presence. Well, he could only keep trying . . . and waiting.

'Perhaps you'd like to view the hydroponics section,' Brantley suggested, trying to regain the attention of his wandering audience. 'Maintaining an even ecological balance is, of course, the other limiting factor in our expansion, as well as the need for shielded quarters. We could import food, but in the long run it's better to grow it here; if enough plants are grown to provide food, they will automatically meet the oxygen demands of the people. That means approximately three hundred square meters of growing area per person, and a photosynthesis energy requirement of thirty kilowatts per person. If we increase the demand for oxygen faster than we build up the 'ponics, the whole ecosystem will go out of balance and we'll have serious problems. Same thing if we expand the growing area significantly beyond the needs of present personnel. *Balance* is the key to success in any closed ecological system,' he said earnestly.

'Mmm,' said Acorna as they ducked through the low tunnel to reach the hydroponics area. No space wasted here! She and Pal had to crouch to make it through; it was a relief to stand up in the spacious dome allocated to hydroponics, with its moist atmosphere and reflected solar light. She sniffed the air. 'You have a little problem with excess nitrogen.'

'Why, yes,' Brantley said, surprised. How had the girl managed to read the gauges from all the way across the dome? 'We're increasing the number of soybean tanks; they're our principal nitrogen-fixing legumes. Later we'll add peanuts, too, for a more varied diet.'

'Good. That should take care of it. It's a little much for me to manage on my own,' Acorna said.

Brantley shook his head. On her own? Something about this conversation . . . these people seemed to be speaking Basic, but some of the things they said made no sense at all.

While he was trying to regain his momentum, Acorna plucked a leaf of chard from the nearest tank and chewed it daintily, a thoughtful expression on her face.

'Needs potassium,' she said. 'Better check your mix.'

'I'd do it if I were you,' Pal said cheerfully at the blank look on Brantley's face. 'She has great intuition about these particular things . . . no intuition whatever about some others, though, so it balances out.'

'What do you mean, no intuition?' Acorna demanded.

Great. She might be annoyed with him, but at least it was attention. Pal grinned.

'Don't you ever think about the future?'

Brantley Geram sidled off to activate the water testers. It would take a few minutes to verify that the girl had been talking off the top of her head when she claimed the 'ponics tanks were low on potassium, but the satisfaction would be worth it. He knew this system; he'd built it, he maintained it. No pretty girl could do a better job than his AI-driven automatic ingredient-balancing system!

'Of course I think about the future,' Acorna snapped at Pal. 'That's practically *all* I think about – how many children can we house up here, and how soon we can start bringing them up.'

'I meant your personal future,' Pal said patiently.

'Calum is working on that.'

'Finding your home? Yes, but that's not all there is.'

Acorna's pupils narrowed to vertical slits. 'Without other people like me,' she said, 'I *have* no personal future.'

'That,' said Pal, 'is what I mean about your impaired intuition, Acorna. There are other people like you right here and you never even noticed. Don't we want the same things? Don't we care about the same things? Do I have to grow white fur on my legs before you'll notice me? Or is all your love reserved for small, helpless

330

people? Maybe I should break my leg. Would you notice me, then?'

'I would not recommend that,' Acorna said. 'I do not know if I can heal broken bones.' They had already discovered some limitations to her healing power. Delszaki Li's nerve paralysis was far too advanced for her to do more than relieve some of his minor symptoms.

Pal threw up his hands. 'You're impossible! You're deliberately missing the point!'

Acorna took his hand. 'Had it occurred to you,' she said softly, 'that maybe this particular point had better be missed?'

'No, it hadn't, and I don't see why,' Pal said.

Acorna took a deep breath.

'Pal. We don't know anything at all about my genus. Your people take twenty years to reach physical maturity; I've done it in four. For all we know, I could be old in another four years.'

'I don't *care*,' Pal interrupted her. 'And even if it were so, is that any reason for not living now?'

'We don't even know if our species are inter-fertile.'

'I'd be willing to run some tests. We wouldn't even need a laboratory—' Pal smiled '—and I'd be happy to repeat the experiment over and over.'

'Don't you want children?'

'Dear lady of my heart,' Pal said, 'we're going to *have* children. Several hundred of them, for starters!'

As he checked the results of the water test with unbelieving eyes, Brantley Geram heard them laughing and thought they must have been running their own tests on the tank mix. OK, so the girl had been right: potassium levels were down. A lucky guess, that was all. A lucky guess.

Ed Minkus took the call which came into the Guardians of the Peace offices. When he realized the origin of the call, he covered the mouthpiece and hissed across the room at Des Smirnoff.

'We've got the inspector on our neck. Over that dock shooting. The grieving parent is on his way here and we have to prove it wasn't *our* negligence that caused his death.'

'Negligence? Negligence?' Des said, blustering because any call from the inspector was startling – and dangerous. One day the man was going to figure out just how little he knew about this department. When he started taking an interest in things, there would be an awful lot of 'things' that would need to be rapidly 'lost.'

'Yes, sir, we certainly will, sir. All the files ready and the tri-d documentation of the . . . ah . . . regrettable incident,' Des was saying, almost falling into the phone to project earnest, and innocent, sincerity. 'Yes, yes. I got the name: Hafiz Harakamian.' He put the unit down as if it carried skin-eating plague.

'Harakamian the father is coming here?' From his surfing of the trade nets the name was instantly familiar to Smirnoff, and suddenly he realized who the man known as 'Farkas Hamisen,' with his connection to Rafik Nadezda, must really have been. The planet seemed to grow aliases the way some people grew . . . ears. 'Did we save the files? I thought we gave the stuff to Nadezda?'

'He got copies, but our files sure show the tungsten bomb, and *that'll* save our liver and lights.'

Smirnoff glowered at his subordinate. 'You hope!'

Then the door to their office swung open and in came their new clerk, Cowdy, a very shapely young woman, herded inside, back first, by the prodding finger of the man who was barging in without proper introduction.

'How many times must I tell—' Smirnoff switched gears the moment he saw their visitor, who was unctuously backing Cowdy into the room. 'Oh, sir, we didn't expect you so quickly,' and he rose, as gracious as if he had never started to ream his underling out of her tights. 'May I, and my partner, express our deep sympathy and regret for the unfortunate way in which your son met his end?'

'I want to *see* the records,' Hafiz Harakamian said in an absolutely expressionless voice, taking a seat at the vid-screen and looking from it to Smirnoff expectantly.

Minkus nearly fell over his own feet and Smirnoff's to key up the necessary file. And there it was: the perp's unswerving progress towards a certain ship, the scanners' discovery of the tungsten bomb, their race to intercept him, and then their neat skewering of him with stunner shots. Then the all-important close-up of Des defusing the tungsten bomb.

'He couldn't have been that stupid,' Hafiz was heard to mutter, at which point both Minkus and Smirnoff began to relax.

'You see, Honorable Harakamian, how little option there was! For that device to have been planted . . .' Smirnoff shrugged eloquently.

'Yes, I see.' He rose from the desk and turned with a very cold and distant expression to face them. 'I have come to collect his remains.'

'There were none. He was cremated,' Ed blurted out.

'Cremated? You donkey! You horse's ass, you camel's slime spit . . .'

'Rafik said that was the way—'

'Rafik?' Hafiz lowered the arm with which he was dramatically gesturing. 'Rafik here?' Relief flooded his features. 'Then it was done as the Prophets have ordained?'

'Of course. How could you doubt our efficiency in such a detail?' Smirnoff said. 'And, of course, we had Nadezda to direct the ceremonies. But, he is on his way to you. He felt it only necessary.'

Hafiz's expression altered and he regarded Smirnoff as one would camel's green cud on formal attire. 'So the bomb was meant for my nephew!'

'It was?' Ed Minkus looked innocently at the Honorable Harakamian.

'There was bad blood between them, that is true,' Harakamian said, dropping his head as if in deep sorrow. Then, tilting his head a trifle, he asked, 'I don't suppose you would know where

334

the ward of my nephew would be? On the ship with him, returning my son's ceremonially blessed ashes?'

'No, he went by himself. The others are still at Mr Li's,' Ed replied, and managed a sickly grin as Smirnoff's expression told him he should probably have reserved that information for a price.

'Not Mr Delszaki Li?' Hafiz exclaimed.

'The very man,' Smirnoff replied.

'Thank you. And good day,' Hafiz said, and made as speedy a departure as his arrival.

'You stupid twit! You ninny-hammered log-head! You anvil-pated numskull. Have you any idea how much that information would have meant in good House Harakamian credits? And you *gave* it to him?'

Ed Minkus drooped. It would take him a long time to get over that.

It did not, however, take Hafiz Harakamian very long to reach the house of Mr Delszaki Li. And there he sat, observing who came and went. When the skimmer pilot seemed restless, Hafiz reminded him that he had agreed to the hire of his vehicle and if he, Hafiz, wished to spend all day across from the house of Mr Li, the meter was ticking and what difference did it make to what the vehicle did with its time?

'Who was you looking to find?' the driver asked. 'Lotsa people go in and out of that house.'

'Well, why not?' Hafiz said to himself. 'Would you have noticed a female with silver hair and . . .'

The driver swung to face his client, his eyes wide with surprise. 'How wouldja know anything about the Lady of the Lights? I only picked you up at the spaceport.'

'Lady of the Lights? My sweet little Acorna has achieved the distinction of a title?' Hafiz said.

'You better believe it. Cured my sister of a birthmark which uglified her to the point no decent man would look at one so cursed. And, without the stain, she's not that bad lookin'.' The transformation seemed to have surprised the driver.

Hafiz sighed. He had thought it might be easy to smuggle her back to his ship and away. But if she had achieved this sort of adoring notoriety, the odds had turned astronomical. The Didi had suggested that the girl had acquired unusual protectors.

'Anyway,' the driver went on, all affability now, 'she ain't here. She and the big red-beard and the little guy went off to Maganos two days ago. To see the moon installation. But they're goin' to have trouble with that,' he added, frowning.

'Oh?' Hafiz said encouragingly.

'Yeah, only they haven't figgered it out yet. If I'd of been the one to take them to the spaceport, instead of a House Li pilot, I'd of told them a thing or two.' He laid an oily, broken-nailed finger along the side of his nose and winked at Hafiz. 'You wanna know anything around here, you ask drivers. They hear a lot even if they do sit up front, pretending they're deaf.'

'Do tell,' Hafiz said, making a paper plane out of

a large denomination credit note which, with a practiced flick of his wrist, lofted over the partition, where it flew straight into the driver's quick hand.

'That I can, because we're all wantin' the Lady Epona to get the better of the Child Bonders and clean up Kezdet's reputation. Why, just the other day, there was some kinda fanatic trying to blow up the docks with a bomb!'

'Really! Is there some place nearby where a man like yourself and I might have a quiet meal and discreet conversation?'

The driver revved the engine of the skimmer in answer. 'Know the very place!'

Judit listened politely, Gill with growing enthusiasm, to the mining subcontractor's description of the simple three-drum drag scraper which was already in operation as they tested feasibility of Dehoney's first-stage designs.

'This is one of DPW's stated objections to the Maganos proposal,' Judit told Gill and the subcontractor. 'They say the drag scraper is an outdated twentieth-century technology.'

Provola Quero, the subcontractor, sneered. '*They* should talk! Kezdet's mines aren't just outdated, they're medieval! Besides, haven't they ever heard of the saying, "If it ain't broke, don't fix it"?' She jammed both hands deep into the pockets of her coveralls and paced to the next viewing window, talking nonstop. 'The scraper *is* outdated for planetary use; it's inefficient and inflexible. And it's not worth setting up for quick in-and-out asteroid jobs. But as a starter system for Maganos, it is ideal. It's simple, rugged, and required very low mass to be lifted up here. When we scale up, of course, we'll replace this with more efficient, high-volume methods . . . using equipment fabricated right here on Maganos, in the pressurized repair shop we have already set up to deal with scraper repairs and working with the high-purity structural metals we reduce from the first batches of lunar regolith. Dehoney planned this operation to bootstrap itself from the git-go. He always said that the whole point of lunar industrialization was to do what you *couldn't* do dirtside, not to throw away credits lifting machinery designed for gravity and atmosphere into orbit and then fixing the inevitable problems.'

Gill's eyes lit up. 'You *knew* Dehoney personally?'

'Studied with him for five years,' Provola said, running a hand through her yellow crewcut. 'Helped assemble the designs for his prize-winning solar greenhouse habitat.' She tapped the stud in her nose, which Gill now recognized as a miniature version of the space-station icon that was the famed Andromeda Prize, worked in black enamel and diamonds. '*I* plan to be the next Andromeda prizewinner,' she added, 'and Maganos is going to do it. Just tell me what you need to make DPW happy, and I'll bury them in documentation proving the worth of Dehoney's plans . . . and *my* implementation.'

She and Gill moved happily into a discussion of

duty cycles, component replacement, and
modular designs, while Judit stared out the view-
port at the monotonous drag, scrape, lift of the
cable-driven machinery. She didn't need to follow
the engineering discussion in detail to be reassured that both Gill and Provola knew what
they were talking about; years of working with
Amalgamated had given her a sixth sense for
which engineers knew their field and which ones
were shooting out clouds of technical terminology
to disguise their incompetence and laziness. Gill
and Provola Quero were both in the first class. If
they were satisfied that this three-drum whatsit
was the best way to initiate lunar mining on
Maganos, she had no doubt they were right.

What she did doubt – very seriously – was the
usefulness of any engineering argument to
convince Tumim Viggers of the Public Works
Department. Accustomed to reading nuances of
speech and slight gestures of body language in
order to survive with Amalgamated, Judit had
picked up far more from that brief, inconclusive
meeting than Viggers had actually *said*. The man
wasn't really concerned about the technical specifications for Maganos; he'd thrown out those
objections almost casually, as if he were only
playing for time. More disturbing, he had evinced
no interest in Delszaki Li's hinted bribes either.
When a Kezdet bureaucrat didn't take a bribe, you
knew you were in real trouble.

She tried listening more carefully to the technical argument, to take her mind off what she

suspected were their more dangerous political problems. Gill was querying the need for the large-scale pressurized repair shop. It had been relatively low on Dehoney's original list of priorities; why had Provola chosen to make it the first major construction?

'Because we need it now, and we're going to need it more every day!' Provola tugged at the one long braid dangling at the side of her short, bristly haircut. 'Sure, some of this work can be done suited and on the surface, but why should we? Give me one good reason for rewinding an electric motor in a vacuum! You've worked asteroids; you should know that dust is the worst problem of low-G, low-atmosphere environments.' *Even you*, her contemptuous tone implied.

'We managed our repairs on the ship,' Gill said.

'You,' Provola flashed back, 'had to be portable. We don't. We're going to need an industrial-sized shop soon enough to fabricate the next generation of mining machinery, so why not build it now and save the cost of expanding later?'

Gill put up his hands to register capitulation. 'All right, all right,' he said pacifically. 'You're right; I'm used to small, quick operations, not to permanent base construction. I wouldn't mind learning, though.'

Provola gave him a sudden, flashing smile. 'And *I*,' she admitted, 'have more theoretical than practical experience. Are you going to hire on to the Maganos project? We'd make a good team . . . unless you have problems with a woman supervisor?'

'I like women,' Gill said.

'That doesn't answer the question. I wasn't asking what you like to do with your hands when you're off duty.'

Gill reached out for Judit and pulled her close to him. 'My hands, and my off duty, are already committed, lady,' he said, 'and I wouldn't object to working for any student of Martin Dehoney's . . . if that answers your question. Unfortunately, I'm not free to stay on Maganos.'

'Why not?' Judit cried. She had just begun spinning a picture of how pleasant their life here could be. Delszaki Li had already shown her plans of the private living quarters he intended to allocate to the woman in charge of welfare and education for the rescued children and had hinted strongly that he would like her to be that woman. If Gill took a job on the mining side of the project, he could share those quarters . . . and he loved children. There couldn't be a better man to restore the children's faith after the horrendous experiences some of them had been through.

But, of course, he hadn't actually *said* he wanted to stay with her. He had only been putting an arm round her at every opportunity, and wanting her to go with him wherever he went, and . . . Judit swallowed her disappointment.

'Can't ditch my buddies,' Gill said. 'We've always been a team, the three of us. Calum and Rafik need somebody with some muscle to do the heavy jobs, and somebody with some common sense to get them out of the crazy complications

341

they're always getting into. I'd be a real jerk if I asked them to buy out my third of the *Uhuru* just because I'm a little older than they are and feel like settling down in a cushy construction job.' The words were directed at Provola Quero, but his blue eyes were on Judit, begging her to understand.

She swallowed again and nodded slowly. Of course he wouldn't break up the partnership. She should have understood that was why he never said anything about the future, even when he was most enthusiastically demonstrating his desire for her company in the present. 'I wouldn't want a real jerk to . . . work on the project,' she said in a small voice. 'But perhaps you'll visit occasionally.'

'As often as I can arrange it,' Gill said, a wistful look on his broad face. 'Oftener.'

It was cold comfort, but it was better than nothing, Judit told herself. Anyway, what did she have to complain about? She had been incredibly lucky in her life so far. And now, at only twenty-eight, she was being offered the chance to do what she loved most: working with children, designing their education and overseeing their welfare and healing the invisible wounds that she herself knew all too well. It would be asking too much for the fates to throw in a fortyish, broad-shouldered, red-bearded Viking throwback as a life's companion in that work.

Hafiz Harakamian found the skimmer driver an invaluable source of information. Not only did he know the day on which Acorna was due to return from Maganos, he claimed to know the very hour of her return. But he also warned Hafiz that waiting for her at the shuttle port would not be a good idea.

'Too many folks wants to see our little Lady of the Lights, now that the word's getting out about her,' he warned. 'Goin' to be a crowd at the port. If she comes out in it, you'll never get to her; if she's smart and gets Security to let her take a back exit, you'll miss her like the rest of 'em.'

He suggested that he bring Hafiz back to the Li residence at the exact time when Acorna was scheduled to return.

'I have always preferred to be in place well before anybody else is expected,' Hafiz said with the firmness of a man who had survived the thirty-year Harakamian–Batsu feud and had negotiated a partitioning of the planetary business without, like the two elder Harakamians, losing his head ... literally. 'We will take our position outside the Li mansion two standard hours before the arrival.'

At the time, this had seemed like an excellent idea. Before the two-hour safety margin was even one-third past, though, Hafiz Harakamian recognized that his tactical instincts had been impaired by too many years in the tropical clime of his home planet. Nobody had mentioned to him that Kezdet's rainy season was about to begin. Or that the rainy season was accompanied by a biting cold wind from the northern mountains. And, since it had been warm and sunny until this morning, he hadn't noticed that this particular skimmer had a leak in the roof and allowed an irritating draft to whistle through from one ill-fitting window to the next. He shifted his position so that the worst of the drip would fall on the driver and told himself philosophically that it was always a mistake to rely on hired equipment and staff, he should have brought his own people and transportation. But after the way young Rafik had cheated him over the unicorn girl, he had rather wanted to pull off his coup single-handed – the way he'd done in the old days, before he became head of House Harakamian. Just to let Rafik see that the old man wasn't past it yet.

The iron-studded front doors of the Li residence swung open, revealing the fantasy of thin-sliced, colorful Illic self-lighting crystals that illuminated the inner doors. Hafiz admired the play of lights and colors while at the same time registering that no other skimmer had pulled up; somebody was coming out, not going in. No need to do anything except slump down in his seat and be inconspicuous . . .

A light tapping on the window beside him was the end of that notion. When he pushed a button to make the glass sound-permeable, it stuck. Cheap, rented equipment! He had to physically open the window. A fine cold rain slanted in, accompanied by a yellow hand holding a holo-card.

'Mr Li sends his compliments,' said the servant, who, Hafiz noted irritably, was protected by a rainshield extending at least a foot around his body, 'and suggests that the head of House Harakamian might be more comfortable keeping him under surveillance from *inside* the house.'

At least Delszaki Li knew how things should be done between equals. It would probably be insulting to hint that the sudden disappearance of Hafiz Harakamian would cause untoward repercussions upon several branches of the Li consortium. Hafiz insulted the servant anyway, and received a graceful reassurance that this was merely a social invitation, nothing more. Of course, the man would have said that anyway. . . Hafiz grunted agreement and climbed stiffly out of the rented skimmer.

'Wait here,' he told the driver.

He could perfectly well have called up another and better-quality skimmer when he was ready to leave, but after the miserable hour he'd just spent, it suited him to think of the skimmer driver sitting and shivering in his drafty vehicle. Besides, in delicate business negotiations, there was always the possibility that one might have to depart in haste, omitting the usual polite formalities of leave-taking.

The servant extended his personal shield to cover Hafiz on the short walk across the street. Once inside the double doors of iron and crystal, he was invited to hand over his lightly sprinkled turban and outer robe for drying while he took kava with Delszaki Li.

The head of the Li consortium was older than

Hafiz had expected, considering the energy with which he directed the galaxy-wide network of the varied Li manufacturing and financial interests. He looked with interest at the shriveled, yellow-faced man in a float-chair, a blanket covering the wasted body whose absolute immobility betrayed his growing paralysis, only the snapping black eyes still showing the life that burned brightly inside. The man was older than Hafiz by a generation or more, older than any living member of House Harakamian. Hafiz's sense of danger went up a notch. Unlike some people, followers of the Three Prophets knew better than to underestimate the aged. In his long and successful life, Delszaki Li had undoubtedly used, analyzed, and countered every trick Hafiz knew, and then some.

While they sipped the first small cups of hot, fragrant kava and murmured conversational nothings at one another, Hafiz felt his brain working furiously. There was no point in clinging to his first plan of snatching Acorna, claiming she was his wife by the Books of the Prophets, and removing her from Kezdet while the Guardians of the Peace were still asking the religious courts for a ruling. Not only had he lost the advantage of surprise, but he doubted his ability to fool Delszaki Li as easily as one could fool or bribe the Guardians. A straightforward, honest approach was more likely to be successful . . . that is, a *reasonably* straightforward and honest approach. His ancestors would reconstitute their corporeal substances if he let down House Harakamian by laying all his cards on the table at once.

After the necessary exchange of condolences from Li on the loss of Tapha and apologies from Hafiz for the boy's idiotic behavior, he made his first oblique approach.

'Regrettable though the death of my son may be,' said Hafiz, reflecting on the matter with little internal regret whatsoever, 'it is written in the Book of the Second Prophet, "When you embrace your wife or child, be aware that it is a human being you are embracing; then should they die, you will not be unreasonably grieved." As is enjoined upon me by my faith, therefore, I have put aside care for the dead and am now concerned for the living. Before his death, Tapha informed me that my nephew, Rafik, had brought to this planet my young ward, Acorna, a child whom he kidnapped from my home last year. These rash young men!' Hafiz sighed with a conspiratorial smile at Li. 'They will be the death of us with their escapades and exploits, will they not?'

'On contrary,' said Li, his black eyes twinkling, 'I find escapades of young people most rejuvenating force in this ancient life. But Rafik has brought no child named Acorna here.'

'Perhaps he changed her name,' Hafiz suggested. 'She is unmistakable – a rarity, deformed, some would say, but in a most attractive way. Tall and slender, with silver hair and a small horn in the middle of her forehead.'

Li's face creased into a smile and Hafiz let out the breath he had not been aware of holding.

Thank the Prophet, the old man was going to admit Acorna's presence!

'Ah, you are speaking of the one our people of Kezdet call the Lady of Lights. But she is not a child. She is a mature woman and no man's ward.'

'That's impossible!' Hafiz protested. 'I tell you, I saw the child less than two standard years ago. She seemed to be about six, then – I mean, she *was* six,' he corrected himself firmly, remembering that she was supposed to be his ward and that he would be expected to know her exact age. 'Even on Kezdet, are children of seven considered adults?'

'Ah. There is concept of chronological age, and there is concept of developmental age,' Li said serenely. 'The one whom I know as Acorna is most assuredly a grown woman. Allow me to show you.'

For a wild moment Hafiz thought that Acorna had been smuggled into the house by a back way and that Li was actually going to have her brought in; then the holo-paintings on the far wall dimmed, to be replaced by obviously home-made vids. The image of a graceful, six-feet-tall Acorna moved, life-sized, across the wall, plucking flowers in a walled garden, playing with a toddler, gracefully lifting a long, full skirt to run up a flight of golden limestone stairs.

'Perhaps,' Li suggested, eyes twinkling at the astounded expression on Hafiz's face, 'is not the one you know as Acorna? Perhaps is coincidence of name and appearance?'

'Impossible,' Hafiz said. 'There can't be two like that.'

Nor could she possibly have grown so fast. The vids must be some trickery. He decided to forget the argument about Acorna's age and press on to his second point. He had the skimmer driver to thank for the gossip that gave him this additional argument.

'It was most irresponsible of my nephew to bring her to this superstition-riddled place,' he said, 'and I shall speak severely to Rafik when I see him. She is in danger from hired assassins, some possibly actually in government pay. It is my duty to take her back to a place where she will be kept safe, loved, and cherished as the unique being she is.'

'Perhaps is not wishing to be "safe, loved and cherished" in museum of rarities,' Li smiled. 'Perhaps prefers danger and important work which only she can do.'

Hafiz took a deep breath and counted to thirteen slowly. It would be most impolitic to accuse his host of talking nonsense. But what important work could a child like that be doing? This was just another lie to delay him, like those faked vids.

He had only reached ten when the door burst open and a short, fair-haired young man burst in.

'Delszaki, I think we've got it!' he exclaimed. 'Probabilities on this latest run show a ninety percent chance that it's somewhere in the Coma Berenices area—' He halted and stared at Hafiz with an expression of horror-struck recognition. 'Ah, that is, never mind, I'll come back later . . .'

'Please.' Li stopped him with a single word. 'Do

349

be seated. I feel sure that Mr Harakamian will be as interested as I in the results of your research.'

The young man bowed and tried to surreptitiously brush the crumbs off his wrinkled coveralls. His eyes were red-rimmed, as though he'd been working without sleep for several nights.

'Delszaki,' he said, 'I don't think you understand. This guy tried to kidnap Acorna once already.'

'Excuse me,' Hafiz said, 'I do not believe I have the honor of your acquaintance.'

'Calum Baird,' the young man said. He wasn't so young, now that Hafiz looked at him closely: late thirties, perhaps. It was the awkwardness and the exuberance that had misled Hafiz. 'And we *have* met . . . at your home on Laboue . . . although you may not recognize me. I was Rafik's senior "wife",' he said with a demure smile. 'The ugly one.'

Hafiz burst into uninhibited laughter. 'That rascal, how he has tricked me again and again! Truly a worthy successor to House Harakamian! How did he persuade you to put on *hijab*? You do not look like the sort of man who takes a secret delight in putting on women's clothing . . . although appearances can be deceiving. *I* certainly was deceived.'

'Rafik talked me into it,' Calum said. 'Rafik, as you may have noticed, can talk anyone into almost anything.'

'Of course he can,' Hafiz nodded. 'He is my nephew, after all. The Harakamian strain runs true in him, at least.' Tapha, on the other hand . . . Oh, well, Tapha was no longer a factor. 'But I interrupt. You wished to tell Mr Li something?'

An almost imperceptible nod from Delszaki Li reassured Calum that it was indeed all right to go ahead.

'I think we've pinpointed Acorna's home world, sir. Once I normalized the astronomical data bases . . .'

'Home world?' Hafiz interrupted in spite of himself.

'Yes. Where her people come from. Of course, she wants to get back to her own race,' Calum said.

'Her own *race*? But I thought . . .'

'That she was human?' Calum shook his head. 'No way. We don't know much about her background, but the pod she was found in shows that she comes from an advanced space-faring race with technology far beyond our own in some ways.'

'The pod she was found in,' Hafiz repeated. He seemed to be reduced to repeating phrases all the time. He didn't like the feeling that everything was shifting and changing under his feet. 'You mean there are others like her?'

'I doubt,' Calum said, 'that it would be possible to sustain a high-tech, space-faring civilization with a population of less than, say, several million at the absolute lowest estimate. The need for specialization alone would preclude any smaller grouping.'

'Several million.' By the Three Prophets, he was

351

repeating himself! Hafiz pulled himself together. 'You could have told me this before,' he said severely. 'It might have saved us all a lot of trouble.'

'I didn't *know* where her planet was until this morning,' Calum protested. 'Where it probably is, I mean. There's only one way to be sure. Someone will have to go and see . . .'

The look of naked longing on his face surprised Hafiz, but he did not have time to consider what it might mean. Another person had entered, as unceremoniously as Calum.

'I might have known you'd be here,' Rafik snarled at his uncle as he barged into the room. 'I turned around as soon as I heard a Harakamian ship had applied for clearance into Kezdet space. It didn't take you long to track down where Acorna was staying, did it? Well, it won't work! She's not here, and you're not getting her back to add to your museum!'

'I am delighted to see you too, my beloved nephew,' Hafiz said urbanely. 'As for the matter of Acorna . . . perhaps we can come to some arrangement that will be satisfactory to both of us.'

'Tapha's ashes?'

'Better a live nephew than a dead son,' said Hafiz with his benign smile.

Rafik's whole body tensed slightly. 'Well, then. I was going to give them back to you anyway, you know. And the cremation was performed according to the orthodox rituals.'

'I know that,' Hafiz said. 'Just as I know that you

have not really let that Neo-Hadithian nonsense rot your brain and supplant your decent religious upbringing.'

'How . . .' Rafik croaked.

Hafiz smiled and gestured at Calum.

'Well, now, boy. You would hardly be letting your senior "wife" run around without *hijab* if you were truly a Neo-Hadithian, would you? I must admit, you completely took me in at the time,' he went on. He felt he could afford a little generosity, since Rafik was so completely off balance. It would soften the boy up for the final agreement. 'But I hold no grudge. You have shown me that you have the true Harakamian mentality.'

As Rafik only goggled at him, Hafiz continued, looking away from the boy so that his words would not seem too pointed.

'Having lost my only son, I am in need of an heir. A worthy heir,' he emphasized, 'one of my own blood, one almost as clever as I am myself. Such a one would, of course, have to be trained in the complex affairs of the House. Training him would be very nearly a full-time occupation for me. I suspect I would have very little time left to pursue my hobby of collecting . . . rarities.'

Rafik gulped audibly. 'I am committed to finishing the Maganos Moon Base project,' he said at last.

'House Harakamian honors its commitments,' Hafiz said.

'My partnership with Calum and Gill—'

'Is it a lifetime contract?'

'It's not a formal contract at all,' Rafik said. 'It just, well, things worked out well for the three of us together.'

'Perhaps,' Hafiz suggested, placing each word as delicately as a surgeon cutting out overgrown flesh, 'it is now time for the three of you to work apart.'

Rafik glanced at his partner. 'Calum?'

'Actually,' Calum said, 'I *would* rather like to go check out my findings on Acorna's home planet myself.'

'Gill . . .'

'If Gill can be compensated for loss of partnership,' Delszaki Li said, 'is offer of Mr Harakamian acceptable to you?'

Rafik looked sternly at his uncle. 'You'll leave Acorna alone?'

'I swear on the Three Books,' Hafiz said.

'Well, then.' All the tension seemed to drain out of Rafik's slender body. 'If it suits you . . . I, too, will swear on the Three Books to return to Laboue for training in the ways of House Harakamian – as soon as I have completed Maganos Moon Base . . . *if* you will compensate my partners appropriately.'

After some formal haggling, they agreed that Hafiz Harakamian would buy out Rafik and Calum's shares in the *Uhuru* from Gill and would provide Calum with a subspace-equipped scout ship from the Harakamian fleet for his search. Rafik and Calum left, limp with exhaustion from the bargaining session, to revive their energies with something stronger than kava, while Hafiz and Delszaki relaxed with the satisfaction of old men who have seen matters properly arranged.

As soon as they were well out of earshot, Rafik began chuckling to himself.

'Uncle Hafiz drives a hard bargain . . . he thinks! But if you're really OK with breaking up the partnership, Calum . . .'

'I've been dying to get out to the Comes Berenices and check my results in person,' Calum said, 'but I didn't like to say anything to you and Gill. Anyway, we're getting a bit old for this asteroid-hopping life. Gill, too. I think he's about ready to retire into a planetside job . . . especially if it's a planet Judit Kendoro is on!'

'And I,' Rafik said with satisfaction, 'have discovered considerable talent for trading during the process of setting up Maganos on a commercial basis. I had already been thinking what fun it would be to have the Harakamian assets to play with. We'll go on letting Uncle Hafiz think he's driven a sharp bargain, though. It makes the old man happy.'

Meanwhile, Delszaki Li and Hafiz Harakamian were enjoying their own interpretation of the bargain over their third cups of kava.

'My nephew is sharp,' Hafiz chuckled, 'sharp enough to cut himself. If he had not been in such a hurry to extract a promise from me, he would have seen what I think you had already noticed.'

Li's face crinkled. 'That you had no more interest in Acorna, now that she is believed not to be unique after all?'

Hafiz nodded. 'When this Calum finds her home – and he strikes me as the sort of obsessed fanatic who will not rest until he has solved the problem – unicorn people will be as common as Neo-Hadithians. What a fool I should have looked, collecting and announcing one as a rarity, when shortly thereafter they would be walking the streets everywhere. But it is well as it ends. I have an heir of the blood to carry on the affairs of my house, and young Rafik has a settled position in life. I keep thinking of him as a boy, but he's not getting any younger, you know.'

'None of us are,' Li said calmly.

'Yes, but you and I have done our work. Rafik needs a wife – a real wife,' Hafiz smiled, 'to give us another generation of traders for House Harakamian. I will settle the matter as soon as he comes home.'

'I have no doubt you will,' murmured Li, 'but might be wise not to announce plans to Rafik just yet. Leave him illusion of choosing his own woman. More kava?'

Twelve

The team of four returned from Maganos early that afternoon, with vids, datacubes, construction records, air and water quality analyses, and every other bit of evidence they could think of to support their contention that Maganos Moon Base was not just potentially habitable but *already* habitable.

'Why must we wait for Phase Two?' Acorna demanded of Delszaki Li before she was well in the door. 'The base is in use *now*. The construction crews are living there; how can this Tumim Viggers say it is not safe? And there is much space available within the pressurized sectors. Provola Quero has caused to be built the very large repair and manufacturing facility which will be wanted later, only she does not need it *at all* yet – well, only a tiny bit of it,' she said with a reproachful glance at Gill's choked-off expostulation. 'We could wall off a small section for repair work and put children's bunks in the rest – use it for a dormitory until the proper living quarters are completed. Why should they live so miserably any longer than is absolutely necessary? Further, Brantley Geram now understands how he can expand the 'ponics system rapidly enough to cope with a sudden increase in population.'

'Acorna is responsible for that,' Pal put in. 'While we were there, she found a nitrogen imbalance in the air, identified a potassium deficiency in the water, and showed Geram how to triple 'ponics production practically overnight without destroying the atmospheric balance.'

'The first two things were data that could have been read from instruments, and I am sure Mr Geram would have thought of the ecobalancing system on his own if he had had time,' Acorna murmured. 'All that is not important, Pal – please do not interrupt!' She turned back to Delszaki Li, her pale face glowing with the cool silvery light that showed when she was excited, her eyes opened so wide that they were silver orbs in her face. 'Truly, Mr Li, there is no technical problem with beginning to use the base immediately – not one!'

'Unfortunately,' Delszaki Li said, 'technical problems are not the only ones. The Kezdet Authority has forbidden us to go forward with Maganos Moon Base, or to add any more personnel, until is completely satisfied by report of independent commission that all construction meets Kezdet building codes.'

Pal snorted. 'If the match factory where I used to work meets the building codes, Maganos is so far beyond that it's not even applicable!'

'Match factory has probably never been inspected by building commission,' Li said gravely.

'Who's on this independent commission?' Gill demanded. 'We can meet with them right now, show them the data. *I'll* convince them Maganos meets code, if I have to ram the cubes down their throats!'

'Members of commission have not yet been appointed,' Li said. 'Informed sources within Department of Public Works say selection and appointment of commission may take several years.' He regarded the four young people – from his perspective they were all children – benignly. 'Is not technical problem. Is political. Someone does not intend plan to succeed.'

'Who?'

Li's left hand lifted slightly, his approximation of a shrug.

'Many people profit greatly from exploitation of children on Kezdet. Could be any of them. Or all of them. But at this time, is still mystery. We know, for instance, that owner of Tondubh Glassworks has bought two judges and a subinspector of Guardians. Very well. I pay them better bribe than Tondubh, now I have them. Child Labor League has list of other corrupt government officials, paid by this factory or that to ignore abuses of Federation law. But even if we buy off *all* minor officials, is still blocked from top. Someone with much power and position in government is stopping plan. Someone so respectable, and so well concealed, that even Child Labor League does not know true identity of man called the Piper.'

Gill's shoulders sagged. 'Then what can we do?'

'Do not despair,' Li said. 'You have on your side Delszaki Li, veteran of many years political and financial double- and triple-crossing. Also have now secured independent services of consultant with even more experience than Li in handling corrupt governments, because has run seriously corrupt organization himself. Hafiz Harakamian.'

Gill turned white. 'Get Acorna out of here!'

'Harakamian no longer wishes to acquire Acorna,' Li said. 'Talk to Calum and Rafik. They have much news for you.'

But the talk had to wait, because Chiura got wind of Gill's return. At this point she came flying down the lift-chute, squealing happily, 'Monster Man! Monster Man!'

'He's big and ugly, all right,' said Calum, who had entered the hall just in time to catch Chiura executing a flying leap far too soon to reach her objective, 'but don't you think it's a bit over the top to call him a *monster*?'

Gill's face was almost as red as his beard.

'It's . . . uh . . . a game we play,' he explained. By now Jana had arrived after Chiura and the girls were tugging Gill by both hands toward the lift-chute. 'Umm . . . maybe we can talk upstairs?'

The talk was again delayed until Gill had been exhausted by chasing Chiura and Jana around the suite on his hands and knees, roaring like a bull and occasionally reaching out one large hand to snatch at flying hair or the hem of a kameez, while they squealed in pretended terror. Even Khetala, who at thirteen considered herself too old for such games, got caught up in the excitement and laughed and giggled like the other two.

'He is giving them back their childhood,' Judit murmured under cover of the noisy game. There were tears in her eyes. 'I don't know how to do that.'

'You never had a childhood.' Pal put an arm around his sister's shoulders and hugged her. 'You had to grow up too fast, to save Mercy and me.'

She looked up at the 'little brother,' who had shot up so fast in the last years that now he stood half a head taller than her.

'Oh, Pal, we *need* Gill at Maganos. The children need him. Can't we persuade Calum and Rafik—'

'That,' said Rafik, grinning, 'was what we wanted to talk to you about.'

'You want to talk business while Chiura's crawling all over him and climbing his beard?' Calum muttered under his breath.

'Safest time,' Rafik replied out of the side of his mouth. 'He won't turn violent while he's festooned with kids.'

They explained their arrangement with Hafiz Harakamian, somewhat apprehensively, and were relieved when Gill's broad face broke into a beaming smile.

'That,' he said cheerfully, 'simplifies *everything*.'

'We were, um, hoping you'd see it that way,' Rafik said.

Gill looked at Judit.

'That's a nice living suite Delszaki Li has put into the Maganos design for you. Plenty of space for two people, wouldn't you say? Think Li would hire a couple to work with the children, instead of leaving it all on you?'

'The proposition would have to be put to him,' Judit said, lowering her eyes.

'Well, then!' Gill made to get up, but he was too weighted down with children to make it on the first try.

'And first,' Judit said, very demurely, 'the proposition would have to be put to *me*. I'm old-fashioned about these things.'

Gill looked at her.

'Me, too,' he said, 'and I draw the line at proposing to you in front of two miners and a gaggle of giggling kids.'

'Then we'll have to do it for you,' said Calum and Rafik in unison.

Calum went down on one knee in front of Judit. Rafik laid his hand on his heart. Gill started turning red.

'Dear Judit,' Calum said, 'would you do us the immense favor—'

'—and Gill the great honor,' Rafik put in.

'Of providing a home and family for this poor, old, arthritic—'

'I am *not* arthritic!' Gill bellowed. 'That trouble with my right knee is an old sports injury.'

'—broken-down, lonely, unloved—' Rafik continued over Gill's protests.

'Oh, stop it, you two!' Judit interrupted them. 'He is by no means unloved.' She looked meltingly at Gill, who was now more purple than red. 'But I think he might have a stroke if you don't knock it off.'

'Then you'd better accept him,' Calum said promptly. 'You wouldn't want to be responsible for the poor old fellow's demise from apoplexy, would you? A kind-hearted girl like you?'

'We'll ask Li to name that suite at Maganos after you,' Rafik suggested. 'The Judit Kendoro Home For Stray Miners.'

'Get *out* of here,' Gill roared, having finally divested himself of children, 'and let me propose to my girl in my own way and my own time!' He shooed Calum, Rafik and all three children out of the room. 'And no eavesdropping!'

That the two former partners did not spoke volumes for their self-discipline and the fact that they had both decided Gill and Judit were exactly suited to each other.

Each went down the lift-chute with a much lighter heart to see what they could do to solve the major problem now facing the Maganos Moon Base scheme.

'Bribery will only get you so far,' Rafik said. 'I suspect there is more at stake than money or prestige or mere power.'

'There's nothing "mere" about power, Rafik,'

Calum said in a sudden fit of depression, brought on as much by the happy scene being enacted in the children's quarters as anticipation of facing an unknown quantity of opponents.

It couldn't just be this mysterious Piper person, not when Mr Li was confounded by the machinations behind the scenes.

'Well, what Mr Li can't find out, Uncle Hafiz can.'

'Don't you mean Papa Hafiz?' he said almost snidely.

'Uncle, smunckle, papa doppa,' Rafik said, shrugging indifferently, 'we are both Harakamians and nothing will daunt us!' He raised a fist in respect of his determination as they reached the door leading to Mr Li's domain. The fist altered and its knuckles rapped most circumspectly for admission.

During their absence in the children's suite, Uncle Hafiz had joined Mr Li, and so had the scruffy man they identified as Pedir, the auxiliary skimmer driver who had attached himself, limpetlike, to Acorna and Judit for their excursions.

'Ah, is good you have returned,' Mr Li said. 'You know Pedir?'

After Rafik and Calum had exchanged greetings and seated themselves, Mr Li continued. 'Is source of much local knowledge and gossip.'

'Knows where a lot of bodies have been buried, you might even say,' Uncle Hafiz added, stroking the chin beard he was cultivating.

'We,' and Mr Li's delicate hand gestured to

Uncle Hafiz, 'who feel is time to introduce Lady Acorna to society—'

'—such as it is,' Hafiz put in.

'—are inviting,' and he gestured now to Mercy who was seated at the console and furiously typing away, 'every person of wealth and standing in city to splendid gala banquet and dancing the night away.'

'Anyone who is anyone in Kezdet will come,' Hafiz said, 'because it will be borne in on them that not to be invited would indicate social or industrial inferiority to those also on the guest list.'

'But Acorna,' Rafik and Calum were instantly on the *qui vive*, 'would be in jeopardy.'

Hafiz flapped his hand dismissively, grimacing away their caution.

'Not from this house,' Mr Li said. 'Not with so many watching her all night long with eyes of hawk and claws of tiger.'

Hafiz leaned back in the comformable chair, at almost a dangerous tilt, steepling his fingers and staring up at the ceiling, a slow smile creasing his face.

'She will be clad in raiment fit for a princess, a queen, an empress . . .' he extended one hand ceilingward, opening his fingers at the apex, indicating magnificence beyond imagining, '. . . bejeweled . . . and also,' he pulled his eyes down to his nephew, 'warded from every possible danger by the built-in systems hidden in the jewelry.'

'Ah, ingenious!' and Rafik relaxed into a chair, stretching out his legs, hooking his thumbs in his belt and preparing himself for whatever pearls of wisdom and crafty conniving were sure to be revealed.

Calum, with a droll smile, wandered over to Mercy's desk position and perched on a stool.

'There will be music . . .' Uncle Hafiz went on.

'Several groups,' Pedir said, 'for I am promised to promote three groups and undoubtedly, once this is noised about, I will have to help others. All worthy and all good musicians . . .'

'Only good musicians,' Mr Li said, raising a slim finger.

'Only the very best,' Pedir nodded, 'for there ain't no bad guys around here as play well. Get you good extra boys, girls for serving, too.'

'I'm doing that, Pedir,' Mercy said, looking up from her screen.

'No problemo,' Pedir said, wriggling both hands to assure her he would not interfere. 'What about a skimmer strike? Would that be any help?'

Mr Li shook his head with more vigor than he usually displayed for poor ideas.

'Strike is ours to do,' he said. 'A different strike. All will see.' Now he raised his frail arm, closing the fingers to a point, retracting his arm, then darting it forward in an unmistakably reptilian strike.

Uncle Hafiz pretended to recoil in terror, his eyes sparkling with amusement. But no more was said. In fact, Pedir was excused, and so were

366

Calum and Rafik, though they were enjoined to have the skimmer driver transport them to the most prestigious tailor in Kezdet, to be measured for masculine finery.

'To talk of the sumptuousness of the coming evening of Mr Delszaki Li's prestigious house,' Uncle Hafiz said. He buffed his nails on his lapel. 'I have already commissioned elegant evening attire. Unless you wish me to deprive you of acceptable female companionship for the entire evening, you had best look less like camel drivers than you do now.'

Rafik snorted. He had hurried without changing from his usual shipboard gear to Mr Li's, and Calum had come dressed as he was because he was uncomfortable in anything but the casual clothing he was now wearing.

'Come, Calum,' said Rafik, rising, 'let us do as we are bid, for if my dearly beloved uncle has commanded us to appear in sartorial elegance, he will certainly be willing to pay for the best there is to be had.'

While Hafiz was sputtering about impudent, improvident imps, the two made their escape, pushing the laughing Pedir ahead of them as Mr Li cackled in appreciation of the taunt.

'I have finished the list, Mr Li,' Mercy said, instantly diverting them to the more important task of contriving a most exhaustive guest list.

Mr Li's house was more than adequate for such a social evening, but rooms long unused for entertainment had to be turned out, refurbished in the newest fads, decorated in the latest color schemes, and exotic viands ordered from all over the galaxy.

'Is going to be a legend in this time, this evening,' Mr Li often said while Uncle Hafiz fervently seconded him, but had to be discreetly restrained from providing a few bizarre entertainments. 'Is not to distract guests from main purposes of all this, good friend Hafiz.'

'True, true.' Though Hafiz sighed, remembering the most amazing contortionist act he had happened to catch at one of the more elegant of the casinos on Kezdet, stimulating jaded tastes and appetites.

The invitations, miracles of calligraphy and illustration in their own right, were dispatched to the recipients, and shortly it became difficult to manage necessary calls from Mr Li's house to suppliers, merchants, and even acquaintances.

Acorna, accompanied by a glowing Judit and a more sedately excited Mercy, made many trips to the couturier who had been chosen, of the many available, to supply their gowns. Excitement was high in that establishment, which had made certain that every other couturier in Kezdet realized how much they had lost by not securing these commissions. Acorna was often so besieged by those wishing her miracles that Rafik and Calum joined them at the dressmaker's.

Rafik was actually helpful, for he had inherited, among other things, Calum said sourly, the

Harakamian dress sense and was able to comment knowledgeably about fit, line, and color.

The jewels were, however, left to Uncle Hafiz, who had sent for skilled craftsmen as well as the raw materials of precious metals and uncut gems, and supervised the styles and elegance of what each girl would wear. That special adornments were also being made for Mr Li's evening banquet was discreetly mentioned and several invitees finally decided to attend upon hearing that news.

Calum and Gill had been busy, too, with electronic and engineering effects which would guard the already well-guarded Li household. They even did their best to protect against such ingenuities as contact poisons, sleepy powders, and other deadly elements. Special beams could render the most popular of these substances neutral. Not that Acorna could not neutralize venom but they wished to avoid such problems in the first place.

And so the great day arrived, and the coiffeurs came with their preparations and oohed and aahed over Acorna's magnificent mane. Her gown had been cut to free her hirsute splendor and a tiara had been designed to crown that silvery glory. (One of the many jealous females was later heard to swear that Mr Li's ward had had to be glued into her costume, for how else could it have stayed anchored so firmly when she gyrated on the dance floor.) The dark hairs of both Judit and Mercy were also teased into fetching styles, but nothing outré, since quiet elegance suited them better, and as a foil for Acorna's unusual appearance.

Khetala, Chiura, and Jana watched, almost as glued to their vantage seats in the 'tiring room,' speechless with the beauty they were seeing, and the subtle ways which natural loveliness could be enhanced. They had received permission to watch the guests arrive and were to receive the same foods that would be served for dinner.

'So you can feast even as we do,' Judit explained. 'There will be so many people, small persons like yourselves would get lost and that might be scary.'

Khetala had agreed. She still liked lots of space around her and felt safe around strangers only if her 'uncles' were nearby.

Chiura had put behind her all the terrible memories which still woke Jana, sweaty and trembling in the night. She was forever leaving her little bed and creeping in with Kheti for comfort. But she was truly excited about the party and knew exactly where she could crouch, unseen, on the first landing of the great stairs and see everyone arriving.

Finally the ninth hour came, an hour which the fine clocks in their niches, corners, and surfaces celebrated with melodious, arrogant, or demure chimings. At precisely the third stroke of the hour, the front door was opened to receive the first guest, a very minor official and his wife, splendidly garbed for the occasion. Jana didn't think much of her dress: the color was garish and the flickering light display adorning the neckline made her look like a washed-out sketch. On the stroke of the eighth, another minor official, his wife, oldest son and daughter, were admitted. Jana liked what the daughter was wearing – the very prettiest shade of pale blue – though it didn't really suit the girl. Her shoes, with their very high heels, studded with sparkling jewels, and straps that started at her toes and went up to her knees, were nice.

The trickle of guests became a rivulet and then a river, with no time to close the door between their comings. Kheti and Chiura got bored with looking at what people were wearing, but Jana feasted her eyes on the colors, the patterns, the combinations, the swags and the trimmings, the feathers and the furs. She could not quite believe there could be so many variations of dress and suit: she, who had lived much of her life in darkness, in a black to gray environment, lapped up all the colors as a desert dweller would drink from an oasis.

Then, he stood in the doorway. Jana was frozen with fear. Kheti and Chiura had left their positions when the undermaid had called them to eat their share of the banquet. Not that Jana could have uttered a word. She could only stare at him, seen in the bright lights, in a deep blue suit which gave off subtle glitters, with a white-white shirt collar barely showing at the neck of it. But it was he, and he was here where she thought she could be safe.

Rigid with terror she watched as Mr Li greeted

him and introduced him to Uncle Hafiz, who introduced Acorna, who smiled and made Judit and Mercy and Pal known to him in this silly ritual they had been performing for every guest that entered the house. Nearly fainting, she saw Gill and Judit usher him into the main salon, where he passed from her sight. Then she collapsed in a little heap.

That is how the undermaid found her when she went to collect the third of her charges for the evening.

'He's coming for us,' was all Jana could say when she first recovered from her faint. 'We've got to hide Chiura.'

'Who?'

'He's *here*. I *saw* him. They *invited* him.'

There could be only one 'him' who would elicit that terrified note from Jana. Kheti's face went gray. 'The Piper?'

Jana nodded. She snatched up Chiura, eliciting a wail of protest as the little one was seriously involved with the tray of sweets, and wrapped both arms around her as though to shield her with her own body.

'We have to get away,' she whispered. 'The lift-chute's too dangerous, it lets out in the front hall. The windows—'

'Wait!' Khetala sank down on the floor, not quite as gracefully as she had been trained to do by Didi Badini; her knees were trembling too hard for that. 'Let me think.'

Jana crammed sweets into Chiura's mouth randomly, to keep her happy while Kheti thought. She was shocked, though, when Khetala reached for a jellabie and bit into the sweet, crystallized-honey crust.

'Is this a time to be stuffing your face?'

'Sugar helps when you got the shakes,' Khetala said. 'You eat something, too. Even if we do run—'

'We *have* to. Now!' Jana interrupted.

'Even if we do, you won't run far on an empty belly. You eat. I'll think.'

Khetala washed down the jellabie with a long drink of iced madigadi juice while Jana obediently picked at a witifowl pastry. Each crumb seemed as if it would choke her.

'Now then,' Khetala said at last. 'I been thinking. The Lady Acorna is *good*. She wouldn't invite the Piper here.'

'I tell you, I *saw* him! The gray man who came to the mine with Didi Badini. Ain't he the Piper?'

Kheti nodded and folded her hands to conceal the shaking of her fingers.

'Oh, yes. I heard him talking to Didi Badini, many and many a time, when she had me locked in that closet where they keep – Well, never mind that,' she interrupted herself hastily. Jana didn't need to know about Didi Badini's dark closets and the means she employed to make sure new girls would be docile when she finally let them out. 'I got to hear him talk again to make sure, though. If it *is* him . . .' she shivered '. . . it's bad. Very bad. See, I don't think they know who the Piper really

373

is. He's got himself another name this side of Celtalan. I heard them talking about it the other day. It's a big secret, the Piper's real name. Maybe the biggest secret in Celtalan. If he finds out we've seen him *here*—' She mimed slitting her throat. 'Best we could hope for is he kills us quick. He ain't taking us back to the mines, Jana. He ain't taking us anywhere. Did he see you?'

Jana shook her head. 'He went straight into that big room with all the lights and pretty ladies.'

'Did the Lady Acorna go with him?'

Jana shook her head again.

'Good,' Kheti murmured. 'She should be all right here, anyway. He wouldn't do anything to her here, where he's passin' under his real name.'

'What would he do to *her*?'

Khetala looked at Jana pityingly.

'He wants her killed, too. He told Didi Badini she's making too much trouble here on Kezdet, getting the bond kids and the Child Labor League all stirred up.'

Jana stiffened and squeezed Chiura so hard that the sleepy child cried in protest. 'You didn't tell me that before!'

'Told Delszaki Li,' Khetala said. 'He knows. He's been seeing that the Lady's safe. Why do you think he sent her off to Maganos? I heard them talking about that, too. I hear a lot.'

Jana went unerringly to the weak point in Khetala's argument.

'But he doesn't know the Piper is that dressed-up man I saw downstairs. Nobody knows. You said that yourself. So he doesn't know the Piper is here, in this house. How can he keep the Lady safe if he doesn't know?' She felt more frightened than she ever had in her life, more than when Siri Teku came at her with the whip that last time. She'd thought she might as well die then, she was hurt so bad and Chiura was gone. But the Lady Acorna had made her live again and had brought her back to Chiura. Debts had to be paid. Jana forced the next words out. 'We got to warn her.'

'We'll find Mr Li. Or somebody we can trust,' Kheti said sharply to force down her fear at the idea of going among all those strangers. 'But I still think he won't move against her now, in this house, where everybody knows him by his real name!'

'He could put poison in her food or something.' As none of the children had experience with Acorna's ability to detect poisons, this seemed all too probable to Khetala as well as to Jana. 'Or maybe he's going to lure her out into the garden and there'll be a bomb. Or . . .' Jana's invention failed. What did it matter? She only knew that the Lady Acorna, *her* lady, was in terrible danger and she had to do something about it. Even if she was so scared all she wanted to do was hide and cry. 'Come on. We got to warn her!'

She stood up with some difficulty, because Chiura had become frightened by the older girls' evident tension and was refusing to let go of her 'Mama Jana.'

'He sees us,' Khetala said, 'we're dead. You know that?'

'I know that,' Jana said, wishing her voice wouldn't wobble so much. 'But I got to go. She took me out of Anyag.' She gave Khetala a scornful look. 'You want to, you can stay here. Maybe the Lady didn't take you out of Didi Badini's bonk-shop. Or maybe you forgot already?'

But Kheti was on her feet now.

'You're an idiot, Jana,' she said, sighing, 'but I can't let you go and be an idiot all by yourself. Got in the habit of taking care of you little kids too long ago, I guess. Come on. Let's go and get ourselves killed, if that's what you gotta do. Only let's leave Chiura here. He don't need to know about *her*.'

But Chiura wound her arms tighter about Jana's neck when Jana tried to set her down, and screwed up her pretty face in the grimace that they knew was preparatory to one of her ear-piercing screams.

'All right, all right,' Jana hushed her, 'you can stay with me. But you got to be real quiet, you understand? Quiet like a ghurri-ghurri, like a shadow, like you're not even there. Or Piper'll get you.'

To Chiura, the Piper was just a name used to frighten her into acquiescence, like Old Black, who lived down in the bottom of the mines and ate little girls for breakfast. So she was scared enough by the threat to hush up, but not scared into screaming hysteria.

Acorna was in fact in the garden, where (under the watchful eye of Hafiz Harakamian) she had

376

retreated from the noise and social chitchat of the party to talk with some of Delszaki Li's distinguished guests about matters of more importance to her.

'Is not only social occasion,' Li had instructed all his people. 'Is testing of the waters. Must talk little, listen much, try to find source of high-government secret opposition. Perhaps head of Public Works says, "Is not my doing, gracious lady, is warning from Orator of the council that would be unwise for political appointee such as myself to further projects undesirable to certain of his constituency." Perhaps orator of the council says, "Having duty to protect interests of glass-working and related industries." Then perhaps we say, "Aha! Is looking closer at Tondubh Glassworks." Only example, you understand,' Li had said, almost purring. 'Personally, do not expect to find source of opposition in Tondubh. Have already bought most of judges and public servants bribed by Dorkamadian Tondubh. He is cheap man, does not pay workers, does not even make good bribes. But perhaps you find some other thread. Listen! Listen! And if must talk, then be obnoxious.'

'Why?' Pal had queried.

'How?' That was Calum, who looked more interested than alarmed at this suggestion.

'Accuse justicers of taking bribes, claim that politicians are put in office by industrial interests, hint that civil servants are in second service of the Piper. See who looks nervous and changes subject. All people here are wishing to be seen as respectable, good people, personally obeying Federation law as well as Kezdet local law. Someone is not. Be offensive, my children.' He smiled seraphically. 'Someone already hates us. Be charitable. Give him good reason to hate and fear us.'

Acorna did not feel that she had any real talent for offending people, so she had been dutifully following Li's first directive and listening. But she doubted she would learn anything from this particular conversation except that Dork Tondubh lived up to his nickname and that Tumim Viggers, head of Public Works, and the politician Vidra Shamali were equally smug, self-satisfied, and impervious to suggestion. All three of these social and political leaders of Kezdet society were more than happy to stroll in Li's exotic gardens with a lovely young lady, even if she did have an odd protuberance in the middle of her forehead. Acorna had followed Li's suggestion and, instead of trying to disguise her physical differences for this party, had accentuated them. Her tight sheath of Illuc spidersilk showed off the lean, flat planes of her body; a spiral of jeweled ribbons accentuated her white horn. The result had been exactly as Li had predicted: after a few surprised looks, the *haut monde* of Celtalan had decided that anything so flamboyantly displayed must be an asset, not a deformity. ('It's a feature, not a bug,' Calum had said sardonically, and when questioned, added, 'Old Earth saying. I'm not sure exactly what it means.')

Unfortunately, the avuncular tone adopted by Dork and Tumim was not likely to give Acorna any results except extreme boredom and a growing desire to turn around and kick them where it would do the most good with her sharp, hard feet. As for Vidra, at least she wasn't accompanying her lecture with the sleazy looks and surreptitious touches Dork added to his talk, but the bossiness of her manner more than made up for that.

At present all three were happily 'explaining' to Acorna exactly why it was impossible to eradicate Kezdet's practice of child labor and why employers should be considered charitable guardians rather than slave owners.

'Of course there are children around the glassworks,' Dork said. 'It's hot work, there among the furnaces. The workers need water; the children bring it to them.'

'I saw a little boy running among the furnaces with a seven-foot iron rod loaded with molten glass,' Acorna said.

Dork made a mental note to ream out the security guards at Tondubh for ever letting this pretty thing inside the compound. She hadn't just been giving away shoes; she'd been *noticing* things. He shifted to his second line of defense.

'Alas, yes, there have been some lapses. You must understand, my dear, Kezdet is an undercapitalized economy. Our people must work to eat. What can we do when parents bring their children to the factory and beg for work? Should we let them starve?'

'Don't wrap it up in pretty ribbons, Dork,' said Vidra in her harsh voice. 'The glass industry on Kezdet requires children. Adults can't run so fast with the molten glass. If Dork and others like him didn't hire children, not only would those poor families starve, but production would go down.'

'That's true,' Dork said with more animation. 'Profits might drop by as much as thirty percent. I have a duty to my shareholders, you know.'

'Yes, it *is* expensive having workers whom you have to pay and provide medical care for.' Acorna smiled agreement. 'Still, most industrial planets manage it.' She thought she could get to enjoy Li's instructions on being offensive, after all. 'What's wrong with Kezdet, that you people can't figure out how to run a factory without slave labor?'

'Now, now, dear, do not upset yourself,' Tumim Viggers counseled her. 'You are young and a stranger to our ways, and perhaps those terrorist zealots of the Child Labor League have been telling you misleading stories. The fact is that the few children working on Kezdet are very well treated. They are fed and lodged at their employer's expense, have years of free training in their chosen career, and enjoy the knowledge that their earnings are sent home to help support their beloved families. Why, if you sent a team of Federation inspectors to any of our mines or factories, I do believe the children would run away and hide rather than be taken away! They love their work, you see, and the overseers are like parents to them.'

380

'Possibly,' Acorna agreed. 'I understand that some parents also beat their children.'

Tumim Viggers sighed. 'There may have been excesses. It is no easy matter to train and discipline young children, but I assure you, they are learning lessons which will be invaluable when they grow up.'

'How many of them *do* grow up?' Acorna asked in a tone of bright interest.

Tumim Viggers chose to ignore that question. 'Child labor is one of the harsh realities of life on an overpopulated, under-developed planet. Extremist groups like the CLL only make matters worse. Why, if we were to eradicate all child labor on Kezdet tomorrow, what do you think would happen?'

'I don't know,' said Acorna brightly. 'Why not try it and find out?'

She rose then. 'I must really circulate, but it has been so nice to get to know you better. Do enjoy the garden. The night-blooming scented plants are in that corner.'

'Do show us exactly where?' Tumim said and reached for her arm, a maneuver she evaded by swaying away from him and out of reach.

As she walked back toward the house, she happened to glance up at the windows and saw three figures hurrying down the staircase: three figures that ought to have been fast asleep in their beds, stuffed with all the food and sweets she had asked to be sent to them. Where was the undermaid who was supposed to watch out for them? If they should be seen . . .

She hurried inside and spotted Calum, who had a desperate look on his face: the anorexic daughter of the shipping magnate she had met in the receiving line was clinging to his arm with a death grip. Acorna gave him the old EVA danger sign. He peeled the girl off him and, muttering some sort of apology, he made his way quickly to Acorna.

'The children are up. They must not be seen,' she said in an urgent undertone. 'On the stairs. If I go up . . .'

'Leave it to me.'

The skeleton had clattered after Calum, but Acorna intercepted her, taking her by the arm.

'I do hope you are enjoying yourself this evening, Kisla,' she said, fortunately recalling her name and steered her towards the refreshment table, where a new display of subtleties and delights had just been arranged. 'With your father so prominent in the shipping industry, do you get a chance to travel to far-off planets and places? Or are you forced to remain here in a dull school?'

Kisla stiffened and almost sneered up at Acorna. 'Fraggit, but you know nothing, do you? School? I've been a qualified navigator for three years. The only reason I'm at this party at all is because the whole family got invited. And then you have the nerve to skive off with the only interesting chap here.'

'An errand only he could do for me,' Acorna said, 'and see, here he is back.'

However, Calum grabbed Acorna by the hand and pulled her so close to him that Kisla swore, more as a deckhand than a navigator might, and flounced off to find another target for her attentions.

'They're terrified. They've seen the Piper here.'

'They have? They could identify him?' Acorna looked around the room for Mr Li's float-chair or Uncle Hafiz, trying to hide the terror she felt. Calum peeled her hands off his arm.

'Khetala and Jana are both certain, but they're terrified for your sake. They're afraid he's here to kill you.'

'Here? In front of everyone?' Acorna ridiculed the notion. 'Not likely.'

'You'd still be dead, sweetie pie,' Calum said soberly. 'Besides which, very few people here are enchanted with your interference with their profitable operations employing child labor.'

'Then why did they come?' she asked, annoyed as well as frightened. Dreadful people. Smile at your face and pull a stunner once your back was turned. Although, where many of those present could hide anything in the sleek, tight-fitting garb that was currently fashionable, she did not know. Very little was left to the imagination, and one could count spine ridges and . . . all sorts of things. She could have appeared at this dinner clad in only her own skin and given away nothing of her gender, but these people covered it all up and then flaunted what they covered.

'They came for the food and to say they had

been here tonight. Mr Li is excessively pleased with the turnout, but I must go tell him that the children can identify the Piper. That will be one more obstacle out of our way, so we can find out where you really belong.' Calum grinned up at her and then squeezed her hands. 'I'll go tell them. You circulate.'

He gave her a little push toward the nearest clutch of chattering men and women. Kisla intercepted her.

'My father wishes to speak with you, Acorna. He says you've been avoiding him all evening.'

There was a remarkable strength in her skeletal arms as she towed the taller girl past the nearest group and toward a quartet, which mercifully included Uncle Hafiz. Acorna stopped resisting.

Hafiz rose and kissed her cheek. 'You are more beautiful every time I see you, Acorna. Here is Baron Commodore Manjari and his wife, Ilsfa, wanting to meet you. The baron claims he ships anything and everything, anywhere in the known galaxy. And, as I'm sure you realize, Acorna, the baroness' family, the Acultanias, were one of the first to settle Kezdet and recognize its importance in this sector.'

The baroness smiled a social smile, while stuffing her face with the dainty petit fours on the table beside her. Baron Manjari rose courteously to his feet and, removing his hand from his pocket, patted his lips before he reached for Acorna's proffered hand. He didn't look very impressive, Acorna thought: medium height, spare build, which might account for his daughter's anorexic-looking body. He had very piercing eyes and a gaze that wished to penetrate her skull. She managed to suppress a shudder as he brought her hand to his mouth. Instead of miming a kiss above the skin, he planted a very moist one on the back of her hand.

'Charmed,' he said, drawling in an oddly dry voice, almost a whisper, as if he had some impediment in his throat. 'I have been waiting all evening to have a few words with you.'

As he released her hand, she began to feel unwell and, with the pretext of mending her coiffeur, brushed her hand to her horn. She could feel it tingle through her forehead and the poisonous kiss, for that was what it had been, was neutralized. Baron Manjari might have ships that traversed the known galaxy and be able to find contact poisons undetectable by Li's guard beams, but he had never encountered one of her species. Her problem now was how to react to having just been given an undoubtedly 'lethal' dose of poison. She noticed that he now brought out a handkerchief to blot his treacherous lips, and then a small pill box, explaining as he withdrew a tiny white oval, that it was time for his medication.

'I did not mean a discourtesy,' Acorna began with social civility, nodding to the baroness, who was having a hard time deciding which small delicacy to try next. 'The littlest ones are filled with raspberry liqueur,' she said, and got a blank look from the woman and almost a sneer from the baron. 'I think I should sit for a few moments,' Acorna said abruptly to Uncle Hafiz, who immediately handed her into the chair he had just vacated.

She began to rub her hand, as if unconscious of what she was doing. She caught the avid expression in the baron's eyes and the tension in his wife's bare shoulders. 'Uncle, a glass of something cool, please?' she said making her voice rise with urgency.

'Of course.'

Acorna used the ornate fan that dangled from her left wrist. 'I don't know what's come over me.'

'Why,' Ilsfa leaned towards her, one hand outstretched to touch her knee, but Acorna managed to avoid the contact, 'I expect it's no more than any young girl experiences during her introduction to society. Why, my Kisla was a nervous wreck until the evening had started, and then she danced all night.'

'Really?' Acorna managed politely in a soft voice. Should she be feeling weak so soon?

'Here you are, m'dear,' Hafiz said, offering her a glass of the madigadi juice he knew she liked, so cold the glass was beaded with moisture.

She drank it all down, hoping thirst was one of the symptoms of the poison working. The baron looked so satisfied that she was sure it must be.

'Just what I needed,' she said gaily, and rose. 'So nice to have had a chat with you but, before I find I have inadvertently ignored someone else, I really must circulate. Come, Uncle Hafiz, there is someone I want you to introduce me to . . .' and she pulled him away despite an initial protest.

'That man just tried to poison me,' she muttered in Hafiz' ear. 'Keep walking. Do I fall down in a faint, or just collapse somewhere? A contact poison. He had a very slimy kiss.'

'By the beards of the Prophets!' Hafiz began, and tried to pull loose from her to deal suitably with Baron Commodore Manjari.

'No, he may be the Piper.'

'Oh!'

'Where is Mr Li? We must inform him.'

'Who identified him? There are many people here who might wish to poison you.'

'Khetala and Jana. They watched the guests entering and saw the Piper among them. They've been quaking with terror ever since, but they overcame their fears to warn me. Well, actually, they found Calum and he told me. Who else would want to poison me?' Acorna demanded.

'Just about every man and a good many of the women here tonight,' Uncle Hafiz said, and signaled the butler.

Acorna wondered if the man had been cloned, or was one of triplets, for he had been so assiduous in his duties.

'Hassim, no one is to leave yet,' Uncle Hafiz said in an undertone. 'And where is Mr Li at this moment?'

The butler indicated the card room with a discreet gesture and glided toward the front door, deftly opening the panel and tripping a switch that would close every exterior door and the garden exits.

Mr Li's float-chair was surrounded by some of the loveliest women at the party and not a single man. He was obviously enjoying himself, and the women were laughing at some joke when Hafiz, smiling to see the quality of the company he was about to join, approached.

'Ah, but ladies, your glasses are empty. Come to the table and I will pour for you all.'

That left Acorna free to inform Mr Li of her suspicions as well as the children's ability to identify the dread Piper.

'Take them to my study. Tell Hassim to secure the house. Immediate confrontation now. Who?' And Mr Li stared at her as he suddenly assimilated the information he had just been given. 'Not . . . how extraordinary! Is most remarkable. Is last man this person would suspect.'

'That's often how it is, isn't it? But how do we entice him to the study? I am supposed to be dying of his poison. Will he not suspect?'

'Is my job. Get children. Get to study. Hafiz?' and he drifted his chair. 'You forgive?' He beamed back at the ladies even as he was moving out of the room, with Hafiz almost running after him. 'I give beep call and assemble cavalry.'

Acorna had already disappeared up the staircase, Calum taking the steps two at a time with Rafik trying to keep up.

Judit intercepted them at the stairs. 'What is the matter?'

388

'Oh, is nothing. Keep guests happy,' Mr Li said. 'Is that not Baron Manjari I see? No chance yet to show him my new acquisitions. Is now the time.'

Judit was too well trained to ask what new acquisitions, and obediently followed the float-chair to where the baron commodore, wife and daughter, were now standing, his expression slightly smug, theirs rebellious.

'Ah, dear Mr Li,' the baron said as suave as ever. 'We were about to take our leave of you. Your lovely Acorna has only just left us to our own devices.'

'She asks me to show you mine, is all,' Mr Li said and, laying one finger along his nose, winked at his guests. 'Have only just acquired.' His finger now bridged his lips to indicate secrecy. 'You travel much and can advise me on how to keep all safe.'

'Surely, Mr Li, you have no need of my advice?' the baron commodore said.

'Ah, but is to see my treasure first and then advise. We go now. Ah ... some devices not suitable for ladies, you understand?' Li added in an undertone. 'My Judit will entertain lovely wife and daughter while you come with me.'

There was something in the tone of the old gentleman that made it impossible for Baron Commodore Manjari to refuse. With an apologetic shrug toward his womenfolk, he followed Li's float-chair to the study, at the far end of the house from the glittering party. Hafiz unobtrusively followed to make sure the baron was cut off from any possible allies who might notice their exit.

The children were gathered in the study, Chiura half asleep in Acorna's lap and the other two holding tightly to her dress. When the baron entered after Li, Khetala gasped and backed behind Acorna, but Jana jumped in front of her protectively. 'Don't hurt her!'

'My dear little girl,' the baron said in his slightly hoarse tone, 'why would I wish to harm this lovely young lady?'

At the sound of the dry, husky voice, Khetala gripped Acorna's shoulder.

'It's him,' she said, her own voice no more than a thread. 'He always whispered before. But I know him. I do!'

'So do I,' said Jana.

Chiura woke up, looked at the baron's face, and wailed in fright.

'Piper!' she shrieked, trying to burrow into Acorna's lap.

'The Piper,' Jana said. 'You came with Didi Badini and took my Chiura away – but we got her back!'

'The Piper,' Khetala confirmed. 'You came with Didi Badini and took me to her bonk-shop.'

The baron sputtered, gobbled, and turned red.

'Nonsense!' he finally managed to rasp. He turned to Li. 'You'd take the word of these raga-muffins from the mines against a man of good family? I've never seen these children before.'

'You spoke with Didi Badini many times,' Khetala said firmly. 'I remembered your voice.

390

There was not much to think about in the closet where she kept me. I remember all the words you have said, from the day when Siri Teku sold me to you until the day the lady rescued me. Do you want me to repeat all I heard you say?'

'Ridiculous!' Baron Manjari said. 'This is a tissue of fabrications, and I can prove it! The child at Anyag had a whip scar on one cheek . . .'

His voice rustled to silence, like a pile of dry leaves when the wind comes to stir them. Delszaki Li and Hafiz Harakamian, one on each side of him, let the silence draw out.

'Interesting,' Li said finally, 'that you know these children came from Anyag.'

The baron made a gesture of denial. 'I must have seen them . . . a business trip . . . arranging shipping discounts . . .'

'A clerk's task, one would think,' Li said.

'The Lady Acorna healed my scar,' Khetala said. 'But she cannot heal *you*.'

Chiura twisted round to face the man who had haunted her baby nightmares, the man who had played with her and tormented her in the skimmer that took her away from Mama Jana. She kept one hand firmly twined in the silvery curls of the Lady Acorna, who had brought Mama Jana back to her. All three children stared unblinking at the Piper, their eyes a silent accusation.

Finally, Baron Manjari looked away. 'No one will believe this story!'

'You wish to make experiment?' Li asked.

'Be seated, Baron,' Hafiz invited. 'We have some

serious discussion to do.' He nodded at the children. 'Should not these little ones be in their beds, Delszaki? It offends me that they should continue to breathe the same air as this camel-sucking filth.'

None of the children felt safe away from Acorna, so she too left, taking them upstairs, where she and Gill told stories and sang songs and promised a thousand times over that the Piper would never come near them again.

'Why didn't you tell us at first you had seen the Piper at the mine?' Gill asked at one point. 'You could have identified him from a vid without ever coming near him.'

'Wasn't sure until I saw him and heard the voice,' Khetala said.

'What's a vid?' Jana asked.

'Poor little mite.' Gill stroked her forehead. 'I keep forgetting, there's so much you've never seen. We'll get a vid player up here for you. You'll love *Jill and the Space Pirates*. I've got all the episodes. Acorna loved it when she was a little girl.' *Just two years ago*, he thought sadly. Well, those days were gone forever. How could Acorna's people stand seeing their children mature so quickly? You scarcely had time to love them before they had become tall, independent strangers.

When all three girls were finally asleep, the lower floors of the house were dark, the lights in hall and gardens dimmed. Acorna rose stiffly.

'I wonder what's happening? We shouldn't have left. What if he poisoned them?'

'Calum and Rafik were with them,' Gill pointed out. 'I don't think the Piper was prepared for violence . . . at least I hope not. I'll be very annoyed if Calum and Rafik got a chance to beat the living daylights out of him and I didn't get my share.' He gently disentangled Jana from his coat and beard and laid her down in her cot, brushing a gentle kiss against her forehead.

'Has been no violence,' said Delszaki Li, appearing at the entrance to the suite in his float-chair. 'Has been some serious negotiation, but all is resolved peacefully.'

Hafiz, behind him, was wearing the beatific smile of a man who has just sold thirteen blind and lame camels for a bale of Illic silk.

'If I could ever feel sorry for that bastard,' Calum said, 'I would now. Anybody caught between Hafiz and Delszaki . . .' He whistled. 'I just hope you two gentlemen don't team up and form the Harakamian-Li Consortium. You'd be ruling the galaxy in no time.'

Hafiz and Delszaki glanced at one another. 'Interesting idea,' they said simultaneously.

'Uh-oh,' Gill murmured to Acorna, 'I think we've created a monster. Come on. Let's leave the kids to get their sleep and find out what kind of deal these two cut with the blessed baron.'

Once more in Mr Li's study, Acorna listened intently, but the results of the negotiations were not entirely satisfactory to her. The price of Baron Manjari's cooperation was their silence. If he was allowed to retain his social position, if no whispers of his peculiar habits and his extra sources of income got out, then they would find that all official constraints on Maganos Moon Base would be quickly removed. Furthermore, Manjari Shipping would subsidize the lunar colony by providing free transport for all materials brought to the moon and all minerals mined there in the next five years.

'Must give to get,' Li said patiently to Acorna. 'If we destroy Manjari, have no hold over him. If we keep silence, can ensure success of lunar colony, make safe place for children.'

'It's logical,' Calum said.

'But not satisfactory,' said Gill.

Rafik grinned. 'Well, think about this. The baron just lost three-fourths of his income – or will, when we take all the bonded children away – and his shipping company is going to be in the red for five years, if Maganos is as productive as I expect it to be. And he won't be able to tell the baroness and that ratty daughter why they're suddenly broke. Does that help?'

'It's a start,' Gill allowed.

'We will finish,' Li said softly, 'when children are all safe. Old family motto: "The best revenge is revenge."'

'I have some ideas,' Acorna said.

'You,' Hafiz informed her sternly, 'will stay out of sight until we have the necessary permits. Remember, you've been poisoned. You're extremely ill and your life is despaired of. You may even have to die for a while.' Acorna looked shocked and then smiled. 'That's right. We don't want Manjari tempted to have another try at you.'

Baron Manjari was hardly able to conceal his rage and fury after leaving Delszaki Li's party. Indeed, he hardly bothered to conceal it. His wife and daughter had learned from long and painful experience how to survive his dark moods. The baroness thought he was angry because she had eaten too many sweets again, the girl because she had been chasing after that blond miner instead of making a push to attach somebody who could be a useful business connection for Manjari Shipping. The baroness babbled nervously. Kisla sulked, but stayed well out of range of her father's hand; she had had to explain away too many bruises as 'accidental falls' already. That, she considered, was the price she paid for the money that had put her through nav training and now paid for the collection of top-of-the-line fliers and small spacecraft she enjoyed for her private use. She couldn't actually work as a space navigator; that would be beneath her family's status. So she accepted the baron's heavy moods, occasional casual blows, and tight hold over her allowance as the inevitable inconveniences of life. And she controlled what she could control: the flight patterns of her ships, and what she put into her body, and how much fear she displayed when her father went into one of his black spells. She despised her mother, who stuffed herself with sweets and then apologized that she 'couldn't help it,' almost as much as she despised the baron himself. At least *she* had some discipline, Kisla thought.

The baron, brooding over the insults he had just suffered, was all but unaware of his womenfolks' feelings. They were afraid of him; good, they would not question him. Not now, anyway. Even if he had to retrench and retire to the country for a few seasons, his wife would be afraid to ask what had happened to their lavish income. Kisla, though – Kisla would raise hell when she found out that he could no longer support a hangar full of private small craft for her personal amusement. He would have to find some way to shut her up . . . If it came to that!

But then, Manjari thought, what were the odds that Li's insane plan would succeed? He would have to ensure that official blocks to the development of Maganos Moon Base were removed, but that did not mean the project would be a success. If Li never managed to get the lunar mining facility in operation, his own expenses in providing free shipping would be minimal. And Li would never make a go of the moon base, because he meant to staff it with the bonded children of Kezdet. Children who had been well trained to hide themselves whenever *anybody* unknown to their supervisors came to a compound.

Let him collect a few strays, Manjari thought. *Much good it will do him!*

The system on Kezdet was too well entrenched,

the children too well trained in fearful, unques-
tioning obedience, for any one man to overthrow
it. That pathetic Child Labor League had not even
managed to keep schools going near the factories
to teach the children their letters and numbers.
Literate, numerate workers could read their
contracts and calculate their indebtedness and
their wages. Couldn't have that sort of nonsense.
Manjari hadn't even had to quash the schools
himself; a word here and there in the ears of the
factory owners most directly affected, and buildings were torched, teaching-vid machines
wrecked, maybe a young idealist beaten up or
'accidentally' killed from time to time to warn
anybody else who might have such ideas.

So Li would make his gesture and collect a few
stray children, and he would think himself
triumphant for a little while . . . and finally he
would understand that his plan would not work,
could not work. The children would never trust a
stranger.

As for that deformed girl who was getting some
sort of reputation as a miracle worker, who might
have been a figurehead for organized resistance –
she would be dead by morning. By this time the
slow-acting poison would make her feel headachy
and sleepy. She would go to her bed and fall into
a sleep from which she never woke, and by the
time her body was discovered, the traces of poison
would have dissipated.

Manjari was almost relaxed by the time his
personal skimmer reached the heavily guarded

compound where his family and servants lived in walled luxury. He need not worry overly much. All he had to do was wait . . . oh, and dispose of those three children. Without his witnesses, Li could prove nothing. And children were fragile; they died every day in the mines and factories of Kezdet. It should be easy enough to get rid of those three. Better to wait a little while, though, until Li thought himself quite safe.

Thirteen

'As good as his word,' Judit said the very next afternoon, as the sheets of permits from every reluctant inspector streamed from the printer.

'Is not good his word,' Mr Li said. 'Is good his fear of disclosure. That works well for men such as this baron commodore. Is there all that are necessary?'

'I think so,' Judit said, scanning the first sheets. 'Pal's doing something on the other unit, though. Nothing from the baron; just a routine legal search, he said.'

Rafik reached for the last one to emerge from the printer and worked backward, moving toward her as he glanced at the official permits, mumbling about which department and what sector and which quadrant. Then he gave a burst of laughter as he cavorted about, wrapping himself in the sheets and tearing some of the peripheries with his antics.

'Stop it, Rafik, oh stop it. You'll ruin them and we've waited for long to get them,' Judit exclaimed.

'They came?' Gill burst through the study door,

Acorna behind him and the three girls following her like the train of a bridal gown.

'We got 'em!' Rafik held the sheets up over Judit's head, wheeling around. 'We got 'em! For once, the baron commodore is as good as his word.'

'His word is not good,' Mr Li repeated, but he was beaming. 'His fear is.'

Judit slapped at Rafik, trying to get him to surrender the rest of the permits. Gill reached up and deftly nipped them from Rafik's hand. He delivered the slightly creased sheets, pressing the wrinkles out, into Judit's eager grasp, and she went back to the console.

'I'll enter them into our records, and send timed and dated confirmations to the respective departments,' she said.

'My, there were a lot needed,' Acorna said, moving with her three shadows to observe Judit as she dealt with the necessary procedures. 'How much longer must I stay dead?'

'But you aren't dead, Lady Acorna,' Khetala said, confused.

'I am as far as the Piper is concerned, sweetie pie,' Acorna said, hugging Khetala to her side. Chiura crept in under her arm, as well, while Jana was content to stand within arm's reach. 'Did you not help Hassim hang the mourning banners?'

'Is not to let the little ones out of the house!' Mr Li exclaimed, anxious.

'Hafiz, Gill, and Calum were with them all the time, and they were crying most piteously.'

'Kheti pinched me,' Chiura said, rubbing her bottom.

'All I had to do was think of Siri Teku's whip and I could cry for weeks,' Jana said, rather proud of her performance.

'But won't I have to be buried?' Acorna asked.

Hafiz shook his head. 'Cremated as befits the first wife of the scion of House Harakamian,' he said, grinning. 'I shall carry the urn with me to repose next to that of my son on my ship when Rafik and I return to Maganos tomorrow. And you, little ones,' and he patted the heads of the three little girls, 'will be among my baggage: the very first to enjoy the hospitality and safety of the Li Moon Mining Company.'

Khetala clung more closely to Acorna, and Chiura sniffled.

'But I shall be carrying you,' Gill said, wagging a finger at them, 'and I want not a whimper, a tear, or a gasp from you when you are supposed to be miners' clothing in my sacks.'

Jana giggled at playing being 'clothing' and even Kheti smiled, for all three girls loved Uncle Gill.

'But you can't tell stories to clothing?' Chiura asked, her eyes wide with regret.

'Who says I can't?' Gill responded, scowling fiercely, and she giggled as he swooped down and tickled her neck with his red beard.

'I've work to do and must concentrate,' Judit said.

'Is, after all, office-study,' Mr Li said, trying to

look severe. 'Rafik must now call suppliers A to M to be sure they have received permit. Judit do M to Z.' He clapped his hands together to suggest urgency.

'Come, girls,' Acorna said. 'We must pack the clothing just so in the sacks.'

Li's assistants quickly learned that there was no hope of keeping Acorna safely in the house while they completed the long task of collecting bonded child laborers from Kezdet's factories, mines, and brothels. Without Acorna, they could not even begin; the children had been too well trained to hide when strangers approached the compound, and what with the recent rumors of a horned goddess coming to liberate the children, most overseers were more stringent.

After the first frustrating day, Judit and Pal conferred with Delszaki Li. As Calum, Rafik, and Gill all reported the same inability to get children to come out of hiding, Li reluctantly agreed that Acorna might go with them the next day.

'But she is not to waste energy with too much healing,' he instructed. 'Is already long task, one person to visit all places. If she exhausts herself with healing every child, will never complete the work. I send medical team with you.'

'I'm not worried about Acorna burning herself out,' Gill said, 'as much as I am about the baron. If she starts collecting children from the factories, you know, he's bound to notice she's not dead.'

'And we went to so much trouble with the funeral banners!' Judit sighed.

'Will speak personally to Baron Manjari,' Li said. 'No trouble there. But you watch Acorna!'

And, with those somewhat contradictory reassurances, they all went together on the second day. Acorna was eager to go to Anyag first, but Calum had overnight produced a revised skimmer schedule showing the optimal path to allow them to clear mines and factories sequentially while making the best use of their skimmers. Anyag was far from the first on the list.

They began at the Czerebogar carpet-weaving factory, where on the previous day Pal had found only empty sheds, quiescent looms, and vague talk from the supervisor of some kind of holiday for the workers – all adults, of course!

Today, as soon as Acorna stepped out of the skimmer, pale children began collecting silently in the central compound. They seemed to come out of nowhere, from cracks in the walls, from shadows. The supervisor cursed them and told them to get away, that they had no business in his factory. The children seemed not even to hear him. They moved slowly forward until they encircled Acorna. The nearest ones reached timidly to touch her with cut and bleeding fingers.

'It is Lukia of the Lights,' one whispered.

Others repeated, 'Lukia! Lukia!' in rising tones until the word became a song of praise circling the courtyard.

'My brother,' a ragged girl said. She pushed a

403

taller boy forward, guiding him with both hands. 'Can you give back his sight, Lukia of the Lights? He had an infection of the eyes and we had only water to wash them, but it was not enough.'

Acorna caught her breath on a sob, but before she could reach out to the boy, Rafik had gestured for a med-tech to see to the lad.

'The infection is reversible, with proper treatment,' the tech said. She straightened and glared at the overseer. 'You would have let the boy go blind for want of a five-credit jar of antibiotic ointment! I am ashamed to be of Kezdet. But I did not know,' she said to Acorna, 'one hears whispers, always whispers, but I did not know . . . I did not want to know.'

By the time the flight of hired skimmers, led by Pedir, had collected the last of the children from the Czerebogar Carpet Factory, the medical technicians hired by Delszaki Li had all volunteered their services, just as the skimmer pilots had done after a little encouragement from Pedir.

At Tondubh Glassworks, the news of Acorna's visit to the Czerebogar factory had preceded them. They were met by a furious Dorkamadian Tondubh, threatening to obtain an injunction from Judge Buskomor against any attempt to remove workers who were legally bonded to work for the glass factory in payment of their debts.

'I wouldn't even try,' Pal said pleasantly. He ruffled through the papers he had been printing out from the com unit two nights earlier. 'I recently performed a routine legal search. We have here . . . no, that's the Vonzodik statement . . . ah, here we are. This is your sworn statement, attested by palm-print before Judge Buskomor himself, that no children under the age of eighteen are employed by any Tondubh concern. Clearly,' he said, looking at the children who had come out, as at Czerebogar, when the word of Acorna's visit spread, 'these children, being well under eighteen, do not work here and hence cannot possibly be bonded to you.'

Acorna looked at him with delight. So this was what Pal had been quietly working on! How clever he was! But she didn't have a chance to tell him so just then; children in filthy rags and clean, nearly new, cheap sandals were pressing all around her.

'You came back, Lady Epona,' one of them breathed.

'Epona, Epona,' the others repeated in a low rhythmic chant that filled the compound and echoed from wall to wall until Dork Tondubh covered his ears and made no more protest against their removing the children.

The skimmer pilots were busy through the day, flying loads of thin, pallid children from east of Celtalan to the spaceport, where Judit and Gill awaited them. When the first children were brought in, Judit gave a triumphant glance at Baron Commodore Manjari's portside manager.

'*Now* do you believe that there are passengers to transport to Maganos?' she demanded. 'Where's the transport the baron promised?'

'I see you want transport,' the manager said, 'but the baron didn't tell me anything about laying it on. 'Sides, our ships are all busy with *real* cargo.'

'Call him,' Judit said.

The manager grinned and spat to one side. 'Told you, lady. I din't have no orders, and I don't have no ships.'

Gill took the man's arm.

'I strongly advise that you accede to the lady's request,' he said. The tone was mild enough, but there was something in the look of his blue eyes – not to mention the size of the hand grasping the manager's arm – that suddenly made using the portable com unit to page Baron Manjari seem like a very, very good idea.

When Manjari answered, Judit took the com unit.

'You were told that ships would be required today to shuttle passengers to Maganos. Will you honor your undertaking, or . . . shall Mr Li honor his promise to you?'

The Baron Commodore refused to believe that Judit and Gill really had passengers for Maganos until the manager confirmed their statement. Very shortly thereafter his personal skimmer touched down at the Manjari private pad.

His face first turned gray when he saw the crowd of waiting children, then slowly suffused with color as he grasped the meaning of their chatter about the lady whom some called Lukia and others Epona.

'She's dead,' he insisted, his voice a gravelly protest. 'Everybody saw the funeral banners . . .'

Gill raised his eyebrows. 'The funeral banners? Those were a sign of respect from House Li to House Harakamian in their mourning for the heir.'

'Whatever could have made you think they were for Acorna?' Judit added with a slight smile.

'Acorna is alive and well,' Gill emphasized. 'And Mr Li suggests that it would be best for everybody if she stayed that way.' He lowered his voice. 'The children you met the other night are already in a safe place. You cannot get at them, but they can be brought back to tell all Kezdet who you really are . . . and if Acorna is harmed in any way, you can be very sure we *will* bring them back.'

The baron's face sagged, as if the muscles had been suddenly cut, leaving only unsupported, aging flesh.

'The Manjari ships are employed elsewhere,' he said. The dry voice was once again level and betrayed no emotion. 'I will make . . . alternative arrangements.'

He spoke into his com unit at some length. Shortly thereafter several things happened. First, obsequious men in Manjari uniforms arrived to invite Gill, Judit, and the children to Baron Commodore Manjari's personal storage hangar. Next, a second Manjari skimmer discharged two women: one short and plump, the other gaunt to the point of emaciation. The older woman wore a bejeweled robe and had a look of pleased expectancy on her round face. The younger one was dressed in unrelieved black and began shrieking before she even got out of the skimmer.

'Father, how dare you commandeer my personal ships! They're *mine*, you said so! To make up for not letting me have a real job as a navigator, because it was supposed to be an unsuitable occupation for the Manjari heiress. Anything I wanted, you said, and when I said I wanted my own collection of private spacecraft, you said yes. You can't go back on that bargain now!'

She stared, suddenly speechless in horror, at the dirty, ragged children being led into her personal skiff with its luxurious interior fittings.

'Hush, Kisla,' Manjari snapped. 'I am only borrowing your ships. I would not do so if it were not absolutely necessary, I assure you!'

'They're *mine*,' Kisla repeated.

'Then, Kisla, if you want to keep them, you will allow your father the use of them for as many days as this takes,' Manjari said so firmly that Kisla's narrow mouth closed on her next complaint. 'You have no conception of the difficulties I face.'

'How should I? You never tell me anything!'

'Well, I'm telling you now. We face ruin, girl. The House of Manjari is going to lose three-quarters of its income for years to come. Maybe forever.'

'Manjari, what is it?' The baroness touched his sleeve. 'What is the trouble?'

'Oh, don't bother me. You've never been any use – one child, and that one a scrawny girl – and you certainly can't help now. Go watch one of your romance vids and eat a box of sweets and stay out of our way!' Manjari turned back to Kisla. 'You *will* help me out in this crisis. And we *will* rebuild the fortunes of House Manjari. You and I, together, as many years as it takes.'

'By letting these stinking beggars on *my* ships?' Kisla's thin face twisted in disgust. 'Forget it! You go too far, Father. They'll get bugs on the upholstery.'

'Quite likely.'

'They'll get space-sick.'

'Almost certainly.'

'They're dirty, and they stink, and some of them are *bleeding*. They are absolutely disgusting, and I'm not having any more of them anywhere near my ships. Stop them, do you hear me? Stop them boarding! Now!'

The baron cocked his right hand back over his left shoulder, but the baroness was beside him before he could strike his daughter.

'Wait a moment, Manjari,' she said calmly. 'While I do believe that this once I sympathize with your desire to beat Kisla, there is something she must know first – and you, too.' She looked at the gaunt young woman with something approaching pity. 'Kisla, *you* would have been one of those children.'

409

'I?' Kisla gasped. 'You're crazy! I'm your daughter! No child of House Manjari was ever even close to one of those filthy beggar brats!'

'No child of House Manjari, true,' the Baroness Ilsfa agreed, 'but you see, Kisla, I learned of some of Manjari's more disgusting habits very shortly after our marriage. There was a little maidservant . . . well, never mind. I vowed then that I, an Acultanias, descended from the First Families of Kezdet, would never bear a child to him. But he would not leave me alone until I produced an heir, so . . .' She shrugged her plump, white shoulders. 'While he was away on one of his half-year business trips, I made a small payment to a Didi in East Celtalan for a relatively new baby. The . . . ah . . . donations to the Celtalan Medical Center to certify that you had been born to me and that I would never be able to have another child were considerably more expensive. I had to sell a lot of my dowry jewels – gaudy things; I never liked them anyway, and Manjari certainly never noticed they were gone. So you see, Kisla, it becomes you ill to sneer at children whose fate – or worse – you might well have shared.'

Baron Manjari and Kisla stared at the baroness in shocked silence.

'Which Didi?' Manjari finally asked.

'One of those you hired to procure children for your filthy habits, Manjari dear,' the baroness said sweetly. 'How else would I have known where to find a Didi? So you see, there is even a possibility that Kisla is your own daughter. Although it seems unlikely to me, since you always preferred children too young to become pregnant—'

Baron Commodore Manjari had lowered his hand during her disclosure and, with an insouciance that was almost laudable under the circumstances, had slipped it into his pocket. Now he withdrew that hand. There was a glint of metal; Gill sprang forward with a warning cry, but he was too late. The plasknife had neatly sliced through the baroness' neck. Blood spurted over Manjari's hands.

'No, Father! Don't kill me, too!' Kisla shrank away from him.

'I had to stop her talking. Surely you see that,' Manjari said in a conversational tone, his dark eyes glittering and staring. 'If people found out that you were a brothel foundling, it would ruin our position in society.'

He looked around him at the horrified faces of Judit, Gill, and half a dozen Manjari Shipping employees. 'Stop talking . . . stop them all talking . . . It's too late for that, isn't it?' he asked Gill, like a child. 'Isn't it too late?'

Gill nodded heavily.

'I was afraid of that,' Manjari said heavily, and turned the plasknife upon himself.

They had tried to keep the children from seeing the removal of the bodies, but Kisla's piercing screams attracted all eyes until she, too, was removed, under restraints and shot full of tranks.

'The Piper's dead,' one child reported to those already on the shuttle.

'The Lady Lukia killed him for us.'

'How could she? She ain't here!'

'She can do anything. Prolly she put *mal ojo* on him to make him kill hisself.'

Gill shook his head as the children calmly took their places on the shuttle.

'I thought they'd be upset,' he muttered.

'They have always known death,' Delszaki Li said. He had come upon them silently, in his float-chair, and Gill jumped half a meter at the unexpected sound of the old man's voice. 'Death is no stranger. Now it is for you and Judit to teach them about life.' He looked down, where the Manjaris blood stained the floor of the port, and sighed. 'But it is great pity about the baron commodore.'

'I don't see why,' said Judit. She was somewhat pale, but she was no longer leaning against a wall and fighting nausea. 'He was an evil man. He deserved to die.'

'Judit, Judit,' Li sighed. 'Have I taught you nothing of business? Now will have to pay own shipping costs instead of extorting from Manjari. Is great pity,' he repeated.

Acorna, still east of Celtalan, heard nothing of the happenings at the spaceport. The enormity of the task was exhausting her – so many places to

412

visit, so many children hidden away and working as slaves! But it grew easier as the day went on. The same secret, subterranean channels of communication that had once spread tales of Epona, of Lukia, of Sita Ram, now carried the word that the promised day of freedom had arrived. Those who hid would not be taken away into the sky; they would have to remain as slaves. And so the children began coming out even before they saw Acorna.

'Tomorrow you won't have to do it all,' Pal said cheerfully. 'Anywhere they see a Li consortium skimmer, they'll come to us. You should go home and rest now.'

'The skimmer pilots have been flying all day,' Acorna said. 'If they can keep on, so can I.' She beckoned to Pedir. 'Can you and your friends manage one more flight today, Pedir? Good. There is one place more that I must visit now. For Jana and Khetala.'

At Anyag, the news of some crazy woman who was taking away perfectly good bond-laborers had reached the overseers as well as the servants. Some locked their gangs in the sleep sheds. Since Siri Teku's gang was just coming off shift at the end of the day, he simply told them to stay Below. There would be no off-shift until this Acorna person had come and gone. She wouldn't find Anyag as easy to ruin as those city-type factories with their soft managers!

But the news had not mentioned a small army of skimmer pilots, medical technicians, and

House Li guards coming along with Acorna. While Delszaki Li's people swarmed over the Anyag workings, breaking open sleep sheds and escorting the dazed, blinking children to skimmers, Acorna looked and looked for the faces she remembered.

'You won't find 'em,' Siri Teku taunted her, grinning. 'They belong to me and Old Black.'

Mention of the underground demon whose name was used to terrorize the children was all the clue Acorna needed. She stopped briefly at each open shaft, delicately testing the air with her horn until she came to the one where the air was heavy with the breathing of many small people left all alone in the darkness of Below.

The engines that moved a cage up and down the shaft were stilled, but there were emergency ladders at the side.

'Laxmi,' Acorna called down into the darkness. 'Faiz. Buddhe. Lata.'

There was a shuffling sound deep in the shaft and a scuffling noise behind Acorna, as Siri Teku moved toward her and three pilots joyfully sat on his chest. Acorna took no notice; all her attention was concentrated on the slender thread of her own voice, drawing the children toward her. 'Ganga, Villum, Parvi,' she called.

As she named the children, they slowly, fearfully, climbed the long ladders to the top of the shaft. Laxmi was first.

'Sita Ram.' She sighed. 'You did come back!' She fell to her knees and kissed Acorna's skirts.

Acorna gently lifted her. 'I will need your help with the younger ones, Laxmi,' she said. 'Lata, Ganga, Parvi?' she coaxed again.

'These are the last ones at Anyag,' Pal said tensely beside her. '*Now* will you come home and rest? If only so you can come with us tomorrow?'

'Yes,' Acorna said. 'Come, Faiz, Villum, Buddhe,' she called. 'We are going home. We are *all* going home.'

That the home she would eventually go to – if Calum's researches were true – would be many light-years, and possibly many subjective years, of travel from Kezdet was not important now. And certainly not to be mentioned to these children until she saw them happy on Maganos under the care of Judit and Gill. Perhaps she and Calum would wander the stars without success, but, in helping these children, was she not earning the right to find her own people? Had she not made good her vow to the destitute and abandoned of Kezdet?

Smiling, she swung Lata up into her arms and walked toward Pedir's skimmer, trailed by children, whose grimy hands clutched her skirts and her long silver hair.

No one at Anyag dared to stop them.

THE END

A LIST OF OTHER ANNE McCAFFREY TITLES AVAILABLE FROM CORGI BOOKS

THE PRICES SHOWN BELOW WERE CORRECT AT THE TIME OF GOING TO PRESS. HOWEVER TRANSWORLD PUBLISHERS RESERVE THE RIGHT TO SHOW NEW RETAIL PRICES ON COVERS WHICH MAY DIFFER FROM THOSE PREVIOUSLY ADVERTISED IN THE TEXT OR ELSEWHERE.

08453 0	DRAGONFLIGHT	£5.99
11635 1	DRAGONQUEST	£5.99
10661 5	DRAGONSONG	£4.99
10881 2	DRAGONSINGER: HARPER OF PERN	£4.99
11313 1	THE WHITE DRAGON	£5.99
11804 4	DRAGONDRUMS	£4.99
12499 0	MORETA: DRAGONLADY OF PERN	£5.99
12817 1	NERILKA'S STORY & THE COELURA	£4.99
13098 2	DRAGONSDAWN	£5.99
13099 0	THE RENEGADES OF PERN	£5.99
13729 4	ALL THE WEYRS OF PERN	£5.99
13913 0	THE CHRONICLES OF PERN: FIRST FALL	£4.99
14270 0	THE DOLPHINS OF PERN	£4.99
14272 7	RED STAR RISING: THE SECOND CHRONICLES OF PERN	£5.99
12097 9	THE CRYSTAL SINGER	£5.99
12556 3	KILLASHANDRA	£5.99
13911 4	CRYSTAL LINE	£4.99
14180 1	TO RIDE PEGASUS	£3.99
13728 6	PEGASUS IN FLIGHT	£5.99
13763 4	THE ROWAN	£5.99
13764 2	DAMIA	£5.99
13912 2	DAMIA'S CHILDREN	£4.99
13914 9	LYON'S PRIDE	£4.99
09115 4	THE SHIP WHO SANG	£4.99
08661 4	DECISION AT DOONA	£4.99
08344 5	RESTOREE	£4.99
10965 7	GET OFF THE UNICORN	£4.99
14436 3	THE GIRL WHO HEARD DRAGONS	£5.99
14098 8	POWERS THAT BE (with Elizabeth Ann Scarborough)	£4.99
14099 6	POWER LINES (with Elizabeth Ann Scarborough)	£4.99
14100 3	POWER PLAY (with Elizabeth Ann Scarborough)	£4.99
14271 9	FREEDOM'S LANDING	£5.99
14273 5	FREEDOM'S CHOICE	£5.99

Transworld titles are available by post from:

Book Service By Post, PO Box 29, Douglas, Isle of Man, IM99 1BQ

Credit cards accepted. Please telephone 01624 675137
fax 01624 670923, Internet http://www.bookpost.co.uk
or e-mail: bookshop@enterprise.net for details

Free postage and packing in the UK. Overseas customers: allow £1 per book (paperbacks) and £3 per book (hardbacks).